**Also available from Carla de Guzman
and Carina Press**

The Laneways Series
Sweet on You

Also available from Carla de Guzman

The Cincamarre Series
The Queen's Game
Stealing Luna

If the Dress Fits (2021 Edition)
How She Likes It
Chasing Mindy
Alta: A High Society Romance Anthology

Coming soon from Carla de Guzman

Love Is All Around: An Alta Holiday Anthology
Making a Scene

MATCH MADE IN LIPA

———

CARLA DE GUZMAN

carina
press

carina press®

Recycling programs
for this product may
not exist in your area.

ISBN-13: 978-1-335-62199-3

A Match Made in Lipa

For questions and comments about the quality of this book, please contact us at CustomerService@Harlequin.com.

Carina Press
22 Adelaide St. West, 41st Floor
Toronto, Ontario M5H 4E3, Canada
www.CarinaPress.com

Printed in U.S.A.

To the time before, and the time after.

There are just some characters who demand their own stories, and I felt that way about Santi and Kira. Their scenes were some of my favorite to write for *Sweet on You*, and I had no doubt that their fluffy, sweet story, with chocolate and matchmaking, and the universe in general, would be the one to follow in this series. The first scene was of Kira and Santi facing off at La Spezia while Kira is chaperoning a date, eating brick oven pizza and handmade pasta, and bringing out the best and worst in each other. I started writing this story in April 2020, at a completely different time and in a completely different headspace.

But then my grandfather died. And I felt that the story had to change. I had always known that Santi would have a complicated history with his family, but I never seriously considered *how* complicated, until then. So I wondered if I had the range to write about death— what it means, what it leaves behind, the things we Pinoys believed in when it came around.

But no. Ultimately, I wanted to write a story about hope and love. The things that we so desperately need in times like these. A story of what justice could feel like, that was attainable in this life. (Thank you, Mina V. Esguerra and Alyssa Cole, for giving it a name.) Lord only knows how many times I had to write and rewrite this entire story to get there, which tells you what 2020 (and 2021) has been like for me.

So here's hoping that this "last best effort" doesn't feel like it was made for anyone else but for me. For my family, and for the life we still have to live after.

A MATCH MADE IN LIPA

Chapter One

December 31
New Year's Eve
Three years ago
Osaka, Japan

Cracking: The process of applying so much pressure on the cocoa beans that the husk will break away. Do not expect clean breaks all the time.

So Anton Santillan was wondering what the fuck he was supposed to do now.

As the panganay, the First Born Son, the Golden Boy of his family, his entire life was a series of people telling him what to do, and him doing it without question. Eat your ampalaya. Beso this tito, mano this tita. Be an outstanding student. Be valedictorian. Get an MBA. Run the business. Don't trust anyone but us, because we know what's best for you.

He had been content (because was anyone ever truly happy?) to do what he was told, because he trusted his family. Trust that his family, of all people, wouldn't hurt him, wouldn't steer him wrong. Wouldn't pull the ground out from under his feet, when they needed him to keep that ground steady.

That had been a miscalculation on his part.

So now here he was, walking the deathly silent streets of Osaka, wondering what his next move should be. This trip was not supposed to be an exercise in re-grouping. But now that he was here, walking the silent street alone, frozen from his nose to his toes with nothing but the cold and the darkness, it felt…like a blessing.

New Year's Eve in Japan, Anton realized, was a much more sedate affair than he was used to. The lights and sights of Dotonbori were only a train ride away—surely the Glico Man wouldn't protest being a part of a tourist's New Year's Eve—but even that visual assault was too tranquil for him. There was a stillness to Japan that not even the brightest neon signs could take away.

Anton was used to the loudness of a holiday in the Philippines—that audible buzzing in the air from the throng of people around you as the anticipation for midnight built and built, the food that accompanied it, the music that seemed to blast from every crevice possible in the countdown to midnight. Fireworks and smoke would fill the air, getting only louder as people scared away the evil spirits, jumped up to get taller, and hoped for a better year.

Even without the holiday, Manila had more noise than this. There would be someone singing karaoke in the distance, the glow of someone else's lights, or the perpetual sound of cars inching through the traffic of C-5.

In Japan, especially in a quiet street in the business district, all was calm, all was only slightly bright. It was so clean it was almost unbelievable, and there was not another soul in sight. Establishments were closed and streets were silent, like the city had shut down for the evening.

It felt slightly apocalyptic.

"Kuya, where are you?" Miro's message cut through the silence, as Anton wrapped his nearly frozen fingers around his phone. Damn, it was cold. Winter was no joke, especially for a guy currently wearing four layers of clothing and living in a country that had temperatures that never went below 25C. "Lolo looking for you. He's making sermon. It's BORING."

Anton ignored Miro's message for now, and stuffed his hands deeper into his pockets (lest the cold seep into his fingers permanently) and kept walking the streets.

The facts were as follows:

1) He'd been fired from his family's company. Maybe. It seemed that way, given his desk had literally disappeared from his office three days ago. But there had been no official notice, no one waiting behind him to tell him exactly how he'd fucked up. It was just gone. Like he'd never been there in the first place. Like Santi hadn't dedicated his entire life to proving himself worthy of being there, like he hadn't increased the Carlton Hotels and Resorts profit margins consistently with his innovations and ideas. Like he hadn't mattered at all.

2) His grandfather was never going to tell him why. It was in Vito Santillan's nature to speak in double meanings and half-truths, always so terrified someone would call him out on it. All he knew was that.

3) He lost all access to the family accounts, and was

no longer getting a salary from the Carlton. He also lost access to his work email, so there wasn't even going to be a turnover. He was, however, expected to show up for the family Christmas celebration, which was… fine. But New Year's had been his limit. So he got on a plane to Osaka without telling any of them. It wasn't like his grandfather was speaking to him.

In fact, he hadn't said anything to Anton during the holiday. Not at the Misa de Gallo, not at the Noche Buena. Not even when he opened Anton's Christmas present—Vito's favorite Kavalan whiskey, fresh from the airport in Taiwan. He'd smiled and thanked Anton like he hadn't illegally dismissed him from the family corporation. Wished Anton a merry Christmas even after he'd called a board meeting to remove Anton's directorship.

No. Confrontation wasn't Vito's style. Manipulation was. Which led to:

4) Anton had to figure out what he was going to do next, and fast. Moping was unacceptable; he was just going to have to accept what happened and move on. That was the only way he could keep his pride and dignity intact in this situation. He'd spent the first day of his vacation on the phone with his banks, checking and re-checking what his financial position was like, where his name was, where it wasn't. He had…just enough, perhaps.

Now the question was: where was he going to go? What was he going to do?

The doors to the convenience store automatically whooshed open. It was overwhelming to walk into a Japanese convenience store, regardless of the weather. The rush of warm air brought the feeling back in his fingers and nose, immediately making his cheeks flush as heat crawled up from where his heat-tech inner-wear was.

Santi's entrance triggered an electronic voice that greeted him with a robotic "irrashaimase." The lights, that had already been pretty intense outside, seemed ten times brighter inside, and he squinted as his eyes adjusted. He surveyed the room, and the rows and rows of Japanese goods waiting for him to pick them up, and nodded politely to the shopkeeper, who smiled politely at him.

Anton quickly spotted the cold goods refrigerator and walked toward it. He had discovered very early on in his trip what he wanted out of a Japanese con-venience store, and very rarely strayed from what he knew. Onigiri triangles and milk tea. Maybe a beer if he was feeling extra melancholic, but not yet.

He spotted the onigiri triangles. There was only one tuna mayo left. Santi reached out to take it, only to have another hand shoot forward and grab it, leav-ing him with nothing but air.

"Sumimasen," he said gruffly, wondering if he was pronouncing that right. "That's—"

"*My* onigiri? Yes it is." The English sounded famil-iar, making Anton turn his head to face his opponent.

Which was how he saw Kira Luz again after twenty years.

And wow. She was beautiful.

Still beautiful, actually, with those dark, upturned eyes that hadn't changed since she was ten. They were eyes that could see everything, see through him with-out much difficulty. It was the same face he used to know, just older. Changed.

Santi used to be told a lot that he had "grown up well." Kira Luz had grown up well too, into someone beautiful and self-assured, as self-assured as someone could be, when she was stealing onigiri from him. And with her, she brought back memories of Lipa, of those endless days he used to have as a child.

He'd forgotten that. How odd that he'd forgotten, playing in the streets with the neighborhood kids, getting his knees scraped and his clothes dirty almost every day. How odd that he'd forgotten that his father used to get up and go to work at the Villa Hotel every day, that his mother could only *dream* of owning a real Manansala. That Miro used to enjoy staying indoors to watch TV, not a care in the world about anything else.

And back then, when you played with the neighborhood kids, you had one leader—Kira Luz.

Kira Luz, who decided that instead of playing just one game, they would try to play them all, so everyone got a chance to choose. Kira, who always picked him for her teams, despite the fact that he wasn't very fast and could never remember the chant for Ice Ice Water. Or Langit Lupa, or patintero, or agawan base.

Everyone had been a little bit in love with her back in the day. He remembered waiting for her at the school gate, helping her when she struggled with the staggering amount of Christmas gifts and Valentine's Day candy she got every year. He remembered the two of them stopping by the sari-sari store across their houses to get soft drinks in plastic bags (she loved Royal Tru Orange, just like him), running outside when Mang Estong and his fishball cart parked in front of the Luz house, because Kira's dad always slipped him an extra

Php 20 so Anton could buy himself and Kira gulaman after their squid balls.

Seeing her brought it all back, and that rush of memory was so strong and so sudden that it felt like being punched in the stomach. He felt like he could tumble backward at any moment.

He'd forgotten that whole other life, that old life where he was called something else. Where he and his family had been completely different people, and when the name Santillan meant nothing at all. Kira blinked at him now, with those dark brown eyes that could always see right into his soul, her cheeks as red as his from the cold.

"Santi?" she said softly, his old nickname on her lips a gasp, like she couldn't believe it. "Is that really…"

"Kira," he said, nodding once. Her eyes went wide, and the next thing he knew, she was reaching up to touch his face with her free hand. No, wait. Not his face. His hair. Her hand was still very, very cold, but it was steady as she reached up and brushed that small, delicate hand against the hair on his forehead, lifting it up like she was searching for something.

A rush of warmth filled him at her touch, and he almost leaned into her hand. Almost.

"It is you." She smiled, seemingly satisfied, and withdrew her hand. Santi pitched forward slightly, but managed to hold himself steady. "You still have that scar."

"Was that the only way I could prove my identity?" he asked, and wow, was he actually starting to sweat? Why was he suddenly wearing too many layers?

"Seeing as you got that scar because of me, yes."

He remembered. He'd gotten that scar when he was

ten and she was eight, and they had been chosen to be flower girl and ring bearer at one of her many, many, many cousins' weddings. He told her that he and his family were moving to Manila, and she'd thwacked him on the head with her flower basket, giving Santi a little scar on his forehead that still lingered.

"You *almost* look like Harry Potter," she told him after his stitches healed, because she always knew how to make him feel better at the worst times.

Kira grinned and took a step back today, like she was trying to take a really good look at him. He wondered what she saw with her assessment. Would she think he grew up well? Would she see the bags under his eyes, or the fact that he hadn't shaved in three days? Would she like what she saw? "Damn. It's really you."

"Of all the convenience stores in the world." He returned her grin.

"Of all the convenience stores on this street," she corrected, and he had to agree. He had to have passed three other conbinis on his way to this one, what were the chances? "One would think the universe was trying to tell us something."

"You're still doing that?" he asked her, chuckling, just because it was nice that she hadn't changed that about herself. Kira read signs from the universe as closely as Santi read his schoolbooks when they were kids. They were sure to ace today's exam because the sun was shining. The universe didn't want them to pass that particular science project because it had gotten drenched in the typhoon.

"Yes, I am still doing that. And you can't argue that it hasn't brought me to some very interesting places," she said without defense or argument, just a statement of a fact that this was where they ended up in this moment in time, two friends who lost touch twenty years ago.

"It also brought you my onigiri," he pointed out, looking at the triangle in her hand, as well as the bag of chips wrapped around her arm, and the bottle of milk tea in her other hand.

"Nope, I already established ownership of the onigiri, and you were just too slow," she tutted, turning away from him in a blur of pink silk and dark hair. Santi followed after her as she perused the aisle. "Ooh, peach beer!"

"At least take my basket," Santi said, offering her the basket he'd picked up near the entrance. "I feel like you're going to drop something."

"You're still doing that?" she asked, smiling to let him know she was just teasing. Kira dumped her items in his basket without taking it from him, walking forward and humming along to the song playing on the speakers, which was in Japanese.

"You haven't changed," he pointed out, watching her look at the items on display and choose and consider them.

"I haven't," she agreed, chuckling. "I'm the same, people-pleasing, universe-believing Gemini you knew twenty years ago. You haven't changed, either."

"I haven't?" he asked, and he wondered how, when he felt like Santi of twenty years ago was completely different from Anton Santillan, the drifting shadow person who didn't know what to do with himself.

"You've always been the tall and silent type," she said with a little shrug, walking down the aisle. "Never a foot wrong, always perfect. You're actually wearing the right winter clothes. While I am going to die freezing in this silk jacket."

She shivered, and Santi immediately pulled the scarf from his neck. His skin practically hissed at the warmth it released. Then, before he could overthink it, he handed it to her while she was considering which of the flavored KitKats to get. Kira turned her head and looked at the scarf before she looked up at him.

"You have to keep your neck warm," he argued. "The base of the brain helps regulate body temperature."

When she blinked at him curiously, Santi sighed and stepped forward, waiting for a moment for her to give him a tiny nod before he wrapped his scarf around her neck with his free hand. Her lashes fluttered as she looked down at where his hands worked, and he caught a slightly floral scent that was coming from her. He noticed her lips looked soft and pink, matching the warm flush that spread across her cheeks.

When he stepped back, she smiled at him, tugging at the end of the scarf to wrap it a little tighter.

"Like I said," she told him. "You haven't changed a bit."

So they were apparently shopping together now. Santi placed a can of beer into the basket, why not. Kira continued walking forward, considering the Calpis, the Ramune, before deciding against all of that and just adding another bag of chips with her onigiri and peach beer. She was just about to add a cream bun when she suddenly laughed, and turned to look at him.

"I just realized. You broke your promise," she told him. The little frown on her face reminded him of when he was ten years old, and he said he couldn't come out to play today because he needed to study. "Do you remember?"

He did. He remembered the both of them sitting in the back of his family's old pickup, frowning and scowling like sitting there was a form of protest against the Santillans' impending move to Manila.

"*You have to promise,*" she'd said to him. "*That you'll come back. When I'm old, like, thirty, and when I need you most. Like a knight in shining armor. With a horse and everything!*"

"*Where am I supposed to get a horse?*" he protested, because even back then he knew how to ask questions. It was, in his grandfather's words, his least attractive quality. "*Why do I have to come back? Why can't you just come to me?*"

"*Because we're going to live in Lipa, duh.*" Eight-year-old Kira had rolled her eyes like the answer was obvious. "*Where else would we go?*"

Where else, indeed. Back then, Lipa City had been their entire universe. Their street near the Cathedral had been their entire planet. There was nowhere else to go, and Manila had seemed like a fantasy place you visited every few weekends, the rest of the world even more so.

But now, standing there in a convenience store in the middle of Osaka, the world had suddenly become much smaller.

"I didn't," he told her twenty-ish years later. "You're still twenty-six, aren't you?"

"Yes," Kira said, wrinkling her nose like she hated that she was twenty-six. "And you're twenty-eight. But the statute of limitations on that promise is going to run out very soon. Which is probably why the universe thought we needed to meet up again. I'm going to assume you're here for the holidays? A vacation of sorts?"

"Yes," he said, if going on a one-week sabbatical to rethink his whole life could be considered a vacation. "You?"

She nodded. "I'm here with my family. I'm supposed to meet my siblings at this temple nearby," she explained, and the amount of snacks in her basket suddenly made sense. "Actually, I just finished from a spying mission."

"Spying mission?" Santi echoed, picking up a box of the Meiji macadamia chocolates.

"Altair Chocolates," she said, whispering the name like someone could overhear them.

"Chloe Agila's brand," Santi noted, because of course everyone knew Chloe Agila's brand. It was a name spoken in the upper-and middle-class echelons of Manila society, the land developer's daughter from Davao who had made a name for herself as an influencer, eventually using that influence to jump start an entire industry of artisan Filipino chocolate.

She claimed she was the first to make chocolate from cacao beans grown in the Philippines. It probably wasn't true, but Altair Chocolates took off, selling in retail stores and popping up in every gift basket in the country. More brands followed her lead since then, making Davao the epicenter of the artisan Philippine chocolate revolution.

All of that Santi just knew from periphery. Families ran big businesses, and it was hard not to know who ran what. Especially when you were supposed to run the Carlton Hotel and Resorts Group, the chain of hotels that were these rich families' hotels of choice. Anyway.

"Yup." Kira nodded, popping the "p" as she peered at a little nail polish bottle in the home goods section. "They just opened a store in Dotonbori, of all places, and I wanted to try it out."

"Are you making a chocolate brand in Davao?" he asked her.

"No." She chuckled. "Lipa. I'm starting something in Lipa." she said, smiling at him, and in that moment, he envied her. He envied her being so sure of her place in the world. "Maybe. I'm not sure yet. I just started learning how, with Davao beans, and Altair is from Davao, so I wanted to taste it. I can already see myself wearing shiny red stilettos and a red cape, going where the wind takes me, spreading the secrets of chocolate."

Santi had no idea what she was talking about, but she seemed completely taken by the fantasy of it.

"You remember the Tomases?" Kira asked.

"I remember Sari Tomas." Santi winced. "She hated me."

"She hated you because you figured out a way to beat her team at patintero," Kira pointed out, going to the front of the store where you could order hotpot, smiling good-naturedly at the employee manning the counter. "Her little sister Sam runs the Tomas Coffee Co. farms in Sta. Cruz now, and they just found an entire *forest* of cacao. It'll take a while before any of that is ready, but it could be something. So I thought I would look at what Chloe Agila was doing. I just wanted to know what my business will end up being like, because you know how terrifying it is, to start something yourself?"

He didn't, honestly, but he supposed that was the

curse of the grandchild-of-the-owner status he used to enjoy.

"I mean, I know the basics, since I started this family business in—you don't want to hear about that."

He was actually interested, but decided not to press her on it.

The next few minutes were focused on Kira pointing at various hotpot items on the menu and the server nodding and smiling. Santi was sure neither of them really knew what the pictured balls were made of, but the hotpot soup itself was warm and fragrant, the kind of scent that made you hungry just by being around it.

"Still impatient," Santi noted.

"Bunso, eh." She shrugged, like that explained everything. "And I know what you're thinking."

"You're psychic now, too?"

"Oh sarcasm! That's new." She laughed, like she was absolutely delighted to hear it. "But you were thinking, 'what would I, a fine arts major, know about running a brand and making chocolate?'"

"I wasn't thinking—"

"Sometimes people just have to accept that their destiny lies in places outside where they expected," she continued, a defiant tilt to her chin as she said that. "We were eighteen when we chose our future careers. How can you make any solid decision at eighteen? And I already had the dream job, but it wasn't…um, it *really* didn't pan out for me, and as much as I love running the Laneways, it's not *mine* per se, but—"

He didn't know what the Laneways was, but it didn't seem to matter so much, because Kira had more to say.

"Basta! This, I can do this well. This, I can make myself, you know? I just need someone to believe in me. I already believe in me. Like really, truly, I can do this. But I don't want to fail at a dream again."

He should say something. He knew he should. She was much too wonderful, both now and in his memory of her, to be this upset. Kira was the kind of person who could conquer the world if she wanted to, and that look in her eye told him that she very much wanted to.

"Order?" the person manning the hotpot asked, looking at Santi.

"Yes," he managed to say, ordering the same items as Sari by pointing and nodding. When he turned to Kira she was looking up at him again, his scarf around her neck and her eyes still studying him. Her food arrived then, piping hot and waiting for her to eat, with a separate bowl of the soup that the balls were cooked in, and another bowl of an unidentifiable brown sauce that might be satay-based, but looked delicious.

"You know I always wondered what happened to you after you moved to Manila," she said, letting her balls cool on the counter as she sipped the iced (in this weather?) milk tea she ordered. "We never figured out how to get in touch. I would have looked for you on social media but it didn't seem like your thing."

It wasn't. He didn't even have accounts, just a vague awareness of social media's existence. Messaging apps for work matters were his limit. Not that he needed those apps at the moment, but they were all still on his phone. He couldn't quite bring himself to delete them yet.

"One of your cousins said years ago that you got into Ateneo for college, but I didn't see you there, so I just assumed—"

"I studied in Canada," he explained, because he remembered getting into Ateneo, remembered taking the exam with those 25 math-based word problems you had to finish in 25 minutes. He remembered how excited he was to continue his education in the school he'd attended from prep to high school. But then, that didn't happen. "My parents stayed in Van for a while, just long enough so Miro and I could go to UBC. But my grandfather didn't like his grandsons being so far away, so I went to AGS for my MBA, and…here we are."

"That's…a lot of letters." Kira chuckled. "What a shame, though. I think we would have been friends again, if you went to Ateneo with me."

He could almost picture it. He'd seen college kids walk up and down the campus in perfect stride, holding on to their books and their laptops like they had all the time in the world to cross from Xavier Hall to Bellarmine. Kira would talk, because she always had something to say, and he pictured himself smiling and nodding along, content just to listen to the way she saw the world.

Just like when they were kids.

But that wasn't how their lives had turned out, and now here they were in a completely different country, caught up in nothing but a coincidence, a bag of convenience store snacks between them. It was five minutes to midnight, and they were supposed to be in different places—Kira ringing in the New Year with her family, and Santi sitting through another sermon. But neither of them seemed to want to leave this place, this moment.

"Are the Villas still running the hotel?" Santi suddenly asked. And he knew he should know the answer to that—he was a Villa too, after all—but he didn't.

When his family moved, his mother had cut herself off from all communication to her relatives, like she'd stripped off a coat and revealed someone much shinier and elegant. Santi hadn't been close enough to his cousins to reach out, or at least that was his excuse.

Kira's face changed then, like he'd managed to find something that she would rather not say out loud. He knew that *she* knew that he hadn't spoken to that side of his family. That was just the way things worked, like Santi knew the Luz family was one of those families that could trace their roots to before the first coffee and cacao trees were brought to the Philippines (yay, colonization).

"They closed their doors last year," she said, and in those few words he knew how she felt about it. He had memories of that place too, sliding down the bannisters, having Villa family gatherings at their restaurant in front. "Lally Villa's kids had their own businesses, and most of her grandkids—including you, and your brother, obviously—moved on to work in Manila or abroad, and nobody was left to run the place. Last I heard, they were looking for someone to take over."

Anton Santillan did not believe in signs, or in the universe. To him, his life was a sprint, a series of hurdles he had to learn to be fast enough to leap over. There was no all-seeing being that helped him along or told him how things could be; there was what is, and what was. There was the divine, and there was intervention. Two very different things.

But if he did believe in signs, he would point to tonight as the one time he was the closest to believing in it. And it wasn't because out of the fifty thousand convenience stores in Japan, they both walked into this one. It wasn't because it was nearly midnight, and for the first time in a long time, Santi wished for someone to be waiting for him at a nearby temple to ring in the New Year. He wanted that normalcy so bad that it almost hurt.

But this felt like a sign because of what she said. The words seemed to ring in his ears, make his heart leap.

They are looking for someone to take over.

Because now he was thinking, *why couldn't it be me?*

No. He couldn't. He couldn't possibly have enough to afford the Hotel Villa. It was a property along the highway, it was sure to come at a high price. He would only have enough for maybe half of it, there was no way he could—

You can't. But your family can. Imagine Carlton opening a hotel outside of Manila, holding weddings and events better than Tagaytay?

Maybe if he could get them excited about this, they could start talking more, and he would be forgiven for whatever it was he'd done. His grandfather liked it when he took initiative, liked it when Santi approached him with ideas and requests. Miro would get a kick out of designing the hotel; he built an entire influencer career around interior design. His father could dust off those old skills he learned from Villa to keep it going, his mother could reconcile with her family.

He could bring them all together. *Like a knight in shining armor.*

"You're smiling," Kira noted, bringing him back to the moment, to this girl who had stolen his onigiri and redirected his entire life in a span of what, thirty minutes? Twenty? What was time? "It looks good on you."

She speared a ball with her chopstick, the steam rising up to his nose. It was fragrant and made his stomach grumble, even if he already had dinner. She held up the ball toward him in offering. He opened his mouth and ate the whole thing. It was delicious.

"Mph!" he exclaimed as he bit into it. Cheese burst from the inside, coating his tongue with hot, melty goodness, as the saltiness and warmth of the broth filled his mouth. "It has cheese inside."

"Does it?" Kira looked absolutely delighted. "That's a good thing, isn't it?"

He nodded. "Unexpected," he said. "But really good."

"We should change up the terms of the promise," Kira announced, chomping on a ball, which might have been mushroom-based, after dipping it generously in the sauce. "Seeing as you're not planning on marrying me anytime soon?"

"I'm not?"

"Well, a knight traditionally marries the princess." Kira laughed. "But I like the idea of having someone out there looking out for me, and looking out for someone. So we should promise to be there for each other when we need it."

"Need is…subjective, isn't it?" Santi asked, wrinkling his nose. "What is that supposed to feel like?"

"Hmm," Kira said thoughtfully, stirring her shabu shabu soup with a plastic spoon. She pressed a hand lightly to her heart, like the answer was there. "You feel it here," she explained. "It's an ache, or a twist in your chest that you can't get rid of. And there's no one else in the world that can understand it, but the other person. That's need."

"Okay," Santi agreed, looking at her. She caught his glance and her eyes just...sparkled. Like she was truly, incandescently happy to hear it. How did she do that, in a combi so flooded with bright light? "When you need me most, I'll be there."

"And...?"

"And...bow?" His brow rose in confusion.

"No." Kira rolled her eyes, but she was laughing. "And if you need me, *I* will be there. Patas lang. Warning, I'm very persistent. My levels of kulit are legendary."

"I remember." He nodded. He hadn't realized that he was touching the same spot in his chest until he saw her smiling at his hand. She held out a hand, nails painted a sparkly gold, and Santi took off his glove before placing his hands in hers. Her fingers were still cold, and her hand was small, but the touch made him feel like something warm and good tingled up and down his arm. Like sunshine.

"It's a promise." She nodded, squeezing his hand. Then her phone started to ring. It was an alarm. Santi glanced at the clock he'd seen above the cashier. It was midnight. Kira immediately gasped and grabbed his arm, using it as an anchor to jump up excitedly.

"Happy New Year!" she exclaimed, giggling as she continued jumping. The rest of the store was silent, like nothing extremely important had happened—the person behind the counter said a casual, "happy new year!" and continued to serve Santi's food, and the street outside was still quiet. But they might as well have been standing in the middle of fireworks, the way Kira was so excited.

"You're not going to get taller, even if you do that,"

he told her, a smile playing on her lips as her cheeks flushed red from the exercise. She was just so happy.

"And yet I see you're wearing red stripes for luck and more bills," she told him, poking the little exposed part of his sweater under his wool coat. "Clever and sartorial."

"Coincidental," he pointed out, because he didn't know wearing stripes was a New Year thing. Polka dots for more coins, yes, but stripes? Really. "But I think you're forgetting the more important midnight tradition."

"The kiss?" she asked, wrinkling her nose. "It doesn't really do anything, does it?"

"It can seal a promise," Santi pointed out, unsure why he was pushing for this. He didn't need this. Didn't need a midnight kiss to feel better. But she was here, and it was midnight. He just needed to do *something* to firmly put his bad year behind him, and start looking forward to a new one. *One last blessing. One last good thing to end this.*

"Okay," she said, with a little nod. Then she closed her eyes, and Santi lowered his head, just enough to capture her lips in his. The kiss was soft and lasted only for a moment, but Santi felt warmed up, and comfortable, like the cold under his skin had finally thawed. He could remember what it was like to feel like himself again. Maybe he was the one who'd needed a kiss to wake up.

"Happy New Year," he said, pressing his forehead against hers as they caught their breath together.

"Happy New Year, Santi," she giggled, giving him

a kiss on the cheek, and somehow that was much more intimate than the kiss they just exchanged.

And just like that, their promise was made. Or re-made.

Chapter Two

January 4
Three years ago
Lipa, Batangas

"So you're not going to tell us about your secret New Year kiss?"

It was a cool evening in January when the three of them gathered. The Luz family's gazebo was lit with candles and twinkle lights and a parol dancing in the breeze. There were no other sounds except the rustle of the trees and the birds of paradise plants chiming in with the rustling to join the symphony, led by the tuko announcing itself in the distance.

"No," Kira Luz said with a coy little smile. Some things were best kept to herself, including really serendipitous New Year kisses with an old childhood friend. And she really would have been able to get away with *not* telling anyone about it, but Santi had insisted on walking her to the hotel that night, where her Ate had coincidentally been hanging out at the lobby for the Wi-Fi. Then, of course, Kira never heard the end of it. "A lady doesn't kiss and tell. She does, however, kiss and do oracle readings. So shh and focus on the inner-most desires of your heart."

It was the perfect night to ask the universe for a little bit of guidance. Kira Luz looked at her friends, Sari naturally trying her best to look uninterested, and Sam all too interested in every move of Kira's hands. She wanted to think there was a magic in the air as the three of them sat around the low table in the middle of the gazebo, her hands inexpertly shuffling the oracle cards she got for Christmas.

"Are you sure about this?" Sari asked, nursing the cup of tsokolate in her hand as she pulled her gray cardigan closer to herself. "We're not summoning any-thing naman?"

"Like what? A demon that will do your every bid-ding? Clean your house? I would not be mad." Sam Tomas shrugged.

"Relax, Sari. This is an oracle reading, nothing more," Kira assured her like she'd had more than three days' practice with the cards. "No predictions, just a little guidance before we go do our things in the New Year. Nothing occult, more spiritual than any-thing else."

And she really did believe in that. If there was any-one who always tried to attune themselves to the cues of the universe, it was her. And right now she needed that bit of guidance. The questions in her heart were getting too loud to ignore, and sometimes it was the universe who knew best how to guide her.

It came to her soon after she lost her dream job, and realized that she wasn't exactly where everyone else was. The world was moving at a pace she couldn't fol-low, down a path she couldn't see. She was supposed to graduate, get a steady job, make money, fall in love, get married, have kids. Kira wanted all that for herself, but had no idea how she was supposed to go about it. The path had been so muddled and lost, that she couldn't even see where she was going.

Enter astrology. It was funny at first, how much a general, non-specific description of a Gemini just felt so…*her*. Then she learned about rising signs and moon signs, learned about the different houses and how the planets aligned when she was born. Then she was introduced to oracle readings, which were so insightful. They helped her remember how to find joy, how to look at how her life was going, and course correct if she needed. How to find the path that everyone seemed to be on.

To her, astrological signs and oracle readings were the equivalent of a matchstick when you were walking through a dark forest. It was better than nothing.

There were three of them tonight. Kira the Gemini, with her questions about her life, if she was doing the right thing, trying not to forget that she was very prone to the most spontaneous decisions. Sam, the Leo, who already knew all the answers. And Sari, who was a Capricorn through and through, rooted and grounded, almost immovable in her steady ways…and could maybe use a gentle push.

"Here we go," Kira said, after she asked her friends to close their eyes and breathe evenly, just to open up their minds. She shuffled the cards, her hands still fumbling a little over them as her limbs loosened, and she allowed herself to breathe evenly and let her mind clear. Three cards, she decided (was it really her, or someone else deciding for her?). One card each. This one. This one. That one. Done.

Okay, universe, she thought, laying three cards face-down in a row in front of her. *What do you have for Sari, Sam and me?*

Each girl picked up their card, choosing without prompting from Kira.

The middle one, she thought, and picked up the card. The wind picked up, and her mother's wind chimes sang. It seemed to be the right choice.

"The belonging you seek is not behind you—it is ahead." Sari Tomas read, her frown immediately deepening, as she stared at the picture on the card. This particular oracle deck was insight from the movies. And while Kira thought the movie selection was *very* limited, it didn't make the insights any less important. "It's Star Wars. I have no idea what this is supposed to mean."

"Nobody puts Baby in a corner. I *loved* Dirty Dancing," Sam announced, showing them her card and chuckling before she flipped the card facedown again, like she wanted to tuck it away. If there was any more insight she gained from it, she wasn't about to say, which Kira found very curious. "What did you get, Kira?"

"I dream of a love that even time will lie down and be still for." Kira showed her friends the card, which featured an illustration of the moon, with white flower petals rising from a bowl, just like in the movie. She remembered the scene, but Kira had a sense that there was a deeper connection behind the drawing, a connection that transcended love, if such a thing existed. "Practical Magic."

"Huh," she said out loud, flipping the card over as if it had more answers for her. "Labo."

"How is it malabo, you're the one doing the reading?" Sari teased. Kira laughed with her friend.

"It all depends on how you see it, I guess. Or I just made a bad pull." She highly doubted that was possible, but decided not to think too hard about it.

But really. A love that time would lie down and be still for? Kira had too many other things in her mind to think about love. She had a condominium unit in Manila to give up, a family business to keep running. A life to figure out, and that wasn't even factoring in that she wasn't ready for love. Love was a hard concept to grasp when the things you thought were a given— a good job, a sure way to be a happy, fully realized adult—were all murky and a huge question mark. Love was not supposed to be in the cards yet.

Still.

She thought about it throughout the reading, and was still thinking about it hours later, sitting out in the gazebo and looking up at the sky. Lipa in December was no joke when it came to cool breezes, so she'd grabbed one of her new Christmas presents—a soft, sage green woven blanket her mother bought her from a trip to Ilocos—and wrapped it around her body for warmth. That, and the little tub of milk chocolates she made, was her only comfort.

"Hey," a voice behind her said, and she looked up to catch her older brother, Kiko Luz, still wearing leather boots, jeans and a bomber jacket like it wasn't nearly midnight. Kiko's cheeks were slightly flushed with the breeze, but his skin was tanned from a recent trip to the beach with his boyfriend. "You still up?"

"You still wearing shoes?" Kira teased, wiggling her toes at him from behind her fuzzy tsinelas. "Also, I should be mad at you, chismis-ing about me like that with our parents. Traitor."

"Oh. So you *did* hear that," he said, and her brother at least had the decency to look guilty as he sat across his little sister. Kira tucked her toes under his thigh and glared at him. "You weren't supposed to."

"I wasn't?" She gasped, her voice dripping with sarcasm, waving around the hand holding the piece of milk chocolate. She was biased, but she thought it really was helping comfort her. "I know I technically haven't been inducted into the post-dinner chika club like you have, but I can hear everything you guys talk about. In fact, I have since I was a kid. Which was how I found out that Ate Kamilla was moving to Singapore, and how I found out that you and Kuya Jake were together, even though I was the one who told him about you at the wedding."

She didn't mean to sound bitter, but it was a symptom of the bunso to always be the last to know anything, and there was nothing she could do about it. Parents tended not to notice there was one kid missing when they were a couple of glasses of wine in, and the chika just flowed out.

"So, yeah. I wasn't supposed to hear that Mom and Dad are worried that I'm never going back to Manila, and that I gave up too easily on my dream job. I wasn't supposed to hear that setting up the Laneways, pouring my time into it, was just because they didn't know what to do with me."

Kiko opened his mouth, but Kira wasn't done.

"And I wasn't supposed to know that they have their

doubts about my idea to open a chocolate shop," she said, frowning at Kiko. "I'm not complaining, by the way. Thank you for the job—I mean, sorry, the distraction."

"Hay," Kiko sighed, pressing his thigh over Kira's toes, rolling his eyes when Kira tried to squirm her toes away, because she didn't exactly love saying all of those things out loud. He held out a hand for chocolate, and she grudgingly handed him a square.

"Mmm," Kiko said, after he took a bite. "You know, this is really good."

"I know." Kira sighed. "I'm shockingly good at making chocolate. And I have a friend who's getting married, and he wanted me to make gift boxes for his ninongs and ninangs."

"Let me guess—"

"I matched them? Yes I did." Kira nodded. "Art directors are fun if you manage to find out that they're into art world gossip. Nida from the gallery in Karrivin was perfect for him, okay?"

"You found a wife for the guy who recommended against your dream company retaining you." Kiko chuckled. It sounded bad when he said it like that, but Kira was okay with it. It had been three years since she lost the job with the company she thought would make her truly, professionally happy. But that dream hadn't panned out. Time to move on to another. "Iba ka talaga."

"See, that's the problem," Kira sighed, picking up another square. "I'm the youngest, I'm…*me*, so no one takes my ideas seriously. You see this?" She held up the chocolate, which, although shiny, was starting to melt between her fingers. "I made this with cocoa nibs from Davao. Imagine what a cacao bean from *Batangas* would taste like, Kuya. I have a feeling it will be amazing, and I can see myself making it happen. And in order for me to do that, I need to do all of these other things, set up a shop, open a business and it's not great to hear that your own family doesn't think you know what you're doing."

"Do you?"

"Of course I don't!" Kira grumbled. "Did you, when you started your firm?"

"No," Kiko admitted, and she gave him a look that was all "see!"

"You know when you frown like that you look like a kid."

"I'll always look like a kid to you guys."

"Mom and Dad just don't want you to get hurt again," Kiko told her, and he looked away, like admitting it was hard for him. See, feelings were hard. But the darkness helped. The cool breeze, the rustling of the trees helped. The chocolate certainly had something to do with it, too. "You were so upset when you lost the job at Serendipity. And we all thought it was your thing, you know? You're the sister that does the art thing."

"Now I'm the sister that makes chocolate. The sister that watches over the Laneways." Kira sighed, dropping her shoulders. "I thought Serendipity would last forever, too. But it didn't. Now I feel like I'm being led to this new dream, Kuya. And it's exciting to me. I'll do it with or without the family's help. But I really wish you guys would get on board, because I want you to be part of my life, because I love you guys. Even you."

"I'm shocked," Kiko said wryly as Kira wriggled

her slippers under his thigh even harder. "If this is what you think you're meant to do, then you should pursue it, Kira. If you dream of making a Batangas chocolate, think it's worth giving up your condo in Manila, worth dropping everything and pursuing…then you should do it."

A love that time will lie down and be still for, she thought, and it made her smile. It seemed that the universe still had her back. And much like Kiko, was vehemently agreeing with her.

Kira looked up at the twinkling parol, uncertain, but already excited about what was to come.

"I think I will," she told him.

Chapter Three

December 22
Three years later
Carlton Hotel, Makati

> *Fermentation: a step in the chocolate-making pro-*
> *cess where the beans start developing most of their*
> *flavor. This will depend on several factors, like tem-*
> *perature, weather conditions, exposure to other*
> *plants around them. Depending on how long and*
> *where the beans were fermented, they will develop*
> *different flavors. Patience and much care is re-*
> *quired.*

If Santi were to really think about it (and he never really did), December was probably the worst month to
get married. Sure, the weather was "cooler" in those
months, enough to make that reservation in Tagaytay
really worth it, and your relatives were all here for the
holidays.

But Christmas was a beast to be reckoned with, especially in Manila, where hell-on-earth levels of traffic were guaranteed, and you were shuffled to and fro
to Christmas parties, family reunions, friend reunions,

Simbang Gabi, Christmas Eve and all the other required trappings thereof. That and the million and one details and events required to actually *have* the wedding in the first place?

He felt bad for the couples who still managed to smile and not collapse to exhaustion in the aisle. Congratulations and best wishes all deserved.

But Santi must have been missing something, because the numbers didn't lie.

After three years of running Villa by himself, he learned that December was still the peak of the wedding months, May and February following close behind. Villa's Azotea ballroom was booked solid two years in advance, with very little wiggle room from December to February. So there must be something to a December wedding that he wasn't seeing.

But as far as Santi's work was concerned, it wasn't his business to think about *why* it didn't make sense, it was his business to do his job, which was mostly to make sure these weddings happened.

"People don't care about your opinion," his grandfather had told him. "They care about you saying the right thing at the right time."

Santi was good at saying the right thing. He'd said the wrong thing only twice in his life—the first time when he argued with his grandfather about adjusting salaries for all of Carlton's employees, given the huge earnings the company had seen since Santi took over. His grandfather had said no, and the next day he found his desk just gone.

The second time was when he came back from Osaka and excitedly offered to lead a joint venture with his younger brother and his grandfather to revive the Villa Hotel. Vito had laughed him out of the room, Miro had rejected the offer, and Santi was issued a challenge.

"Go ahead. Make it successful. Prove to me that you're worthy to come back to the Carlton. By yourself."

That was three years ago. Three years of working, with very minimal support, and zero visits from his family to the place they exiled him to.

Santi was not going to make the mistake of saying the wrong thing again.

So when he walked into the Carlton Makati for the first time since he was "banished" from the company, he said all the right things. Smiled at staff, nodded politely at those who recognized him, and said nothing.

But seeing the all-too-familiar marble and glass lobby made his heart ache, made his exhale shuddery. It was like walking into a relic from his past, because his past was shiny marble lobbies, a modern sculpture that changed every season, a chandelier that would have made the Phantom of the Opera jealous, and a faint vanilla scent in the air. He remembered this place when it was smaller, remembered when they started to pull in bigger clients, bigger events. He remembered the work he put into this place.

Today, he was seeing it all as a stranger. More specifically, a wedding guest.

"Kuya," Miro Santillan's voice said cooly, as he walked down the lobby staircase, casual as ever, like he was fully expecting someone to take a picture. He tossed his head back, permed curls flying away from his eyes.

Santi knew that always staying photo-ready was a

hazard of his little brother's socialite/influencer life (follow him, @makemiromoves), but it did mean that Santi wasn't sure which mask of Miro's he was about to contend with.

Santi supposed he and his brother were close, in a way two people lumped together during a disaster would become close. There wasn't anyone else in the world that understood the special brand of frustration, the emotional exhaustion and irritation the Santillans wrought. But still, there was a distance between him and his little brother that Santi couldn't quite bridge, no matter what he did.

It started around the same time Santi made the deal with Vito. He got the funds to take over Villa, and paid it all back, with interest in three years. Miro hadn't visited the place once, had rejected Santi offering to pay him to do all the interiors (which he thought was the point of starting an interior design-based channel?) and started to snark at him, instead of with him. Like Santi had turned from his semi-reluctant ally/brother into persona non-grata.

But it was fine. Miro was entitled to whatever hurt he was feeling. Santi was patient enough to wait for his little brother to tell him his problem when he was ready.

"Miro," Santi said, noting his little brother was already pulling off the orchid boutonniere attached to the lapel of his jacket, tugging off the pale pink tie that all the groomsmen had donned for the wedding. "Leaving so soon? The reception hasn't even started."

"I've been up since five a.m. for this damned wedding. If I stay longer, I'll have to start charging a talent fee," he said with a bitter chuckle. This was Miro on top of the world, without a care for anyone else but himself, happy enough to say what was really on his mind because there wasn't anything Santi could do about it. It usually happened when he was about to leave a room, be somewhere he was more likely to be adored. "I don't know how much longer I could have pretended to smile and be happy for Kit."

"He's your cousin," Santi reminded him.

"*Second* cousin," Miro scoffed, rolling his eyes. "I was chosen to be a groomsman because I'm the handsome one, and they probably wanted to make Lolo feel like we weren't excluded. Anyway. I'm leaving. Places to be, stories to post, you know."

Santi didn't, but said nothing.

"And I just wanted to let you know that Mama was very proud about the fact that she didn't give the happy couple a gift, despite her and dad being Ninang and Ninong," Miro said, his brow raised as if daring Santi to comment on how outrageous that was. "Said it was more than enough that we didn't charge them the peak rate for the wedding venue."

"So not only is she a bad Ninang, she's also a liar." Santi sighed in resignation. Vito Santillan did not believe in giving a family and friends discount, unless there was something in it for him, and a second cousin's wedding definitely did not count. "And now we have to fix it."

"We?" Miro laughed. "I don't think so. *I'm* off to this secret bar that's supposed to have arcade games and an even more awesome bartender. You're going to fix this, because I know you, and I know you already have a solution. You probably handed Kit the cash right after the wedding."

He wasn't wrong. Santi had already approached

the groom after the wedding, offering his congratulations during the family photos before he slipped him an envelope with thirty thousand pesos of his own money—enough to cover the couples' expenses for the Santillans' dinners, at least ten thousand "from their Ninang and Ninong" and the rest as a gift from Santi, Miro and Lolo Vito, because it was a polite thing for the guest to do.

He wasn't going to say out loud that he never really expected any of his family to give a wedding gift.

"And, Lolo is looking for you," Miro said, and Santi immediately dropped his shoulders as he wondered what his grandfather possibly had to say to him. Last week he drove to Manila for three hours just to listen to his four-hour treatise on why taxes were an illusion, and he shouldn't pay them (they were not, and he had to). The time before, it was to rub in Santi's face that the Carlton was doing *absolutely spectacular*, without actually adding the words, "ever since I fired you."

But Santi was a good grandson. A dutiful one. So he sat down and said nothing. Absorbed all that bullshit and never truly let it wring out.

"Hmm," was all Santi said, but Miro could sense the blood in the water, and pounced.

"I thought you would be a little happier to get face time with Lolo, since you exiled yourself to the probinsya and all," Miro commented. "We can't all be lucky enough to get away, you know."

"You could have come with me," Santi said, raising a brow. "You could have cut yourself off from the family funds, worked for yourself."

"Oh no, my allowance keeps me too comfy for that. Lolo thinks I'm too dumb to be put to work, and I don't have to live in the province." Miro shrugged. "Huh. I guess *I'm* the lucky one."

Santi would have loved to argue with Miro on that, because they both knew that there was not a dumb bone in Miro Santillan's body. But there was little point in doing that today. Instead he smiled at his brother, assured him that he'd already taken care of the problem ("of course you have") and said goodbye.

Santi watched Miro walk away for a moment before he went up the staircase to get to the reception venue, which was, as expected, full of wedding guests.

Another one of the pitfalls of a wedding was the time in between—figuring out what on earth guests were supposed to do when they were hungry, bored and waiting for you to finish taking all the pictures and the same-day-edit video.

Today's happy couple had decided on a classic solution, with a photo booth in the corner, standing tables, iced tea and pica-pica of garlic peanuts or crispy fried kangkong with dip. Not enough to get guests drunk or full before they had their dinners, but enough to tide them over until then.

"Ton-ton!" One of his distant relatives waved at him as he walked past, and Anton smiled blandly and waved back, hoping they wouldn't approach. Family gatherings were prime places for gossip, and Anton didn't have the energy to explain that no, he wasn't actually "banished" to Lipa per se, he just chose to go there after Vito didn't give him any other option, which was totally a different thing.

When he'd walked out of that convenience store three years ago, he'd pictured himself working with Miro and his grandfather, making improvements on the

Villa's hotel, making it another diamond in the chain of Carlton Resorts and Hotels. Instead, Miro had rejected the idea outright, claiming disinterest, and his grandfather had laughed in Santi's face and said "good luck" without any emotion or care, and signed the check.

Santi made the best he could with the situation. But still that feeling that he didn't belong in Lipa followed him. That Manila was where he had to be, because this was where his family was. Even if Manila didn't feel right anymore.

"An-*ton*!" A shrill hiss pulled him out of his reverie, just as he was about to take a bite of the plate of crispy kangkong in front of him. He really did like it, but only if the garlic aioli dip was made right, and the chef at this particular Carlton had the perfect recipe.

"Mama," he said, giving her a perfunctory but still polite kiss on the cheek. "Where's Papa?"

"Oh you know your father, he finds the first opportunity to leave and takes it." Joyce Santillan shrugged. "He's at the mall across the street, but he'll be back. Did you just get in from Batangas?" she asked, straightening her back as her eyebrow rose. She carefully gave him a once-over glance, looking for a point of attack. She wasn't going to find anything. "I did not see you at the wedding."

"I was sitting in the back," he explained.

"Hmm," his mother said like the answer was satisfactory.

Joyce Santillan very closely resembled Miro in the looks and charm department, but where Miro had inherited his naturally, Joyce had learned hers. Moving to Manila from Lipa to her had meant leaving everything behind and not looking back. Santi wondered what she made of her son going back there. She certainly never said anything to him about it.

"I heard from Choning that you slipped Kit thirty thousand pesos on behalf of the family," she told him, her canary diamond earrings shaking as she did. "I would have thought you would be a lot less reckless with Tatay's money."

It's my money, Santi thought. He saw every peso his brother and his own parents spent, how they charged the family for a sneeze, thanks to an email thread that always conveniently forgot to remove him. But *Santi* was the one reckless with the funds. Santi was the one who was "lucky" enough to still have a life, was the one who had abandoned them.

Santi who had lost access to all those accounts when he was fired, who was too guilty not to refuse a request from Vito. Sure.

"It's polite," Santi pointed out. "Especially since you're now their Ninang."

"I don't care if I birthed them myself!" Joyce exclaimed, rounding in on Santi, poking him in the chest with a perfectly manicured acrylic nail. "Anak naman. You just *had* to be the one to hand the envelope. You could have given it to me, and I would not have to look cheap!"

That had been…a miscalculation in Santi's part. But he wasn't going to admit it to his mother. So he said nothing. But he did notice that a few guests' heads had turned, most notably the titas that had waved at him earlier, and the titos who somehow procured cans of San Mig Light and were trying not to stare.

"Let's talk inside," Santi said, gently taking his mother's elbow to lead her into the ballroom.

"Oh, un*hand* me, you ungrateful child," Joyce hissed, pushing Anton's hand away before she marched to the ballroom. Anton barely had time to look at the decor when his mother redoubled her efforts to tell him off. "Don't think I don't know that you're deliberately trying to make me look bad in front of the family! Do you hate me that much?"

"I'm not that smart," Anton said, crossing his arms over his chest. Conclusion: it was a bad idea to come to the wedding. A *really* bad idea.

"Yes you are." His mother sighed like she was just as tired of this argument as he was. "You know it, I know it, everyone does. There was a reason you were asked to leave the Carlton and suffer in Lipa these last three years. But if you loved me even a little bit, you would have thought of me first. What about my needs, anak?"

"Just like you thought of me, while I was suppos- edly suffering in Lipa?" he asked.

"What was that?"

"Nothing," Anton said, resigned but not apologetic. It would do very little to apologize, and at least he still had his pride. "What's done is done, Mom."

Joyce Santillan huffed and said something else about once again having to fix everything, before she flounced out of the ballroom in a storm of diamonds and tulle. Santi heard himself sigh when she left, felt his entire upper body relax and drop. Then he slowly turned around and found himself standing inside a can- opy of flowers and chandeliers, with soft yellow light- ing that gave the place a dreamy feel.

He had to admit, it was nice. Almost worth having a wedding in December for. Could even picture his fu- ture, definitely-not-happening-anytime-soon wedding happening right here. Santi was never one to indulge in fantasy, but the setting was right. He was wearing a barong, a really nice one, too. All he had to do was picture a bride. One waiting in the ballroom, walking across the canopy of flowers, skin glowing under the light of the chandeliers. Maybe "Moon River" could play; he'd always liked that song.

He walked across the dance floor, still observing. He was humming the song too, giving himself just a second to picture a moment that seemed too far away, too impossible for him to comprehend. But here he was, picturing a wedding. His.

"Santi?" a voice said behind him, making him turn and blink in surprise. Kira Luz was, quite suddenly, standing in front of him in a soft pink ball gown of tulle, her long dark locks curled under a flower crown, her impossibly warm brown eyes made even more impossibly warm by the lighting. She looked like she'd emerged from a fairy tale, speaking to the mere mortal who dared interrupt her slumber. Almost like he'd summoned her.

We should promise to be there for each other when we need it.

Santi shook off his cloudy vision. "Kira," he managed to say. "You didn't hear any of that, did you?"

"Well, I wasn't listening, if that's what you're asking. And hi," she said. That little smile of hers could have melted hearts, if Santi wasn't too busy being disoriented as hell. "Did I know you were going to be at this wedding?"

"I didn't know you would be here either, so—"

"Wow. It's almost like destiny," Kira noted thoughtfully. He wanted to disagree, point out that destiny was merely a string of coincidences, but decided against it. Who was he to question what she believed in? She held up an open box, foil sticking out at the top. A chocolate bar. "Eat this."

He'd known she was part of the wedding, but not until the ceremony actually started. He'd seen her walking down the aisle as a bridesmaid, tucked under Miro's arm. What was she doing in the ballroom already? Why was she looking at him like that? How much of his conversation with his mother had she heard?

There was a reason you were asked to leave the Carlton and suffer in Lipa these last three years.

See the thing was, it hadn't exactly felt like suffering, these last three years. He missed Manila, missed the feeling of being there, but Lipa hadn't been awful at all.

He wondered what Kira made of that, if she'd heard. Not that he'd ever explained any more to her than he had that night three years ago in Osaka.

In those three years, he and Kira had developed a… not quite friendship, not quite relationship. He'd managed to keep his distance from her, from everyone in general. Lipeños were never quite sure of what to make of someone who came back, and it suited him just fine. This was supposed to be a temporary exile, even if he still didn't know what to do to stop it. Approaching her was never the plan, because staying wasn't the plan. And if there was anyone who could potentially make Santi want to root his life to Lipa, it was the fairy queen standing in front of him, handing him chocolate.

"Is it poisoned?" Santi asked, and Kira rolled her eyes.

"It's fifty percent milk chocolate, jerk," Kira explained with a little chuckle, lifting a bar of foil before she broke it with her fingers. The chocolate made a satisfying *snap* sound, and she opened her hands for Santi to take the piece of chocolate. Santi picked up the square and gave Kira a look. "Just eat it, okay."

Santi took a bite of the chocolate. It was fruity. Almost tart, and dried his mouth in a good way. It was hard to believe that something that tasted so complex had only 50% cacao. Santi swallowed, then took another bite. And just like that, he was out of chocolate.

"Can I have—"

"Here," Kira said, snapping off another piece, slightly smaller.

"So generous," he said sarcastically.

"I figured you could use something soothing," Kira pointed out, and he heard that little catch in her voice, that hesitation of her wondering if she should say it out loud, then letting the dice roll, bahala na what Santi's reaction could be. "Okay, I wasn't listening, but it was hard not to hear. It was a bit loud."

"Great." Santi wished the earth could just swallow him whole now, even if he greatly appreciated the chocolate. Thank god it was a little dark; he prayed she didn't notice that his cheeks were probably red, because they felt hot. She wordlessly passed him the rest of the bar, and he popped another square into his mouth. "So this is ano, paawa chocolate?"

"Of course," Kira said, but the way she said it made him feel like it wasn't a bad thing, necessarily, to get pity chocolate. Especially not one that Kira had very obviously made herself. Gemini Chocolates was on its own tier of chocolate greatness to Santi, and he had to admit, it did help somewhat. "Also, I'm in here because I was checking on the wedding favors. I can't tell you how much of a strugglebus tempering was. But the chocolate is fine, and you looked like you needed it, so…you're welcome."

"Strugglebus? What does that even…wait. You *stole* this," Santi realized, looking at the packaging in his hand, where sure enough, Kit and Clara's names were embossed in gold, and the same motif from the invitation was all over the packaging. "You've turned me into an accomplice."

"Oh relax, Grim Reaper-nim, I always bring extras for my wedding clients." Kira smirked, taking back the chocolate.

"I still don't understand why you call me that." And no, he wasn't pouting. Definitely not.

"It's your own fault. I told you to watch *Goblin* and find out." Kira tut her lips, biting off the bar itself before she handed it back to Santi, who winced before he snapped off a piece from the opposite end of the bar. "Or do you Virgos not have sixteen hours free from work you definitely don't have to do?"

"It's like you're speaking another language." Santi sighed, shaking his head and trying not to laugh. Because this was the first time in the entire wedding that he was actually enjoying himself. "So how do you know the happy couple? I'm sure we're not related."

"Lucky you," Kira said, giving him a little wink. "But like most of my custom chocolate clients, I know the couple because I matched them. We were blockmates, me and Kit and Cla. He had a crush on her since orientation, and I told him her favorite cake was Swiss Chocolate from Becky's. Cla's birthday was on a Monday, and he went to Becky's fully expecting to get the cake and win her heart, but they were closed, and Kit was *devastated*."

"Kit, devastated?" Santi echoed, because he couldn't imagine his cousin, second or not, so lost in the throes of love that he would be devastated, with italics implied. He also couldn't imagine being as open to, well, everything as Kira. So in touch with everyone she met that she could claim the title "matchmaker," without a problem. It was fascinating, and terrifying to know that she'd held other people's feelings in her hands, and helped them along.

What would she do, he wondered, if she was faced with *his* feelings?

"On the verge of tears, or at least that's how I remember," Kira said, waving a hand at Santi as if to scold him for interrupting her. That was when he noticed that her lips looked very soft, and slightly more pink and shiny than usual. It made her look prettier. As if she wasn't already. "Anyway, he starts knocking and begging Becky's to open up for him, because he *needs* this cake. And I had to stall Cla from going home somehow, because she couldn't go home without knowing how Kitty felt!"

"They should put this story on the back of the dinner menu," Santi deadpanned.

"I told the story for the same-day edit, don't worry. And *then*," Kira said, because he was sure at this point that she was both ignoring him and making the story much more dramatic than it should be. "Just when Cla was about to give up on me, because tutoring me in Math 10 is no easy feat, there he was. Kit, his grin wide and happy because the people in the shop were actually baking in the back and they took pity on him. I passed Math 10, they fell in love, and then they lived happily ever after."

Santi doubted that it had been that simple. But far be it from him to correct someone who had actually been there.

"So they will." He nodded, looking around at the spectacle before them. For all his complaints about weddings, he really did enjoy them. Liked the idea of two people pledging to be together, through the best and the worst of times. To commit to each other, and just…love them. For as long as they were allowed.

He sighed. It didn't seem like it was for him.

"But matchmaking sounds like a terrible marketing strategy," he said, turning his attention back to Kira and those eyes of hers. "You wouldn't have known that matching them all those years ago would mean business for you."

"I didn't, but it makes making chocolate for them now extra special," Kira said, and her face just…lit up. "And I must be doing *something* right with my businesses, because one of us had to go behind my back to open up a store on the Laneways, and I'm looking at you, Mr. Silent Partner Kuno."

Santi groaned. She was never going to let him live that down, will she?

The Laneways was a row of old warehouses in Lipa that, by the Luz family's renovating and Kira's operating, had turned into a lively, profitable retail space that commanded more foot traffic than most of the other open-air commercial spaces in Lipa. Santi's decision to financially back Sunday Bakery without telling Kira had rightly earned him her ire, because everyone knew he was behind it the moment Sunday Bakery opened its doors.

But it was okay. He actually didn't mind it. It made him feel like he was part of the Laneways somehow. He felt more welcome than he had that first day he showed up at Hotel Villa with Vito's money, and ready to work.

"Real G's move in silence." He quoted Lil Wayne, only because Gabriel sent him the meme. "Like lasagna."

Kira blinked at him for a moment, her face completely shocked and still before he saw her lips curl up, her eyes light up, just before she started to laugh. Really, really laugh, laugh so hard that she had to grab the sleeve of his jacket to keep herself upright.

"So glad I could amuse you," Santi noted.

"Oh my god." Kira laughed, and there were tears in her eyes, that she carefully wiped off with her fingertips. "Is this the kind of dry humor that won over all the local suppliers in Lipa?"

"It was my winning personality," he said dryly, sending her into another fit of laughter. "Goes well with that Batangas tapang I keep hearing about."

That was how Santi managed to get a foot in the door, through sheer force of will, and speaking to each and every local supplier he could find. Batangueños didn't mince words when they accused him of having a short fuse, too demanding, too much of a perfectionist. But hey, they still became his suppliers. Even if they weren't quite his friends.

"Well, I suppose it worked. Everyone keeps flocking to Villa, and I can't open social media without seeing someone post about it, or get married there, or talk about the food," Kira noted, and Santi let the pride swell in his chest. Because he deserved it, didn't he? After three years of working on the hotel, making it beautiful, making it a place people wanted to be in, and spend their time in, he deserved to agree that it was a good idea. "You made it way, way bigger than anyone could have imagined."

And yet it isn't enough for Vito Santillan, Santi thought, pushing that aside immediately. Something he could process later on, preferably never.

"And everyone who isn't in Villa is in the Lane-ways," he pointed out to her instead, and she laughed.

"SM and Robinsons found shaking," she joked. "I'm surprised you ended up in Lipa, actually," Kira contin-ued, taking a bite of the chocolate before passing it to him. "I would think your family would love someone as good as you here in Manila."

Santi winced, sure that the sudden bitterness in his mouth wasn't the chocolate, because the pride that had swelled in his chest had instantly deflated like a bal-loon. He was about to tell her that his family was the whole reason why he was in Lipa in the first place, but was interrupted by a woman with a headset walking into the ballroom and seeing them.

"Hala, errant guests!" they exclaimed. "Excuse me, you shouldn't be in here."

"It's a wedding reception, everyone will be in here in about an hour anyway," Kira pointed out.

"Nevertheless, I have to insist that—" The wom-an's eyes widened when they saw the chocolate bar in Santi's hands. "Is that a wedding giveaway? Did you *steal* a wedding giveaway?"

"Um, what?" Kira asked, her voice suddenly high-pitched as Santi groaned. "He didn't—"

"Stop, chocolate thief!"

He wished he could explain why this was his first instinct, but he really couldn't. Santi just saw the possible danger, and reacted.

"Run," Santi said, taking Kira's wrist and pulling her out of the ballroom, just as the wedding coordinator was about to lunge at them to get the half-eaten chocolate back.

"Keep running!" Kira shrieked as they ran past the other wedding guests, past the photo booth and down the stairs, until they made it to the relative safety of the lobby lounge, Kira laughing all the while as Santi sunk into the plush chairs he'd grown up with.

Sitting in the lounge was so familiar it almost ached. He knew which seats shielded you from which views, and which seats made sure you were instantly visible. He and Miro used to play spy games from the lobby lounge, too. Sure, the face of the lounge changed, but the placement of the seats was the same. The four-member orchestra that played every day still stayed in the same place.

Anyway. Pain he could set aside.

"That day we met in Japan," he said, and he appreciated that Kira didn't seem confused by his tangent. "I'd just been fired from the Carlton."

"What?" Kira gasped, putting the chocolate down. "Why did they fire you?"

"My grandfather and I were arguing about salary advances and raises," he said, and was surprised to find he could say it without too much emotion. Like he was talking about something that happened to someone else. "We had different opinions on how it worked. The next day, I came to work and my desk was just…

gone. My stuff was in boxes, all the files were taken somewhere else. I'm the owner's grandson, I couldn't exactly complain to HR about it."

While Santi had never experienced the need to spend money that he hadn't earned yet, he understood that sometimes, bills and salaries just didn't line up. He suggested that the Carlton be a little more lenient in allowing salary advances, proposing that they be just as low or affordable as a government loan. Vito thought otherwise.

But Santi didn't think that was why he had been so unceremoniously unemployed. Santi didn't want to seem like the ungrateful grandson—god only knew anywhere else he wouldn't be in this high a position. So he left quietly, moped quietly, until New Year's Eve.

"When I came back with the idea to restore Villa, I proposed that we do it together. Santillan and grand-sons, working on a project together. When he heard, my grandfather laughed in my face," Santi told her, and realized that he'd never told anyone else this. Who was there to tell? His family already knew, and nobody else…there really wasn't anyone else *to* tell. "He gave me the money, put the hotel under the Carlton chain and just…left me alone. My accounts tied to the family were cancelled, my cards were cut, and I was sent off to Lipa. They still tell me that Villa's success isn't enough. That I am not enough to deserve coming back."

"Shit," Kira gasped, and Santi heard himself chuckle mirthlessly. Shit didn't even begin to cover it. But he was glad someone else said it. "That's…sorry, but that's fucked up."

"Poor little rich boy, I know," Santi said.

"Rich boys have feelings, too," Kira pointed out,

smiling kindly. "Your grandfather hurt you because he didn't agree with you. Who does that?"

Santi didn't have the answer to that, either. Kira turned her head to the windows, three stories high and gave guests the full view of the Makati skyline.

"It's raining," she noted, even as the sun was shining, and a rainbow streaked across the sky. "A tikbalang is getting married."

"Lucky tikbalang." Santi looked up. It was raining in sheets, but it was a gentle drizzle that felt like mist when you walked through it. He used to hate days like this when he was a child, as rain like this only made everything hot and even more humid when it went away. He didn't mind so much at the moment, if it meant luck for the happy couple.

"How do centaurs wear pants?" Kira asked suddenly, and she looked like she really was wondering. Santi blinked at her a few times, as he realized just how complicated the question was. "Tikbalangs have horse heads, so obviously they wear pants like everyone, but what about centaurs?"

"How do giraffes wear scarves?" Santi asked back. "And other nonsense questions."

"Important questions," Kira insisted, and there was a moment when he caught a glimpse of the neighborhood kid that dominated the roadside. He smiled and leaned forward, picking up the chocolate bar. Only to realize that there was only one serving left. He offered it to Kira, who shook her head.

"You're the chocolate thief," she joked, smiling at him. "And it really does make you feel better, no? Eating the chocolate."

He had to admit, it really did. Surely there was some

scientific explanation about sugar and oxytocin and other chemical reactions. But it was also Kira, sitting next to her and being able to talk, in a way that they never got to before, having him consider how centaurs wore pants, or giraffes wore scarves.

It was her making him laugh and roll his eyes, saying impossible things, and her making him feel like he was just a little bit wanted, making him consider that his feelings really did matter.

"I have to say though," Kira continued, leaning back against her seat, rotating her ankles in her silver heels. "I'm glad you ended up in Lipa. That you brought Villa back to life. That you went behind my back and opened Sunday Bakery."

"Really?" Santi asked, in disbelief, although he hoped she couldn't see just how much.

"Really," Kira insisted, and Santi felt an inexorable pull in his belly, one that led him closer to her. He knew the distance between where he was sitting, and where she was, had played in these spots for a lot of his life. Almost as if it was to lead to this moment, of them sitting together, the chocolate all gone.

"Kira. I moved to Lipa because of you. It means more, because it was you."

Santi still didn't know what his destiny was. Was it to stay in Lipa? To keep pushing Villa to its limits to earn his place back in Manila? He didn't know. He wasn't even sure he believed in that kind of thing. But tonight, as the rain fell in sheets outside the floor-to-ceiling windows of the Carlton, as the candles flickered orange light into Kira's eyes, he didn't care.

"You're about to kiss me, aren't you?" she said, and

that cheeky little grin of hers was enough to make him give in to the pull of her.

"Would you like me to?" he asked.

"Yes please," she said, a little breathily.

So he kissed her. He came in close and slow, following that pull toward her. That little gasp she made before he did almost made him pull back, but Kira sank herself into the kiss, and Santi's hesitation melted away as he gave in, too.

He held her face in his hands, gently brushing at the still-soft skin, as things like patterns and plans made sense in his head. He finally understood why people married in December, why New Year's mattered, why you wore stripes instead of polka dots. Why being born under the right stars could bring you to this place, to this exact moment.

And that was all this was, a moment. But stars and planets were born and died in moments like these, and even Santi could believe in destinies revealed by chocolates, in the stars determining who he was going to be.

Until, of course, it was interrupted by a very loud, very rude cough. And with that single cough, the moment shattered, gone as soon as it had come. Every muscle in Santi's back tensed, as a pair of eyes bore into his back.

"Anton." His grandfather's voice was a low warning.

"Oh." Kira pulled away, and he saw her cheeks flush when they pulled apart, her eyes wide and her pupils slightly dilated, her lips still that sweet shade of pink, a little more red now that Santi had kissed them. She turned her head away, as if she'd heard that cough from the direction of the ballroom. "I should…"

Santi didn't want her to go. He wanted to talk about

the kiss, what it meant, what she wanted. But it was more important to him that Vito Santillan didn't cross paths with her. Santi moved to the right, totally shielding Kira from Vito's gaze. She tilted her head slightly, as if to ask him what he was doing.

"We'll talk," he said softly. "I promise. Thank you for the chocolate."

"Another promise?" Kira asked wryly.

"One of many I intend to keep."

He could see she was trying really, really hard not to look over his shoulder. She smiled at him instead before she left the chair, the lobby lounge, and showed nothing but her back as she made her way up to the wedding reception. Some of the muscles in Santi's back, his arms relaxed, but only slightly.

Then he stood up to his full height, took a last little breath, before he turned to face his grandfather.

At the age of 90, Vito Santillan showed no signs of slowing down anytime soon. He still came to the office every day, still wore suspenders and a long-sleeved shirt like he didn't live in the Pacific Ring of Fire, and still muscled his way through his business's problems. Even after the events of three years ago, Santi had a great respect for his grandfather, and would likely never lose his admiration of the man who built one of the biggest hotel brands in the country.

But admiration could still come with distrust. Could still come with resistance, and…fear. Gods craved devotion, after all, and Vito made himself the god of his family a long time ago. He made himself and his money the center of the family's universe—enough to make Santi and Miro's parents leave them in Vito's hands to raise. Enough to make the family feel like utter failures when they were put at a distance.

"Busy?" Vito asked. "I told Miro to fetch you thirty minutes ago."

"Miro already left," Santi said, which wasn't an excuse or an explanation, and not something Vito could use against him. He had to learn to be careful with what he said that way.

"I need to show you something upstairs," he said, turning and walking away unassisted, because he still walked perfectly fine, so much that he strictly maintained six feet of distance from his nurse, Melba, at all times.

Santi wordlessly followed his grandfather to the elevators. Vito swiped a card against the reader and the elevator moved steadily up the hotel floors, and the silence was horrible. Santi legitimately didn't know if his grandfather was going to berate him about Kira, or Lipa, or whatever it was they were going.

"What's in the penthouse?" Santi asked.

"We're renovating the suite for your little brother," Vito said, glancing at Santi as if wondering how that would hit. Santi schooled his face into mild interest, which was the only way he was going to make it through this. "He asked for a place in Makati, and I was only too happy to indulge him."

The unspoken words hung in the air. *Meanwhile, when you asked me for a condo, I adamantly refused.* It had been a practical consideration then, because he was getting his MBA and the drive from QC to Makati every day was hellish at best. Vito had refused, saying Santi had done nothing to deserve it.

Santi was still making payments on the condo he

purchased back then, sure it would be a good investment. And here was Miro, getting a penthouse suite to himself.

The elevator doors opened, but Santi couldn't really absorb any of it—the furniture, the view spread out all the way to Laguna de Bay, the marbled floors and the chandelier. He didn't listen as his grandfather listed how much each renovated item cost, how it was selected with love and the utmost care. It was petty, but he didn't want to know. He really didn't.

"Lolo, I think the reception is starting, we should—"

"This could have all been yours, you know," Vito said, and could Santi detect wistfulness in his voice? "You were doing so well with Carlton. People know the Santillan name with class, and power. You were such an integral part of my legacy. And yet you chose to squander it away."

The conscience he was alluding to had grown from Santi's own explorations. Because unlike the rest of his family, he'd actually gone out into the world, and changed his perspective on money and life. He met the CEOs and leaders of his batch—Cora Ciacho, Isabel Alfonso, Regina Benitez—and molded his philosophies and moral compass after them. He'd read articles about Joaquin Aritz and learned their approach to business. He studied under people who knew better than him, and didn't pretend he knew more.

But all of that knowledge, all of that skill and improvement, wasn't enough to earn him this. No matter how much he loved Hotel Villa, loved making it better, making it Estate and Lands' "favorite place to get married outside of Manila."

"Are you sure you still want to stay in that little

probinsya of yours?" Vito asked Santi, like being relegated to the provinces (when Lipa was just as big as any city now) was a punishment. Like Vito would actually let him back into the fold of the Carlton if *Santi* could just let go. "Say the word, and I can bring you back, hijo."

Santi thought about talking with Kira earlier, how happy she was selling her chocolate to her friends, how she knew him well enough to understand him. He thought about Villa, and how he managed to make the old place a little more welcoming, made the place feel like home, for him and so many other people. He thought about the Laneways and sitting in Sunday Bakery with Gabriel, about the recent Christmas Party where he ate too much cupcake and hummed along to the karaoke contests.

"His" probinsya didn't feel so little to him. But still. Manila was Manila, and you couldn't be anyone if you couldn't make it in Manila.

"What would it take?" he asked. Paths and possible outcomes fell away with every choice you made. This was Anton making his choice, his stand.

"What is it going to take?" he repeated, emboldened by his grandfather's surprise. "For you to ask me back to the Carlton. Back to Manila. Back to the family."

There was silence in the penthouse. His grandfather seemed to consider it. He was silent, staring out at the view, at the dust on the table, at anything but Santi, who was so nervous he could hear his pulse beating.

No wait. Those were his temples throbbing. He was getting a headache. Cool.

"Villa is already top of mind for hotels in the region," Santi continued. "We've already more than made back your investment. What else would I have to do, for you to trust me again?"

How much would you sell your soul? a voice whispered in the back of his mind. He knew this was a deal with the devil. But what could you do, if the devil was the person who raised you, who taught you everything you knew?

"The Lai Group recently purchased a lot in Lima," he said, and Santi's stomach sank to the ground. Because of course he knew that. And because he was so smart, he knew what his grandfather was about to ask him. "Hotels would do well across mall lots like that, especially if they're making it a commercial and office space."

He had to have known. Somehow Vito had to have known that Santi had a stake in the Laneways, the only property left in the area. Why else would he bring it up? Why would the Carlton even want to be in Lima when they had a strong hold on Lipa?

"That's what you can get me," Vito said. "If you can get me that space, then I'll let you back in. I'll make you CEO, if that's want you want. You're a smart boy, you can figure it out."

Santi felt like he'd been punched in the gut. Twice.

"You want the Laneways," he said. Even if the mere thought of asking Kira to sell the Laneways to him already made his stomach churn.

It was a row of commercial spaces in an old warehouse. Santi wouldn't be the first to say that it wasn't the most innovative idea. But it was special, both to the people who set up businesses there, and the people that came to the Laneways. Even Santi had business on the Laneways—Sunday Bakery was shared with a business partner, but it was still partly his. His grandfather didn't know about it, but suddenly the bakery, Kira's chocolate shop, Sari's cafe, Ate Tiana's restaurant, all of that was in Vito's crosshairs, and he couldn't let it happen. Vito had already taken Lipa away from him before, had taken the Carlton away.

Was Santi really going to let him take this?

He wanted to sit down. Wanted to ask if there was literally anything else he could do. But one look at Vito's face was enough to stop Santi from asking. Sentiment was unacceptable if money was on the line, which was one of the many, many reasons why the Santillans should never have the Laneways.

"I want you to get it into your head, hijo," his grandfather said. "Lipa is meaningless. And until you get me that deed of sale, this penthouse will belong to Miro."

Then he turned and walked away. Santi looked around at the suite, at the stunning view, and at the crystal chandeliers and the pretty coffee machine on the kitchen counter. These were things he should want for himself, and maybe he did. But he also felt tired, suddenly. Exhausted. And the evening had only just begun.

Chapter Four

December 26
Gemini Chocolates
The Laneways, Lipa

Today's Horoscope: Twins are most powerful when they're in sync, and you're feeling that sync with the universe today, Gemini. The world is yours to experience and feel in the way you need. Don't let the earth signs get you down.

When the Luz family moved to their big, new house in Haraya Subdivision, after years in the bayan, Kira had insisted on growing flowers on her windowsill. Her family, who all had gardens of their own, were only too happy to donate. So she had fragrant rosal from Lola Luz's garden, small, delicate dama de noche crawling up to the roof from one of her Titas, and beautiful sampaguita that Kiko had given her as a birthday gift when she turned twenty-nine that year.

And while these plants loved the summer heat, Kira left her windows open at night in December, and the smell that wafted into her room in the mornings was always incredible. That, and the cool air, always made her December mornings special. She woke up to the heavy, musky scent of her rosal flowers, the birds singing in the mango tree in the Luzes' front yard, and the wind whistling in the trees.

Yes, she was a Disney princess, basically. Now all she needed was a Disney prince with slightly sleepy eyes, fancy hair, surprisingly soft lips and—oh my god, it was barely 8 a.m., how was she *already* thinking of Anton Santillan?

She'd left Makati shortly after the wedding the other day. She would have loved to stay in Manila a little longer, actually spend time with friends she barely saw anymore (she couldn't believe how many of her blockmates were already engaged/with child/moving in/moving away), but with the holidays truly setting in, there wasn't time.

She realized that it wasn't as easy, keeping up conversation with her friends—she no longer knew what the hot new food trend was (people were very into ramen, apparently), what people were lining up for (again, ramen).

And it wasn't like she could really talk about her chocolate, how hard it was when it didn't temper, when the Laneways lost electricity (as it still did sometimes), her frustration when the chocolate bloomed, and she didn't know why. She didn't really talk to anyone about that, not that there was anyone she could talk about it to.

But she supposed that was just a consequence of living in the provinces, away from Manila. If Kira had stayed, she had no doubt that she would be just like her friends, aware of the newest thing, excited about new places to try, parts of the city still left unexplored. She would have found some kind of corporate job (because nothing says "stability" like working for a multi-national!) fallen in love, married, had kids.

It wouldn't be a bad life at all, really. But not one she would give up Lipa for.

Girl, why are we thinking of a jowa when you've got a business to run? she thought, chuckling to herself as she watered her plants. She wasn't even thinking about love, much less babies and marriage.

Kira preferred love when she could give it to other people in the form of chocolate or matchmaking advice. *That* she was comfortable with. Love was meant for other people, much braver people than herself. Her job was to make sure that they got their shot at it.

When she was about fourteen, fifteen, just starting to understand the concept of love, and relationships, her mother told her to be patient. *Wait for love. It will come to you. Pray for it. Manifest to the universe that you want it, and it'll come. You'll fall in love faster than you realize.*

So, she waited. She manifested crushes, waited for guys to make the first move, because they had to. And love came, easily enough. Kira was likeable and fun, and said yes to dates when guys asked. But they never really turned into anything more than that, a night or two together. The guys in Manila said she was "fun," but she was a bit "too much to handle." Like she was some kind of frying pan or something.

So, she thought, "okay, then maybe I can pour my love into my work instead." She'd always dreamed of being part of Serendipity Studios, a stationery shop that made everything from notepads and stickers to rugs, water jugs and wallpapers. She'd cried of happiness when she passed the interviews, showed up to work even when she didn't know what a junior accounts manager was supposed to do half the time. Continued to show up even when the cracks of their perfectly made foundations started to show, and was left to fend for herself, mostly.

Six months later, they said, thanks, but no thanks, maybe this isn't for you, so bye.

Which brought her right back to Lipa. Where all a guy had to do was breathe wrong in her direction and everyone would know about it. It made her a little more judicious, a little more hesitant. She loved running the Laneways, loved running Gemini, and everything that came with it. But by the time she came back to Lipa, she'd gotten used to waiting. Whatever was meant for her would come if it was time. If it didn't...then maybe it just wasn't for her.

She would much rather focus on her chocolate, something she had control over, something she could create with her hands and make other people happy. Who would have thought that *Kira* would figure it out? And when the days were good, when the chocolate tempered and snapped as it should, it was good.

But the other days? The bad days? Oh god. Those were the worst.

"Is this a long-winded explanation of why I'm not getting my tableya today?" Sari Tomas asked, her brow rising at Kira from across the countertop at Café Cecilia in the Laneways, two hours later. "My customers will riot."

Kira had her morning coffee every day at Sari's cafe. She loved it because the space was nice and airy, with enough plants and seating to feel comfortable, and Sari's music taste was excellent. It helped that Sari was also one of her best and oldest friends. Cafè Cecilia exuded the same energy the rest of the Laneways had—stylish and comfortable. It was Kira's favorite place to have her morning coffee.

Well, breakfast *and* morning coffee, now that Sari was officially boyfriending the baker next door, and Café Cecilia now had good food. Long story. Cute story, but a long one.

"My aircon sputtered and died the other day, and I know it's December, but all those appliances generate heat, so it was melt city all day. *All day*, Sari. Including me," Kira explained.

"Poor baby," Gabriel, the aforementioned baker boyfriend next door, said, patting Kira's head as he continued to eat his bowl of tocino and kesong puti on rice. He treated Kira exactly like he treated his younger siblings—slightly annoying, even if his heart was in the right place. "Did you get someone to fix it?"

"Mang Roldan knew a guy, and Ate Nessie watched the shop while he fixed it," Kira explained as she stole a slice of kesong puti from Gab's plate. It had been fried in olive oil, making the slightly salty white cheese extra salty and crispy and delicious. "Kasi I went to Kit and Clara's wedding."

"Why do those names sound familiar…?" Gab said, scratching his chin, clearly ignoring the way Kira was now stuffing her pan de sal with his kesong puti. It was really good. "Are they from Ateneo?"

"Yup. Blockmates," she explained. She was about to start her usual roll call of all the ways Gabriel, an Atenean, also knew Kit and Clara, also Ateneans, because that was just the way they worked, when Sari stood in front of the two of them with a mug of her own coffee. The UP graduate stared at the two of them with that little look on her face, that I'm-so-glad-I'm-not-from-Ateneo face. "They had it in Manila."

To be fair, Sari seems…more settled somehow, Kira thought. A little more mellow, as much as Capricorns could be mellow. And it probably had a lot to do with the Libra sitting next to Kira who was currently holding Sari's hand and kissing the back of it. Cute. Air signs were usually good lifting forces on earth signs.

"Dimples, didn't Anton Santillan *also* attend a wedding the other day?" Sari asked her new boyfriend, and god, the way Gab's face just lit up at her mention of his little nickname was so sweet. Like those milk chocolate and caramel buttons her aunt used to bring home as pasalubong from London. "At the—"

"Carlton Makati, oo na, oo na," Kira groaned, reaching over the counter the way she really wasn't supposed to, and grabbed a to-go cup. "He was there. I was there. The world is too small."

"So did you see him?" Sari asked as Gabriel gasped exaggeratedly. Kira knew it was pointless to lie to her friends and tenants. But really, more friends than tenants. Point at a tenant in the Laneways and Kira could tell you how they became friends. But it also meant that they knew everything—her life, her love life and lack thereof, what she had for breakfast, where she had lunch. It was a lot.

"I saw him," she admitted, trying not to think about Santi in that creamy white barong, the way his lashes fluttered when he tried to smile, or that sad look on his face whenever his family was brought up. "His baby brother and I walked the aisle together. We—"

Kissed.

"Said hi to each other," she finished, quickly pouring her remaining coffee into the to-go cup, not bothering with the lid. "Okay, I have to go. Chocolates to make, orders to fill—"

"Things to keep secret?" Sari asked, her brow rising in suspicion as Kira groaned and stuffed her pan de sal into her mouth. She'd known Sari since they were kids, and she was sure it was only a matter of time before her friend sussed out the truth, because Kira was such a generous person when it came to gossip. Even if it meant gossip about herself.

"I plead the fifth, whatever that means!" she managed to say, quickly making her escape from Café Cecilia, and out to the Laneways, where from there, it was a quick walk across the cobblestone street to her own shop, Gemini Chocolates.

Gemini was the first shop you saw when you entered the Laneways, and it was the only establishment that was actually a building and not a repurposed warehouse. It used to be an office, at least according to the plans she'd seen when the Laneways was under construction, but was now repurposed into Kira's chocolate shop.

Kira really liked her space. It was chaotic, but in a way that didn't overwhelm anyone. Like walking in to your rich tita's house in a fancy subdivision for the first time.

Her floor was a checkerboard tile of emerald green and white diamonds, an original from the building. She'd painted her walls a cool teal blue, warm enough to be appetizing, but cool enough to be easy on the eye. The menu board hung on the wall across from the door and was the first thing a customer saw when they walked in, the chocolate selection changing as often as Kira's moods dictated. Today, it was milk chocolate bars with banana chip crisps, one of the earliest chocolates she'd developed, and a customer favorite.

Right now, a surge of customers were in the shop, tasting the different chocolates and exclaiming over the tableya, recently announced as a favorite at some year-end list by Gentleman's Guide, and was now flying off the shelves faster than Kira could make it. And now with her aircon fixed, it shouldn't be a problem.

She frowned at the space, at her staff serving customers, at customers trying samples, exclaiming about the chocolate. There was something missing in this scenario, but she couldn't quite put her finger on it. What was off?

We'll talk. The memory of Santi murmuring into her ear suddenly sprang up, in a way that memories tended to. *Thank you for the chocolate.*

Kira shook her head vehemently. Santi was definitely *not* the thing that was missing. If anything, he wasn't really here. They were friends again, sure, but the last three years, they hadn't really talked, and bickered more often than not because they didn't talk. And *anyway*, that wasn't what she was missing, it was something else, it was…

"Fuck!" she exclaimed, making more than a couple of heads turn to her in shock as she made a run for the kitchen.

It had been the quiet that had surprised her. Making chocolate was very, very noisy business. From cracking to winnowing, roasting to melanging, chocolate demanded attention and made its presence felt in terms of smell and sound (or lack thereof). Cacao nibs, sugar, cocoa butter—all the good things that made chocolate—needed to be left in melangers for at least 24 hours to break down and turn into chocolate, constantly mixing and grinding and whirring all the while. And as far as her timings went, it definitely had not been 24 hours since she added the ingredients, and yet she hadn't heard anything.

"Astroboy, how could you," she sighed at her finicky melanger, which she called Astroboy in an attempt to get it to love her a little more. But sure enough, it had stopped, and the chocolate was still grainy. And seeing as Kira didn't personally know anyone who used melangers on a daily basis, and the service center was in the US and couldn't answer her call right now, Kira was going to have to figure this out on her own.

Yay.

Kira took a deep breath, willing herself to calm down. Her yoga teacher always said that breathing would help her calm down and center herself, gain the mental fortitude to do the thing she just needed to do. *Breathe.* Then recite an intention to help. *I can handle fixing the melanger. I can handle fixing the melanger.*

And no, Kira wasn't stalling, she just really needed a second to...

"Kimberly," Ate Nessie's voice cut through her centering.

"Thank god," Kira said, turning to see her former nanny, current superintendent of the Laneways, Nessie Soriano, walked into the kitchen. Kira had a lot of mother figures in her life, and Ate Nessie was one of them. It was understood among the Laneways that while Kira was the one that signed documents and sent billings and answered concerns, Ate Nessie was the one in charge. Kira loved her immensely, especially when it meant she could delay doing something she really didn't want to do yet.

"Sus, hija. Please do not take the Lord's name in vain," she said, making a quick sign of the cross and looking up at her ceiling as if to tell God, "do you see what this child is making me do?" before she moved toward Kira's toaster oven.

"Ate Ness, the word 'sus' was taken from 'sus-maryosep,' which is a shortened version of 'Hesus, Maria, Joseph,' so do you really want to scold me about taking God's name in vain?" Kira asked.

"Itong batang irè." Ate Nessie shook her head, again at the ceiling. "By the way, that candle shop, Eternal Flame, pulled out their letter of intent for that spot next to yours."

"Ah," Kira said, nodding. "Not *so* eternal, then."

"Boo," Ate Nessie argued, making Kira laugh. "And doesn't it mean that the spot next door is cursed? This is the third tenant that pulled out."

"Not cursed, just waiting for the right lessor," Kira pointed out. "InLab came close, but Nero decided he was perfectly happy where he was. And that duwende everyone keeps telling me that lives there is a good one, I can feel it."

"Feel feel naman." Ate Nessie chuckled before she waved around a brown paper bag. "I need to borrow your toaster oven."

"Okay," Kira said, looking over her shoulder because she already knew what was in the bag. "The fee is two pieces of bonete."

"Hay, nako." Ate Nessie sighed, unloading the bread

bounty onto the oven tray. "First Gabriel eats more than his share, and now I have to give some of my share to you. Your generation, ha."

"Yes, my generation of needy children who will never experience bonete as good as you make it, Ate Ness!" Kira exclaimed, walking over to her and giving her a quick hug.

"Shouldn't you be making chocolate or something?" Ate Nessie asked, her brow rising in suspicion. "I thought you said you were 'so busy you don't even have time for a boyfriend,' or are you a liar, hija?"

"No, I'm just…delaying a problem," Kira admitted, glancing surreptitiously at the melanger that she really was supposed to be trying to figure out. But what if she broke the machine? What if she lost a part, and couldn't put the thing back together?

She smiled innocently at Ate Nessie, who smiled back before she reached up and squeezed Kira's cheek. Hard.

"Lusot ka pa," she said, as Kira complained. Yes, she was aware that Ate Nessie still thought she was adorable when she pinched her cheek like this, but twenty-nine years later it still *hurt*. "Trabaho na!"

"Fine, fine, I'll work na," Kira groaned, rubbing her aching cheek and marching to her errant melanger. The machine was made up of two large, stone grinders shaped into wheels that spun. But it did have a tendency to stop when a bit of cocoa nib got stuck in a particular part of the wheel. She glared at it, sighed and finally got to work.

And as she worked, up to her elbows in chocolate as Ate Nessie poured herself her third a cup of coffee for the day and waited for the bonete to cool just right. Kira's brain couldn't help but start wandering all the way back to Manila. To that night, and that kiss on the lounge chair. That moment where she felt like Rose from *Titanic*, except of course she wasn't naked, he wasn't an artist and they weren't careening toward a ship crash.

Ship crash? Was that right?

But anyway, it was a kiss. A good kiss. Better than the one she got in Osaka, by her estimation, because she didn't remember thinking, *holy shit Santi is a good kisser* last time.

We'll talk. I promise.

That was all he said before she fled the scene and went back up to the reception. But he hadn't called or texted, messenger dove-d since that night. Nobody seemed to know if he was even in Lipa, or had stayed in Manila. It was like the setup of a teleserye, or maybe even a K-drama.

She could picture it now. The setting? Lipa City. The soundtrack? An eclectic mix of folk-pop Filipino and Korean pop music. The filter? The kind that made everyone look like they had perfect skin, were constantly glowing, with just the barest hint of lip tint. Kira could picture herself as the plucky heroine in a Korean drama, complete with a montage of her working in her shop with a spotless, pretty apron, music in the background. Then the door to her shop would ring, and she would look up, and Santi would walk in wearing a suit—because the chaebols always wore suits—and look absolutely stunning in it.

Then he would smile wryly over at her as he listened to her singing to herself and continue to fall deeper and more madly in love. And it was good, and happy, and it would feel like all of Kira's waiting had come to fruition just by seeing his little smile.

But then, gasp! Santi's family would find out about their budding romance and try to keep them apart!

Kira knew the drama that surrounded the Santillans—eventually she'd overheard Ate Nessie tell her mother that Santi's grandfather Vito had demanded his grandsons be close to him in Manila, that he refused to let his flesh and blood be Batangueño, and apparently it was enough for Santi's parents to uproot the kids, never speak to the Villas again and stay in Manila. The grandfather was supposedly as strict as he was rich, and the next everyone heard of the Santillans was the day Santi drove into his Lally Villa's house in a flashy red Mercedes making an offer on the Hotel Villa.

Anyway, it would play nicely into Kira's imagined drama. There would probably be a scene where the grandfather would persuade Kira to leave Santi for an exorbitant sum, and she would laugh and get water tossed in her face (ala Cherie Gil). But Kira would be too in love to care, and exit the fancy Santillan mansion in Loyola Grand Villas (featured in a magazine for being extra McMansion-y) just in time to see Santi, still in a suit under the blazing Manila sun, leaning against his fancy red Mercedes grinning at her. And the music would swell, and they would slow-mo run toward each other, then…bam! Amnesia. Play end credit music and spicy previews for the next episode.

This is why you read fanfic, and not write it, she reminded herself with a silly chuckle.

By the time Kira managed to finish cleaning out, taking apart and restarting the melanger (the cacao nib in question was the size of a pebble, understandable that it had gotten stuck), it was lunchtime, and she was officially too hungry to even think about Santi and his decision not to call her. Which was good, because she was due for a meeting at Cantina.

Kira stretched her arms over her head as she stepped out into the sunshine. The Laneways was, more accurately, a laneway, a single row of warehouses with a cobblestone walkway in the middle, a few Talisay trees to provide shade, and a wall of bougainvillea in the end. People were walking around casually from store to store, peeking at the goods, considering the restaurants. The days between Christmas and New Year were usually their weakest, but still there were quite a number of people out and about.

Kira walked past Hope's Garden, waving to the shop girls, who said hello. She stopped by Sophie's Sounds too, to ask the storeowner if her order of the new BTS album was already there (they were making a killing off of pasabuys in Korea). It was always a nice walk, and made even better at night, when the Edison bulbs they strung across each wall lit up. She'd gotten the idea to hang little lanterns in between the lights and encouraged the owners to raise their own plants after walking through Huashan 1914 in Taipei. It made the Laneways seem like it had been there much longer than it had been, made it seem more welcoming.

And as always to Kira, this was home. She walked to the very back of the Laneways, the spot closest to the bougainvillea wall and everyone's favorite Fil-Mex restaurant.

"Kira!" Tiana Villa, who Kira *just* remembered was Santi's first cousin (was there no escape?), waved her over and pointed at Kira's usual table. "Late ka na!"

"I know, sorry, Ate Ti," Kira sighed. "But I did manage to bring…"

"My tableya!" Tiana exclaimed, accepting the pale pink paper bag, holding two kilos of tableya. Kira had also dropped off Sari's order on her way to Cantina. "Sakto, I was thinking of baking a cake for the dinner rush. Sit, sit. Your usual order?"

"Yes please, thank you!" Kira smiled, as Tiana disappeared into the back. Cantina's customers preferred the al fresco seating more than the indoor, especially in the cooler months. If it was already dinnertime, Kira would have ordered one of Tiana's excellent sinturis margaritas, but as it was too early, she ordered the juice instead.

Kira was not surprised to find that someone was already sitting in her usual table, waiting for her. The man looked nervous, glancing around the banderitas and twinkle lights, the zapate draped over palochina chairs, the candles in mason jars at the center of each table. His foot was shaking, tapping the side of the table in a quick staccato rhythm as he bit his nails. Kira called his name, and he looked up.

"Help," Alfred Tiongson, one of Kira's neighbors in Bolbok, groaned as she sat across him, and a plate of adobo flake nachos was placed between them. "I'm in love."

"Sounds serious," Kira giggled, eating a nacho. "Does she know?"

"She knows. She's actually here," Alfred said, holding his hand up enthusiastically and waving like whoever it was, was fifty feet away. "Mikaela! Over here! Hello! Yes, please have a seat, my love, you look radiant today!"

"Thank you, dear. Hello, Kira." Mikaela Aguilar smiled, and Kira suddenly understood why Alfred had asked her to lunch. Mikaela was her family's *unica hija*, and even at twenty-four, was famously *not* allowed to date. Her parents were so strict that she had to put her phone on speaker and call home whenever she made her way home from work at the Laneways. But Kira could see why Alfred would fall for her—a Pisces and a Cancer would be a deeply affectionate match, full of understanding and love. If the Pisces managed to draw out the Cancer's feelings.

And Kira knew that if there was anyone who could do it, it was Alfred.

"Oh my gosh, the two of you are so cute together," Kira cooed as Mikaela blushed, sitting next to Alfred, holding his hand under the table. "What's the problem?"

"Well, *we* would like to go out on a date," Mikaela said. "But…"

"Her parents don't actually know that we're together yet," Alfred finished, pouring Mikaela a glass of water. "So we could really use your help to figure out a way to do it without her parents knowing."

Kira wasn't sure when she became everyone's go-to girl when it came to love, it just sort of happened. Sometimes people just needed a little push, and Kira was good at that. In fact, she wasn't just good. She was *excellent* at it. So much that she loved it, built an entire chocolate shop just so she had a reason to keep doling out advice. Whether it was pushing Gab to sing a duet in the karaoke contest with Sari, asking Cla to wait for her one true love to confess his feelings or this, Kira always knew exactly what to say, and today was no exception.

"Not telling your parents is a bad idea, Mikaela," she said slowly, as her usual lengua burrito and sisig nachos arrived on the table.

"What? Why?" Mikaela asked, and Kira had never seen her so indignant.

"Because that's lying," Kira said, stating the obvious. "And when it blows up in your face, which it will, because your mom is friends with Ate Nessie, and Ate Nessie knows everything, you do not want them to be caught left-footed. Flat-footed? Whatever."

"So what do we do?" Alfred asked, his face serious, even if Kira knew that the nachos were his weakness. The man was ready to work, and Kira appreciated that.

"Mikaela, your parents are traditional, no?" Kira asked, and the younger girl nodded. "Then you have to take on this ligawan in a traditional way."

"What, gather my friends and sing under her window?" Alfred asked. "Because I'm a terrible singer."

"And is it courtship if we're already together?" Mikaela asked curiously.

"Oh it's not a courting for you, it's for your parents," Kira said. Traditional ligawan in the Philippines was all about impressing your intended's parents. If you managed to follow their rules long enough, you were "granted permission" to go out.

It was horribly, horribly antiquated, in Kira's opinion. But changing an adult's mind wasn't going to happen if you didn't consider their concerns in the first place. "They have to know that Alfred is not a threat to you. That he's worthy of your trust and affection, and they'll come around, too."

Gosh they were both adorably clueless. Kira wondered if she was like this when she was twenty-four.

"The shop sells a tub of 88% dark chocolate triangles," she said suddenly, seemingly apropos to nothing as she picked up a nacho.

"My dad's diabetic," Mikaela pointed out.

"I know," Kira said, nodding. "I make the triangles with coco sugar, and it's mostly cacao. He can't eat too many, but he can eat a little. I know your mom also loves Sunday Bakery, Mikaela. So if I were you, Alfred, and I'm not saying I am, I would get a tub of chocolate, an order of those gorgeous cheese rolls Gabriel makes, then I would go to Mikaela's house and offer it for merienda as Mikaela's friend. Your intentions are clear without having to overstep her parents, which is what they don't want."

Kira couldn't pretend to know why Mikaela's parents were the way they were, but that's just how it worked. In this country, you took the bad with the good, and worked around it, because you had no other choice sometimes.

She saw Alfred cast a wary glance at Mikaela, and she looked worried, too. Kira wanted to sigh, it was so freaking adorable. She'd always been part of the club that saw other people in love, and reacted with, "sana all!" in a lovingly joking way.

As much as she was used to waiting for love, it didn't mean she wasn't jealous when she saw it happen for other people. How was it so easy for her to find love for others, but not be able to see love for herself except in the form of teleserye fantasies and chance kisses?

People told her that it meant that she just wasn't ready yet. Apparently falling in love meant being vulnerable, and vulnerability was a very real fear for someone who felt like the lone family member that needed adult supervision (a Luz trait more than astrology, really). Easier to be the all-seeing being that helped other people fall in love. Then maybe it would come back to her, one way or the other. Ready or not.

"Don't worry, you two," Kira told them with a small smile. "Love favors the brave. So be brave, and give it a try. If all else fails, I'm happy to chaperone your date from a very respectable distance."

Chapter Five

December 27
The Luz House, Haraya Subdivision
Bolbok, Lipa

Today's Horoscope: Entering Capricorn season doesn't come without challenges, and this is a big one. But with your usual ease and effortlessness, Gemini, you can get through it! Trust your decisions, and you will be fine. Let the waning gibbous moon bring enthusiasm.

"Tita Kira?" Cassie Luz-Ang, Kira's one and only niece, asked as Kira paced the room.

It had been five days. Five days since Kira and Santi kissed at the Carlton, and *still* she hadn't heard from him. Not even a peep. In the five days since the wedding, Kira had helped Ate Tiana perfect her chocolate tableya recipe, had discussed the merits of white chocolate pain au chocolats with Gabriel, helped Sari repaint her bedroom, while Alfred and Mikaela secured permission to go out on a date (with Kira as a chaperone, but hey, we love compromise).

But still, Kira hadn't heard a thing from Santi.

"Tita?"

She'd considered calling him, of course, but it didn't feel right. It felt *weird*. Because their interactions over the last three years since he came back in that shiny red Mercedes were always in the realm of professionalism (him) and being a caring but nagging friend (her). Before this, Kira saw his business partner Gabriel more often than she did Santi, and Santi was supposed to be *her* friend. She could always count on Santi to dole out business advice once she wore him down a little, and he seemed to enjoy explaining "rent escalation" and "escrow" to her when she wheedled him for it. But it wasn't anything beyond that, until that wedding.

Remnants of her upbringing in all-girls Catholic schools from prep to high school had taught her that feelings are things you repress, and not share with anyone. The first act of having a crush was to deny, deny, deny. Deny until the world ends, because god forbid people find out that you actually *desired* someone. Ngek.

"Tiiita…"

Not that she "desired" Santi. She didn't. She would just prefer to know his thoughts on him possibly desiring her before she reciprocated. Totally normal. Hay, sometimes her being an air sign really bit her in the ass.

"Tita!" Cassie exclaimed, and Kira snapped to attention.

"Cassie?"

"What's a gibbous moon?"

Despite living in Singapore, Ate Kamilla, Kuya Harry and Kira's one and only niece, Cassie, never missed Christmas in Lipa—much to the delight of Kira's parents, who loved Cassie much, much more than their own children (they were happy to say every year). Between the Luz-Angs and Kiko's boyfriend also in residence in Lipa for the holidays, it was a full house. It made thinking out loud very difficult.

"Um," Kira said, tossing a pair of silver sequin pants, a pleated skirt and a satin maxi skirt on the bed next to where her niece was using Kira's horoscope app of choice to see what the stars had in store for her this season. "Gibbous today our daily bread?"

"Ti-*ta*," Cassie groaned.

"Do we like the silver sequin pants or the satin tangerine maxi skirt with the white shirt?" Kira asked, holding up both options from the bed to her niece, who seemed to give it serious thought.

"Depends," she huffed. "Is this for your super-secret spy mission you don't want me to go with you to?"

"Cass, I would love to take you out to dinner at the most romantic place in Lipa, I really would, but your tita is broke from the holidays, " Kira explained. "La Spezia is like, Singapore expensive."

Cassie winced, because even she understood the difference in value. Kira hadn't really thought through volunteering to chaperone a date, when said date would require her to pay more than a thousand pesos to eat. So she might as well put on a great outfit, pretend she was taking herself out on a date in La Spezia. Which also, coincidentally, happened to be at the Hotel Villa, and was Santi's restaurant, and just on the off chance that someone decided to finally show up—

No, no. Kira shook her head and reminded herself to focus. Santi wasn't even in Lipa. He was in Manila, at least according to Gab and Sari. Kira was dressing up because she was about to spend a lot of hard-earned money on a meal, and she wanted to look good.

"Well, your nail polish is jelly red with glitter, so I would go with the tangerine," Cassie said after a moment of careful consideration. "Then wear it with the brown sandals! Ooh, you will look so effortlessly casual."

"I don't know," a voice said from the door. "I kind of feel like wearing a white shirt to eat out is asking for disaster when your boobs are as big as ours."

"Ate!" Kira groaned, rolling her eyes at Kamilla Luz, fourteen years older than her and smiling in amusement as she leaned against the doorframe. "Knock naman? What if I was naked?"

The problem with blasting music and getting ready to go out like a lead actress in a rom-com was that none of those leads ever lived in the Luz house. The Luz house that was supposed to have enough room to comfortably fit a family of five was currently straining under the weight of nine people. Sure, she loved having the whole family over, but it just felt a *tad* crowded at the moment. Kira was perpetually running into someone in the hallway, having to explain to someone where she was going. Today was not going to be an exception.

"Why would you be naked in the house?" Kamilla's brow furrowed, as if it was the most ludicrous thing she'd ever heard. "Anyway, you can't go. Dad wants a family meeting since the Luz meeting is happening next month."

Kira groaned and collapsed backward on the bed next to her niece, and crossed her arms over her chest, preventing her boobs from tilting back, for maximum drama. When your family consisted mostly of Earth and Fire signs (seriously, Kira had at least three cousins born on the Aries-Taurus cusp; it was a thing) every decision was made rationally and democratically, via vote. And since it was all so neat and tidy anyway, they decided to formally run things as a corporation—Luz Holdings, Inc. Very straightforward.

Kira thought it was cute, the way her father's siblings—and actually, the entire family—flocked to Lipa to make a year's worth of business decisions in one go, but her father was always quick to remind his kids that the Meetings were Serious Business. You had to know your shit to participate, and seeing as Kira was running two businesses—the Laneways, under the family corporation, and Gemini Chocolates, funded by the family under her single proprietorship—participation was mandatory for her.

It wasn't unusual for the family corporation to fund the nephews and nieces' projects (Kiko's architecture firm started off under the family's wing). But Gemini, at three years old, was still very much a baby bird to Kira's mind. It still needed a little more time to dry its wings before she really flew.

Which meant she had to walk things through with her father before everyone else. It was fine, it was necessary, but did it have to be *now*?

"Where are you going anyway, dressed like that?" Kamilla asked, wandering over to Kira's vanity and browsing through her nail polish collection.

"To the most romantic restaurant in Lipa," Cassie sighed, as Kira wondered what was so provocative about a tee shirt and a skirt. Was it the slit? Maybe it was the slit.

"La Spezia?" Ate Kamilla asked, turning to the two

sharply, and it said volumes about the restaurant's reputation that her sister's face was lit up at just the mention. "I read about it in the in-flight magazine—The Treasures South of Manila. Sosyal!"

"I'm actually chaperoning—" Kira started to explain, when Kamilla clapped her hands excitedly.

Kira and her sister may not live together anymore, but Kira was still very familiar with Kamilla's "I've got a bright idea" face. Which led to things like Kira opening a chocolate shop, Kiko studying architecture and the three siblings knowing all the lyrics to "Read U Wrote U" from Drag Race.

"We should have the family meeting at La Spezia," Kamilla spoke, and so it was going to be true. Kira groaned again. She loved her family, she really did. But there were just some things you needed to do yourself, like chaperoning other people's dates and paying an exorbitant amount to do it. "I'll pay."

Okay maybe there were *some* pros to having her family tag along.

"Yay! Fancy dinner!" Cassie exclaimed, getting up out of bed to start looking around for an outfit. Kira glared at her older sister, who was now spraying Kira's perfume on her wrists.

"Must you spoil my fun, Ate?" Kira asked.

"Yes," Kamilla said, laughing and taking another sniff of Kira's perfume. "I'll tell the others about the plans. Be ready in ten minutes, Kira!"

If you were to ask Kira to imagine a restaurant owned wholly by Anton Santillan, she would probably picture a conveyor-belt sushi place. Not because Santi was particularly fond of sushi (was he?), but because she was sure that the concept of food appearing by button and conveyor belt would appeal to him.

He couldn't do any of that with Hotel Villa. It had a reputation to uphold, a legacy of care that he was simply picking up and continuing. A restaurant of his own, though? Kira would think he would take every opportunity to do it from a distance.

So one could only imagine her surprise when she walked into La Spezia for the first time, and immediately thought, *It's...so warm.*

The success of a restaurant in the Philippines hinged on two things: hype and ambience. Hype was made by La Spezia's positioning—everyone was fascinated to see just how fancy it could be. Ambience was easy, and this place had a whole bayong of it. Like someone held up an Italian postcard to the space and said, "I want that, here."

It was a testament to Kiko's architectural (architecturing? architectable? nothing sounded right, she should ask Kiko) skill that he managed to recreate the feeling of being by the Italian Riviera, despite having never visited it himself. But Kiko insisted that the entire vision had been Santi's. "He chose everything. I just brought it all together."

Anton Santillan, the former boy next door. Anton Santillan, who had driven in from Manila in a flashy red Mercedes twenty years later and bought the crumbling Hotel Villa off of his relatives. Anton Santillan, who remodeled the hotel with antique furniture and all the plants in Laguna and turned it into a premier wedding destination booked solid into the next two years.

The walls were painted a soft peach, slightly unfinished to seem more rustic. Almost all the walls were flanked by arched windows with wrought iron frames that peeked out into a garden that had, of all things, a lit fountain. The one wall that didn't have windows had arched built-in shelves, stuffed to the brim with what looked like every wine and alcohol bottle available, and would have made Dionysus proud. The ceiling was high, and the fake plants cascading down from the trellises should have looked cheap, but in the warm glow of the lights, it looked like a scene from *Mamma Mia*.

They still tell me that Villa's success isn't enough. That I am not enough to deserve coming back, Santi had told her five days ago. But as Kira stood under all that splendor, she couldn't help but think that there must be something seriously wrong with Santi's family, that they couldn't see how wonderful any of this was. And this, she said with the confidence of someone who still managed to go to a place or two when she was in Manila, and knew what successful places looked like. La Spezia was it. Hotel Villa was it. How could they not see that?

"Kira!" Mikaela interrupted her thoughts, as she and Alfred finally appeared at the restaurant entryway, which had now turned into a spectacle, where Ate Kamilla was getting them a table, her mother was fussing over her father's pants, the other Luzes were browsing the menu, and now Alfred and Mikaela. "You're here, good! Alfred and I requested a table near your..."

"My family," Kira said apologetically as the rest of her family turned and waved. "You are now officially chaperoned by the Luzes, congratulations."

"Oh, that's good!" Mikaela exclaimed. "Um, good evening, po."

"Good evening Mikaela, where is your date?" Kira's father asked.

"Mikaela, I actually had something to ask about the capital gains tax on the—" Kiko began, but Kira leaned to block Kiko's view, and shushed her older brother.

"Kuya, it's a weekend. Call her on Monday if you really have a boner to pick with her."

"A *what* now?"

It took some time for their little mishmash party to arrange themselves into seats—the Luzes occupying a long table for nine in the middle of the restaurant, while Alfred and Mikaela were in a booth directly under one of the arched windows that looked out into a garden with the fountain. Close enough for everyone to keep an eye on them, but far enough that they could still have privacy.

Once Mikaela and Alfred were settled, and they discussed their signals in case of emergency, Kira felt herself relax and ease into the experience. She released a slow breath as she dipped a bit of her focaccia bread in olive oil, balsamic vinegar and crushed garlic. The bread and the olive oil just went perfectly together, with that acidic tang from the vinegar that made it addicting. As if it was made for her.

She didn't really know Santi at all, did she? She understood him, knew a little about that pain behind his eyes, knew he would make good on his promises just on sheer force of will. But this was a piece of him that she hadn't expected. Just like that kiss, just like that look in his eyes whenever he talked about things he liked. She didn't know him. And there were very few things Kira admitted to not knowing.

So maybe she should do something about it. Like

call him and ask what he wanted. Because it was becoming increasingly clear to her that she 1) was maybe tired of waiting for love and 2) she also maybe liked him as more than a business consult/childhood friend. And all she had to do was ask, and she would find out which outcome she was going to get—her teleserye happily ever after, or not? She would prefer to have one over the other, and admitting it to herself was terrifying.

"Now that we have that in order," Raymond Luz began, as Kira munched on her antipasto plate. It had parma ham from an artisanal maker in Laguna, sliced melons from Blossoms Farm, a mound of soft and stretchy mozzarella from Luz Creamery, sprigs of arugula and fresh tomatoes that they grew on the Villa property, and the most perfectly toasted bread Kira had ever had, made in-house. "Let's talk about the Luz meeting. It's happening at the end of next month."

Crap. Kira had forgotten that they had come to talk about this. Serious face, serious face.

"Chika on the group chat is that Tito Nico's eldest, Uno, is joining," Alice Luz said. "He's the cousin that graduated Wharton and worked for those fancy finance firms in Tektite."

"MVP graduated Wharton, too," Kuya Kiko pointed out as he finished dispensing his tomatoes onto his boyfriend Jake's plate, and Jake gave up his melons. It was very domestic and cute.

"I think what he's trying to ask," Jake said, "is why that's important, Dad?"

"Uno asked to add an item to the agenda," Raymond said darkly, or as dark as a man could look enjoying a candied fig and balsamic salad with burrata. "A third-year review of Gemini Chocolates."

Cue silence. Kira suddenly felt the eyes of every person in the restaurant on her, even as she was mid-chew of her parma ham and melon. By the time she finally finished swallowing, her food tasted like ash in her mouth.

"What!" she exclaimed a little sharply. *"Why?"*

Her immediate reaction was *No. Fuck no!* She wanted to wrap her arms around her business, barricade herself to her shop door and snarl.

"Because your business plan predicted you would make back your capital expenses by now," her father explained, calm as ever.

"Yes, but I didn't expect that I needed to buy the tempering machine to keep up with the demand! Plus, getting my beans from Davao and South Cotabato entails shipping cost that I had only guesstimated," Kira argued. "And isn't the point of an estimate just that? To *estimate* things?"

"Yes, but it's a new year, and anyone in the family has the right to bring it up if they want, and Uno in particular wants to do it," Kamilla argued, and Kira wanted to tell her sister that she wasn't helping, but really, she was making an excellent point. Because that was the way the family's democracy worked. "You borrowed that money from Luz Holdings. And my guess is, Kuya Uno wants to put his experience to good use for the family, and wants to use Gemini to look good."

"Relax, Kiki. It's not unusual for them to ask questions," Kiko pointed out, a little more firmly. "They did it to me naman din."

She knew Kiko was saying that to commiserate with her, but it wasn't exactly the same, was it?

It didn't matter that she made so much chocolate she dreamed about it; didn't matter that she loved being able to personally talk to each and every one of her customers, or that her matchmaking clients crossed over to buying her chocolate every time. Basta, she wasn't getting that ROI back, therefore she wasn't doing well. She was *enjoying* herself in her business, so she was definitely doing something wrong. Kira narrowed her eyes at Kamilla's perfect calm, at Kiko's serious expression and her mother's sudden inability to look at her.

"Oh my god," she said, nearly dropping her fork. "Is this…an intervention? Are you all trying to intervent me?"

The look on each of her family members' faces was more than enough. Even Harry, who usually tried to keep away from Luz family drama, was suddenly very focused on his food. Nobody even bothered to correct her.

"Oh my god!" Kira hissed, leaning forward. "This *is* an intervention!"

"We're worried about you," Kiko said, because he was the only one she could still listen to when things were escalating. "Running Gemini hasn't been easy for you, obviously, but—"

"The way we see it, there are two ways to go about fixing your ROI problem," Kamilla added, and Kira could not believe this. She hated this, the concerned looks on her family's faces, because it seemed that she couldn't be trusted to run her own business. And because Fire and Earth signs were solutions-oriented folk, she was going to be handed the solutions without her asking for them. "One, you can find a way to decrease your cost to produce the chocolate."

"Decreasing costs means lowering quality," Kira pointed out, seeing right through the business doublespeak, ha! "I can't do that. People like my chocolate the way it is." Because she could be stubborn too, if she needed it.

"Fine, then you'll have to do the other thing," Ate Kamilla continued. "More sales. A *lot* more sales. You have regulars and occasional custom orders, but you're going to have to do more."

"And matchmaking isn't a marketing strategy," Kiko said.

That was the second time in five days someone had told her that. Was that actual, real-world advice that people got?

"Um, the three custom wedding orders I booked this month, all for couples I matched, would like to disagree," Kira said, her cheeks heating. "I can make things special for these clients because I know them. *And* lest we forget, my matchmaking has also led to Kuya Kiko and Kuya Jake getting together, *and* Alfred and Mikaela."

The family all peeked at the couple, who currently seemed too preoccupied with gazing into each other's eyes to notice. Kira sighed and stabbed her melon and ham. Sure, her custom orders were great, but they were sporadic, and clearly not constant enough for her to keep up.

"I don't think we were denying that, Kira," Kuya Jake said gently, breaking the impasse. Kira didn't know what expression she was wearing, but Jake must have seen something, because he immediately backed off. "Oh my god, babe, take over, I can't, she's like my little sister."

"She *is* my little sister," Kuya Kiko pointed out. "Kiki, you know we're just worried about you."

Kira believed that. She really did. Because that was what her family did, they worried about each other, broke things gently to each other, helped each other out. But this…this was so personal to Kira, it felt like someone was trying to invade her space. Take away something that she built herself.

She took in a deep, shuddering breath and held it in, waiting patiently for her heart to unclench before she slowly released it. Yoga breathing really did help.

"Thank you, all of you, for your concern." she said slowly, and it was almost satisfying to see the surprise on her father's face. "And all of this has been duly noted. I have a month pa naman to figure out what I'm going to do, and I am not going to that board meeting without a plan."

"Good." Ate Kamilla nodded. "And you can ask us if you need help."

She knew that. Knew that very well, if this dinner was any indication. Her parents were willing to spend way too much on family dinner just to get Kira to accept the fact that she needed to do *something* about Gemini. It was sweet, and overbearing at the same time.

But the con to asking for help from her parents or her siblings was having to explain herself to them. None of them *quite* understood what Kira was doing in the first place. Kiko and Kamilla were great at building things, making things happen, her parents were good at keeping things practical. But still, Kira couldn't make them understand why it was important that she acquire so much machinery, why her operations stopped when her melangers stopped. Why she had to import beans from Mindanao. Why she felt alone a lot of the time, and why she felt just a little lost.

As the youngest, with a thirteen-year age gap between her and Ate Kamilla, Kira was used to being the last in everything. The last to know the chika, the last to know what the family's plans were. She was used to falling behind to her parents, who ran their businesses with nary a hitch, and her siblings, who fell so naturally into professional jobs. Their lives followed an obvious, straightforward line. And Kira was happy for them.

But it comforted her that her being left behind was just because she was younger. Surely she wouldn't be left behind, in the outside world, where everyone was her age and going through pretty much the same things. But the older she got, the more she realized that it wasn't true. People her age were getting married, having kids, settling into lifetime careers where they turned from awkward underlings to the ones people relied on.

And suddenly Kira was left behind again.

Universe, if you have a plan, I'd really like to know, Kira thought, resisting the urge to look up at the ceiling. *I could use some help.*

"Have I showed you my favorite newborn calf?" Alice Luz asked the table suddenly, whipping out her phone and holding up a photo of the sweetest-looking baby cow, with a perfect star on her forehead. Nothing like a picture of a baby cow to break the tension, for which Kira was eternally grateful. "They named her Ning, for Bituing Walang Ningning."

"What does that mean?" Harry, Kamilla's husband, whispered beside her.

"A star without the kumukutikutitap," Kira said with a straight face, making Kiko nearly spit out his wine.

"That's a sad name for a cow to live up to," her father commented at the head of the table, and Kira saw him squeezing his wife's hand, and her heart wrenched. They must have hated that as much as she did. "They couldn't have named her Shawie, or Cherie?"

"Ning was cuter," Alice argued. "Better than Tala, at least."

"I've always thought Cherie was a badas—I mean, impressive name," Kiko coughed.

"Ha-ha, Tito was about to say a bad word," Cassie snickered beside Kira. Kuya Jake was busy engaging Ate Kamilla with the latest from Manila—which restaurants were currently making waves, which restaurants' shine had since faded (and had faded quickly), which places were being lined up for, who opened them.

The waiters poured another round of wine for the adults and served the brick oven pizza, which featured balsamic onions, mushrooms from that fancy farm in San Benito, bits of blue cheese, on even more cheese. The crust was pillowy and soft, the dough slightly salted but still tasteless enough for Kira to want to dip it in spicy honey. And Kira needed carbs at the moment. They really did help soften the blow to her ego.

Was it worth it? her traitorous brain asked her. *All that drama, all that hirap. Was it worth it?*

"Remind me again why you called this a spy mission, Cass?" Ate Kamilla asked, the only one eating her pizza with a fork and knife. Kira gasped and widened her eyes at Cassie, who was suddenly very interested in the fountain outside. Kira groaned. This was what she got for telling her niece everything.

"We're spying?" Jake asked excitedly. "On who?"

"Oh god," Kiko sighed. "Kira, did you really make the family go to this restaurant so you could spy on Santi?"

Kira made a noise, something like a squeak and a choke on her bread, because how did Kiko even *know* about that.

"Yes!" Cassie exclaimed.

"No!" Kira said at the exact same time. "Santi's not even here."

"The fact that you know he's not here is—"

"Santi? Officially friends na kayo ulit, hija?" Alice asked, leaning forward on the table to get a better look at Kira. "Not because I don't want you to date him, or anything, because I *do* want you to date him—"

"Mother, please!" Kira groaned, wishing she could burrow herself under the focaccia bread until the conversation was over. She looked at Alfred and Mikaela, and thanked god they were still in their own little world.

"I don't want you to date him," Raymond argued. "For the record."

"Dad," Kira said in the exact same tone, because it didn't help. "Didn't you use to slip him twenty pesos to buy me gulaman when we were kids?"

"If I had known it would lead to this, I wouldn't have done it!"

"I am only saying this because you were so unhappy when you lost your friends when you moved back here," Alice said, reaching out across the table to squeeze Kira's hand affectionately. "So it's good that he came back."

Kira winced, because her mother was right. She knew full well that losing friends was a part of the process of growing up. People just fit differently, or didn't fit at all, as you became the person you wanted to be. When she moved to Lipa, her Manila friendships just…fell away. Because they led other lives, because Kira didn't bother to keep up with what was the latest in anymore.

But it hurt like a bitch every time, giving someone so much of your heart, only for them to trample on it and walk away. To dive eagerly into a new experience, only to be left alone, and then unceremoniously fired, like you never mattered. It had been better to stay in the sidelines, helping other people build more lasting relationships. Here. In the place she loved.

But hey, at least her family's normal equilibrium had restored itself. All was right with the world, at least until next month's board meeting. Argh.

"Isn't that Kuya Santi right there?" Cassie asked, doing her grandparents proud by using her pursed lips to point in the direction of the back of the restaurant.

"Nice try, Cassie." Kira took a deep swallow of her wine. Mmm. Dry. "How do you even know what he looks like?"

"Ate Nessie had pictures!" Cassie said cheerfully, because of course she did. Cassie was smiling with all the adorable innocence of…er, whatever grade she was supposed to be in now. "She said he came back for you after twenty years."

I moved to Lipa because of you, he'd said. *It means more, because it was you.*

"He didn't come back *for* me, he came back and I just happened to be in the same place," Kira argued, and this heat on her cheeks was from the wine, it had to be.

"But you like him, don't you?" Cassie asked, as the next course was served, an aglio olio with hand-made linguini, slow-cooked bolognese with Angus beef meatballs and pesto in nubby little pasta twirls. Yummm.

"Hay naku, she has a crush," Kamilla sighed. "Now she's never going to leave Lipa."

"Why would I want to leave?" Kira scoffed, and shook her head. "Pass the aglio olio."

"Because if the chocolate boom was going to happen anywhere, it's going to happen in Manila, isn't it?" Kamilla asked, tilting her head curiously like she was ready to drill holes into anything Kira said. "Can I have the Parmesan?"

"Ate naman, I would really appreciate it if you didn't try to parent me in the middle of dinner," Kira narrowed her eyes at her sister. Thankfully the noodles were perfectly al dente, enough that it was satisfying to bite down on them a little. "I'm doing *fine*."

"Are you sure, because the board meeting next month—"

"How are we enjoying our meal so far?" a voice interrupted, and it was like the fight just whooshed out of Kira in a rush, so quickly she nearly staggered.

All because Santi was standing right in front of her holding a bouquet of deep, crimson red roses. And he was smiling like he knew something she absolutely didn't. Not even the Grim Reaper had ever looked as devious as him, standing in front of her family. Yes, her heart was flip-flopping in her chest, around the same time as the butterflies in her stomach decided to drink fuzzy lifting drinks and were now trying to get her to float on cloud kilig.

And where have you been? she wanted to ask him. *What the hell was "we'll talk" supposed to mean? Do you know how many times I've thought about kissing you again, you jerk?*

"Oh Santi! We were *just* talking about you," Alice exclaimed, her cheeks already flushed pink from her alcohol consumption. Kira wanted to slide under the table. "I never tried making mozzarella with our milk."

"I wouldn't have done it if it wasn't the best, Tita." Santi nodded, very pointedly not looking at Kira as he did so. "I'm glad you like it."

"How very interesting that you're here." Kamilla narrowed her eyes and seemed to be studying Santi from head to toe. She was looking at his artfully tossed hair, at the way he was just casually wearing a suit jacket in the Philippines that Kira was 100% sure was purchased from Uniqlo. "I've been told several times this evening that you weren't around."

"Oh my god, *Ate*!" Kira hissed, but both Santi and Kamilla ignored her.

"I was supposed to be in Manila. But I realized," Santi explained, then he looked up at her like there was nobody else in the room, "there were other, more important things here."

San Sebastian, Kira thought, because if she was going to pass blame around, she might as well involve Lipa's patron saint. *Please don't let me die of embarrassment and kilig at the same time, amen.*

"What pasta shape is this?" Raymond asked, holding up a bit of the trofie pasta with his fork, looking very unimpressed. "It looks like libag."

How could you, Kira thought immediately, wanting to glare up at the patron saint Ate Nessie-style, if she could. Both Kira and Jake coughed, and Kiko had to rub both their backs to support them.

"It's trofie pasta, Tito, a Liguirian specialty." Santi didn't look fussed at all as he slowly turned his gaze on Kira.

She didn't know how he did it; had anyone else seen him, they would think, "ah yes, that's Anton Santillan and his usual expression." But there was a heat in his gaze that she absolutely felt, like someone had poured thick chocolate ganache down her throat and it was now pooling and settling in her stomach, between her legs. *Bakit. Ang lagkit. Ng tingin niya.*

"Kira, may I speak with you privately?" he asked her, in front of her entire family, and honestly, just take her away now. Even Alfred and Mikaela had looked up, and god, how many more people would have to witness what was clearly the weirdest moment in Kira's life?

"Bakit?" Kiko asked suddenly, and Kira spotted Jake patting his boyfriend's arm and whispering something about not being such a "toxic tito."

"Yes! Talk!" Kira exclaimed a little suddenly, needing this moment to happen somewhere else. "We should! Okay!"

Was that too much? She was sure she saw her mother try not to laugh. Kira shot up out of her seat and left her phone on the table, telling Cassie to watch her phone.

"Roger, 007." Cassie winked conspiratorially at her.

"Um, over and out." Kira nodded once, and now

it was her father's turn to chuckle as Kamilla sighed wistfully, while Cassie was left completely confused.

But Kira didn't see the reactions of the rest because she was already walking away from the table with Santi, and she felt she couldn't release her held breath until they reached the bar near the kitchen. How far were they from the table? Could she speak now?

"Breathe," Santi soothed. "They can't hear."

"But are they watching?" Kira asked, not daring to turn her head.

"Yes," Santi said, pulling a rose from the bouquet and holding it up to her. "Let them."

"You realize they're going to ask me about this later." Kira accepted the rose. Her heart was beating erratically. God, she was going to get hypertension in a year, she knew it.

"Just one?" she teased him, waving the rose around, so perfectly fresh that Youko Kurama could have easily made a rose whip out of it. Ugh, she used to love Yu Yu Hakusho. "Tsani."

"I don't know what that means."

"It's…" Kira began, but decided against it. "Secret."

"I'm going to Google that. Also, I would give these to you," he explained holding up the others. "But these are not for me. I picked them up from Hope's Garden for tonight's debutante at the Azotea ballroom. I didn't think she needed more than eighteen."

Kira sighed. Because she was relieved, obviously. Nineteen roses would have been too much. (Assuming they were for her, of course, and they weren't!) Was it terrible to say that she was *slightly* disappointed? Because she was. As reality star, and star-in-her-own-mind, Valentina said, "this doesn't fit into my fantasy," and hers in particular included maybe a string quartet and a fountain that came with those roses.

Not that this one rose wasn't nice, or sweet, it was just…well, she just really needed to talk to him, is all. Because this waiting was terrible. Because this crush (because that was what it was) was starting to crush her, and she needed to settle it all. To quote another famous Ru girl, "because what you want to do, isn't necessarily what you're gonna do," so just because she wanted this to happen, didn't mean it was going to.

So better to ask now, diba?

"You um, wanted to talk to me," she reminded him.

"Let's talk outside," he said, clearly unaware of her turmoil. He handed off the flowers to one of his staff, and got a nondescript box and two forks in exchange. He extended his hand toward a nondescript door off the side of the restaurant. "Privacy awaits."

Kira walked through the door and was met with Lipa's chilly late December air. They were in the garden, the one with the lit fountain that she could only just see through the restaurant's many windows, in a corner that was just out of sight.

Almost every santan bush was topped with twinkle lights, making them look like they were glowing. It was well into the evening, but the gumamela flowers were still open and in full bloom, their petals dancing in the cool wind. The lightest scent of ylang ylang lingered in the air from the trees nearby, and rosal from the bushes.

It was like stepping into a fairy tale, if you didn't mind the occasional tricycle roar in the distance. Kira took in a deep inhale of the cool evening air.

There were just some moments in your life you knew were important. The day Kira decided to make chocolate, the first time she ever matched a couple. This, for some reason, felt like one of those moments.

She turned to face Santi, and smiled. He looked like a god that decided to walk among the mortals, and he might as well have been, with his fancy MBA and Canadian degree, his money and just the way he carried himself. He was different. No matter how much he tried to hide it, Santi hadn't been part of Lipa for a long time now. And even as he stood there in the garden, Kira could see that loneliness in his eyes. That longing for something.

"I need your help," he announced, and it was a good start. A very good start, indeed. "I have dessert."

Chapter Six

December 27
The garden outside La Spezia

*Roasting: a step in the chocolate-making process
that involves delicately roasting the beans to achieve
a particular flavor. There are no rules to roasting,
but it's best to let the heat in gradually, and let the
beans develop the flavors that fermentation already
created.*

"Is that cake?" Kira asked, practically bouncing as
she settled into the bench near the door, placing the
rose next to her. Santi smiled. She was nervous. The
person who sold him that bench had called it a gallinera and explained that it could also hold a chicken in
its wooden cage base. Santi had to tell to the man that
he wasn't really interested in raising chickens, but the
bench was really nice.

This would be the perfect time to ask her, he thought,
suddenly. *Would you sell the Laneways to me? Would
you help me make everything right with my family, in
exchange for everything I built here?*

Because that was the trade-off, wasn't it? Even if he

did manage to convince the Luz Holdings board to sell the Laneways to him, Kira would hate him for taking it away. Gabriel would lose Sunday Bakery, as would Sari and all the other retailers there. They would stop selling their goods to Villa, which relied a lot on local sellers, and Villa's reputation would be in tatters.

But hey, that wouldn't matter, if Santi was in Manila, diba?

A knot in his stomach twisted. He couldn't ask that of Kira. Regardless of his feelings for her (and her status as Reigning Patintero Champion of Lipa), it was made clear to him in his last three years that the Laneways were Kira's place. A place the Luzes carved out for her when she needed a soft landing, until she grew it into something spectacular enough that Vito wanted it for himself. Every time she came to him to ask for business advice, he saw it on her face. How it ate her alive that she didn't know the answers, that she needed to come to him, because not knowing might mean someone taking it away.

It was magic. Hers, how she built a community there.

And Santi had experienced some of that himself, part-owning Sunday Bakery. People deferred to Kira on decisions, they greeted her in the morning. The place was hers. He couldn't ask her to give it up, not for all the redemption in the world.

In short, he told himself, *it's hopeless.*

And besides, he hadn't asked her out here for that.

"Something better," he assured her, making a gesture for her to move a little so he could sit next to her. It felt nice, sitting next to Kira here. It felt right. And Santi had long since lost that feeling. How strange to have found it again, three years and one hotel later, in this very spot. Santi opened the box containing the dessert and showed it to her. "Or at least it could be."

"Ooh," Kira said, her eyes growing wide at the sight. Santi tried to hide a smile. He liked seeing her so intrigued. "What is it?"

"This is a tartufo," Santi explained, handing her one of two spoons. "An Italian dessert I once had at the Piazza Navona in Rome, or a replica of it. It has the right elements, but there's something not quite right with it. I can't figure out what it is."

One of the reasons why Santi had thought to open a restaurant was because he liked feeding people. It was an instinct of his, to have food ready to share anytime. And with La Spezia, it felt more special, more intimate, to be doing it in such close quarters. The restaurant's menu changed as often as he and his chef could talk about it, and he spared no expense when it came to sourcing the best ingredients. Because if he was going to put himself out there, there was no better way to do it than with food.

It sometimes surprised people what food Santi called nostalgic. He liked the thick, almost marinara-like tomato soup from that Italian restaurant in Mindanao Avenue. He held caramel cakes with buttercream flowers close to his heart, because that was what he always had for his birthday. He loved mais con hielo when it had a scoop of vanilla ice cream and cornflake bits. It wasn't all lumpia and halo-halo.

With La Spezia, he was sharing memories from a trip abroad, a trip that had ultimately made him realize that he'd changed. That he had become completely different from his family. So to have his tartufo be not quite right? He wasn't going to stand for it.

He handed Kira the box, and she eagerly tucked in, running her spoon through the layer of whipped cream, the chunks of chocolate and chocolate ganache, until her spoon met with the dark chocolate ice cream, and the mousse inside. She seemed to have no trouble balancing all of that on her spoon, then took a bite.

"Mmmmm," she said, and Santi felt his breath catch at the sound of that little moan of ecstasy. His heart actually leaped in his chest. She seemed to like it.

"Good?" he asked. But then her face turned thoughtful, and Santi started worrying. No good came of someone suddenly becoming thoughtful after eating chocolate.

"I'm biased," Kira explained. "But I see the problem. This dessert is all…frippy. Nothing comes together."

"Frip…it's all frippery?" Santi clarified. Kira nodded. "Can it be fixed, you think?"

"Of course." Kira chuckled, placing the dessert on her lap. "I think recreating a dessert you had in Rome is a great idea. But maybe…"

"Maybe?" Santi asked, his brow furrowing.

"Maybe what tastes good in Rome is different in Lipa," Kira told him. "Your tomatoes and basil are different, your cheeses are different, people's tastes are different. How we enjoy something varies place to place."

Santi frowned, considering.

She was right, of course. He'd spent a lot of time cultivating relationships with his local suppliers. How could he have just forgotten, when it came to the chocolate? Come to think of it, how many times had international brands come to Manila and admit to adjusting their menus for Filipinos? They came fully aware they were bringing something new to the table, but knew that it still had to fit the people eating it. It was all about the audience.

And Santi's audience loved that both La Spezia and Hotel Villa sourced everything they sold locally. At the time, it had saved Santi on transportation costs, but the effect had been that it gave Hotel Villa a style that was classy but homey, gave La Spezia's Italian dishes a familiarity.

Come to think of it, why *didn't* Villa and La Spezia have more chocolate? They could have more items on the dessert menu in the lobby lounge. They could offer chocolates on pillows for their suite guests. They could have champorado for the breakfast buffet.

"It will be something new," Santi conceded. He remembered what Kira's chocolate tasted like. Could only imagine what it would do to a tartufo.

He should be asking her about the Laneways, about the possibility of the family selling it. But Santi had already decided that his returning to Manila was not worth the collateral damage of Kira's unhappiness. It wasn't worth the collateral damage to anyone, really, but even more so when it was someone he'd known since he was a kid, someone who knew him, and remembered who he was, before he fully became Vito Santillan's grandson. Since she'd showed up at that convenience store in Japan, she told Santi what she needed. She needed someone to believe in her.

He could do that, which was why he never minded

when she came up to him at the last Laneways Christmas Party and made him join the karaoke contest.

He liked being the one she turned to when she was lost about Gemini or the Laneways. He used to be merely content with it, but that kiss in Makati had changed a lot of things for him.

But if he brought up selling the Laneways, he would lose her. And the thought of losing someone as…special to him as Kira Luz was terrifying. He was better at being a hero than he was a grandson.

"Kira, I…" he said. "How would you feel about being Villa and La Spezia's chocolate supplier?"

Silence. She blinked at him once, twice, three times. There was a moment where Santi thought he hadn't said it out loud, but he was sure that he had.

He didn't think he said anything particularly funny, but Kira's face just absolutely split into laughter, and the next thing he knew, she was leaning into him, her hand on his arm, like she couldn't believe he just said that.

Santi was confused. Or maybe he was still a little tired from his drive from Manila—the traffic had been hell, even more than usual. But at least SLEX and Star Tollway had been clear, which still didn't explain Kira's laughter. She smelled nice.

"It's like you're asking me how I feel about centaurs wearing pants," Kira told him, wiping tears from the corner of her eyes. "God, universe, what are you *doing*?"

"What?"

"Just…can you…can you ask me again?" She got herself together, cleared her throat, sat up straighter. "I'm a professional. You want me to what?"

"Kimberly Raine Luz," he said, serious and mostly because he knew she didn't like it when people used her full name. "Would you like to become the official chocolate supplier for Hotel Villa and La Spezia?"

"I... I don't know." Kira said.

"You don't?" Santi blinked back in surprise.

"Well, yes, I know. I mean, yes, I know, but..." Kira shook her head. "Look. The universe is wonderful and weird. But it has never given me an answer this fast. I'm adjusting."

"You asked the universe about me, Kira?" he asked, a little slow, a little deliberately intimate.

"Um," was all she said, and he knew it was dark, but there were just enough lights for him to notice that she was blushing. It brought him right back to that moment at the hotel, to that kiss that he still thought about, one that he agonized about days after. "Yes."

"And what did she tell you?" he asked, moving in a little closer. He could catch the scent from the rosal flowers behind her, could see her eyes widen slightly. Maybe she was trying to break the tension, but Kira suddenly swiped her spoon through the tartufo and stuck it in her mouth, like a barrier between them. Santi chuckled.

"They said that one of us promised the other that we would talk about what happened at the wedding," Kira said, licking remnants of chocolate from her lips. Santi was momentarily distracted by the motion, but only momentarily. "Were you in Manila this whole time?"

"I was. I escaped," Santi explained, pulling back. He considered the next thing to say as he plucked a little santan flower from the bush beside him.

How could he explain that he'd come back to Lipa

because he didn't want to be in Manila? That he was weighing one place against the other, deciding which to give up?

He twirled the santan between his thumb and forefinger. Santi had memories of them pulling out the filaments of the flowers to suck at the little bead of nectar inside when they were kids. Kira used to be an expert santan chain maker, if stuffing one end of the santan into another made one an expert.

"With nothing but your Mercedes and the clothes on your back?" Kira joked, and the playful smile on her face dropped when he flinched. Damn, he hadn't meant to flinch. "Really?"

"More or less," he said, keeping his eyes on his fingers, slowly pulling out the filament of the santan in his hand. "I can buy clothes in SM."

"They did just open a Uniqlo."

He narrowed his eyes her way, but he smiled, and having her smile back at him made his cold, dead heart melt a little in his chest.

"I wanted to come back," he explained, but it didn't feel like the right word. "Needed to come back."

"Did something happen?" Kira asked, taking another bite of the chocolate.

"A collision of things," he said, almost putting the end of the santan in his mouth to suck at the sap before he decided that he wasn't a kid anymore, and tossed it aside. "My parents decided to skip the holidays altogether this year. I went to my grandfather's house on Christmas Eve, and it was…empty. Nobody was there, or Lolo was asleep, but…did you know that Gabriel and I were supposed to sign a lease agreement with the Lai Mall after the holidays?"

"I figured," Kira said. "You only took a year's lease for Sunday Bakery. I thought it was weird, but Ate Nessie…"

"Knows everything?" Santi asked.

"She does," Kira agreed. "But I'm guessing that's not happening anymore."

"Gabriel had a change of heart," he explained. "Decided that we should just revisit our mall plans next year, or maybe the year after that."

"Maybe never," Kira said.

Santi's business partner had all the practical reasons why they shouldn't go through with it—they needed to gradually ramp up their production, he needed to figure out how to streamline things. But what Santi didn't really hear was the actual reason why. A mall deal for Sunday Bakery was the way forward. The way up, in a sense.

But Gabriel just decided, *nope, no thanks. Let's overturn all of our plans.* And it had nothing to do with logic, or needing time to standardize his baking, but the fact that he'd fallen in love with the barista next door, and he didn't want to be away from her. It was that easy for Gabriel, and Santi didn't understand why. Or how he could alter his entire life around that.

"I just don't know how people can make decisions based on their emotions." Santi's brow furrowed as he remembered. "It's unfamiliar to me."

"Well…wasn't moving here an emotional decision?" Kira asked, leaning back against the seat. "Not because we met in Japan, or whatever. Lipa still meant something to you, obviously, or else you wouldn't have decided to come here. It's the same for Gabriel. He thinks he belongs with us in the Laneways. It means something to him to stay."

There it was. *He belongs with us.* And Santi couldn't help the little surge of jealousy that sprang up from his stomach, green and nasty. Why was it that Gabriel, who had been in Lipa for all of three months, was suddenly accepted, and happy and satisfied, while Santi, who had been here for *years*, was still…yearning. Wanting to belong here, or Manila, or anywhere that would take him.

"It goes against everything I was taught. Lolo would hate that, if I told him we were forgoing a deal with the biggest mall in South Luzon." Santi frowned, ignoring his feelings. "The goal of a business is to make profit, and increase its profits until you have more money than God. Staying would be counter-productive."

"Goals are changeable." Kira shrugged, like it was that simple to change the way you were trained, the way you were raised. "Gabriel opened Sunday Bakery to prove something to his family, but now he realizes he did it for himself, because he just really enjoyed baking. I opened a chocolate shop because I insisted that I needed to do something for myself, by myself, but I realize I've mostly been using it as an excuse to meddle in people's lives."

She frowned then, like she'd bitten into something nasty, and Santi didn't like that. He wondered who made her feel like her chocolate was a bad thing. It really wasn't.

"I love your chocolate," he told her. "And I don't think you could run your business if you didn't take it seriously."

"Oh," Kira said, and there was that blush again. He

quite liked being the one to make her blush. "Thank you."

"The 60% dark is my favorite," he continued. "Not too sweet."

"You would be the kind to like chocolate that wasn't sweet," Kira agreed, and it was good to see her smile. "Santi, what a business should accomplish should be up to the one who put it up," she finally said. "Don't you think?"

Talaga ba? he almost said, because that was exactly the opposite of what he thought. But then again, who was to say what good was supposed to be like?

He was raised to think that money was a good thing. It was essential to living a good life. He learned that businesses made money, and that none of those things—money, business and a "good life"—could ever be found in the provinces. Manila was supposed to be good, *the* place to live. But experience had told him that Manila had her horrors. Manila could be the Most Terrible and Expensive Place in the World To Live In, even with all its conveniences.

Eventually he realized that the analogy was false. There were more than enough families in the country making good money from businesses born outside the capital. He'd learned that a "good life" wasn't always a sprawling house in Loyola Grand Villas. He learned that money was important, but so was family. So were good relationships with people around you.

Everything about his family was supposed to be good. They had money, they ran a good business, they were all healthy. But Santi had still spent Christmas alone, wishing he was brave enough to just drive back to Lipa, until today.

"You make it sound so easy," he said with a sigh.

"My mercury is in Aquarius eh." Kira shrugged, waving a hand to brush off the statement. "I am very good at coming to a logical conclusion."

"No, you…" Santi coughed, almost saying *no, it's not that, it's that you're beautiful, and you are so happy with where you are that things become easier. It's because you're so loved.* But he didn't say things like that. "It's you, Kira. You just have this way of making things make sense. Which is how I got convinced to try Royal when we were kids, and my life has been better with it."

She laughed, and it was good to know she seemed to remember it, too.

"I guess this means you just have to trust me," she said, tapping her rose against his nose.

Sitting there on the gallinera today, the lights soft against Kira's face, ylang ylang and rosal in the air, and he knew that he did. It was maybe the easiest thing he could admit to her right now. He trusted her, completely. He always had. He took a bite of the tartufo. Memories of Rome came rushing back to him, but he couldn't help but be excited for what a tartufo with Gemini chocolates would taste like, too.

He didn't know if it was the sugar, but Santi's mind slowly started to wander. He could picture walking hand in hand with Kira on the cobblestone streets of Rome. Could see them walking to the Piazza Navona at twilight, where the summer sky in Rome was an incredible pink and purple hue. Could picture taking her to the restaurant that served the illusive tartufo, and listening to her talk about how wonderful it was. She would probably like it.

He shook himself quickly away from the fantasy, because dreams like that were for other people. He was an exiled grandson who was just trying to get his family to love him. She didn't need to have his mess on her lap. Selling him her chocolate was more than enough for him. It should be more than enough for him.

"So is that a yes?" Santi asked. "Are you going to help me by selling your chocolate?"

"I'll need to test out the tartufo thing myself, figure out which chocolate would work best," she said thoughtfully, waggling her eyebrows because she had the upper hand against him. He liked to think that she always had. "But full disclosure, if I help you, I would actually be helping myself out a lot."

"Why?" he asked. "What's wrong?"

"No, just…money things." Kira wrinkled her nose. "More specifically Gemini and money things. In that she doesn't have much."

"I'm good at money things," Santi offered. "In case it wasn't obvious."

"Ah, weh?" Kira asked sarcastically, looking up at the lights above their heads, at the restaurant nearby, at the fountain not too far away. "Hindi nga. We don't have to talk about everything today, but I could use your insight, too."

And for the first time that holiday, things seemed right. He knew how special the holidays could be because he'd spent them in Lipa as a child—one of his titos would dress up as Santa and leave presents for him and his cousins at midnight, if they sang their Christmas carols loud enough to wake the dead. His Lally would play an old Christmas album (usually a Basil Valdez, because, tradition) and the adults (even

his parents, back then) would dance while the kids bus-
ied themselves with presents. That kind of magic was
long gone, but it only meant that Santi wanted nothing
more than to have it back.

He suddenly remembered that he was taking her
away from her family, who were probably well into
their own desserts inside.

"I should let you go back," he said. "Were you and
your family celebrating something? You seemed very
happy."

"Not celebrating per se." Kira wrinkled her nose,
and Santi wondered what had happened before he
showed up. "Just being together. We do that a lot."

"Lucky you." Santi didn't mean to sound bitter, but
oh well.

"Is that why you asked me to come out here? Because you were jealous?" Kira asked, tilting her head,
curious. "Was this tartufo a ruse?"

"Oh no. I really was worried about it. It's been bothering me for the longest time, and I realized you were
the right person to talk to when I saw you with your
family. And I admit I did feel a bit of jealousy," Santi
admitted, but he was used to that pain in his chest
whenever he saw other happy families in his restaurant. "But more than that, I was happy to see you in
the restaurant. And I realized you were the only person in the world outside of the Santillans who knows
about what happened, with me and Lolo."

He'd thought of it on the drive to Lipa. Who had he
told? How had he processed any of it? He didn't know
anymore. Because he'd told Kira, he realized how free-
ing it was, to be able to talk about what happened out

loud. He'd just needed someone else to know. Some-one else to understand.

"You can talk to me about it anytime," Kira as-sured him, and reached out for his hand. He knew it was meant to be a comforting gesture, but he didn't need comfort. Not right now. "That's what friends are for, right?"

"That's the problem," Santi said slowly. "We're not just friends. Are we?"

He made it sound like a complication, and it was. Add it to the long list of complications he was already carrying around. Because he would have wanted to stay in the garden for the next three days and talk to Kira about how he wished he could have more with her. How they weren't just friends. Why he'd kissed her that day at the hotel (because she was lovely, and she made him feel like he could be happy).

But Santi already had too many complications that he was carrying. And he couldn't afford to drop her, be-cause he wanted her to still be in his life. It was selfish, but it was better than nothing. It was him confirming something they both knew perfectly well, that noth-ing about any of this was happening in the right order. They'd kissed the first night they met again, then they didn't really speak to each other, only to go to where every couple seemed to start—talking, being friends, smiling and holding hands in romantic gardens.

"Santi," Kira said gently. "We're going into busi-ness together."

"Can't I have both?" he asked her, leaning closer, and he could smell her, that pleasant scent of Kira just being herself. His forehead pressed against hers, and Santi closed his eyes, loving the feel of having her so close, his heart aching for her. "You. Your chocolate. I want both. I'm selfish like that."

"You're not selfish," Kira scoffed, but didn't pull away. "You were probably told that wanting things for yourself is selfish. That's different."

"Boss Santi?" a voice asked through the doorway, and they broke apart, Kira suddenly very preoccupied by the half-eaten tartufo. Santi chuckled at her before he looked up at Danny, one of the waiters for La Spezia. "Table six would like to ask if you've taken their daughter hostage."

"Hala," Santi said to Kira like this was totally her fault.

"Ka dram-ah." Kira rolled her eyes. Her years in Manila might have softened her language, but the sharp, crisp edges of her Batangueño couldn't be denied.

"What course are they having?" Santi asked, as Danny's eyes darted between Santi and Kira. He made a mental note to personally speak to Danny about keeping secrets after this.

"We're about to serve dessert, sir."

"Alright." He nodded. Anton Santillan was a businessman's grandson, and if there was anything a businessman knew how to do, it was to smooth over little slights, to make the people they were talking to feel like they could trust him. He knew what was polite, what was galante, and he was not ashamed in doing it. "Can you ask Lauren to make palista the meal for table six?"

Beside him, Kira suddenly choked, and he fought to hide his smile. He remembered when they were kids, and they'd discovered the power of the palista, thinking that they had to write down which food they got from the sari-sari store because they were free, only to find out Aling Pusay sent bills to both their parents every week.

"Comping a five-star meal for nine people is *not* making palista," Kira hissed at him under her breath, and he grinned. "And you don't have to do this."

"So you admit my food is five-star," he said, and yes, he was being mayabang now, but he didn't care. He was sure she found it amusing. "And I know I don't have to, I want to. It's an apology to your family, at least, for interrupting your dinner. Danny, could you wrap up this tartufo, and anything Kira didn't get to eat, have wrapped for takeout. The fried seafood is a specialty, I don't think you got to try it."

Then, because he really wanted to impress her, he added, "Wrap up a second tartufo, too. For further study purposes."

Santi honestly didn't know who looked more perplexed. Danny, who knew full well that La Spezia never did takeout, or Kira, who was looking at him like he had three heads.

"It's an exception, Danny," Santi told him, knowing his concern. "You can get take-out boxes from the lobby lounge."

With a nod, the waiter turned and left with the half-eaten tartufo. Santi nodded in satisfaction.

"Weirdest night of my life," he thought he heard Kira mutter beside him. He was about to ask her to repeat it, just for clarity, but she shook her head. "You know, everyone will know about your little exception by the time I go back into the restaurant. Are you sure you want to—"

"As much as you want me to taste your chocolate,

I want you to taste my food," Santi explained. "And besides, I owe you a Christmas gift."

"Your Christmas gift is pasta, risotto, fried seafood and a chocolate bomb. I feel loved."

"As you should," Santi said in a tone that brokered no argument, no witty comeback. Because she really did. She deserved everything good in life, everything she wanted. She always had, he thought.

"I should head back," Kira said, standing from the bench, taking her rose and smoothing her skirt. Santi quite liked the way it showed off just enough of her legs. "You know, I had all of these reasons to come to La Spezia. But I think I just really, really wanted to eat your food."

"And? What's the verdict?"

"Oh, I'm not going to say. Your head might actually explode."

"I'm looking forward to working with you on this." Santi grinned. He realized then that he wasn't all that different from his little brother. Where Miro could slide in and out of his masks easily, Santi could open and close himself up, depending on what the situation needed. Defense mechanisms vary, apparently.

"Look at that," Kira said softly. "You're actually smiling."

Santi felt his cheeks heat, and he cleared this throat, shook his head as she giggled. "That was an accident. Good night, Kimberly."

"Good night, Santi." She smiled, using the rose to wave goodnight. "For the record, I like it when you smile."

Then she exited the garden, leaving him outside, by himself. Smiling.

Chapter Seven

December 29
Somewhere along Ayala Avenue
Makati City

> *Winnowing: the process of separating the shells*
> *from the roasted beans. A pain. Always a pain.*

The map of Metro Manila in Santi's mind was pretty clear. Quezon City was North, and whatever came after it was Too Far. At the center of Manila was his home base, Ortigas, a business district with subdivisions a stone's throw away. Going south, in rapid succession, was Mandaluyong, Makati, Manila and Pasay, all places he had to pass on his way to the highway to get to Lipa.

From where he was standing, he could see most of that map spread out almost entirely before him. He liked this exercise, trying to recognize the places he frequented from a different angle. Like trying to see if home was still familiar, no matter how he saw it.

"A thousand pesos says he's going to do it," Miro said suddenly beside him, as the Santillan brothers pretended to be preoccupied by the view from the top floor of the Tan-Sy building. Views were essential to purchasing buildings after all, especially ones along one of the most expensive avenues in the country.

"He won't," Santi insisted, taking a slow sip of the coffee Miro had bought him. His little brother was enthusiastic when he said that it came from this cafe that was originally in Japan, or something. Santi personally preferred the Tomas Coffee Co. beans he had on stock in Villa. "He just likes the idea that he could."

"If you knew that, then why would you bother driving all the way up here in the first place?" Miro asked, rolling his eyes, and Santi knew this Miro. This was "Upset At Everything" Miro, the one that showed up when Santi wasn't cooperating with him. "Or are you really trying to suck up to Lolo that much?"

"I was promised family lunch," Santi reasoned, which was true. Vito had promised lunch with his grandsons, but could they make a little stopover at this building first? "You remember those?"

"When Lolo would talk to the chef, convince him to make something off-menu? We haven't had a meal like that in a long time."

"I'm nostalgic like that." Santi shrugged.

"Says the one who left in the middle of the night." Miro rolled his eyes.

"That's a lot of judgement from someone getting the penthouse at the Carlton," Santi pointed out, raising a brow at his little brother, who rolled his eyes.

"I asked Lolo for a condo in Poblacion. The decent side of Poblacion, mind you, maybe even Rockwell. But nooo, he *had* to insist on getting me the Carlton because he wanted to rub *your* nose in it."

"Beggars can't be choosers." Santi shrugged, and

he didn't miss the irony in that statement. There was nothing about Miro Santillan that even hinted at begging. All Miro had to do to get what he wanted was to smile, and say, "You're absolutely right, Lolo."

While Santi and Miro could commiserate with each other (in fact there was nothing else they could talk about but their shared misery), having each other's back was a completely different story. Miro was too attached to what he was getting from Lolo Vito to fight for Santi. Santi was too attached to his little brother to resent him for it.

When Santi told Miro about his idea, about Hotel Villa, Miro told him it was never going to work. "Just stop working so hard, Kuya. Lolo would never hurt you if you didn't do anything to deserve it." Then when Vito laughed and told Santi to stay in Lipa, since it was what he wanted so badly, Miro hadn't fought for him, hadn't disagreed. He even made it sound like Santi had purposefully gotten himself kicked out of Manila to spite *Miro*, which was ridiculous. He understood Miro not wanting to rock the boat, if it meant living on a daily allowance that could feed a family of six without having to do a single thing.

But even as Santi stood there, the world at his feet, he knew that it wasn't worth it. Because Miro was standing in an old building in the middle of the day against his will, and Santi was here because his grandfather had asked him to come. The motivations were just different.

A strange peace had settled over Santi. Well, not quite peace, but...detachment? Like he knew very well that this wasn't the way real life worked for anyone.

That they were (sadly) wasting someone's time. Again. "Miro, did Lolo tell you about…"

"I think I've seen enough," his grandfather suddenly announced, his way of saying, "I've done the mental math, and I can totally afford this building, but I'm not going to buy it."

"Anton, what do you think? Is this building fit for my legacy?"

Santi honestly didn't know what came over him. Maybe he was just feeling all of his thirty years and couldn't believe he was still doing things like this. Maybe he realized he could be somewhere else right now—either sitting at Sunday Bakery, early for his afternoon meeting with Gabriel, or at Hotel Villa, taste-testing new food with his head chef. He could also be in Gemini Chocolate, trying his hardest not to buy every chocolate bar in sight.

But whatever it was, he still shrugged, and said, "I don't know."

And shit. He'd slipped. Santi could have given Vito any number of valid reasons not to buy the building— they were in hotels, not leasing, the capital gains tax they would have to pay would outweigh its benefits, nobody had mentioned *why* the building was being sold in the first place.

But no. Saying he didn't know was akin to saying he didn't care, and to a man who needed attention, it was the rudest thing Santi could have said to his grandfather.

Beside him, he heard Miro splutter. The men standing behind his grandfather, touring them around, suddenly looked like they wanted to be anywhere but here.

Vito looked like he couldn't decide if he wanted to laugh or scream.

"Well," Vito said with a huff, turning to the others. "Shockingly, something he doesn't know."

Stupid. Really stupid.

Lunch had been extremely stilted and quiet, Vito brimming with all the things he wanted to say, and both Santi and Miro wishing they were anywhere but here. There was no special menu, no discussing their favorite old hobbies, none of Lolo talking about his prized fountain pen collection. Just…stony silence. Everything Santi didn't want.

"I'm starting to wonder if you really want to come back to Manila, Kuya," Miro had said after. It had meant to be teasing, Miro was always teasing, but it still hurt. "So much for family lunch. Lolo, I'll go back with you to the house."

Then he was left to stand there alone in a street corner in Arnaiz, his stomach full of really good Japanese food that he'd barely tasted. Santi sighed. He took his car and drove to Chino Roces Extension, across EDSA, because he was already here, and he might as well buy fancy bread while he was at it.

He had just finished, and was about to head to his car when he got a text. Kira.

Grim Reaper-nim, My informants tell me that you're in Makati and that you have a car.

Santi chuckled, despite himself. He was surprised that everyone in Lipa was appraised of his whereabouts; he didn't think they noticed when he left to go back to Manila.

Yes. Was about to leave for Lipa. What can I do for you, Sunny-ssi? he replied, because he could be smooth that way.

Can I hitch a ride? I'm in Legazpi.

Ironically, Santi had been closer to Legazpi Village before lunch. Oh well.

Also, OMG YOU WATCHED GOBLIN. I am so proud!

The address led him to a restaurant on Rada Street, a row of restaurants mixed among condominiums and office buildings (because urban planning? Was that a thing?). Santi watched Kira step out of the restaurant wearing ripped jeans and a sheer magenta blouse, her hair pulled back in a ponytail that swished when she turned her head. So different from the loose pants, soft shirt, chunky black sandal combos that she liked to wear. This was Kira blending in to Makati and the other similarly dressed people in the restaurant. She was even wearing dark lipstick. It suited her.

"Thank god!" she exclaimed, and the way she beamed at him when he lowered the window to call her over made him much more busog than anything he'd eaten at the restaurant had. "You saved me."

"From?" Santi asked, reminding her to put on her seat belt before he peeled away from the curb and headed for the Skyway.

"Small talk, urgh." Kira stuck her tongue out, and placed a paper bag Santi hadn't seen before on her lap. "I mean, she's my friend, and I know she works in advertising, but I don't have to know anything about advertising to be her friend! Am I supposed to care what her boss said to this other person? I don't even shop there!"

"Shop where?" Santi asked, confused. He'd only seen her this flustered, or talk this fast, when she was coming to him to ask about the difference between a bond and an equity, or why her uncle insisted she get a credit line for the Laneways. Which, he figured, only meant that this really, really bothered her.

"I wanted to ask her how her family was doing, how her trip to Singapore was, if she had a hard time finding the shop I asked her to buy from." Kira shook her head. "We used to be close, you know. Now she's... anyway. Thank you for picking me up. I would have had to hang out at the mall until Kuya Jake finished tonight otherwise."

"So why did you meet her, whoever she was?" Santi asked curiously, as the buildings and structures of Makati fell away. Driving on the Skyway always made him feel like he was driving far, far away, and it made him feel like it was a little easier to breathe, somehow.

She was quiet for a bit, like she was seriously considering her answer.

"Well, because she's still my friend. I still care about her enough to rearrange my entire day just to see her. I asked to make pasabuy from Singapore," Kira explained, indicating the paper bag on her lap. "Hay, the things I do for KPop merch. What's your excuse?"

"I need an excuse to be in Manila?" he asked her. "I live here."

"You have three businesses in Lipa," Kira pointed out. "And a house across the park from mine, also in

Lipa. You don't fool me, Anton Santillan. You're just as Batangueño as I am at this point."

He'd told himself that buying that house in Haraya Subdivision was an investment choice, but that of course didn't stop him from buying the more comfortable bed for the place, from having the kitchen built out the way he wanted it because the oven that came with the house wasn't as good as the one he had in Ortigas.

"So you're really not going to tell me what you were doing in Makati?" Kira asked, and he quickly threw her a glance as if to say she was being nosy. "Are you secretly seeing someone? Did you need to buy something that *wasn't* in Uniqlo Lipa?"

"What is it with you and Uniqlo?" Santi asked.

"Uniqlo is the chosen wear of the Ateneo/La Salle millennial when they want to seem relatable." Kira shrugged. "I don't make the rules."

"They're comfortable clothes that fit me well." Santi didn't know why he was defending his sartorial choices, because Uniqlo really did come with a variety of styles, but good to know that Kira found it amusing. "And hey. *You're* an Ateneo millennial, too."

"Yeah, but their jean sizes are for tiny people." Kira laughed.

"Yes, because Birkenstock sandals and flared cotton pants are the true peak of fashion," Santi said, which made Kira laugh even harder. Look at him, making jokes. He was feeling better already.

"Lakas mo mang-asar, ha," she warned him, but there was no actual anger in her tone, just a playful glare that made Santi smile. "The last time I saw you,

you were wearing a suit jacket and leather shoes. In Lipa."

"I always dress appropriately when the hotel has events," Santi argued. "Luckily I did, the debutante's father invited me to drink with him for a bit."

The next two hours flew by that way, the two of them arguing about style, about the best place in the city for lomi, if Lobo or Laiya was closer by driving. They made a definitive ranking of all the food Kira tried at La Spezia (the pesto was number one, surprise) and talked about their friends ("I *knew* Sari and Gab would be well matched!") and their childhood memories. She talked to him like they were the oldest of friends, and they hadn't lost the last twenty-plus years to Manila, to his family, like he hadn't been keeping his distance from her for the last three years.

She'd always known how to draw him in to her, whether it was the offer of Royal Tru Orange in a plastic bag, the manong with the fishball cart showing up at his house, or sitting and talking with him in a car headed back to Lipa. Her eyes sparkled with delight every time he said something she agreed with ("Chinese garter should *definitely* be an Olympic sport"), and he liked that she turned to face him while he drove, her back to her window, her knee on the passenger seat. He would have liked to look at her, if he wasn't driving.

He was picturing them in Rome again.

Kira even managed to convince him to try drive-through McDonald's coffee, and while Santi regretted that particular coffee choice, he didn't regret taking that detour to pick her up. And for two hours, everything was good. He actually felt like…himself again. Not the rotten apple of his grandfather's eye, not the brother who stubbornly refused to get with the program. Just…himself.

"I'm heading to the Laneways, can I drop you off there?" Santi asked, as they exited Star Tollway and found themselves in Lipa. Like the spell of their impromptu road trip had lifted.

"Yes, thanks." Kira nodded as they headed down the highway. "You seem different, did you know that?"

"Different?" Santi echoed, curious.

"You're smiling again."

He couldn't deny that. Was surprised that she had actually noticed that he didn't do it that often.

"I've always enjoyed my time here," he admitted. "Even when I was made to think it wasn't enough, I still enjoyed it. I used to think there was something wrong with me, that I was enjoying what I'm doing here. But I'm starting to think that maybe my goals could be changeable."

Then he pulled the car over to a parking space, and turned to Kira. It was difficult to describe the happiness he felt, that someone was looking at him the way she was, that she was glad to be next to him. It made him feel warm inside, for someone as wonderful as her to see him.

"Whoever said that must be very, very wise," she told him.

"Wise enough." He shrugged, before she pinched his side and made him laugh. Of course Santi had to retaliate, which meant she had to retaliate again, and she was so brilliant at breaking through his defenses that he actually had to carefully take her wrists to stop her. And suddenly her face was inches away from his.

The air in the car suddenly seemed warm, and was that a blush spreading across her cheeks?

"Santi," she said, and her voice was a little breathy. She was a little close, but he let himself come even closer. When she smiled, and tugged at the hem of his shirt a little, he obliged and came even closer.

He wanted to kiss her. It was no longer surprising to him, to feel that urge. Like he'd had it in him all along. Except now, he was tired of holding himself back from what he wanted, and what he was feeling. Sitting with her in his face for the last two hours had made him feel loose, and comfortable. Safe, even. Safe enough to ask for what he wanted.

"We have a business deal to fix. You haven't even tasted the new tartufo yet."

"I know," he said. "But that's tomorrow."

"Always a day away," Kira joked.

"Kira, I—"

A sharp knock behind Kira made them both jump, Santi's head hitting the ceiling of his car. They both turned to see Gabriel Capras and Sari Tomas smiling smugly at them, the couple holding hands like they had just found two more possible members of their little Love Club.

To Kira's credit, she didn't look at all embarrassed, simply clearing her throat and lowering the window on her side with the press of a button.

"Yes, mamsir, may I help you?" she asked her friends in a sugary-sweet tone, even if Santi was sure her face only said, "go away, go away now."

"Did we interrupt something?" Gabriel asked innocently, his voice equally as sugar sweet. He tilted his head so he could get a closer look at Santi. "Or were you thinking of joining me and Anton Manansala V. Santillan for our meeting at Sunday Bakery?"

"Manansala?" Sari next to her boyfriend asked, her lips quirking in amusement. "Like the—"

"Like the National Artist, yes," Santi sighed, not that he was particularly proud of the name. At this point, there was only one thing he could say to them to get them to go ahead to Sunday Bakery. "My mother is an enthusiast. I was actually about to head to Sunday Bakery for our meeting. I have bread from Patis."

"What!" Gabriel exclaimed as Kira and Sari looked confused, and Santi reached to the backseat to grab the goods he'd picked up before driving to Legazpi. Patis Bakery in Makati was one of those places that claimed to "elevate" the humble panaderia, as if there was something wrong with the current iteration. But even Santi had to admit that their bread was pretty good, worth some of the hype. Santi had managed to grab the last of jamon and keso de bola croissant sandwiches, pan de coco brioche and raisin bread ala Baguio Country Club.

Santi thought that it would be enough to distract Gabriel from the fact that they'd been caught seconds away from another kiss. But sometime in between the croissant sandwiches and their second cups of Café Cecilia coffee, Gabriel pulled Santi aside, leading him to the landing of the staircase that led up to Sunday Bakery's kitchen. From where they were standing, Santi could just see Kira and Sari talking and taking bites of their food, not so surreptitious about casting them curious glances.

"Just have to talk to him about the Grand Opening!" Gabriel yelled over his shoulder in explanation.

"Santi, do you think we should get doves and release them when we open the bakery?"

"Doves are for weddings, Gabriel, we don't need—" Santi began, but Gabriel shook his head.

"Yeah, don't worry, I already ordered the party poppers. What are your intentions with Kira?" he asked seriously. "She's our landlord, not to mention my friend, so my old-timey toxic male instinct is to protect her. Even from you, Sants."

"I like spending time with her," Santi explained, looking at where Kira and Sari took bites of the pan de coco. "In the interest of disclosure, I have known her since I was a child. She was the one who gave me the idea of moving to Lipa."

"Oh yeah, Sari told me how you were all in a little neighborhood barkada," Gabriel said, waving his hands around as he quickly replaced the bakery's depleting supply of the mini caramel cakes. "Thanks for telling me that, by the way. I *thought* it was super random that you ended up in Lipa."

"You don't seem surprised," Santi said, curious. "About me having feelings for Kira."

"No, because I've read this romance novel. I mean, I had the sense that there was always something going on between the two of you," Gabriel chuckled. "I'm very wise that way."

"I disagree," Santi said. "Everyone is still talking about how silly your courtship with Sari was. With the marching band. And the carnations."

"It was a prank war, Santi! And for the record, I asked her out the first time I met her, my affections were never in doubt," Gabriel said proudly, piling yema rolls onto a plate like they didn't have enough food already. "I mean, you know naman, right? It's not a bad thing to feel things for Kira."

"Really?" Santi asked, chuckling ruefully. "Because I definitely feel like I don't deserve her."

"But you deserve to be happy." Gabriel wasn't looking at him as he ate, but it didn't make the words any less true. "And you think you're in a position to make her happy. So go forth and let yourself try."

But Santi wasn't the kind of guy who tried something. He did it, and always did it well. And he could say he was due to make this declaration for a while now, and he didn't really expect that Gabriel Capras would be the first to hear it, but Santi was trying to be better about being honest about how he was feeling. And it was easier to say to Gabriel, who understood how difficult it was for Santi to admit to wanting things. It was safer too to admit how he felt to someone who wouldn't leave. Gabriel didn't have to know that Santi giving in to his feelings came at a cost, that his grandfather still asked about the Laneways, and had, just that afternoon.

But he had to say it out loud, because his chest felt like it was going to burst into pieces. So he might as well tell Gabriel.

"I want it all," Santi said thoughtfully, not quite sure if he believed it yet, but saying it out loud had its merits. "All the happiness. With Kira. With Sunday Bakery and Villa and La Spezia. I want to be happy, Gabriel. I understand why you decided to stay."

Gabriel blinked at him, and wasn't that exactly why the two of them decided that they needed to talk, to hash this out? But as Kira said, goals were changeable. And today, as he stood in his bakery with his friends, with good bread and even better coffee, Santi knew his goals were changing slowly.

"Dude…"

"Please don't call me dude."

"When we first met you asked me not to call you Santi, Santi," Gabriel reminded me. "Let me have this."

"Fine," Santi sighed. "Gabriel."

"Anyway, I was going to say that I'm glad you made the decision…dude." Gabriel elbowed Santi in the ribs, as if Santi was the newcomer to Lipa. "It's work, though. I mean, you can't just do something without doing the work. That's like me thinking I can make bonete better after eating it a couple of times, or writing something that 'subverts the genre' when you never actually respected the genre in the first place."

"What?" Santi asked, somewhat confused.

"Nothing," Gabriel said quickly. "I'm just saying. Allow yourself to be vulnerable. To be open. To imagine a life here. It's really not as impossible as everyone made us believe."

Santi knew it wasn't impossible. But he couldn't fully explain why he just couldn't give up on Manila yet.

By the time Santi and Gabriel actually finished talking about Sunday Bakery's Grand Opening, and their merienda was all gone, it was well into the evening already. After declining a dinner invitation with Sari and Gabriel, Kira had asked if Santi was interested in grabbing dinner just the two of them.

Something casual, she'd insisted. *Like Lipa Grill or something. I love their inihaw na pusit. Are you a fan of lomi?*

He was not, unfortunately, but Kira didn't seem as incensed by it as other Lipeños were when he brought it up. And now here he was, sitting outside the Laneways in the early touches of the evening, looking up at Kira's twinkle lights while she closed the shop for the day.

Santi had only been inside Gemini Chocolates a handful of times. At first, he'd been too embarrassed, suddenly showing up in Lipa so suddenly after his conversation with Kira. Then he was ashamed because he hadn't told her that he was partnering with Gabriel on Sunday Bakery.

Because it was the holidays (or maybe because Kira just really liked a good outdoor light), twinkle lights were set up overhead, over the big window that looked into the space. Underneath that, she'd hung individual parols made with delicate white capiz and gold frames, subtle but effective when put together with the twinkle lights. Santi sat on a simple wooden bench by the window and found himself surrounded by plants—a large dill plant that had no business being that tall, a climbing plant with curly leaves and deep purplish blue flowers. (*They're clitoria ternatea!* Kira would happily tell him later.) There were other plants there too, more than he could ever name, even one placed inside the basket of a bike that looked like it had seen better days.

With the Christmas music playing in the distance, and the cold snap that accompanied the breeze, the little spot outside Gemini Chocolates felt calm, and comfortable. Santi leaned against the wall, resting the back of his head against the glass of the window.

He took deep breaths, trying to settle the uncomfortable twisting in his stomach, the one that had seemed to follow him from Makati. He had always been good at hiding it, but in a place like this, it felt safe to feel it, to give it a chance to calm itself.

The following were things that he was trying to settle in his head:

1) He was never, ever going to be able to ask Kira to sell the Laneways to Carlton. That was a given. From a financial standpoint, it was making too much money for the Luzes to let it go. Santi would admit he had a mild emotional attachment to this place, he couldn't imagine the depth of Kira's or any of the other shop owners'. Which meant that.

2) Santi was going to have to stop trying to go back to Manila. He had all the logical reasons to just stay here and be happy, but there was still a part of him that wanted his family's love. Which, he really should be smarter than that, because everyone knew the story of the scorpion and the frog.

3) He was currently sitting here, and all he could think of was the woman closing the shop behind him. And he knew what he wanted (more), that he wanted to ask if she was interested in more. But more would mean involvement, and involvement meant that she would have to be exposed to the Santillans. He didn't want to do that, and risk losing her. More than his constant juggle of complicated, he was aware that the people he loved weren't the *best* people. They would judge. Ask questions. Make her feel small, because that was their way.

He couldn't bring that to her door.

And he'd thought about it, over and over, endlessly. Did he *need* her? No. He couldn't need her, because to need someone was a weakness. And Santi had grown up knowing that he shouldn't need anyone.

It's an ache, or a twist in your chest that you can't get rid of. And there's no one else in the world that can understand it, but the other person. That's need.

But wanting was a completely different thing. And Santi wasn't sure he had enough in him to resist that wanting anymore. He'd just inhaled, wondering how the hell he was supposed to tell her all of that, when the shop door beside him opened and Kira's head popped out.

"Bulaga!" she exclaimed, but the door had been too heavy for her surprise to be effective, and he just smiled at her, still leaning against the window.

"Let me guess," he said, tracking her with his gaze. "You have a back door."

"Don't we all?" She winked exaggeratedly at him, laughing at her little joke as she closed the shop door behind her, skipping one of the three steps to street level before she stood in front of him, her hands behind her back. It was like they were kids again, and she was patiently waiting for him to go outside with her to play.

"Very mature," he said dryly, as Kira nudged his knee with hers to get him to move over on the bench.

"Tabi," she said, and he shuffled closer to the dill plant while she eased herself next to the climbing vine, and that was when he realized she was holding two mugs.

"Here," she said, handing him one of the mugs. "Peace offering, and pre-dinner snack."

He peered inside and immediately recognized the silky smooth tsokolate, likely made from Gemini Chocolates' tableya. The mug was hot, and he raised the cup to his lips, where he was met with the hot chocolate. He took a slow, measured sip, and the liquid filled his mouth pleasantly. The chocolate was thick, but not too thick, sweet, but not sweet enough that he couldn't taste the fruitiness of the chocolate, the heaviness of the molasses and the light touch of the milk.

He knew traditional tsokolate was made with a batirol, rolled between the palms until the chocolate was light, airy and frothy. But this chocolate sill had some density, like it wasn't something to be trifled with. It was tsokolate that could only have been made by someone who knew exactly what they were doing.

"They say that cacao has the power to unlock hidden yearnings and reveal destinies," Kira said, looking down at her mug as if she could read its contents. "Makes you wonder."

"Did the ancient Mayans volunteer that information, or did the colonizers just infer it?" Santi asked, taking another sip, deeper than the last.

"Makes you wonder what your destiny is," Kira corrected him. A little smile played on her lips like he'd said something amusing, and Santi wondered if this wasn't exactly what she wanted, to have him drink her chocolate and have him under her spell or something.

He shook his head, and those impossible thoughts away. She wasn't weaving magic spells into her tsokolate. Was she?

"Sarap?" she asked him, sipping from her mug a lot more carefully than he was.

"Yeah, it's super sarap," he said, and winced when he realized how conyo it sounded. But it made her laugh. "Yeah, yeah, make fun of me na. You studied in Ateneo, you should be used to these kinds of mga... words."

"I am," she said. "But it's still funny! Can you say 'tusok the fishballs,' please, just once, for me?"

"I would do anything for you Kira." He scoffed and sipped his tsokolate again. He really should look into getting this for the lobby lounge; the stuff they served was garbage compared with this. "Except that."

They paused, the two of them looking at each other again. They sat next to each other a lot as kids, but this felt...different. Kids' relationships were uncomplicated—you exist, therefore we can be friends. It faded when you lost proximity, as they had. But now they were both adults, and she could have decided to sit with so many other people. And still, she chose to sit next to him. Still, they looked at each other with a little bit of awe, affection and that little zing of attraction, because the other person brought it out in them.

People came and left all the time, but right now, they chose to sit beside each other.

"I don't think I apologized," he told her, lowering his mug. "For not looking for you at the wedding, or talking to you after. I wasn't really sure if you were interested in knowing any of it."

"You didn't owe me explanations, and I shouldn't have had expectations like that on the universe." Kira shook her head. "But please don't feel like I would never be interested in what's happening with you," she said, her voice serious. "You matter to me, Santi. I'm interested."

"A lot happened in those years that I was away," was all he said, which really, was a Pandora's box in and of itself that he was giving her the option not to break open at the moment. "Things that I'm not ready to talk about, I think."

Instead she reached for his arm, just above his wrist, and gave it a squeeze, smiling at him in reassurance.

"Okay. I'll be here," she said, which made Santi immediately frown. He tried to think of the last time someone had been that kind, or gentle with him, and god, his mind was pathetically coming up short. That couldn't be right, could it?

It could, his brain supplied. It really could.

"I really do like this, by the way," he told her, indicating his now nearly empty mug, which, how did that happen? He looked at her and she was resting her head on the back of the window again. "Tired?"

"It's been a *long* day." Kira groaned. "I don't know why going to Manila takes so much energy from me. I don't even drive."

"I get it." He shrugged. "It's an exhausting place. And you had to meet a friend who didn't seem interested in what you had to say."

"I think," Kira sighed, "you just hit the nail on the head. And now I will hold that grudge over their heads forever. I'm a Scorpio Moon."

"I'm an Earth Snake, so I'm not very forgiving either, probably," he warned her, which made her laugh, because obviously he had no idea what he was talking about.

"Completely different Zodiac, dude." She shook her head. "But of *course* you're also an Earth Snake. I need to keep myself awake. I still have a meeting with Eugene and Jenny for their custom wedding order next month."

"Let me guess. Another couple you matched?" Santi asked.

"I can hear your sarcasm, Grim Reaper. But yes,

I did match them," she huffed, but he could hear the pride in her voice. "They were childhood friends, and she's been in love with him since forever, but he just needed a *big* old push. Literally. Basta, it's a whole story."

"You really believe in that, don't you?" Santi asked her, amused. "Matchmaking. Magic."

"Those are two very different things," she pointed out to him, shaking her head. "Also, you say that now, but when I finally match Ate Nessie with someone—"

Santi actually snorted.

"Ala eh," Kira tutted. "Is that *derision* in your tone, sir?"

"Ate Nessie?" he asked. "She's…"

"Old?"

"I was going to say feisty," Santi said. "She calls me pogi, though. I'm not mad at it."

"Don't worry, Santi." Kira chuckled. "If you didn't already like me so much, I would still be able to find someone to match with you. A lot of girls are into the whole 'suplado chaebol thing.'"

"Suplado what?"

"And also," Kira added like she didn't hear him. "I'm surprised at you. How can you not believe in magic, living here?"

"Here?" he asked. He had to admit, the Laneways came with its own brand of magic. People just felt comfortable when they were here. Or he did. Here there was no competition, no need to be the best, as long as you enjoyed what you were doing. He'd seen it first-hand when Gabriel and Sari tried to outwit each other last Christmas, only to end up with them falling in love. Magic.

"This country," she clarified, waving her free hand around. "We've got a strong affinity for weird shit, if I do say so myself."

"Weird shit?" he echoed, disbelieving.

"Don't sweep in the house on New Year, so you don't sweep away the good luck. Siblings can't be married on the same year to avoid sukob. Steps on a staircase are counted, oro, plata, mata, and cannot end in mata." She listed these things, serious as they were. Even Kira's brother, Kiko, a more levelheaded architect than most Santi had encountered, had strictly adhered to the stair thing when they refurbished Villa.

"You live here and you just find yourself following those little things. I mean, life in the Philippines is… well, sometimes it's a fucking trash fire, except there's a neighbor that suddenly has a fireproof house that wasn't supposed to be available for anyone."

He couldn't disagree there.

"So when someone tells you that there's something you can do, that you can appease the spirits by offering them sweets, that you can save yourself from cancer by not wearing a bra to bed, is it really so bad to listen? Or to at least think about it?"

Her head turned to his, and their gazes locked. It was like the world had slowed down around them at her command. Her lashes fluttered and swept as he was given a full view of her dark brown eyes, playful and sparkling, drawing him close to her until his entire world revolved around her.

"And you believe in that," he said.

"Maybe," she said, wincing, and her hesitation surprised him. Someone who had been so sure about what she wanted out of life was suddenly saying "maybe?"

"Lately I've been wondering if I've been listening to the universe wrong. Apparently, just because people used your chocolate and your expertise to find love, doesn't mean you make enough to be able to keep your store. And then, of course, you came."

"Ah," Santi said. "I understand why you found my proposal so hilarious."

"You know what was happening at that dinner? I was just recovering from my family telling me that chocolate is all well and good, matchmaking was okay, but I needed to explain myself to the Luzes. Because they don't understand what I'm doing." She sighed, her shoulders dropping as she shook her head. "They understand ROIs and bottom lines, and revenues. I had *just* asked the universe for help, and suddenly you were there, asking me the right questions," Kira explained, smiling. "Not that I'm dismissing your thoughts, or exploiting you, or saying you're controlled by the universe—"

"No." Santi shook his head. "Kira. I know what being exploited for business is like. This isn't that."

"Okay, I know I said I would wait, but you really have to tell me what happened to you in Manila one day," Kira said, blinking at him like he'd revealed something shocking. "But this is a good idea, the two of us working together. Everyone and literally my mother knows that you have good relationships with your suppliers. I haven't heard a single bad thing they've said about you."

"Maybe they're scared of me," Santi said.

"They respect you, Santi," Kira corrected him. "And I think your customers would *love* a tartufo made with my chocolate."

"It's the chocolate that makes people fall in love," Santi noted. Then he looked down at his cup, remembering what she said about destiny. He wondered if this was how it revealed itself to him, in the form of Kira Luz showing up at the right place at the right time.

"Are you falling in love with me now, Santi?" Kira asked, a little chuckle in her voice told him that she was joking, but still, the question caught him off guard, made him pause.

"I was…" he said, very suddenly, out of words.

"Joking, I know," she told him lightly, looking away. "I just don't want to lose the shop. Don't get me wrong. I love the Laneways, and everything about it."

"It's easy to see why." Santi nodded, looking out at the space before them. He could see Sunday Bakery just across the street, where the staff was speaking to their last few customers. Next door to that was Café Cecilia, warm and welcoming. On and on, the shops went, offering different temptations and comforting things, and it was nice.

There was a reason why he wanted to be a part of it, too. Not just because it was popular, there was… there was a magic to it that he couldn't understand. No competition, no fighting. Just a group of people coming together to make something special.

"But it's not mine." Kira wrinkled her nose in distaste, like it was physically unpalatable for her to say so. "It belongs to all of my family. And I'm happy to keep working for them if they need me, but one day, they won't. On the Laneways, I'm a Luz. But in Gemini, I'm just…myself. I'm everyone's friend. The one they turn to when they need something. Gemini is my haven. My safe space."

A place like this was such a bubble in a country like the Philippines, where business was harsh and competitive, where it was always about one-upping each other and exerting authority that you maybe didn't have.

To Kira, Gemini Chocolates, and by extension, the Laneways, was a safe haven. Santi understood that, because isn't that exactly why he was here? Exactly why he drew a firm line between his Lipa life and Manila life? He was here tonight because he'd needed that safe haven. And just like Kira, her presence here meant the world to him. She mattered because she was here.

Santi should have never asked his grandfather about what he could do. He regretted it the moment he'd asked.

"It's a good space," he assured her. "I feel safe here, too. And I find myself enjoying this."

"The tsokolate," she said, nodding. "It's amazing, if I do say so myself."

"Not just that. It's spending time with you again," he clarified, and it was worth saying something that he never would have otherwise admitted, just to see Kira Luz blush. "Talking with you again. I missed you, Kimberly."

"Same," she said simply, and Santi wanted to exhale in relief. She missed him. She understood how missing the other person felt like, because she felt it about him. She wanted him, and he wanted her. It sounded so simple, so reachable. All he had to do was take it. Say yes. Be selfish.

"Also," he added, "one of us has to believe in the universe. And it has to be you."

"*Has* to?" she asked him curiously.

"It means something to you," he told her. "It has

guided you and led you to some interesting places—
opening the Laneways, making your own chocolate,
building your community, matching couples, convenience stores in the middle of nowhere, Japan."

"But not security for Gemini Chocolates."

"But there's something you can do about that," he
pointed out. "Something *we* can do."

"We. I like the sound of that we."

He looked at her, and knew he saw Kira Luz, and
everything she represented. Good things and magic,
possible happiness. A bit of chocolate had lingered,
just at the corner of her lips.

Their faces were close. Close enough that he noted
the color of her lips, achieved by some kind of lip product. It made her lips glossy and deep berry red, reminding him of the roses she loved so much. Did she still
love them, or had she outgrown them? he wondered.
There was so much about her he longed to know. To
rediscover. To remember. Three years waiting for a
kiss was a long time.

He was about to ask if he could stop waiting, and
just kiss her, when his phone started to ring, loud and
demanding as it vibrated violently in his pocket. Santi
hastily pulled out his phone and frowned at the name
flashing on the screen, as if glaring at it would make
it go away.

"Hotel stuff?" Kira asked, frowning.

"Yes. Nothing too bad, but something I have to handle right away," he sighed. "Rain check on that dinner?"

"I never understood what that meant," Kira mused.
"But yes."

He placed his mug between them. Then before he

turned to leave, Kira tugged his hand and kissed him. It was a soft kiss, a casual press of her mouth against his. But Santi felt his entire body melt against hers. Felt himself curl toward her, like a flower turning to the sun. He kissed her back, in between breaths, and he felt Kira's lips curve when she smiled.

"I'll see you tomorrow," he said softly, tucking a strand of hair behind Kira's ear before he turned and left. His stomachache had miraculously cleared.

Chapter Eight

December 30
Gemini Chocolates
The Laneways

*Today's Horoscope: Your unique point of view and
love of life is what makes you special, Gemini. Your
belief that the universe is still inherently good will
bring you the love that you need.*

Kira was singing. It tended to happen, when her playlist started playing a really good song and her body just needed to move. And Janet Jackson's "All For You" was one of her favorites, even if she'd forgotten most of the lyrics.

"So Curl Up and Dye's landlord renewed their lease near the Cathedral," Ate Nessie announced, as she entered Gemini, brushing past the customers who were curiously watching the owner totally killing it on the choreography that she made up on the spot. "They're not going to get the space here na."

"That's a shame." Kira shrugged. "I was looking forward to the salon…making the cut."

"You're in a good mood," Ate Nessie noted dryly,

shaking her head at the joke. Kira pretended not to notice that the Laneways' favorite Ate's tone was pointed. So pointed it was practically a Seurat (ha! that class on art history paid off).

Ate Nessie was still giving Kira a look as she sat in the lone bistro table and batibot chairs by the window, a set Kira had rescued from her grandmother's storage. Ate Nessie raised a hand, and one of Kira's staff immediately served her usual cup of tsokolate. Ate Nessie preferred hers extremely glossy and thick, and got it without the extra splash of milk the shop usually added first.

Kira tried not to think of the last time she had hot chocolate, because really, she had thought about it *so many times* already.

"Have you ever seen Temptation Island?" Kira asked Ate Nessie seemingly apropos to nothing. "The movie?"

"1980 or 2011?" Ate Nessie asked, and before Kira could chide her for it, she shook her head. "I mean, I would *never* watch a movie like that! Even if I am a fan of Dina Bonnevie."

"Uh-huh," Kira said. "There's that scene where they're on the beach, walang tubig, walang pagkain… let's just start dancing!"

Then she started dancing, which only made Ate Nessie look at her even more worried. Kira stopped and sighed, knowing she was simply using the music to mask her pain. She dropped her shoulders and slid onto the chair across from Ate Nessie.

"I got an email from Tito Nicos today," Kira explained in a soft voice, making sure nobody else in the shop could hear. "They've decided not to renew my contract for next year as manager of the Laneways. Apparently Uno's taking over that. So they want access to all our files, our spreadsheets and reports."

"What!" Ate Nessie exclaimed, the blood draining from her face. "Do you...do you mean, I'm fired?"

"No! Oh god, no, Ate Ness. I would never do that to you." Kira jumped up and gave Ate Nessie a quick hug to reassure her. "We made your contract ironclad all the way to your retirement package, so you're fine. But this will be my last year, so...dance party."

Ate Nessie looked relieved, but only for a moment. "So that's it. It's over. They're taking over the Laneways. And you seem to be taking it well." She even started dancing, the way Kira had earlier. "The Laneways is your baby."

"I'm still processing," Kira admitted. "But I always figured this would happen. It may be my baby, but I'm just a surrogate, and I'm done birthing it." She winced at the awkward metaphor. "The Laneways always belonged to the family. I was put in charge because I needed a place to start over six years ago, and it gave me that."

No need to remind Ate Nessie that the Laneways had solved two of the family's bigger problems back then—what to do with land that wasn't generating income, and Kira's sudden unemployment from what was supposed to be her dream job. That Kira enjoyed running the Laneways, let it grow in the direction it needed to, was just a bonus.

But things grew, and people had to move on.

"I'm okay letting it go," Kira assured her. "But the email also mentioned that Kuya Uno was keeping an eye on Gemini, and I'm actually worried about that.

Gemini is my *actual* baby. Something I made, and gave me purpose, and not just something to do."

That was the difference, wasn't it? One of the world's biggest lies was that you would always be happy doing what you love. But "doing" in and of itself meant work. Meant stress, meant days when you didn't love the thing so much. But it only made the love all the more special. Kira liked making chocolate. She *loved* selling it to other people, loved making them happy, and building memories around things that she made.

It was romantic, a result of her privilege, and almost terribly ideal, but it satisfied Kira. Helped her get through those long days when her chocolate simply refused to temper, when her machines gave up, when her beans didn't come in or got lost in the mail, or when someone told her that they didn't like her chocolate.

It was just that she couldn't fully map out her own thoughts, couldn't explain how those thoughts grew into firm, solid plans, plans that she knew would work. Like reading pegging on-page for the first time and not truly understanding it until someone explained exactly how it worked.

"There are still things I can do for Gemini, Ate Nessie," she said, so full of determination she felt dizzy with it.

"Ah yes. This deal with pogi. Si Santi." Ate Nessie's brow rose sardonically. "He's coming to taste your chocolate today, no? You two seem to be getting closer. Ala eh, don't deny it. Don't think I didn't notice you spending more and more time with him. First the garden, then that ride back to Lipa."

How did she even know about that?

"Look at you! Kinikilig ka ga," Ate Nessie chortled, even as Kira gasped and pressed her hands to her cheeks just to get them to stop blushing. Because yes, fine, she was kilig, but it was really, really hard not to be when she really was spending so much time with Santi.

"No ah!" she said, and god, denial was a bad look on her. "I was…blushing because, BTS is playing!"

"Korean boys are not replacements for true love, Kira. Telly told me she saw you both looking nice and cozy together at the Star Tollway exit when you drove in."

"Ala naman!" Kira exclaimed. "Spying on me, Ate Nessie? Really?"

"It would be spying if I deliberately looked for chismis, but the chismis comes to me willingly," Ate Nessie explained, waving a hand around as if that fixed it. "But be careful with your heart, Kira. You give it away too willingly."

"I don't."

"You do," she said, shaking her head. "You gave your heart to the Laneways and now the Lai Mall is taking over the space across the street, and your cousins suddenly think it's worth notice. You gave your heart to your chocolate, but now Uno wants to take it away. You gave your heart to couples who sought your advice, but once they're together, it's done, they don't need you anymore!"

Kira wished she could argue back, she really did. But it was true. She hadn't heard a peep from Alfred and Mikaela since that first chaperoned date, she just assumed that things were going well. She didn't realize that her friends actually recognized her part in their love stories until she was asked to make the chocolate, but even that was her job. It was something she needed to do.

But it didn't bother her, really. There were always more friends to make, more couples to match. If they didn't need her anymore, it was a good thing.

Even if a tiny voice in the back of her mind said, *but don't you want something that lasts? Something that's just yours?*

"And now you're ready to give your heart away to this Manila Boy." Ate Nessie said the term in the least endearing way possible. Never mind that Santi wasn't born in Manila. "The man could just be buying your chocolate to get into your panty!"

OH GOD.

Kira wanted to take a shovel, dig a hole and nap in it for at least two days. She could recognize when Ate Nessie had a point, but right now it was a full-on Monet; clear from a distance, blurry up close. She tried to speak, but the only sound that her mouth could make was, "wha—"

Yes, she was giving her heart away with every piece, but she was okay with that. Yes, the growth was slower than she anticipated, but it was at a pace that she set, a pace she was comfortable with.

And sure, Santi buying her chocolate would be amazing, but it changed nothing about how being able to make chocolate made her feel—proud that she was able to make something by herself, proud that she had learned to do this and do it well, and excited to keep making more. It was a way for her to connect to people in her community, a way to reconnect with people who might have fallen away from her life (only to come back). When she'd lost sight of what she wanted to do, she found out about chocolate, and the rich history Batangas shared with it. Chocolate became a legacy she'd stumbled upon, and Kira held it close to her heart.

I am exactly where I need to be, her yoga teacher said that morning as he took them through their morning flows. *What would your life be like if you believed that affirmation?*

Pretty much the same, really.

"Ate Nessie," she finally managed to say. "If Santi wanted to get into my panties, all he has to do is ask. And I will probably say yes."

Now it was Ate Nessie's turn to be speechless, which made Kira smile. It was as much of a declaration as she was going to make about the subject. She was sure the entire neighborhood would know she was open to sex with Anton Santillan, but what was the point of arguing about the truth?

Admitting your desires seemed much more fun than pretending they didn't exist. Oh my god, was she growing up? Was she a full adult now?

"Also, my heart is fine," Kira insisted, pressing her hand to her chest as if checking. "A little bruised, but she can still handle it. I can handle this." And because she couldn't help herself, she was on a roll, she added, "And my Korean idols give me joy, let me enjoy them. And their music, obviously."

Ate Nessie's face turned from shock to slight embarrassment, until she finally snapped her fan open and pretended to be preoccupied with the heat. Kira wanted to apologize, immediately feeling guilty, but she couldn't. Give Ate Nessie an inch, and she would take a mile, that was for sure.

"You don't have to do this, you know," Ate Nessie said, waving the fan around, indicating Gemini. "You can just run the Laneways and still have...everything you already have."

"If anything, this whole Luz family meeting tells me that I can't," Kira insisted, putting a few ice cubes in two glasses before she poured tsokolate into them. Batangas tsokolate purists might scoff at the idea of their precious drink iced, but it was suddenly hot today. "Gemini is mine. It's something I built, and something I'm running. If I have to fight my family on it, I will. I can keep doing it on my own."

"Ah siya," she finally said, accepting the glass. And Kira knew that this wasn't going to be the last time they talked about this, but at least for now, she was heard. She didn't need Ate Nessie's approval. She didn't need anyone's approval, really, but it felt good to see her nod. To see her let it go, because she believed Kira.

But before she could say more, the shop bell rang to signal Mang Roldan walking in.

And Ate Nessie just blushed, and melted into a puddle on the floor. Which was understandable, because Mang Roldan was clearly trying to melt her with the heat of that intense gaze of his.

"Kira," Mang Roldan said, that Keanu Reeves smile of his spreading slowly across his face. Ate Nessie was very vigorously fanning herself. "Rosanna."

Hala siyaaaa, Kira almost said out loud, because nobody ever used Ate Nessie's full name. And sure enough, Rosanna Soriano was blushing like blushing was a completely new concept to her. God this was adorable. Kira immediately shipped it. She felt like Tinker Bell getting all the applause she needed to live, whenever her kilig senses started to tingle. And if she could do this for Ate Nessie, one of her favorite people in the world? Well, it would be a small way to pay her back for all the love and kindness she'd given Kira.

"Hi, Mang Roldan!" Kira said brightly. "You should have an iced tsokolate. I just made some."

"Oh, I couldn't," he said sheepishly, smiling politely at her. "Nakakahiya."

"I insist!" Kira said brightly, shooting up from her seat, her tsokolate sloshing dangerously in her hand, but no harm was done to her floors. "I'll make you a glass. I have to check on my tartufo anyway."

"Hija," Ate Nessie said. "If you value your life, you will—"

"Throw in a free dessert? Sure, why not?" Kira asked brightly. "What do you say, Mang Roldan? Tsokolate and a brownie?"

"Well," he said, and she could tell that Landi City, population Nessie and Roldan, was about to happen really soon. "If Rosanna says yes…"

"Oh yes, go ahead," Ate Nessie said. "I…would not be mad."

"Great!" Kira clapped her hands together excitedly. She asked one of her staff to make sure Ate Nessie and Mang Roldan "get cozy" before she disappeared to the back of her shop, giggling all the way. She tied her hair back into a ponytail, threw on a bandana and an apron. Putting on another song (Carly Rae Jepsen this time, because she always sang into Kira's *soul*), she was humming along and pulling the tartufo from the ref.

Kira carefully got out her cooled ganache, her dark chocolate ice cream, her still-warm brownies and strawberry jam while she played her favorite song, danced along when she could. She really should take a photo, because marketing. A before-and-after shot, maybe a time-lapse? That would be interesting. But all her countertops were taller than her hip, and it was really hard to get a good angle…

In retrospect, using the rolling chair and standing on tiptoes just to take a photo wasn't the wisest decision Kira had ever made. But, as soon as that chair started wobbling, and she felt herself losing balance, she knew it was pointless to think about it.

But thank god for guys with strong arms and quick reaction times, because the next thing she knew, she was safely off the ground, her and her arms naturally looped around Anton Santillan's neck.

Oh god, his eyelashes are even longer up close, was the first thing she thought, and her face immediately heated up, like a "kilig" switch had been flipped to its maximum, and now the butterflies that lived in her stomach were creating a huge typhoon of heart emojis that threatened to burst out of her, and she was going to start laughing, because apparently experiencing maximum kilig made her laugh and clench every muscle in her body…help.

Was she breathing? Probably not.

Santi was completely stone-faced, his lips pressed together in a hard line, his hands practically clamped to the back of her knees and shoulders. He didn't look like it was any burden, carrying her like this, but seemed more upset that he had to do it in the first place. The entire room went still, as if the whole world was in shock or in too much kilig that this had actually happened, and time stopped, holding its breath, just for Anton and

Kira. Just like that night in the gardens, that moment in the Carlton lobby, that night in the convenience store.

Their little moments were building. Kira liked that they were building.

"What were you doing?" he asked her, like catching her like this was something that happened every day.

"Taking a photo," Kira explained, wrapping her arms a little tighter around his neck. Wow, he smelled really nice. Like something clean and fresh. Actually, he smelled a lot like her vetiver and tea tree bodywash. Oh god. "Not my smartest moment."

"Correct," he said.

"You're an hour early."

"Also correct," he said, and a tiny part of Kira wished someone else could see them, because she wasn't sure if she was going to believe that this actually happened. "I think I should have gotten you a ladder for Christmas."

"You can still give me a gift for Rizal Day," Kira joked. "Also I had a ladder. It just had wheels. Can you let me down now?"

"That depends. Can you be trusted on solid ground now?" he asked, raising a brow in response, but set her down carefully anyway, and she wasn't too proud to admit that she already missed the feeling of his arms on her, that the places where his hands had been were absolutely tingling.

"Thank you," she managed to say. "For the rescue."

"Anytime," he said back, his palm very suddenly on the back of his neck, rubbing the spot where Kira was sure her hand had been. He was trying very hard not to look at her, she realized, and her fears about him withdrawing were somewhat allayed when she realized

that his cheeks were flushed. She pressed her lips together before a little kilig-induced giggle threatened
to escape her. Anton Santillan was blushing. He was
blushing because of *her*, and could she just explode into
a storm of butterflies and heart emojis now?

"Um," she said, looking around the kitchen. "Make
yourself comfortable."

"How?" There was hesitancy in Santi's voice that
Kira ignored as she put her phone down on the first
empty spot in the counter she could find. To be honest,
there wasn't a lot left. Between unmolding the chocolate and prep ingredients, catching up on her post-
Christmas orders and her insistence that she be the
one responsible to keep the back kitchen clean, she'd
fallen just a little behind.

"Kira, how do you find anything in here?" Santi
asked, walking around a sack of fermented beans,
around the plastic storage boxes she used to store
the roasted beans, the immersion circulator that was
plugged into the last remaining socket under the counter.

"I…figure it out," she sniffed defensively, setting
up the mixer, and crap, where did she put her measur-
ing things?

It was like watching a cat (or a fox? She'd never
seen a fox in her life.) stalk around the room, looking for something that wasn't messy or knocked over.
He walked toward the back wall where she had three
toaster ovens set up with a rotisserie drum for roasting beans. Then to the melangers (Astroboy was doing
much better, thanks), all happily grinding down nibs
and sugar into chocolate. She watched him carefully,
wondering what he was going to say next.

"Look, you can come back in an hour, and everything will be fine," Kira assured him. "I just want to—"

"These are your melangers?" he asked, pointing at the machines.

Kira heard herself say, "oh," in total surprise, felt her back straighten very suddenly. A wave of defensiveness washed over her, and tension seeped into her fingers. "…yes. You know what a melanger is?"

"I've been doing some reading. After you told me about it in Osaka, I wondered what it entailed, so…" He shrugged. And she knew that he didn't mean that to sound sexy, but it did to her. Since when was she into a man who could throw around terms like melanging? Who read up on things because they wanted to understand what you do a little better? "Melangers are the machines that grind and break down the nibs and ingredients into chocolate. Do you use a winnower to separate the cacao shells from the nibs?"

Oh god, be still her beating heart. Among other things.

"She's in the back," Kira explained, using her pursed lips to point at the back door. Santi nodded.

He was standing by the counter where she'd unmolded her chocolate this morning—there were bits of chocolate on the counter from earlier, crumpled-up parchment paper and sil pats that needed washing. Kira winced, bracing for the next thing he would say. "Can I…"

"I know, I know, it's messy, I told you—"

"No, I was going to ask if you wanted me to wash up, while you finish," he said, indicating the cake ingredients that had taken over her side of the countertops. "No more flatlays, though. Please. I can take those."

"First of all, you know what a flatlay is?" Kira asked, smirking at him.

"I'll have you know I have an MBA in marketing. And I have an influencer for a brother," he said very seriously. "I know how to take a good photo."

"Kahit na. I couldn't ask you to clean up." She shook her head. "It's my job—"

"Your job today is to make me a tartufo," he reminded her. "I would like to be useful while I wait. Let me clean for you."

Kira glanced briefly at the ceiling. *Dear universe,* she thought. *Of all the signs you drop into my lap, it had to be a Virgo?*

"Okay." She nodded. "Cleaning supplies are…uh…"

"I'll figure it out," he said, and oh god. He smiled. Anton Santillan with the fancy hotel, with the fancy restaurant, had smiled at the idea of cleaning up her kitchen. Kira wanted to laugh, but he was much too earnest to be laughed at. She really needed to keep her kilig at bay.

And anyway, it stopped being hilarious when he was doing this thing where he rolled up the sleeves of his thin cashmere sweater (she'd seen it at Uniqlo, she was sure of it).

And oh god? His arms were…they were…

Well, it was no surprise he managed to carry her as easily as he had just a few minutes ago.

"Hesusmaryosep," Kira whispered at the sight. They were good arms. Really good arms. Arms that could carry her, with corded muscles and warm skin. Those were arms that had done the *work*. She wondered if he could hold her up with those arms, preferably against the wall.

Fuck, sorry, she thought immediately. But who was she apologizing to? Surely the universe wouldn't put this man in front of her if she wasn't meant to enjoy the view?

"Yes?" Santi asked, his brow raised as he fussed with the sleeve by his elbow.

"Nothing!" Kira said, resuming focus on her work. Tartufo! She was supposed to be making a tartufo, god. There was no time to be distracted by forearms, and Santi making a comment about how she got the good mop (she was not aware that there was a bad mop).

Santi was mostly quiet behind her as he cleaned, the only music in the room being her singing Joni Mitchell. It was...nice. And quite domestic, and Kira would be a liar if she said she didn't enjoy this.

She assembled the tartufo carefully. The Internet had been vague as to what the Tre Scalini restaurant's tartufo was made of, but Kira based it more off of the one Santi had shared with her that night.

She started with the brownie in the center, made with Gemini's baking chocolate (of course) and her own cocoa nibs for a little bit of bite. Then the strawberry jam, an order from Good Shepherd because nobody made it as good as they did in Baguio. On top of that, she put a scoop of the ice cream made with Luz Creamery, and then poured a generous layer of her dark chocolate ganache. Not too thick that it crushed the delicate ice cream, but not too thin that it pooled on the plate. The chocolate looked silky and sumptuous, and topped with a bit of whipped cream, it looked almost exactly like the dessert Santi gave her.

Kira smiled in satisfaction. *Hello, gorgeous.*

"All done?" she asked, turning to face him. He nodded and stepped to the side to show off his handiwork, and holy crap her countertops were practically gleaming. He'd also neatly stacked the molds like books on a shelf for easy reach, and had turned over the bowls on top of paper towels to dry.

"I should have given you a label maker for Christmas," he said, but there was a little smile on his face that made her heart grow six wings and fly off and drop itself into Santi's hands. Who would have thought that the way to Santi's heart was a good mop?

"The tartufo was better," she assured him. "I'm done, by the way."

"May I see?" he asked, as if Kira didn't make it for him.

He turned around to her side of the room (yes, she saw him sigh a little at the mess she made on the counter) and saw the dessert, slightly misshapen, but looking as perfect as Kira was going to make it.

"I don't have an ice cream maker, so this was the Luz Creamery's sample that my mom let me take," she explained quickly as Santi approached it. "And my brownie recipe is pretty basic."

"Are you trying to stop me from eating this?" Santi asked, standing next to the tartufo now. "It looks perfect."

"It does, doesn't it?" Kira smiled, unable to hide that flush of pride that filled her. It *did* look good. "The brownie has 60% dark chocolate, and the ganache is closer to 88%. I wanted there to be a difference in the ganache and the brownie so it wasn't too boring."

Santi said nothing, but kept watching. No, not

watching. Listening. He was listening to her, hanging on to what she was saying. It was a heady feeling, only because she never noticed how intently he listened to her until that moment. Listening and *really* listening to understand what someone was trying to say were two completely different actions. And Santi always looked at her that way, like he was fully trying to understand her.

"When I think about it, Gemini is about connections, memories. I want to make Filipino chocolate. Filipino chocolate is all about what makes people happy. It's surprising and rich, but it's something you share."

She handed him a spoon. "I make every piece of chocolate that comes out of this kitchen, and I want it to mean something, every time. I will never compromise on that. I want it to be clear, this partnership of ours? It will make good memories. New memories for you and me. And it doesn't change the way I feel about you, which…we can discuss that later."

Santi smiled and wrapped his fingers around hers to take the spoon.

Santi cut the dessert with the spoon, and time seemed so slow in that moment, cutting through the layers as butterflies danced up a storm in Kira's stomach. It was like watching those sexy KitKat commercials, if they ever casted a guy.

Santi closed his eyes as he put the spoon in his mouth, tasting the dessert. With each movement, Kira could almost hear her heart thumping in her chest. She couldn't even tell if her own dessert was any good, she could barely taste it in her own mouth.

But before she could tell Santi to stop eating, he swiped his fork through the cake and took another extra-large bite. Kira's eyes went wide at the sight of Anton Santillan with a mouthful of tartufo.

"Slow down, you might get brain-frozen," she cautioned as she poured him a glass of milk.

"Oh god," he said, breathing like he'd just run a marathon after another swig of milk. Kira was ready to launch at him and make him just tell her what he thought. "Kira, this is—"

"This is?" she echoed.

He was smiling. His eyes looked soft, and he looked…happy. It just lit up his entire face, made him seem like the years had been kinder than they were. Made him seem incandescently happy. And it floored Kira that he could smile that way, because she hadn't truly seen it since they were kids. How strange that just lifting the corners of his lips, in that soft smile of his, completely changed the way she looked at him.

Her heart flipped in her chest. She'd always understood moments like this in Korean dramas, when the lead would smile and just sweep the lead off of their feet. But now more than ever, she truly knew that feeling they were trying to convey.

I think you understand me perfectly, she thought, unable to help but smile back.

"It's good. Kira, this is…it's exactly what you said. Happiness," he said, and it made her heart melt. Not just because he understood what she was trying to say, but he enjoyed it, too. "It's exactly what I was looking for."

"Are you sure?" she asked in a small voice, trying to hold in her happiness, a little balloon of joy slowly inflating in her stomach, taking over all the butterflies, all the nerves, all the knots of anxiety.

"I'm sure. I'm so sure. I know there are still details to sort out, but this…" He looked back at the dessert. "You were right. It makes good memories. I want to officially ask if Gemini Chocolates would be interested in becoming a supplier for Hotel Villa and La Spezia restaurant."

And there it was. The balloon burst, and she squealed in delight. There were endless things that could still go wrong—this alone might not be enough for Gemini, they might disagree on price, she might not be able to make enough—but there was plenty of time to ponder that later.

Right now, she wanted to celebrate this.

Santi opened his arms to her for a hug, and she did him one better and launched herself into his arms, laughing as she hugged him as tightly as possible, those sexy forearms easily supporting her thighs as they wrapped around his.

"I'm excited," she said. "I'm so happy you liked it."

There was a pause, which she totally didn't notice because she was just too happy hugging him like this. But eventually, she felt Santi's body loosen, and his arms wrap around her just a little tighter.

"I'm so happy you made it for me," he said, before he pressed the softest little kiss on her cheek. It sucked all the air from Kira's lungs, and she looked down at him, at this face that was so familiar and so mysterious.

They said that déjà vu was a memory from another life. And right now, this moment felt so familiar to Kira she was sure she'd lived it already. Maybe in another life they already had. Maybe in another life they had been together as soon as they understood what falling in love meant. Maybe in another life they had never grown apart, maybe he would have been more stiff and cruel, and her a little more kalat with her feelings.

But then again, in another life, they didn't come together again like this.

"Santi," she said softly, tenderly, but she really didn't know what to say next. She pressed a hand to his cheek. To that jawline of his, sharp and deadly. "I meant what I said."

"Your chocolate was always good to me, even before I realized my feelings for you. I've had three New Year's without you. I don't think I want another," he said very suddenly, and that was all Kira needed to close her eyes and allow herself to sink into him, to press his lips against hers.

He tasted like chocolate. Or maybe it was her. But it was dark and sweet and rich, more and more tempting the more she tasted. His grip of her never wavered, and he kissed her back, waiting for her to cue him, to tell him how she wanted this to go.

So careful, she thought. *But I want to see you undone.*

She arched her back, pressing her chest against his, slipping a hand through that gap in his button-down shirt, and she could have sworn she heard him gasp. She popped open a button with her fingers to trace little circles on the smooth skin of his chest, never once pulling away from the kiss. Santi's hand on her waist gripped her, and Kira slid a little forward, so she could feel him getting hard under his jeans—

A low, buzzing sound filled the room, and it took a second for Kira to realize it wasn't actually her racing heart, but Santi's phone, demanding attention from beside the half-eaten tartufo. His brow furrowed, a little knot forming there, and she giggled, giving in to the urge to smooth the knot with her thumb.

"Ignore it," he said, even as he walked her backward so she could sit next to his phone on the counter. Then he took her hand, brushing his thumb over her knuckles that somehow still had chocolate on them. "This is more important."

Kira looked down at the phone. "It says Doctor Perlas."

That got his attention. Without letting go of her hand, Santi looked at the phone and swiped the screen before placing the phone against his ear.

"Doc?" he asked curiously. "Is something wrong?"

Kira was close enough to hear the sound of the doctor's voice, but not exactly make out what he was saying. The way the color slowly drained from Santi's face, the way he let go of Kira's hand—she knew. Something was terribly, terribly wrong.

"I understand," he said, and Kira could see the way he worked his jaw, saw how he struggled to keep himself together. "I'll be there as soon as I can."

Then he hung up, blinking like he couldn't remember where he was, why he was here. Kira took his hand gently and he flinched in surprise, but took her hand, squeezing it and releasing a tight exhale.

"I have to go," he said, and it was like watching all the happiness he'd built drain away. It ached a little, to see him that way.

"Is everything okay?" she asked.

"My grandfather's in the hospital." He sighed again, and Kira caught a little shudder there, like the very idea of going back to Manila didn't appeal to him at all. "He was having chest pains. They're running tests, but god, the man is 90. I have to…"

"You have to go." She nodded, gently pushing his chest to give her room to hop off of the counter. "Do you need me?"

She knew he was going to say no—there was too much family shit going on for him to agree. But there was a moment (and she'd seen it on his face; since when was his face that expressive?) where he could have said yes. And Kira would have gone without hesitation.

But as it was, he wasn't quite there yet. Santi took her hand, placing it onto his cheek. He leaned into Kira's hand, closing his eyes, she brushed at the slight stubble on that deadly jaw of his. He closed his eyes and sighed again. Then he kissed her wrist, a gesture of thanks, Kira thought.

"It's okay," he said, his voice suddenly small. "We'll talk."

That was officially Kira's least favorite sentence in the world.

Chapter Nine

December 31
Sta. Gianna University Hospital
Manila

> *Bloom: is either of two types of white substances*
> *appearing in the surface of chocolate. Fat bloom is*
> *when the cocoa butter separates from the rest of the*
> *chocolate due to high heat. Sugar bloom is produced*
> *by crystallized sugar, usually caused by moisture*
> *exposure. Bloomed chocolate can be repaired, but*
> *as with all the steps in chocolate making, much*
> *patience is required.*

"Ten-piece crab roe and shrimp xiao long bao, ten pieces hakaw, spicy pickled cucumber, radish cake, Taiwanese tofu with century egg, sweet and sour pork with lychee, lemon chicken, large hot and sour soup, salted egg prawns, broccoli and garlic sauce, large yang chow fried rice." The delivery rider read off the list as Santi examined the bag he was handed, nodding along.

"What about the—"

"Chocolate xiao long bao, it's in the other bag." The

driver handed him a second paper bag with the restaurant logo. "Media noche spread, sir?"

"What?" Santi asked, confused as he juggled the bags of food.

"Media noche. For New Year's Eve?" the driver asked, and Santi blinked back in surprise. He hadn't realized that it was already New Year's Eve. He'd forgotten, in the rush of the last twelve hours. Today was New Year's Eve. The new year was literally four hours away, and Santi was here in the hospital.

I've had three New Year's without you. I don't think I want another.

Santi tried not to picture Kira's cheeks flushed and her pupils slightly wide after he'd kissed her, tried not to remember the smile on her face when he told her he liked her chocolate. Those were not good thoughts to have here.

He managed to give the driver a tip before he headed back into Lolo's room, noting that the hospital was busy as ever even during the holiday. Santi peeked at the chocolate xiao long bao, wondering if it was going to taste any good, and headed to the elevators.

He'd almost violated a couple of traffic laws heading back to Manila at breakneck speeds last night. By the time he made it to Sta. Gianna, he was surprised to find his grandfather sitting up on the hospital bed, yelling at Doctor Perlas, the best geriatric doctor in the country, for being "incompetent."

Which was a good sign, the good doctor concluded. The tests had all showed up normal, and there were no obvious signs for Vito Santillan's heart to be less than...slightly okay. He was 90, after all.

But they did want to put him under observation for

another day, which was why Santi and Miro were arranging their dinner spread on the tiniest countertop ever. His father had rushed off to the hospital offices, looking for a way to claim Lolo's PhilHealth benefits, leaving the two brothers in the room to arrange the family meal. Three and a half hours to go.

"I had plans, you know," Miro groaned to his brother. "Lissy Co was hosting a party at the penthouse in Discovery Suites; I wanted to have a bellini and say 'fuck you' to this past year."

"I didn't realize you were having a particularly bad year," Santi said, his brow rising.

"Well, Kuya, it is possible that you don't actually know everything." Miro rolled his eyes. "I suppose you had plans in Lipa. Chasing pigs, whatever it is people do in the probinsya."

"Miro." Santi knew full well that his brother knew that he was being an ass. He was, for some reason, trying to get a rise out of Santi, which didn't really sit well with the older Santillan. Unfortunately, it was also working really, really well. "Try not to act like such an elitist ass sometime."

"Knock back a few rounds of gin bulag, light a few fireworks," Miro continued, disregarding his brother's obvious agitation. "Kiss a probinsyana."

"Miro," Santi hissed at his brother. "Stop talking. Let's forget about the fact that you were born in Batangas just like I was. Lipa is my home. I won't let you insult it."

"Oh, it's your *home* now, is it?" Miro asked in a mocking tone. He was maybe just teasing, but there was no kindness to it, and it sounded like he was directly trying to hit Santi. "I suppose that begging Lolo to tell you how you could come back was something he just made up?"

Santi did his best not to show any reaction to that. In the past, he thought that he loved Miro enough to ignore those little digs, sometimes direct stabs, into Santi's ego, his choices and his attempts to figure out what having a "good life" meant. But now, Miro just looked like a petulant child, trying to poke Santi into any kind of reaction for what? Satisfaction? Some strange form of revenge?

"What's happening?" Vito asked, groggily, waking up from his nap and narrowing his eyes at his grandsons. "The both of you are loud."

Technically it was the first time he was really seeing Santi in the room. He'd done his best to avoid staying too long inside, speaking with the doctors, getting his prescriptions refilled, finding all the reasons to not have to be there when Vito woke up.

"Do you have the deed of sale?" Vito asked Santi. He couldn't catch a break.

"No, Lolo," he said, as if he had any plans to move forward with that. He knew he couldn't stall forever, but at least stalling for now had to be an option. It had only been, what, a week since Vito issued his challenge?

"Useless," he said, completely glossing over the fact that the Carlton would not have been able to expand to Cebu and CDO without Santi, that he was still contributing to the company now, even after his unceremonious (and quite frankly, illegal) dismissal. "You will never be able to come back to Manila if you continue to be useless."

But see, did Santi really still want to come back to

Manila? Vito was asking him to give up everything he'd built in the last three years, in exchange for what? Feeling good that he'd done right by his family?

On a trip to Tokyo once upon a time, Vito had described their family as similar to the Tokyo subway system—a bowl of noodles someone had tossed to the ground, twisted and tangled, and infinitely messy and complicated. He'd liked that comparison, and still brought it up frequently.

"Ganyan tayo," his grandfather said proudly.

Irreparably tangled together, tighter the more someone tried to break free. Santi supposed he wanted the family to be close, but knots were needlessly complicated things, and impossible to unknot when you needed it to.

Unless you cut yourself off completely, he thought darkly. Which was immediately followed by, *Fuck, I wish I was in Lipa.*

Life there wasn't quite so easy, but at least it was a difficulty he could navigate. A difficulty he could breathe through. Being here almost felt like he was drowning.

There was some commotion in the hallway as Santi stared at his grandfather, completely at a loss for what to say, when the door swung open, and his mother walked in, her face bright red with anger and her hands shaking.

"The *nerve* of her," she said, shaking her head. "Ang kapal talaga! Santi, you tell her to leave, and tell her don't come back na."

There was only one person in the world who could raise Joyce's blood pressure like this. Only one person who could make her so nervous. Santi sighed and walked out to the hallway, where he saw his Tita Valeria leaning against the opposite wall, carrying a fruit basket and smiling wryly at her pamangkin.

"Let me guess," she said, like she and Santi hadn't been estranged for the last ten years. "They've sent you to deal with me."

"Hi, Tita," Santi said, coming over to kiss his aunt on the cheek. Her skin was soft and papery, and he almost didn't recognize her until she'd spoken to him. But other than that, his aunt looked good. Looked happy, almost. "It's good to see you."

"Does Tatay even know that I…" Tita Valeria asked, shaking her head. "Never mind. I heard Tatay was in the hospital and I thought…well, I don't know what I thought, but it's New Year's Eve, and I've got suha."

She held up the basket, filled to the brim with bright yellow-green orbs, all marked with a sticker declaring it "fresh from Davao."

"He does like suha," Santi agreed, accepting the basket. He noted his aunt was still looking at the door like she was seriously considering if she should force her way inside. Santi felt a little pang in his chest. Seeing Tita Ria almost felt like a foreshadowing of what his life could be like, very soon.

"He's fine, Tita," Santi assured her, because if he couldn't let her inside, he could at least give her a little comfort. "The tests were all clear, they just wanted to keep him under observation."

"Of course he's fine," Tita Ria said, tears brimming in her eyes. Vito Santillan's youngest daughter, the one who used to be his favorite, was now standing out in the hall, unable to speak to her father, out of her own volition. Santi had so many questions. "He'll live forever."

"According to him," Santi agreed, and his aunt squeezed his hand affectionately.

"I should go."

"I'll walk you down, Tita."

"Thank you, Ton-ton," Tita Ria said, tucking her arm around his as they slowly made their way to the elevators. "I'm sure you had New Year plans, too."

"I did," Santi admitted with a sigh. "But…family comes first."

"People you share blood with and family are two completely different concepts," Tita Ria said, and Santi could tell that she'd said this kind of thing several times already, to other people. "At the end of the day, the people who love you most are the ones you should stick to, no?"

Ah, love. That complicated thing he wasn't sure he was actually capable of feeling.

Wrong. A pang spread across his chest at the thought, almost like his heart was making its protest known.

"So I have to wonder," Tita Ria said, seemingly unaware of Santi's confusion. "What are you still doing here?"

He was tired. So tired of coming up with reasons why. Maybe it was love. Maybe it was a sick sense of duty, hammered into his head at a young age, a familial obligation. It could be pride too, Santi refusing to let go of a family that saw him as someone to use.

It could be all of that.

But Santi was tired, and he knew there was somewhere else he would much rather be, where he didn't have to come up with reasons to be there. He could just show up, and at least one person would be pleased to see him.

They made it to the lobby, where, after a wave of Tita Joyce's hand, a black SUV that screamed "expensive" pulled up to the driveway. Santi was slightly taken aback, especially when the window rolled down and Johnny Marbella, owner of the Marbella Group and the Carlton's biggest local competition, smiled so warmly at his aunt that it made Santi's heart wrench in his chest. He must have seen something in Tita Ria's face, because the smile faded.

"Shit, Ria. I'm so sorry," said Johnny. "They asked you to leave?"

"That's my family." She shrugged like it was exactly what she'd expected. "But thank god for you, no?"

And Santi felt that. He understood that idea. *Thank god for you.* For people who actually cared, and for people who wouldn't resent you for being there. People who wouldn't ask you to leave when you needed to know something.

He didn't realize his aunt was trying to kiss his cheek until she pulled on his sleeve.

"You're a good boy, Anton," she told him, and it made Santi feel good, to hear his Tita tell him that. "But right now, I need to get drunk with my husband. You're welcome to join us. I feel like there are things you need to say."

"I do," he admitted, surprised to find that he could still speak. "But there's somewhere else I need to be. I'll be okay."

And he realized that he really, really would be.

Chapter Ten

December 31
Haraya Subdivision Park
Bolbok, Lipa

Today's horoscope: As Jupiter moves into your 7th
House, you might find a lot of luck in keeping that
special someone close. Stay with that feeling and
ring in the New Year with all the love and happiness
you deserve, Gemini.

As much as Kira loved celebrating Christmas, she
loved New Year's Eve even more. Not one to be left
behind by, well…anything, the Luzes went all out in
their New Year's celebrations, until eventually the other
residents of Haraya subdivision followed suit.

The village park was a busy place on the day, and
Kamilla was their queen. She had been coordinating
with people since before she flew in from Singapore,
telling the sound guys where they could set up, making sure the cleanup committee was ready the next
day. Cassie had decided to be her assistant this year, a
decision Kira was sure her niece was already regret-

ting as she followed her mother around the space with a clipboard. It was super cute, though.

Kira's Dad, Kuya Kiko, and Kamilla's husband, Harry, had been part of the fireworks committee for as long as Kira could remember. They bulk-ordered the fireworks from Bulacan months ago, and the day was mostly just for figuring out timings—start with the kwitis, the ones that whistled as they shot up in the sky before they banged, then the fountains and the trompil-los. Then at around eleven, the real fireworks—the big ones, the kind that spread color and light against the dark night—continuously until midnight, then all of that would be joined by the loudest, longest Sinturon ni Judas they could find.

Technically, Kira (and Kiko's boyfriend, Jake) were also part of the fireworks committee, if only to be the ones to remember to buy sparklers and lusis for the older kids to join in the fun, and supervise.

"Dream team!" Jake said, giving Kira a high five as they unloaded the sparklers from his car. Sure, they bought the fireworks last minute, dashing off to the highway right after mass to find a roadside seller, but cramming was practically their tradition. "I remember I used to love playing with watusi on the street as a kid. Now that was some hardcore shit, scraping it with your slipper to light it up."

"I know!" Kira exclaimed, chipper and happy as ever because she was fine, and nobody needed to know about what happened with her and Santi. "Whatever happened to those?"

"Banned, mostly because kids kept trying to eat them." Jake winced, and so did Kira. "Okay, I could really use tsokolate, it's so *cold*, and everything is so loud!"

"I love it," Kira admitted, burying her hands into the pockets of her sukajan (bought in Osaka three years ago, and yes she wore it to manifest her desires into the universe, but Jake didn't need to know that). "It feels more magical this way."

As if on cue, a shower of red and green lit up the sky, from the house across the street. Then red, green and gold from houses farther in the distance. Lipeños took their fireworks seriously, started early and finished as late as they dared. The barrage of fireworks and bangs and pops would continue well past midnight, and sometimes even the day after. The streets would be smoggy and add an air of mystery over everything, but really. There was no other way to ward off the bad juju of last year than this.

"Yes, the smoke and karaoke in the distance really add to the entire ambience," Jake said sarcastically. "Not to mention the motorcycles on the highway backfiring to join in on all the fun!"

"Kuya Jake, you are such a killjoy." Kira frowned.

"Why do you think your brother and I go so well together?" Jake laughed. But he must have noticed Kira not being as quick with her response, because she'd caught sight of Santi's house. The lights were all off. He wasn't home. "Kira?"

"Hm?" she asked, looking at Jake as if she'd forgotten he was there, because she had, for a second, lost herself in thoughts of where Santi could possibly be, if he was lonely, if he was thinking of her. He hadn't called, and true to his previous fashion, hadn't talked.

She was worried about his grandfather, but more for Santi's sake than Vito Santillan's.

"Layo ng tingin mo, girl," Jake chided. "What's on your mind?"

"Just," she exhaled sharply, "wondering. By this time next month, Gemini could be gone, and I really, really don't want it to be gone."

"Oh, Kira," Jake sighed thoughtfully, and Kira appreciated that he didn't comment on how out of left field the thought seemed. Air signs stuck together, clearly. He wrapped an arm around her. "Don't be a pessimist now! Manifest it. You're not going to lose Gemini. You remember what your siblings said about asking for help, diba? That applies to all of us. I'm a private school teacher, though. I can tell you about moles and Avogadro's Constant, but I know nothing about chocolate, except that yours is delicious."

"Thanks," Kira chuckled. "And yes. I need advice, but…"

"Someone else's?"

"Yes. Someone else's advice. They're just going through a lot right now, and I don't want them to feel like I'm pushing them."

"Have you considered asking them if they're okay with helping you?" Jake mused. "Like, ask them if they've got the energy to give you the advice you need. I know it's hard, because it's much easier to simply mentally project your needs onto someone else and hope to God they pick up the cues. But that never works out. You just have to be—"

"Brave."

"Exactly." Jake nodded. "When your Kuya and I started dating, I was right in the middle of my review for my LET certification, and my master's. You remember?"

"I do," Kira said. "Kuya drove back and forth to Manila and Lipa twice a week until he finally got the brilliant idea to bring you here to study."

When it came to idols and celebrity crushes, Kira was no stranger to occasionally indulging in a daily dose of delusion (sorry, real-person fanfiction). Imagine a world where they would see you, and make you feel loved, and wanted. But more than that, Kira wanted… well, she wanted the intimacy of it all. She wanted someone to pour her love and affection into, in kisses and tight hugs, in little strokes of the arm. She wanted to have someone she could drive to and from Manila for (if she knew how to drive).

It was just that she was taught not to ask directly for it. She was taught to wait for it, and to wait to be asked if that was what she wanted.

But to have it be Santi? Someone who understood her, and made her laugh, made her think about what she really, truly wanted, speak it into existence, make her *ask* for it? It would be wonderful.

"He spent a *lot* of those visits just watching me study," Jake explained, his face tinged with wistfulness, which Kira could see even in the darkness. "And I felt terrible, because I wanted to be able to do it on my own without anyone's help. And the weird thing was, I was just expecting him to help me, but my boyfriend is stubborn as the rest of his family—"

"Hey!"

"Bato bato sa langit, when you get hit, it's a bitch," Jake said, and Kira laughed, because that was totally not how the saying went. "Anyway, he's not a mind reader, which is why he needed his baby sister's help just to notice me in that wedding years ago. So I told him. Help me, please, I'm sorry I'm a drain on you, but I can't do this without help."

"Oh," Kira said, because she didn't know this story. Sharing the intimate details of his relationship really wasn't Kiko's style.

"But your Kuya didn't make me feel bad about my asking for help. He just did it the best he could. I felt horrible and guilty, but he never made me feel like I was a burden. And after my master's and passing the LET, there really wasn't an alternative. I would go where he would be. Because I knew very well that he would do the same for me."

Jake squeezed Kira's arm affectionately, as if the wisdom of his experience would pass to her that way, and Kira smiled at him appreciatively. While she'd been largely responsible for her Kuya's current love life, the intimate details of it were unknown to her, and she really needed to hear it from Jake, because Kiko would have been way too embarrassed to tell her.

"Babe, come here, you have to see this awesome frame I built for the trompillo," Kiko announced, taking his boyfriend's hand and dragging him over to where the rest of the fireworks committee was nodding and grunting at said frame.

"Heeeelp!" Jake squeaked, making Kira laugh as they walked off.

"Kira!" her mother said, hooking an arm around hers to drag her toward the extension of the open barn that served as the village event area. "Mayette has been talking our ear off about this fancy pan de sal she bought from a panaderia in Makati, and I have run out of ways to say it's amazing."

"Is it?" Kira asked, wondering what could possibly be improved about an already perfect roll.

Alice Luz shrugged, like she'd completely given up on making a fair judgement. "Just come with me, please?"

The members of the food committee greeted the Luzes with choruses of "hello!" They were still serving the "light dinner" before the huge Media Noche at midnight, so the spread was mostly pan de sal with various fillings, quezo de bola (if it's not Marca Piña, we're not having it!) and fiesta ham, or arroz caldo for those looking for something a little heavier.

Among their group was Ate Nessie, cursing a cup of barako and arguing with Josie from three houses down about who made the best bonete in Lipa. Mang Roldan was sitting beside her, very calmly listening and trying to hide his smile at Ate Nessie's wild gestures.

"Kira dear, when are you going to bring a young man with you to New Year?" Tita Vilma asked, and it took all of Kira's willpower not to wince. "Preferably a nice boy who can keep that chocolate shop running for you!"

"Ha?" As soon as Kira put the pan de sal in her mouth. She'd stuffed hers with guava jam and kesong puti, and was chewing so she couldn't answer. "Tita, my chocolate shop will keep running regardless of if I have a boyfriend or not."

"Oh goodness, these millennials, I really don't understand them."

"Don't worry, Tita," Kira assured the neighbor who

really had no reason to worry about her. "I'm not going anywhere anytime soon. Boyfriend or no."

And for the first time in a long time, she really, truly meant that.

"I suppose that Santillan boy is a no-show again this year." Tita Mayette sighed, turning her head toward Santi's house, a bungalow place that currently had all its lights closed. "It's like nobody actually lives there."

In the distance, she spotted Jake and Cassie making their way to the smaller fireworks and saw that as her chance to escape. She quickly made her excuses and joined her niece and brother-in-law to distribute the sparklers to the children, while the older kids were allowed to light the lusis, as long as they didn't take pics from the front.

"Kira." Ate Nessie's urgent voice caught her attention, but she didn't turn away from the kids. "I need to speak with you."

"Ate Nessie, it's New Year's Eve! It's time to cast away our cares and for you to stop looking at me like that." Kira chuckled, wrapping an arm around her shoulders in a side hug as Ate Nessie rolled her eyes.

"Should I be concerned that Dan has yet to kiss me?" she asked. "Am I not kissable?"

Kira paused, realizing quickly that Dan must be what she called Mang Roldan, before she asked Jake and Cassie to cover for her while she led Ate Nessie away from the festivities. She was sure she wanted privacy right now.

"We've been on quite a few dates now," Ate Nessie explained, the furrow in her brow deep. "And they've been fun! He's such a good listener, and we like the same music, and we both love being around nature, ganun…"

"But?" Kira asked encouragingly.

"Every night he drives me home and kisses the back of my hand! Like I'm his grandmother! Hay nako." Ate Nessie sighed, her shoulders dropping. "I am too old for this. Maybe he just doesn't see me as an attractive person."

Kira wrinkled her nose. "Yeah, no."

"Hija, if you're going to speak in tongues, you have to let me know."

"No, I mean he's attracted to you!" Kira interjected, nudging Ate Nessie with her elbow. "Ate Ness, the way he looked at you at the chocolate shop the other day was sinful."

"What!" she exclaimed, and even in the dark, Kira could see the telltale signs of Ate Nessie blushing.

"The man wanted to drop everything and kiss you," Kira said, and honestly, where was the lie? Mang Roldan could deliver a smoldering look better than anyone, and Ate Nessie as the recipient could not have missed that. "But maybe he's looking for a little…um, encouragement from you?"

"Hija, I wore my malandi lipstick, what other encouragement do I need to give him?" Ate Nessie looked genuinely flustered and a little bit frustrated, and Kira wanted to hug her again. She really could go into a whole tangent about how red lipstick really was great, and that Kelly Monago's collection was amazing, but it really was more for herself than for Roldan, and that wasn't the lecture today. Nah.

"I think Mang Roldan will appreciate a more direct

approach," Kira said, carefully choosing her words. "Like...you can ask him if he wants to kiss you."

"Hala, I cannot ask him that!" Ate Nessie insisted, shaking her head. "I would rather just kiss him myself!"

Kira grinned at Ate Nessie, surprised and amused that she would come to that conclusion all by herself. Ate Nessie blinked back at Kira, as if shocked that she had. The two of them stared at each other, forever doomed to be at an impasse.

"I don't think you need my help anymore, Ate Nessie," Kira said gently, giving her the reassuring hug she needed. "You know exactly what to do."

"But..."

"You really like him, don't you?" Kira asked, and Nessie nodded. "Then show him."

"Hay, hija." Ate Nessie squeezed her hand. "You know, you really have a gift for this."

"I know." Kira smiled at Ate Nessie. "Thanks, Ate Ness."

By the time Nessie and Kira went back to the party, someone was playing Christmas music over the speakers, and some of the adults were now dancing in the gazebo/village center. Even Kamilla was dancing.

The cochinillo was brought out ("why is the lechon so *small*?" gasped a tita), as well as Pancit Malabon ("isn't that for birthdays only?" a different tita scoffed) and twelve different round fruits were on display for luck and prosperity ("isn't that for Chinese New Year? That isn't until February!" said another). Kira was wearing polka dots under her sukajan, was ready to jump up and down when the clock struck midnight, and took care that nobody swept in case they swept away bad luck.

In the distance, Kira spotted Alfred and Mikaela sitting in the swings together, their hands clasped and smiling softly as across them Mikaela's parents watched the fireworks. Things seemed good there, too.

She was surrounded by family and friends, good music and fireworks.

Everything was perfect, and yet she knew someone was missing. Someone should be here, next to her, ringing in the New Year, saying goodbye to the old. She sighed deeply. Santi hadn't called, or texted again. And she didn't want to be the one to ask him to come, because he'd been so worried about his grandfather when he left.

Oh well. There was always next year.

"Tita?" Cassie asked beside her, holding a sparkler away from them both. "Is everything okay?"

"Meh," she admitted, ruffling her niece's hair without messing up her French braids. "But I'm sure it will be."

It was about a minute to midnight, the last minute of the year. And Kira figured she might as well spend that last minute a little more hopeful. Was that a New Year's resolution?

And just like that, *everything* happened.

First, the trompillo was lit up, and everyone immediately cheered, clapping, blowing torotots and other manner of noisemakers at it. Kiko had built an impressive frame for the large firework, a brilliant, whirling display of orange, then yellow and white sparks, spinning faster and faster until it ran out of steam.

A few seconds after that, there was a squeak of surprise as Tita Vilma and some of the village titas saw Ate Nessie grabbing Mang Roldan by the shirt collar and tiptoeing to give him a very spicy New Year's kiss. They looked really sweet, and there was nothing but love in both their eyes as they touched each other's cheeks. Mang Roldan looked slightly flushed, but incredibly happy at this particular turn of events. Then he dipped her low and kissed her again. So cute.

And a few seconds after that, just as the smoke from the trompillo started to clear, Kira saw someone marching through the haze. She narrowed her eyes at the figure, trying to see better. But there was something familiar in the way he walked—no, wait. The way he strode across the lawn, his hands in the pockets of his jacket, his button-down shirt slightly open, and the most determined look on his face. Kira gasped.

She'd seen *Pride and Prejudice* enough times to know exactly what was going to happen.

"Cass," she said weakly, needing to somehow confirm that this wasn't a dream, but her niece had already gone off to somewhere else, presumably to give her parents her midnight kiss, because everyone around them was counting down already, and Anton Manansala V. Santillan was...

He was *striding*, with supreme confidence that he knew exactly what he was doing. His gaze was fixed on her, anchoring on her, even when he seemed to be having a hard time looking through the haze as well. But their eyes met, and his face softened, the knit in his brow smoothing slightly as a tiny smile played on the corners of his lips. A smile that was just for her.

Kira's heart swelled. It might have burst already, might have become a puddle on the ground or a thousand glitter particles exploding inside her chest, she didn't know. All she knew was that he was here, that they were together at midnight, and she couldn't have asked for anything more.

"Kira?" Santi asked when he walked up to her, his stride confident as ever, even if he was squinting just a little bit.

"Santi," she said, squeezing his hands after he'd reached for hers. "You're here."

"I'm here," he said, and there was a tightness to his voice that she couldn't identify. Was it the smoke? The cold? Emotion? "And I would rather be here than anywhere else."

As far as romantic declarations went, this was definitely one for the books. A story to tell the grandkids while they watched *Pride and Prejudice* for the twenty thousandth time. Kira tiptoed and wrapped her arms around him in a hug, and he was warm and comfortable, smelled clean and crisp.

But most importantly, he was here, and made her heart feel too big to contain in her chest.

She kissed him, and it felt like a promise. It made up for all the New Year's they missed, all the time they lost. It promised better days ahead, even when the bad ones came.

"We need to talk," she finally said, pressing her forehead against his chest, sighing.

"I know. Business things."

"Other things." Kira shook her head.

"Okay," Santi said gently, lifting her chin. "Like I said, I'm here. Anything you need."

And she knew they should start on a battle plan for Gemini. She knew that they had exactly thirty days to clear up her strategy, to make a case. Ask him to check her work. But she wanted at least a day, one day to celebrate the fact that Anton Santillan actually came to Lipa. That he'd come for her. That he was *here*, and that she was fully accepting the fact that she desired him.

Everyone told her that love would come if you were patient, if you were good, if you were simple, if you prayed, if you manifested it. But Kira was only just starting to understand what that actually meant—love was already here. But it was up to you to take it if you wanted to. Crushing, liking, falling for someone were all active things, and they were all things that ended the waiting.

And today, she chose to end her waiting.

"I need you, Santi," she said, smiling up at him. "I mean, there are other things, but right now I need *you*."

"Right, I said I—oh," he said, seemingly understanding. His face melted into a tiny smile, before he hid it away by kissing her. "Okay. As long as you don't say—"

"Let's start this New Year with a bang?" Kira winked at him, and he groaned.

"That."

Despite all the naughty things she'd ever done in her life (not that there were a *lot,* but there were enough), Kira had never done this before. Never literally snuck out of a family event for a guy, never walked into his house with the full intent of having sex with him, just because they could. And they could, which was as surprising as it was exciting.

In her earlier days, having sex was a Major Operation. It had to be with someone she could trust with her life, somewhere special, somewhere she could leave when she didn't feel safe, someone else had to know just in case. She had to be the one buying the condom because you never knew. How funny that her Scorpio Moon showed up when she least expected it.

But Kira needed some level of control over the situation, because she couldn't afford to lose it. She supposed those were the red flags that told her that she didn't exactly feel as safe as she should. And it wasn't like it was easy in Lipa, where people would always find out.

But walking into Santi's house with him was easy. Kissing him was lovely, and it felt good. She didn't care if people knew, because she wanted this. She was willing to explain this. *Panindigan mo, and use protection,* had been the extent of her family's Sex Ed talk, and she knew she could stand for this.

They kissed on his entryway; neither of them seemed to be able to decide if they should keep kissing or take off their shoes. Kira was wondering how Santi could keep bending his head like that, because height difference.

"Fuck," he growled, and Kira could swear she almost came when she heard that, and he caught one last kiss before he fussed with his boat shoes to take them off. Kira laughed and walked past him, her sandals already off and placed by the wall.

"Ah buti na lang I wear sandals," she giggled, walking into Santi's living room, swaying her hips a little.

"Did you just move in?" Kira asked, looking around at his, um…minimalist style.

There was a couch. It was a good couch, nice and big, but that was literally it. Most of the living room walls were still that primer white, clashing against the hardwood floors. Sure the floor-to-ceiling sliding doors made it seem cool and zen, but this was Santi's home, and there was nothing of him in it. Which was odd, given how personal La Spezia was, how carefully chosen the furniture was in Hotel Villa.

"I haven't exactly settled in," Santi explained, coming up from behind to wrap his arms around her, distracting her with a kiss to her neck, making Kira's entire body shiver and her inner thighs clench. "And my plans to eat you out are not for this room."

"Oh my god. *Plans* to eat me out. Such a Virgo," she said, rolling her eyes, and she felt the low rumble in his chest as he chuckled, loosening his hold on her, his lips lifting from her skin. Kira whimpered a little because, come on, dude, she was really enjoying the kiss, really enjoying being able to just brace herself on those arms of his. "Huy naman."

"Kira," he said; he had to be lowering his voice like this on purpose. Like he was trying to make her come with just the sound of his voice. By saying her name in that private, whispery way, that way that was meant only for intimate moments like this. "Do I have your consent to make you come?"

MALAMANG! Kira almost said. *I mean, yes.*

"Exactly how were you planning on doing it, Anton?" She turned her head so there was no doubt he could hear her. She swayed her hips a little, and he followed, her hands still bracing lightly against his arms as he ran them up the front of her thighs. And what was that weird breathy sound? Right, it was her.

"First," he began, and she pulled his arms up, giving him permission to go higher, higher… "I would like you to come on my mouth. I'm sure you will be exquisite on my tongue, Kira."

A finger brushed against her swollen bottom lip, as Santi's other hand slid just under the skirt of her dress, fluttering against the place he wanted his tongue to be. Kira shuddered.

"A-and?" she asked, knowing this was a dangerous game they were playing, but a little danger was always good.

"And the rest, will be up to you," he told her, resting his hands on her hips. "I've waited three years to do this, but I want you to want me. As much as I've dreamed about you."

"Oh my god," Kira gasped, and she could feel Santi grin, as his lips were currently preoccupied with the side of her neck and shoulder.

"I'm right here," he murmured into her ear, and she felt the little licks of flame that he'd ignited with those three little words prickle on her skin, and shit. Ang hot.

"You are so full of yourself," she told him, turning so she could face him, her arms looped around his neck. He kissed like a man on a mission, a little desperate for her to want him as much as he wanted her. She reached around him and tugged at the hem of his shirt, pulling him down so she could whisper to him now.

"Just like you will be," he reminded her, and she laughed, looping her fingers in the waistband of his jeans this time (not Uniqlo, Kira was only a little disappointed), using that to pull him closer, to bring those lips of his to hers. They danced backward until her back met a console table, and how did she not realize that there was a console table?

Santi placed his hands on both sides of her waist,

lowering his head and caging her in. She still couldn't figure out what he smelled like, but she loved it. Was slightly addicted to it.

"Kira." He was almost chanting her name. "Do you want this?"

"I want you," she gasped, and besh, she was out of breath. They hadn't even done anything and she was out of breath. "I want you just as much. Take off your shirt."

"Good," he said, although she didn't know if he approved of her consent or of her asking him to take off his jacket, then his shirt. How unfair that he also had a gorgeous body. A little on the wiry side, but brimming with strength under those smooth planes.

She started shrugging off her jacket, and flapped it off when the sleeve caught in her wrist. Santi chuckled, but his eyes were all sparkly, melty and sexy when he looked at her. He licked his bottom lip, before he bit it, and Kira could have sworn that she *felt* that little bite.

"What did I do?" he said. "Who did I pray to, to deserve you, hm?"

"You did this to yourself, no." She smiled at him, humming in delight as his fingers traced the neckline of her wraparound dress. Her skin was tingling, her body was starting to feel heavy as her muscles tensed, as he wound her up. "It's your stars and mine, a moment where you and I are both here."

"I don't want a moment," he disagreed, urging her to unbutton herself a little quicker by dipping his tongue in the valley of her cleavage. "I want everything with you, Kira. As long as you'll have me. I want to stay here in Lipa, I want to be happy here. There's nothing else."

"Oh god," she sighed, because he was tracing his

hands around her breasts, his fingers fluttering against her nipples. She tightened her hold on him, and it wasn't just because she could feel herself surrendering to how he was making her feel (hot, beautiful, desired). His words touched her, because they were everything she wanted too—this moment, this place, this man. This possibility of happily ever after, right here.

"I think you mean Santi," he corrected, chuckling as she playfully kicked him. He leaned forward and kissed the middle of her chest, just at the top of the dip of her cleavage, nipping at the spot that he'd kissed, soothing it with another kiss. "Lean back a little."

She did, and it was almost criminal how smoothly he tugged at the tie on her waist, letting the front of the dress fall open, and even Kira was surprised at how flushed she was all over, how he didn't seem to notice the brown stretch marks on her waist, the deeper, older ones peeking up around her breasts.

"I want you," he repeated, and with a flick of his wrist, the dress fell open to give her a full view of her lime green sports bra.

"What the…" he said, and Kira's face flushed furiously.

"Making chocolate is a sport," she explained, and she really would like him to take it off now please, because it was really hot, and she really wanted him to touch her there. "My boobs, my bra, my choice, buddy."

"You really should learn to pick up some Virgo habits," he tutted, pulling the dress aside even more to reveal her favorite panties, dark blue and went all the way up her waist. "Ready for anything."

"Oh, is that why you keep condoms so close by?" she asked, raising a brow, pulling out the little pack she'd managed to pull from the back of his jeans when they were walking to the house. See, pockets were great.

"Touché," Santi laughed, pulling at the band of the sports bra to lift it over her head. And god the sweet relief of one's boobs being freed from a sports bra was unparalleled. She sighed happily. And because he was a gentleman, Santi did her the service of taking off his belt and his jeans as well, as was polite.

Kira was pretty sure she'd said "oh my god," again, because there had to be something godly about that V line of his, and how very obviously he was enjoying this.

He kissed her again, holding up one breast, making her gasp as he tasted the skin, licked her now stiff and erect nipples. Kira's thighs wrapped around his hips and she squeezed, bringing his still-covered erection between her legs. The little grunt he made and the gasp that followed when Kira arched her hips slightly were ones she would keep with her forever.

Santi pinched her nipple a little too hard, and she made a sharp noise of protest, but accepted him kissing the spot in apology.

"Let me show you," she told him, and she was awkward at first, frowning slightly as she pushed up her breasts, closer to her body, tweaked and twirled a finger around the nipple. She'd never had to show anyone how she liked this before, she realized. "Then I can..."

She arched her hips again, and that little touch from his heat made her push harder, squeeze tighter. Kira was enjoying this, enjoyed hearing their breaths get shorter, and shorter, their cries get a little louder.

"Santi," she breathed. "I was promised a good eating out."

"I did." He acquiesced, tugging her underwear down and making her lean back again so he had enough space to press his palm against her mound, making her release a choked gasp when he slid a finger between her legs. She heard the squish of something wet as his finger made its exploration, slowly sliding up until he found her clit.

"Pu-*ta*," Kira groaned, breathy and long as Santi swirled the mound gently. Kira made a little sound of pleasure, and Santi needed a second finger to properly touch it, swirl against it like Kira had on her nipple.

"Who is?" Santi joked, and how did he even have the audacity to joke at a time like this?

Kira moaned, and her hips rose against his hand while he stroked her, adding another finger against her clit while she clenched against nothing. The back of his hand pressed against his own straining erection, making him moan, too. As if sensing his distraction, Kira dropped her hand from her breast and sat up, wrapping her arms around his neck as his fingers slid to where she wanted him, and she lightly squeezed his cock. Santi made an unholy sound, a cross between a moan and a cry, one she was sure he had never made before in his life.

"Distracted?" she teased. He grunted in response and pulled his hand back, tugging her underwear down completely.

"Bed," he managed to say. "Now."

"Briefs," she said in response, her brow rising. "Now."

He was much too impatient for his own good, and

scooped her up off of the console, Kira's arms immediately wrapping around his neck as she squealed in surprise.

"Santi!" she shrieked, laughing as Santi said something about his bed being too far, and his condoms being in the room and how he couldn't wait. He laid her carefully on the bed, big enough for Kira to miss that the room was just as bare as the living room. He smiled down at her, straining cock and all, and hell if it wasn't her favorite smile. He looked truly, truly happy.

"I've wanted you too, you know," she said, smiling, before she kissed him. "Ever since you tried to steal my onigiri."

There wasn't much to be said after. He took off his own underwear, his cock stiff and ready. But before Kira could hand him the condom, he shook his head and grabbed her ankles, pulling her closer to where she was kneeling. He traced a little circle around the thatch of hair. Santi was relentless in chasing her pleasure, licking her slit, sucking on her clit as his fingers curled and stroked deeper inside her, listening to her cries of pleasure, the insistent little tugs she made on his hair.

Kira's entire body tensed, and she braced her feet on the bed as her back arched, as she anchored herself on him. Her pleasure built, and built, until it burst into thousands of stars and constellations, destinies mapping out and fading before she could properly process them.

"Oh…my," she said between shaking breaths, but stopped short of the last word because Santi looked like he wanted to go there. He was grinning when he licked his lips, when he put his fingers in his mouth and sucked before he moved over her, placing a chaste, sweet little kiss on her forehead.

Of all the things this man could do to undo me, Kira thought, smiling.

"Do you want water?" he asked, and she shook her head in response.

"I want you." She shook her head, twisting a little so she could reach his cock, rubbing it up and down a few times. Santi groaned when she touched the head, and she spread the little bit of precome on the tip. "I want it from the back."

Then she turned over so her back was facing him, looking over her shoulder, his face caught between excitement and disbelief.

"I knew you would be insatiable," he told her, rubbing his nose against the side of hers. "It must be a Gemini thing."

"Oh Santi," she laughed. "You know so little about the stars."

When he finally slid on the condom and entered her from behind, his hands splaying up and down her back, her hips raised, her cheek pressed on the pillow as she grabbed his sheets for dear life. She loved that he wasn't shy about thrusting into her, about kissing the back of her neck, of saying how much he liked this, this delicious rhythm of the two of them, together. Neither of them held themselves back, the silence in the room filled with their gasps and cries and moans, the slick, wet sound of him speeding up then slowing down, making the moment stretch, longer, longer.

But Kira needed more. She pushed an arm up, wondering how the hell she was supposed to balance herself if she needed…needed…

"Kira," he said, doubling over so he could grasp her twitching hand. "What do you want?"

"My clit," she gasped as the new angle allowed him to enter her deeper. "Santi, I need… I need…"

He didn't have to be told twice. Adjusting his position, he freed his right hand and used that to brush past her belly, the thatch of hair between her legs and into her slick folds, wet as they clenched with his every thrust. She lifted her head to gasp.

"Tang ina," she said, looking over her shoulder, and Santi kissed her hotly, fiercely. "More."

And she appreciated that he didn't ask questions, already knew what he had to do (because she certainly didn't), placing his foot on the bed, using that leverage to thrust harder into her, and fuck, yes, that was it.

Her hands gripped the bedsheets so tightly she was sure they would tear. But still she met him for every thrust, gripped his body when he coaxed her upright so they were both kneeling. Kira had to place an arm over her breasts to keep them from bouncing too hard. And it wasn't very long before she clenched around his fingers, his cock, swearing at every star and universe she could remember, because, thank you! Thank you for this, for him and her, and the space for them to do this. Moments later, he came too, gasping in her ear, saying her name, saying she was perfect, and this was wonderful.

But most importantly, that he was happy.

I want to stay here in Lipa.

In the end, the answer came to him as easy as making love to Kira. That holding her close, kissing her, being inside her was as easy as it was to admit that he wanted to stay. That he could give up Manila and all its conveniences entirely, because he was happy here.

"You're gripping me a little tight there, Sants," Kira said, but she was smiling as he mumbled an apology, and kissed her fingers. They'd opened the windows to let in the cool December—well, January now—air, and he was holding her hand as she caught her breath again. She assured him she was fine, and repositioned herself so she was lying on top of him. Her arms were flat against his bare chest, her chin resting on the backs of her hands as she looked at him. He could almost see the wheels in her brain turning.

"Something on your mind?" he asked, loosening his grip on her but keeping his hand there, stroking the soft skin of her waist.

"Was not staying an option?" she asked him suddenly, and Santi was a little floored. He'd forgotten how tight-lipped he'd been about the whole staying-in-Manila thing. He mentioned it to her once or twice, but he really didn't want to hash it out with someone who was a huge, huge factor in his decision to stay. "I mean, I know your Lolo has some kind of mega-grudge against Lipa for some reason…"

He chuckled. If only it was just that.

"I was made to understand that running Hotel Villa was a punishment," he explained to her, and the truth sounded too ridiculous when he said it out loud. He hadn't done anything wrong. Had done nothing to deserve that kind of scorn. But he'd gotten it anyway, for daring to run Carlton the way it should be. "That the only way I could earn back my grandfather's love, and stay in Manila with my family, was to make Hotel

Villa a success. And then when I did that, he...asked for something else. Something I can't give."

Because the Laneways wasn't for Santi to hand on a silver platter. His grandfather had asked for the impossible, and Santi was slowly learning that it was okay for things to be that way. That he wasn't the asshole for letting go.

"So Lipa is...a second choice," Kira said slowly, and he could hear the pain in her voice, saw her wince. She looked lovely in the dark of the morning. And he could read every expression that crossed her face.

"No," Santi said, cupping her cheek, brushing his finger over it. He raised his head so he could kiss her, assure her that it wasn't the case. "I don't think it ever was a second choice. Lipa feels like the right choice."

He released her, and Kira rolled onto her back, making a little humming sound as she nestled back into his pillow. Santi caged her in his arms, watching her emotions as they shifted from contentment, happiness, to peace. She blinked sleepily at him, and he wondered what was going on in her head.

He could tell her now. Could tell her that his grandfather had wanted the Laneways in exchange for Santi's return to Manila. But it all seemed moot, now that he'd decided to stay. No need to tell her about things that didn't matter anymore.

"I feel like that, too," she finally said. "I'm glad you came home, Santi."

They stayed in bed for most of the night, talking. She told him about her dreams for Gemini, of mastering the beans Sam found in the Tomas farm to make her own. They were both still naked and already had multiple drinks of water and trips to the bathroom to clean up. Kira could have stayed like this forever. Best New Year's ever.

"Do you ever wonder if you should be somewhere else?" Santi asked, lying back against his couch, where they eventually retreated, as Kira's head rest on his stomach while they both snacked on olive oil fried kesong puti. It was something Santi had just "whipped up" with what he had in his pantry, and when Kira dipped both in egg and breadcrumbs before frying? Ugh, perfect post-sex, so-past-midnight-that-it-was-closer-to-noon snack.

"Not really. I'm happy where my life is," she told him. "Did I tell you I used to work for Serendipity Studios?"

"Really?" Santi asked, because of course he knew the coolest stationery company in the country.

"It was a dream job, and I for sure thought I could stay there forever," Kira chuckled, because it had been so long ago, and it was funny to say it out loud. But of course it had *hurt* back then. "But at the end of my six months they just…decided they didn't need me. Something about how I was a team player but didn't take initiative, when it was literally my first job, and they were in the middle of a crisis, half the time my supervisors weren't even there."

Not that she was saying she'd been a perfect employee, but it gut her to the core, to have that dream taken away from her. She still carried that scar with her, and it was years later.

Which was why it only hurt more that Gemini could just…disappear. Because she hadn't done enough? She wasn't going to take that.

"You know what my Tito Nicos said, when he sent me that email about taking over the Laneways? He said, 'walang personalan, ha.' What does *that* even mean? How can business not be personal, especially in this country, when it's run by families, by friends, when it's supported by communities? If it wasn't so personal, the Laneways wouldn't be what it is today. It was literally built around personal relationships, around a community of people."

Santi remained silent, but she knew it was because he was listening. She liked that he was listening, even if half these things were just things she said off of the top of her head. Things she just needed to say out loud. When they first met again, she'd said that all she needed was someone to believe in her. And how nice of the universe to respond with Anton Santillan.

"I'm good at making chocolate. I'm *so* good at it, actually," she continued, and it should be okay for her to say that. Because she wasn't lying, wasn't making up a story. "How could a retail chocolate shop still be up and running if it wasn't any good? But it's not translating! When I'm in that meeting it's like everyone's speaking a foreign language that I should know. That I do know, but I can't access as easily."

She seemed to be holding her breath, waiting for Santi's response, or maybe hoping to take back how much of her insecurities she'd revealed. His fingers paused.

"I think," he said slowly, as if he was trying to come up with the right words. "That's bullshit."

"Hey!" she said, sitting up, turning to him and frowning. "That's not nice."

"Wait, wait," he said, kissing her cheeks to reassure

her that he was going to say the right thing, wait lang. "I'm sorry. I meant to say, you're Kira Luz. You love everything with all your heart, and people are drawn to that. To you and your chocolate. It can't be wrong."

"But Anton," she told him. "It could be gone in a month. I don't know if I can keep it running forever."

"Nobody thinks they can run something forever, only for as long as they can. That's why the best businesses have exit plans."

"Everyone's telling me to take that exit plan right now. My parents, my siblings, my uncle, this cousin I haven't spoken to since I was a kid when I would only answer to 'Princess Jasmine.'"

"Princess Jasmine," Santi repeated, tucking a bit of her hair behind her ear, and the action was so tender and sweet that it made Kira lean into his touch, just a little. She pretended to bite his hand as if in retaliation, but Santi only chuckled.

She really liked it when she made him smile.

"You have to face it head-on." The words were said firmly, but in a way that didn't make Kira feel like she was being lectured. Supported, yes. "Your chocolate, the business, your problems. You owe it to yourself to face it all with the confidence of someone who knows their shit. Because you do. That other language they're speaking, you understand that. It's just a little lost in translation."

Then he kissed, her, his lips pressing against her forehead, and the action was so suddenly tender that it made Kira want to sink into his arms and listen to him encourage her for at least another year. "You know everything you need. If there are things you need to sort out, I can help. I can do math."

"Oh good, because I am terrible at it," Kira laughed. "Santi, I don't want you to think I'm taking advantage of you."

"Trust me, you're not," Santi assured her with a little kiss to her temple. "I can help you with this. Let me help you with this. Because it makes you really happy. If you were faking it, then the universe wouldn't have sent you a sad sack like me. Then we would have both been miserable."

Kira wrapped her arms around him tightly. "You're not unhappy," she said, burying her face in his neck like she was still just a bit embarrassed. "You just feel guilty about being happy. And you're not alone, Santi. I'm with you. Just like you're with me."

Chapter Eleven

January 5
Haraya Subdivision
Santi's House

Conching: Not just your Tita's nickname. A step in the chocolate-making process where cocoa butter, sugar and other flavoring are very slowly added to the refined chocolate, in set hour intervals, essentially putting the final touches on what your chocolate is going to taste like, how smooth and fine it will be.

Santi didn't know if circadian rhythms were one of those things dictated by nature or nurture. Maybe it was dictated by your star sign (Kira would know, and he really didn't want her to catch him Googling), but if they were, he and Kira would be on the opposite sides of the birth charts. Again.

He'd never considered astrological compatibility before. When someone tried to explain it to him, how your entire personality is defined by the moment you were born, he rejected it immediately. Astrology was too random, too nonsensical to mean anything to Santi.

But here he was, at the start of the New Year, wondering about the stars. That maybe it wasn't a definition of a personality, but a way to see the world. To try to make sense of something that normally made no sense. It was natural, to try to put an order to things, after all. And it was almost…comforting, to know that somewhere out there, there was an explanation for why his life was the way it was.

Maybe the stars didn't know everything, but there was probably a reason why people kept looking to them for answers.

The first night they slept together, he wasn't sure she'd done any sleeping. Partly because they were preoccupied with, um, not Virgo things, and partly because she just didn't seem to. Santi remembered catching glances of her reading on her phone, or feeling her shift restlessly in bed beside him until he kissed her and asked if she wanted him to tire her out.

He was an early riser. Santi was always awake just before 5:00 a.m., and hell or high water, jet lag or no, he was awake at that exact hour of every morning.

You rise with the sun, I wake with the moon, Kira had said to him, which was a nice way to say that she slept late, and he woke early.

But what Santi realized about their situation was that he was the perfect person to rouse Kira from his bed so she could sneak back to hers. They'd been doing that the last few nights, keeping things between them, lost in a lovely, intoxicating haze of kisses and lovemaking (she laughed every time he called it that). One would think she would be used to it by now.

But Santi liked being the one to wake her.

"Kira," he said gently, kissing her bare shoulder as

she continued to sleep soundly on her stomach, her cheek smooshed against his pillow. Sunrise light was filtering through his trees and into his newly acquired curtains, but she was unfazed, continuing her deep slumber. "Kira, wake up."

"Mmm, convince me," she said, burrowing deeper into his sheets. Santi grinned and kissed the same spot on her shoulder. "More."

"It's five," he reminded her gently. "You said you wanted to sneak back into your house before then."

"Too cold to move," was her dissatisfied response, even as her eyes were still closed.

To be fair, she wasn't wrong. He'd forgone the air-con last night, and left a couple of windows open, but the room was so open, and the air so chilly that it felt like there were two aircons on. He suddenly under-stood the wisdom of Kira's insistence that the bed be near the window, although she claimed it to be more of a luck thing than anything practical.

His houseplants, all new, all gifted from Sari Tomas one day after New Year's (she claimed it wasn't too late because "it's not Three Kings yet," and not bad feng shui if he kept them far from his bed), all seemed to be enjoying the cool breeze, swaying just slightly. Kira pulled his bamboo sheet duvet (a Christmas gift from Gabriel when Santi said specifically that he wasn't ex-pecting gifts) over her shoulder.

"I think I can persuade you," Santi murmured, hov-ering so he could bend close to her ear before he nib-bled lightly at her earlobe, which actually made her giggle and swat his hand away.

"Can't we stay in bed forever?" she groaned, roll-ing over and wrapping her arms around his neck, her breasts pressing up nearly to her chin. Her eyes were still closed, and Santi chuckled, kissing both her lids before he wound his arms around her back.

"Sorry, darling," he said, hoping she didn't catch his tiniest bit of hesitation at the affection, burying his face in her neck to kiss her, and she lazily scooted up the bed to give him a little room. "Big day today. Hotels to run, worlds to conquer."

"Oh yes, a very *big* day indeed," she joked, arching her hips slightly and wiggling, and the groan she managed to illicit from him was a sound he was sure he'd never made before—he was sure he never sounded like *that* during sex. "Mmm. Morning, Anton."

"Kimberly," he scolded playfully, moving from her back to trace the curve of her waist, pulling the covers over his head so she could still stay warm and snuggly as he kissed the underside of her bare breast, making his way lower. He kissed the soft skin on her belly, nipping at it lightly and making her giggle above.

"What are you doing?" she asked, lifting his duvet to peer down at him like she had no idea, and he looked up.

"Waking you up," he explained like it was obvious. "May I?"

"Oh," she laughed. "Go right ahead."

And he did. With a light touch, her legs fell open, draping lazily over his shoulders as he kissed the side of her knee, lightly skimming his fingers along her thighs. Kissing Kira Luz was a delicious experience, one Santi savored. He kissed the deepest part of her thighs, close enough to where she needed him that she squirmed, making him chuckle.

"Are you lost down there, Santi, I can—oh!" she exclaimed, because Santi knew exactly where she liked being touched, being licked. He focused his efforts on her clit, coaxing it with his tongue, his fingers stroking lower and lower, enjoying the sounds Kira was making above him, the way her heels dug into his back. She didn't dig her hands into his hair, but thrust her hips brazenly against his face, asking for more.

"Mmm, awake yet?" he asked her, although the words were lost between him nuzzling against her and the blanket over his head. It did have the intended effect of making her shudder at the vibrations.

Santi had always been a fast learner, and it had taken him a mere two tries (both very successful endeavors, tysm) to know how to make Kira Luz writhe, make her squirm. He knew that the fastest way to make her come was via her clit, that she liked it when he focused his attentions there. He knew that when her thighs squeezed around him she was too blissed out to speak, that when she started to gasp he was close.

"Shit, Santi, ikaw—" she gasped, and the covers were thrown off over his head, and he looked up just in time to see Kira watching him, her face completely flushed, her lips dry and slightly parted. It was that look of absolute desire in her eyes that spurned him on, let him slip his fingers in a little deeper with a wet squelch. He wrapped his lips around her clit and moaned.

Kira Luz came undone, filling his space with her sound, her scent, her absolute pleasure. Santi could get used to this.

"Did I do it?" he asked, knowing full well he had, crawling up the bed to catch her lips on his, and Kira lazily kissed him back, licking the bottom of his lips.

He took the discarded cover and threw it over both their heads, and he listened to her catch her breath.

They were going to need breakfast.

"This is so unfair," Kira announced, as she watched Santi assemble breakfast. From across the countertop, Santi grinned and sprinkled Parmesan cheese over his own bruschetta before he took a bite. To be fair, it was delicious. He had slightly old ciabatta he'd made, added olive oil and salt before he toasted up the slices and rubbed a clove of garlic on each. Then he added tomato sauce, a fried egg with a still-runny center and a bit of Parmesan. "You bake bread, *and* you cook?"

"I own a restaurant, and a bakery." Santi shrugged, pouring Kira a glass of water.

"Neither of which you cook or bake for," Kira pointed out, and rightly so, leaning over the counter. She seemed comfortable in his space, and Santi wanted her to be comfortable. It made his heart warm in his chest to see her in his kitchen. "But I did wonder why you decided to open an Italian restaurant, of all things."

"Did I ever tell you about the time I went backpacking along Western Europe?" Santi asked. Here was another story he hadn't really told anyone else.

"Is that…are you trying to get me to sleep with you again? You can just ask me," Kira said, taking a bite of her food and making a little noise of delight (Santi mentally filed that away, because it was the same noise she made when he first put his mouth on her). "I've seen the *Friends* episode."

"I've never seen *Friends*," Santi admitted, and he knew very well that was a source of shock for a lot of people. Really, the more shocked people were that he hadn't seen it, the less he wanted to watch it.

"You haven't?" she asked, and if she was shocked, she didn't let it show. "Tell me about Western Europe, then. If I suddenly come on to you, know that it's your story's fault."

"I'll keep that in mind," Santi agreed, a little confused, but not at all unhappy with the idea. "When I was twenty-five, my family went to Rome to take a cruise along the Amalfi Coast. On our first day, my passport was stolen."

"What!" She gasped, and he had to admit, it was nice having a captive audience. "How?"

"I was the idiot who left it in his back pocket at the Trevi Fountain." He grinned, shaking his head. It was okay to laugh at it now that he was back home, but it certainly hadn't been funny at the time. The police had been very little help, telling him to look in trash bins, and the Philippine Embassy's list of requirements changed depending on whom he was talking to.

"Long story short, my family went on to join the cruise, and I managed to get a provisional travel permit, but had to travel by land by myself. Because I didn't want to fly home right away, and I didn't want to stay in Rome, I asked the concierge where I could go, and he suggested the Ligurian region. That's how I ended up spending the next eight days living above an Irish bar in La Spezia that served the best Italian food I had ever had."

"Is that why La Spezia is La Spezia?" she asked, but interrupted Santi's affirmative when she took another bite of her food. "Mmm, sarap. My god, Santi, you're killing me with a sandwich, I hope you're proud."

"I am a little," Santi admitted, grinning. "And yes. Calling it Irish Pub would have been confusing. But it was eight days where I was by myself, with no other obligation to anyone *but* myself. That was how it all came together. I realized something was…amiss with my family because I had experiences like that outside of them. Things happened to me that they couldn't or didn't want to help me with, so I learned. I realized that we weren't fine when I met other people who had money but weren't completely heartless, people who knew how to love other people. Because of people like you, and Gabriel, and Sari and everyone I've met here in Lipa."

He paused while he was eating as he thought about it. Did the rest of his family have connections to a world outside the Santillans? Miro did, but social media surely had its limits and pitfalls. Tita Joyce had her amigas, but she never really allowed herself to have deeper connections that Santi saw, or at least none that she showed them. Lolo had cut off his parents from the Villas, and they had decided to isolate themselves in Canada. There was Tita Ria and Johnny Marbella, but surely that came after she left the family.

Lonely existences, all of them. But Santi was starting to learn that he didn't have to be alone. At least, not here.

"Is it as beautiful as I think it is?" Kira asked. "Cinque Terre."

He looked across his kitchen island at her, at the lovely person who made him feel less lonely, the person who made him laugh and made him see things a little more clearly. He was thinking about them together again. He could picture them in Monterosso drinking limoncello slushies, holding hands and looking out at the ocean. He could imagine them in Osaka, huddling together in the cold, their path lit by the brilliant billboards and shops. He could imagine them in Lipa on New Year's Day, saying goodbye to the year that passed in the loudest way possible.

Now that he'd said what he wanted, it felt a little more real. Like it was possible, if he stayed on this path. All this time, he'd been so focused on what he wouldn't be able to have if he left Manila that he didn't even start to consider what he would gain if he stayed in Lipa. And these little fantasies were all part of what he stood to gain.

His heart leaped in his chest, and he placed his hand over it, counting out each and every second it beat for her.

"We can go someday," he said, still counting out the beats. "You and me."

"Oh," she said, her eyes wide. "You and me. It sounds good."

"Good?"

"Better, best," she clarified, smiling. "Do we still have time to make out? Just a little bit?"

They did not. But they did anyway.

"I am so going to get caught," Kira groaned, thirty minutes later. They had made a detour to the corner panaderia outside Haraya. It was already eight thirty, and Cassie was probably aware that her aunt had not, in fact, slept in her own bed the night before. Kira was, in short, dead.

Normally, Kira had a lot less shame about where she went, and didn't tell her family unless it was outside the city limits. But with the Luz-Angs leaving for Singapore today, she hadn't wanted to mess up the family dynamic by saying, "by the way, I have a new boyfriend!" hours before they departed.

So they snuck around. It was just easier that way.

"You have said that for the last three days, and so far nobody has questioned the guilt breads you leave at the dining table every morning," Santi said dryly, locking the door of his house behind him as he and Kira started to walk towards the Luzes', taking the long route around the park.

"The best way to distract a Luz is to dangle Spanish bread in their face," Kira explained. "But I don't know. I just have this…feeling. They're going to know the second I walk through the door."

"Is that a bad thing?" Santi asked curiously beside her. He had assumed that keeping their new relationship under wraps was a pipe dream, given they were walking from his house to the Luzes' in broad daylight. He was pretty sure that was Mikaela's mother watching them with her jaw hanging open in shock. Santi waved at her, and Mrs. Aguilar immediately turned away.

"We didn't do this right," Kira sighed, wincing a little and clearly lost in her own thoughts. "I can't just show up at the house with Spanish bread and say oops, I'm sleeping with Santi!"

"Do they not like Spanish bread?" Santi asked, looking at the paper bag full of bread they'd gone out for minutes earlier.

"And it's not that I'm ashamed of myself, or of us," Kira continued as if not hearing him. "But I couldn't stand it if they disapproved, not that their approval matters, but I still want them to like you, because you're wonderful, and this is exactly what I meant when I said that I—"

They stopped, and the house was only about ten feet away. Santi was frowning when he turned to her, trying to think of the right words to express what he was feeling. It was unfamiliar, the rush of warmth he felt, the desire to wrap his arms around her, hold her close and listen to her talk, for as long as she let him.

So he did, the bag of warm bread against her back as he pulled her in close, breathing in her scent—that slightly musky, flowery scent that was so familiar but he couldn't identify. The feeling in his chest overwhelmed him, the warmth and affection washing over in a wave. He recognized it as satisfaction, at being able to help her a little, to show her that he was there for her.

Kira nuzzled her face in his chest, wrapping her arms around his body and squeezing him like she sorely needed it. Santi kissed her forehead, just where her hairline was, to assure her that he was there, that he was happy.

"I shouldn't worry," she said, and he nodded.

"TITA!" a voice shrieked, and Kira absolutely froze in his arms. Even Santi was a little scared now. "WHERE HAVE YOU BEEN!"

Santi slowly turned his head, only to find that the entirety of the Luz household was staring at them both with equal parts shock and surprise. Kira's parents were standing together in the front garden, wearing hats and holding garden tools. Kira's older sister and her husband were staring at them from the doorway among a collection of luggage, presumably to load into the car. Cassie was looking out from the right window, and Kiko was wide-eyed over on the left. Jake was standing beside him and clearly trying not to laugh.

"Um," Santi said, smiling awkwardly as he loosened his grip on Kira. "I think your family just found out about us."

"You don't say," Kira said sarcastically, smiling at them and giving them a little wave. "Howdy, everyone."

Santi had always wondered how it was that Raymond and Alice Luz managed to keep their family so close together. Both Kira and Kiko studied in Manila but came back to Lipa, and while Kamilla lived abroad, it was obvious that physical distance did little to change the family's affection for each other. And it was while he watched the entirety of the Luz family watching him that he realized that he was actually very, very jealous of that closeness.

They were tangled together too, but here, it was okay to pull away when you wanted to, to come back when you had do. They were just…happy. That was perhaps the biggest difference.

"Uh-huh." Kamilla looked like she was struggling between laughing and shaking her head. "And where have you been, Kiki?"

Raymond Luz (who was holding a pair of garden shears, oh god) narrowed his eyes at Santi. "Hm. Good morning, hijo."

"Uh, good morning…po," Santi said awkwardly. Was he supposed to bow? He wasn't. But he really wanted to.

"I knew it!" Alice exclaimed beside him, practically leaping over the marigold bush in front of her to drag her daughter and the man holding her hand up the small set of steps that led to the front garden and toward the Luzes' two-story house. "Ray, look, they're *together*! The village titas owe me *so* much money! Come inside, we can eat that before we have breakfast. Is it Spanish bread? The panaderia outside the village really does Spanish bread well. Kamilla, can you start the barako? We need a lot. Jake!"

"Yes, Mom?" Jake piped up from the second-floor window.

"Can you give Kiko the address to that bibingka place we found the other day, so he and Harry can pick up a few boxes? Cassie and I will make champorado. I still have dilis from Bataan, buti na lang. Ray, if you are just going to glare you might as well eat, too!"

"But I haven't—" Raymond started, lifting his plant cuttings and garden shears.

"You can wash your hands and do your gardening later, hay naku!" Alice exclaimed, tutting. "Kiki just brought home a boyfriend! This is monumental!"

"Fine," Raymond conceded. "As long as I get another grandchild!"

Santi was slightly overwhelmed as they were ushered up to the Luzes' house. Tita Alice was suddenly talking to him about how lovely it was that he and Kira were together, how she'd known since twenty years ago, while Ate Kamilla had wrapped her arm around her sister, asking questions that made Kira laugh nervously.

Eventually Jake and Kiko came downstairs with Cassie, and the Luzes' house was suddenly…alive. It was like the warm yellow walls, the soft cream and dark wood furniture and all the decor that came with it seemed brighter, and more interesting with the family in the house, their shouting and laughing over each other as they set up breakfast. Kira and Cassie were singing with matching dance moves while waiting for the Spanish bread to finish toasting, and Harry was waving around a spatula like he was at a concert. Jake ushered him to the dining table, an impressive thing of yakal and molave that was surely an antique.

"This is your seat," he said, pulling out an extra dining chair from the corner of the dining room that matched the table, woven cane on the base and back. He placed it near the end of the table.

"I have a seat?" Santi asked, looking at Jake with surprise.

"The Luzes are very particular about who sits where," Jake explained, and clearly the man was amused by this whole thing, judging by that smile. "Dad sits at the kabisera, of course, Mom on his right, then it's by birth order of the kids, and not their partners, so Kira gets the opposite end of the table. It's a bit of a squeeze, but you get to sit on Kira's right."

"Right," Santi agreed, touching the back of the seat. He'd never had a place before. He was used to sitting wherever was available, depending on who Vito felt was supposed to be on the receiving end of a long sermon. It was comforting, to have a place to sit.

"Has anyone ever told you that you look almost *exactly* like the Grim Reaper from—"

"I want my new Tito to sit next to me!" Cassie came out of the kitchen, placing a basket of the just-warmed Spanish bread in the middle of the table. Santi swallowed a lump that had suddenly lodged in his throat. "Tita Kira said he knows how to make bread. How do you *make* bread?"

"Wow, talaga? Is there anything your new Tito Santi *can't* do?" Kiko asked, walking back into the dining room, holding boxes of D'Three Sisters Bibingka, his brow raised suspiciously at Santi. How strange that he was now under Kiko's thumb, when Kiko was almost always at the Villa for restoration and repair work.

Cassie was looking at him expectantly, as if he was supposed to pull a rabbit out of a hat, and Santi cleared his throat. He also realized he was just wearing his pajama sweatpants and his sando. Not exactly his best look, but it would have to do. He crossed his arms over his chest.

"I can't juggle?" he said hesitantly.

"See!" Cassie said to Kiko like it proved anything. Santi sighed and looked up just in time to catch Kira standing in the kitchen, smiling at him. He smiled back, a quiet little exchange of affection. Suddenly, he knew what he was feeling.

It was happiness. Pure and simple happiness, the kind he never thought he could achieve.

It felt good.

Several hours later, it was nearly lunch, and Santi was still a bit full. He didn't mind so much, though. Kira was coming over before they headed to his place, where she would be teaching him the fine art of samgyupsal. And if that wasn't enough, he also had a bar of Gemini's 60% dark milk chocolate in his front pocket. In case of emergencies. Kira had slipped it to him before he left her house. She looked happy too, her cheeks never quite losing a happy little flush that she'd carried from the start to the end of breakfast.

It felt so…normal. And so nice. He quite liked it.

"Don't miss me," she told him, kissing his cheek (yes her parents were fully aware of their relationship status, but Kira didn't seem to want to push her luck).

"We have a very serious meeting later," Santi reminded her. "There will be math."

"I'm very excited for all the math," Kira said, nodding seriously. Then she sighed and pressed a hand to his cheek for a second. "I'm so happy you're here, Santi. Oh, I have baon for you, teka…"

He had to admit, it was a different kind of luxury, going through his day with the assurance that there was somebody out there who was thinking about you, who cared enough about you to slip a bar of chocolate she happened to have on hand before sending you off back to your house to get ready for the day.

It was enough to make him smile.

But his smiles were short-lived, it seemed, whenever he thought about staying in Lipa. Because eventually, the shadow of his grandfather's threats would loom, encompassing everything else.

Nobody from the family had called since his great hospital escape from New Year. And maybe Santi was just a pessimist, but he wasn't optimistic about it. It wasn't in a Santillan's nature to leave something well enough alone.

He shook the thought away as he stood up from his desk. Kira was coming to the hotel. Santi wanted it to be completely professional, so he might as well head to the lobby lounge and make sure they had snacks. Brain food was essential for a situation like this, right? Gabriel had recently used Gemini chocolate to recreate the Bruce Bogtrotter cake from Matilda with caramel sauce and Kira's chocolate. It was a huge hit, and Santi was excited to have Kira try it.

And he'd never believed in manifestations, he was

too practical for that, but he was halfway to the kitchen when the universe decided to conspire against him.

"Sir? I think your family is in the lobby to see you."

"My family?" he asked. Santi did a double take, only to see Libby, who was doing her OJT at the front desk, fidgeting. He wasn't sure what else she could have said, because nobody knew that he was *actually* a Villa (because he was a Manila boy, and that was all they needed to know) so nobody would refer to any of the Villas to him as family. Which meant only one thing.

"Yes po," Libby said with a nod. "I recognized your grandfather from the Carlton Group website. He's there, as well as a man I don't recognize."

He thanked Libby, and asked her to lead him to where they were. Sure enough, Vito and Victor Santillan stood in the middle of the lobby, shivering from the cool January breeze and the sudden rains, and glaring down the entire hotel. It was as bad an omen as anything.

Despite Villa being a part of the Carlton Group, Santi's grandfather had never once set foot in the Hotel Villa. None of the family (this side of the family, anyway) had even attended the hotel blessing three years ago, and Santi had personally sent each of them an invitation. But apparently, all it took for Vito to show up was one argument, because here he was, scrutinizing the capiz chandelier that hung between the narra staircases, both originals of the Hotel Villa.

"Mukang cheap," Vito said. "Always has been. Don't you think, Victor?"

"Yes, Dad."

Victor Santillan, Santi's father, didn't have much say in his own life, much less his sons'. He was looking around the hotel too, unable to hide his own awe. Santi wondered what he saw. Did he see how different Villa's classic Filipino style was from the Carlton's more sleek marble and brass? Did he think this was an improvement from the twenty-plus years ago that he worked here as a manager?

"Is that Lally's Manansala?" Victor asked, frowning at the painting taking pride of place behind the check-in desk.

"Lolo, Father." Anton approached them, because this was his space, damn it, and he wasn't going to be worried just because they showed up. At the very least, they were able to see what he'd been working on for the last three years, see what he'd managed to do. At least they could pretend to be proud of him. "You're here."

"Ton-ton, how on earth did you manage to get that painting?" Victor asked, like it was some big secret. He frowned at the painting, which had been in the Villa's possession since before Santi was born. "Lally would never let it go to just anyone."

"Lally knows it's still in the family," Santi explained, keeping his hands behind him to maintain his casual mien, all the while noticing a tic in his grandfather's jaw. Oh he *hated* that. For someone who was in the hospital a few days ago, Santi was pretty sure he wasn't supposed to be up and about and raising his own blood pressure like this.

"All this…decor," Vito spat. "This is what you spent my money on?"

"I spent your money to make people spend their money here," Santi said cooly. "I think you know as well as I do what Villa is worth to the Carlton brand."

Which was true. Almost all of Carlton's hotels were

placed in major cities in the Philippines—they had more hotels in Manila than they did anywhere else. It was more expensive to run hotels in Manila, which meant that despite Santi holding the smaller hotel, he was earning more than some of Carlton's locations.

"And you have no plans of adding more rooms, expanding?" Vito huffed. Santi still didn't know what his grandfather was trying to do. Was he sizing up Villa's value? Assessing its worth for some kind of grade he wanted Santi to chase? Maybe.

"No expansions." Santi was firm in that. "Villa really is meant to be a boutique hotel. We're happy with our 45% GOP. I believe the Manila hotels are at 30%? Adding more rooms would make it less personal, and its size is what a lot of our guests love about it."

"That's all you're dreaming of? A tiny boutique hotel? I built a *legacy* at Carlton, Anton," Vito said, shaking his head, and god, that actually hurt. What a thing for his grandfather to declare, that Santi's desires, his happiness, had not been worth the money Vito had hoarded (for what?). That Santi himself wasn't worth investing in. "My legacy will not include Lally Villa's crumbling hotel. This was a waste of my money."

Santi was sure Vito had said it to hurt, and some part of Santi wished that it didn't affect him so much anymore.

"You would be much better off coming back to Manila, let someone else run this little place," Vito continued, as if a hectare of property on the highway in the middle of a big city was "little."

"And seeing as you have no plans to acquire that property in Lipa, you might as well just come back to Manila."

"What?" Anton asked, his heart stopping in his chest. He wasn't even sure he'd actually said it.

"You heard me," Vito said, and Anton knew his grandfather was trying to be gracious here. "This is everything you've wanted right? I'm letting you come back."

He should feel…well, he didn't know what he should feel.

Elation? Relief? Happiness? But it felt nothing like being in the Luzes' dining room that morning had felt. It felt different, and not quite right. Santi didn't trust it. Didn't trust them, it seemed.

His phone buzzed in his pocket, and he looked at the message.

Where did this rain come from??? Anyway, I'm on the way. Try to resist me until after we talk about the chocolate. ;)

This wasn't right. What was Santi doing, staying here, taking this beating from his family when there was somewhere else he needed to be.

He thought about his morning with the Luzes, how they were all talking about going to Sunday Bakery's opening at the end of April. The Luz-Angs were apparently planning to *fly in* for the occasion, which just blew his mind. They didn't need to, but they wanted to. They had looked up tickets, which coincided with Holy Week, explained to Cassie that she needed to be ready for the coin tosses and to Santi that he should make sure to talk to this priest that was apparently their relative as well, did they need help securing candles for the blessed event?

And Santi's family didn't even know that Sunday Bakery existed.

"Well?" Vito asked Santi, expectantly.

"I don't have an answer for you, Lolo. I have somewhere else I need to be," he announced, looking away before he saw his grandfather huff, and his father still lost in thought.

Santi spotted his hotel manager watching them from a safe distance, and he waved her over. "If you have any questions, you can ask our hotel manager, Carol. I'm sure she knows as much about Villa as I do. Carol, if you can persuade them to try the Lobby Lounge before they leave, you can leave it on my tab."

"Anton," Vito said solemnly. "Think about this seriously. I managed to convince your parents to leave Lipa behind before. It will be easy to do it again. I'm only looking out for you, hijo."

Santi tried to hide the sharp intake of breath he made when his grandfather said that. A part of him still believed Vito when he said that. That was the worst part.

Chapter Twelve

January 5
Around The Same Time

*Today's horoscope: You might just get carried away
with a burst of renewed energy for work, thanks to
Capricorn season. You might experience confusion
in your personal relationships, especially when it
comes to career, but trust in your partner will see
you both through.*

Kira jogged up to the entrance of Hotel Villa, and spied
Santi looking all serious, his hands behind his back
and everything, as he spoke to a group of adults who
seemed to be both in awe and suspicious of him. It was
enough of a strange combination for her to stop and
swipe off the rainwater on her eyes.

This was what she got for riding a tricycle to Villa
from the Laneways, and conveniently forgetting to
bring an umbrella when the skies had threatened rain
all day. Now she was soaked from head to toe in her
jeans and white shirt, sure that everyone could see
through it now.

She walked toward the little group and cleared her

throat. Three heads turned sharply toward her, and she was slightly taken aback at how much Santi looked like his father and his grandfather. It was a little creepy.

"Excuse me," Kira said sheepishly. So this was the highly chismised, almost infamous Pamilyang Santillan. Seriously, it was like looking at a poster to a telenovela. "I need to speak to Anton."

Everyone was aware of the drama that surrounded the family—how Santi's grandfather had insisted that no grandson of his was going to stay in the provinces. How Santi's mother never said hello to her amigas from Lipa when they ran into each other in Manila anymore. How she cut herself off from her own family when she moved away.

And here was Kira, with a wet shirt, dripping on her boyfriend's lobby floor. Wonderful.

"Kira, you're all wet," Santi said.

She swatted rainwater from her eyes and sighed at Santi, who looked like he was very much regretting his statement of the obvious. She would rank this situation a very solid Stressie Tomas. Or did the youths say Stress Drilon now?

"Yes, yes I am. Now can we just—"

"And who is *this*?" said Vito Santillan. She'd heard her parents say that exact thing whenever she was within touching distance of a Y chromosome of a certain age, but Vito had said it like it was a bad thing. Kira had heard stories about selfish, evil, vile people, read about them and heard all the stupid things they said, almost every day on the news.

But it was quite different to look at someone like Vito Santillan in the eye and not ask, "what the hell is wrong with you, your grandson is wonderful!"

"Kira Luz po," she said, before Santi could say anything. Normally Kira would have come forward for a mano right now, but it didn't feel like the right thing to do.

"Oh, I remember you," Santi's father said. "You're that child who always made our son come out and play on the streets."

And you're his father, who made him miserable, Kira wanted to say back, only repeated chants of "not your fight, not your fight," singsonging in her head to remind her to stop.

"I see." Santi's grandfather's frown deepened. "You're from Lipa."

The disdain was clear in his voice when he said it. And suddenly, Kira didn't want to stop. These people were being rude to her, she was wet, and she didn't need this shit, Santi's family or not.

"Proudly," Kira told him, and she was sure the iciness in her voice wasn't because she was cold. She crossed her arms over her chest and wondered if she could stare Santi's grandfather down, because Santi was stiffer than he'd ever been, even as he stood beside her. "Po. And like I said, I need to talk to Anton, could—"

Santi looked...worried. And it was so strange, to see him look worried. Santi never worried, he had plans on plans on plans. Kira could also see Vito mentally going over the list of things he knew about the Luz family: what they did for a living, why he was aware of the last name. Kira was used to that game.

"This is exactly what I was afraid of." Vito shook his head, disappointed as he looked away and spoke as if Kira wasn't standing right there. "That you would think that your stay in Lipa is permanent, Anton."

"It is permanent, Lolo," he insisted, standing next to Kira and handing her his jacket, which was perfect, because she was definitely shivering now. "I made the choice to move here after you fired me."

"It's a distraction," Vito barked, the force in his voice making Kira jolt. "I was trying to make you strong, and resilient, and you decided to get me to pay for everything. Diyan ka magaling eh. Using that big brain of yours to get what you want. And now you're with a Batangueña. Too proud, too self-important. Tapang pa."

"That's not what happened, and you know it." Santi's calm was almost terrifying, even to Kira. She was sure his grandfather's face had gone purple.

"Ayan." He glared at them both now. "I knew it would turn out this way. That my making you strong would make other people want to use you. This is exactly why I want you to come back to Manila immediately. Stop this nonsense hotel in Lipa, and take your place in Carlton."

"She isn't using me," Santi said at the same time Kira said, "*Excuse* me?"

"Victor, call Attorney Bonifacio," Vito continued, speaking to someone who was standing behind Kira and Santi. "Tell him that I want Anton written out of the inheritance."

She gasped. Could he do that?

"She can't do that," Santi said, his voice remaining even and neutral. Kira had listened to enough *Ask A Lawyer* AM radio shows on the road to know all kinds of fascinating things about Philippine law. Like for example, the concept of legitim, and why he would always inherit—if not via his grandfather's free portion, then from Santi's father. She also knew that it was used to prevent disinheritance like this, or passing everything to a random relative, or a cat. "You literally don't have a choice in how I inherit, because I always will."

Kira placed a hand on Santi's arm, and he turned to her. The hardness in his face melted away into a sort of soft tenderness, and he kissed her temple. *I'm fine,* he seemed to say.

Santi turned to his grandfather again. And if Vito wasn't purple before, he definitely was now. Which was probably not a good thing, considering he was in the hospital just a few days ago.

"If I had the choice," Santi said, "I would want you to live forever, Lolo. So none of that burden will ever fall to me."

Then he looked at Kira, and there was that tenderness in her eyes again. *How was it,* she wondered, *that such awful people managed to make someone so... wonderful?*

"We're leaving." Santi decided, leading her though the lobby, squishy wet shoes and all, out to his car, shielding them from the rain with an umbrella. His manager followed him out with a question, and Santi gave them instructions to make sure his family was alright, to comp anything they ordered, if they did. But he didn't want to see them when he came back to the hotel.

"Santi," Kira said, pulling his jacket closer around her, grateful he didn't turn on the air-conditioning. "Are you—"

"No," he said, exhaling a lungful of air. The car

pulled to a stop in front of a traffic light. He dropped his head, and she saw his shoulders sag. "That wasn't how our afternoon was supposed to go."

"It couldn't be helped." Kira shrugged.

"I'm sorry they were rude."

"I'm sorry he talked to you that way," Kira said as they continued their short drive back to his house. "You really love your grandfather, don't you?"

"I don't know." Santi shrugged. "I'm not even sure I know how to properly love anything."

"Yes, you do," Kira insisted, because that was the silliest thing he'd ever said. He loved Villa so much that he pretty much rebuilt it and made it successful. He loved his experience of Italy so much he recreated it for strangers every night. He wanted so much to be a part of the Laneways that he financed Sunday Bakery. And those were the big things. There were so many other little things she could have spent a whole evening listing down. She chose to believe he did them out of love. "You know exactly how to love someone."

They made it to his house. She wasn't sure that he believed her.

"You should shower. I don't want you to get sick," Santi said, taking off his shoes by the door and changing into tsinelas. Kira did the same, because she now had a pair here, of course.

"I'm not going to get sick because of rain—!" Her sentence was cut off by her own loud, weirdly violent sneeze. Which was followed by another. Then a teeny-tiny one, which made a bone in her chest pop. "Aray."

"You were saying," Santi said, and aha, was that him trying not to laugh? She could see that little quirk of a smile on his lips.

"I'll get more towels," Santi continued, heading toward the bedroom. "I'll run the bath."

Kira nodded as she made it to the living room, Santi's jacket still around her shoulders. She sighed and sat on a butaca chair, staring at the cat that was sitting on the arm of the couch and staring back at her.

Wait.

What.

"What the," she said out loud, narrowing her eyes in case her eyes were deceiving her, but nope. That was a cat with orange, black and white fur staring back at her, a tail swishing in dissatisfaction as it clearly found Kira lacking. Kira was sitting on a butaca chair that definitely wasn't here before either, the kind with long arms and a rattan back that made it perfect for naps.

"Santi?" she asked, turning her head toward the hallway for a second, but when Kira looked at the couch again, the cat was gone. The chair was still here though, the extra-long arms a perfect place for Santi to stack three towels in front to her. "When did you get a—"

"The chair? It's a belated Christmas gift from... someone." He shrugged. "She has excellent taste."

"She...?" Kira echoed.

"My Tita Ria," he said, smiling before he picked up one of the towels and dropped it over Kira's head. "I should introduce you sometime."

Kira took off Santi's jacket and rubbed the towel in her hair, so soft that it was hard to believe that they weren't using one from Villa.

"I'll get snacks," Santi said, immediately getting up from the couch. "I should make you tea. I found Lady Grey at South Supermarket."

"Santi, you—" Kira sighed and left the towel draped over her shoulders, and placed another over her lap. "Do you want to talk about what just happened?"

"Definitely not." He sat back down, but crossed his arms over his chest. "We're here to talk about business, and I need to not think about what just happened. I would much rather do that."

She stared at him for a minute, wondering if she should push, if she should try. Processing things needed to happen, because feelings tended to bottle up and fester in one's body. And Kira had the feeling that Santi wasn't in the mood to go into affirmations and meditations right now, so they would do this. Working was a coping mechanism, too.

Kira nodded and sat up straight, although she kept her cross-legged stance on the chair. She straightened her back and adopted a serious mien. If they were going to do this, then they were going to do this right.

"Okay," she finally said. "Did you read my summary of everything?"

"Yes," Santi said, crossing one leg over the other and releasing his crossed arms to thread his hands over his knee. "I have a few questions about specific things, but I'd like to hear you say it first. Give me your point of view. Then we can go from there." Santi got up suddenly and disappeared into the bedroom again before he came back out and produced a soft, cream-colored bathrobe. "Change into this, then start talking."

Then he walked toward the kitchen.

"Now?" Kira asked.

"Yes!" Santi yelled from the kitchen. "I just need to keep my hands moving. Helps me think. Tell me everything."

Kira quickly took off her shirt and her shorts and threw on the robe (which was also soft and fluffy, and unsurprisingly had the Hotel Villa logo) before padding into the kitchen, where Santi was bringing out little wheels of cheese, crackers, honey, meats, biscuits. In short, the man was stress making a charcuterie board.

Kira's heart melted.

"Kira," Santi said, making her look up suddenly. "Talk to me about Gemini."

"Here's the thing," she began. Then she launched into what she understood, in her words. She talked about the process of making chocolate, why her capital expenses had gone mostly into her equipment (because basically no equipment = no chocolate) and the costs of sourcing her beans elsewhere and making sure that those farms get paid right. She talked about the growth potentials of chocolate worldwide, how the chocolate industry in the Philippines was still big enough that a new player like her could enter, and her plan to create her own market while still playing alongside the Altair Chocolates of the world.

She talked about what the chocolate meant to her, how it had allowed her to make connections with people she would have otherwise lost, how people came to Gemini Chocolates looking for that connection. She talked about how much it meant to her that people were happy because of her chocolate.

"But that's the emotional appeal. I don't know the serious, non-personal, businessy appeal," Kira finished. "My family said I had two choices, to lower my costs or to get more sales. So I need to know if I have enough or if I still need to—"

"You're fine," Santi said, finally putting down his fancy cheese knife. "Eat."

She did. The ham was really good, whatever kind of ham it was. It went well with the grapes. "And contrary to what you think, your situation is not as dire as you think. Yes, the tempering machine set you back, but estimates are a guess. An educated stab in the dark. They're not supposed to be the bottom line."

"Exactly, that's what I thought din!" Kira exclaimed, nodding in agreement. "That's exactly why it's called a guesstimate!"

"You gave me your average sales, then the number of custom weddings per year. So I have enough to propose the number of chocolates I need for Villa and La Spezia. Per month, in total, we need…"

He took out his phone and typed while Kira nibbled on brie and spicy honey. It was *divine*. Kira felt a tension in her shoulders loosen, felt her body relax. She knew it wasn't the cheese, the fluffy robe or the warmth coming back into her toes. It was this, him understanding what she meant when she said that she needed something. His seeing that she knew what she was doing. His speaking business in a way that she fully understood.

Maybe that was what made him so effective at his work. He made things understandable, broke them down into simpler parts. For the first time, Kira felt like someone actually had her back. Someone believed in her.

When he showed her the final number of kilos on the calculator, she nearly dropped the cheese.

"Santi." She shook her head and waved a pretzel at him. "Are you serious?"

"You know, I've never been asked that." He thought-fully popped a grape into his mouth. "Ever."

Kira would not be deterred, though, and was ready to disagree until Santi launched into his explanation.

"Sunday Bakery is having its Grand Opening. They will need at least twice the amount of chocolate they usually need. Villa is going to need thirty percent more than we originally discussed. Gabriel came up with a recipe for this cake for the lobby lounge that is selling out faster than we can make it." He picked up a slice of cheese. "I've talked to Gabriel, the chef at La Spezia, my accountant and my purchasing manager. They said this was what they needed. And before you can say that I'm only saying all of that to help you, I'm telling you, it would be much easier for me to just give you the money to cover that capital expense. It's not a lot."

"Santi," she told him, because somehow she knew he wasn't kidding. "What are you going to do with all that chocolate?"

"Eat it all if I could," Santi admitted, chuckling before he pulled the bar of the 60% dark milk chocolate from the pocket of his jeans, and Kira would never be as touched by anything as she was when she realized Santi was carrying around her chocolate in his pants. The thing looked half-empty already. "Villa is launching a breakfast buffet at the Azotea ballroom. A full Pinoy breakfast. The chocolate for tsokolate and champorado alone is a lot. Then there's the Valentine's desserts for La Spezia. I predict the tartufo will be a big hit."

"This isn't much of a negotiation."

"I was just trying to illustrate that I needed you. I'm not getting the short end of this deal." Santi smiled. He pushed the phone toward her. "Now negotiate with me. Price or amount, that's up to you."

Kira gave it some thought. She knew the number she needed to make back her capital expenses, and knew how she priced her chocolate to suppliers. She did a little math of her own, and the calculator gave her a monthly addition in sales that made her eyes widen.

"This is…acceptable," she said, turning the calculator to him. Santi didn't laugh, didn't comment how adorable she was when confronted with numbers (because she was). "But specialty orders will have a different price."

"Of course." He nodded. "I've been hearing things about a white chocolate."

"That is confidential information, sir." Kira narrowed her eyes at him and grinned, and he grinned back. Then he took back his phone, and opened his contacts. "What are you doing?"

"Calling my purchasing manager and my lawyer," he told her. "They have the sales agreements on standby. I want us to be able to sign everything by tomorrow morning."

Let it be said that Anton Santillan was not the kind of man who believed in waiting. Kira also called up her accountant (Mikaela's boss) and explained the situation. The rest of their afternoon was spent clarifying details, getting into specific terms of the contract. Anton spoke to his staff, and they narrowed down the numbers, at one point setting a conference call between all the parties. Kira wanted to laugh at the near absurdity of her making a business deal in a bathrobe and tsinelas, but Santi had taken her seriously, argued when he needed to, negotiated when she was asking for too much.

He made her feel like she was his equal. And they were.

By the time the charcuterie board had nothing but a couple of sad circles of soppressata left, she felt herself shivering in her robe, and her teeth only slightly chattering. The contracts would be delivered to them both tomorrow morning.

"I'll clean up," Santi volunteered. "You should go take a shower. Put your clothes together so I can throw them in the dryer, too."

"Fine. Only because you—" Kira stopped and sneezed, and a muscle in her chest seemed to protest. "Ow. Can I borrow your clothes?"

"Of course," Santi said, giving her a quick kiss on the temple and ushering her out of his kitchen before she headed to his bathroom, which was currently her favorite room in his house. It was a narrow space, with gray stone tile that led all the way to a glass shower the size of a small closet in the back, a wall separating it from one of those fancy Japanese toilets that made a rain sound to encourage you to pee. There was a bathtub on the left, his and hers sinks on the right. It had a freaking skylight, for crying out loud, and because the rains had cleared, created a little square of sunlight exactly where Kira was standing.

Kira made a little humming noise, because this was what cats must feel like when they napped in the sun. She stretched her arms over her head and turned on the bath taps, letting warm water fill the tub. She had tossed the robe aside and examined Santi's bath options (the man had sampaguita bath bombs, also stamped with the Villa logo).

She sighed in contentment as she soaked in the sampaguita-scented bath, laughing when she realized that Santi had co-opted a lot of his own stuff from Villa.

"Can I come in?" he asked from behind the door, and she wasn't modest enough to say no. So, Kira had a very nice view of Anton Santillan leaning against the doorway of his bathroom, his sleeves rolled up the way she liked and his arms crossed as he stared at her. "What's so funny?"

"You," she said. "You steal from Hotel Villa. Tiyani."

"I—" Kira laughed when she saw Santi's flustered face. "The robe is a prototype. As are the towels."

"And the bath bombs?"

"Samples. Those might actually be expired."

"They smell fine from here." Kira settled deeper into the sage-colored water, made possible by the magic of the bath bomb. She lifted a foot above the water and pointed her toe at the soap-and-shampoo set hanging on a ledge at the end of the tub. "And those?"

"Extras." Santi's ears were red now, but he did push himself up off of the doorframe and sauntered toward her, his eyes dark and full of intent. Kira shuddered, and the bathwater was particularly warm. "I wouldn't put these things in my hotels if I didn't enjoy them, you know."

"I guessed." Kira smiled, leaning forward as Santi sat on the floor next to her. He must have seen the hesitation on her face because he smiled softly at her.

"I'm fine," he said.

"No you're not," Kira insisted. How could he be? It

wasn't nice, or kind, what had happened in the lobby of his own hotel. He didn't deserve that. And neither did she. "You don't have to be. Your grandfather barely spoke to me, and I'm not fine."

"I don't have to wallow in my sadness either," he pointed out. How very Earth sign of him. "And I am sorry about them. Lolo and my father. I was trying not to expose you to that side of my life."

"It's a part of you, Santi," she insisted, sighing as he swirled his fingers in the water, as if making sure it was still warm. "It's always going to be a part of you."

"I know." His voice was small suddenly, as he looked at his lap. If Kira wasn't sitting in the bathtub, she would have hugged him. But he sighed and looked up at her, his face softening as he reached up and tucked a loose strand of hair behind her ear. "But it's a part of me I'd rather not show."

"Santi…"

"So. We're officially going to be business partners tomorrow," he said, not really wanting to talk about this. "Are you ready to meet my exacting standards?"

"Ha!" Kira chortled, but leaned her head on his hand. "You're going to love my chocolate as much as I love this tub."

"Gemini Chocolates and bathtubs. A winning marketing strategy," Santi said, and look at her man, making jokes.

"Better than matchmaking?" Kira joked, her brow rising. Santi pulled his hand back, as if embarrassed, and rightfully so.

"I was wrong to have said that," he admitted sheepishly. "The matchmaking is part of your strategy, but… it's also not really the matching, it's the making people feel welcome into your space. It's knowing that you're there for them. They know you, so they'll buy it from you." Santi smiled, and god, it was always so nice when he smiled at her. It was like the world was definitely going to be better. "And if it wasn't for your matchmaking, we never would have seen each other at that hotel in Manila."

"If it wasn't for my matchmaking, I wouldn't have been in La Spezia to talk to you when you came back to Lipa."

Santi moved to sit at the edge of the tub beside her, swirling his fingers in the waters, his eyes trailing across her collar, down to her breasts and the rest of her body that was barely hidden under the surface. Anyone who saw them would think that she took baths in front of him all the time.

"Full disclosure," he said. "When you gave me your chocolate at the wedding, I gave Chloe Agila my give-away bar."

"What!" Kira gasped. "You gave…you gave the queen of Philippine chocolates *my* chocolate? Why? How do you even *know* Chloe Agila?"

"Oh, she was mine and Lily Capras's classmate in AGS. I needed a second opinion on the chocolate, because I couldn't be objective, knowing you made it. I didn't know if I was just clouded by my feelings."

"You? Clouded by your *feelings?*" Kira echoed, flicking a bit of water at him. "Yung totoo?"

"It's new," he admitted, ignoring her sarcasm. "But I sent her the giveaway, and asked her opinion. The first thing she said was 'holy shit, dude,' which might be a compliment."

"Maybe." Kira lowered herself a little more into the

tub because nope, she was not going to blush because her chocolate idol said her chocolate was holy shit. But she lifted her hand out of the water anyway and gestured Santi to say more things like that.

"She said it was complex and fruity. Something about the way it had the best kind of dryness on her tongue. She also said she wanted to meet you," Santi said, that tiny grin on his face knowing full well that he'd just done the right thing. "Should I tell her you're game?"

Kira's brain short-circuited. Whatever she was expecting by coming over to Santi's, she certainly didn't expect *this* to be the end result. All she could manage was a nod before she reached forward and grabbed Santi by the shirt, tugging lightly until he got the picture and leaned forward so she could kiss him, and she could touch his jaw with a wet hand.

"Thank you," she told him, already unbuttoning his shirt as she kissed his neck, and it was her turn to nip lightly at his skin. "For believing in me so much. And not just Chloe, or the chocolates. It's everything. You believe in me, so much, and I said that was all I needed."

"It's a process," he assured her, his gaze focused solely on her. "But believe in yourself, Kira. You have everything you need to keep Gemini running."

And she kissed him, just because she didn't have the words to thank him.

"We are not having sex in the tub," she told him.

"Not *yet*," he said, and kissed her again. Kira gently pushed Santi up, and stood up from the tub, warm, sampaguita-scented water dripping down her body. She heard Santi's breath catch as his eyes roamed her body, and Kira found that she didn't feel insecure about his gaze at all.

"Just to be clear," she told him, picking up the robe she'd discarded earlier to wrap around herself, accepting Santi's help so she could get out of the tub. "We're not having sex because of the deal, or because I feel bad about what happened today. We're having sex because—"

"I'm amazing at it?" He quirked a brow.

"Nice try. It's because you're hot. Because I like you. And because I trust you." She tiptoed up so she could kiss him. Then she turned her head so she could whisper into his ear. "And maybe you are a little amazing at it."

Then she licked around the shell of Anton Santillan's ear. Kira had never seen him unbutton his shirt as quickly as he did at that moment.

The robe came off again as soon as they made it back to her bedroom. Santi pulled her in close from behind, peppering kisses on her neck, the back of her ear as his hands pressed against the swell of her breasts, unable to really fully contain them. Kira moaned leaning back against his shoulder. Normally, she would have been happy to accept this adoration. She really would.

But right now, she wanted Santi to come undone. And she was the one who was going to do it.

She wriggled free from Santi's arms. Ignoring his confusion, she turned to face him, while putting a bit of distance between them. She nudged her head toward the bed.

"Really?" he asked her.

"Ayaw mo?" she teased. Clearly he did want her to,

because he sat down at the edge of the bed, his muscles tense, his cock stiff and erect as he waited for her.

Kira made a little humming noise before she approached him, making him lie back before she spread herself beside him, her face close to his chest, her hand just within reach of his cock. She slaked her tongue around his nipple, making Santi hiss before she grasped his cock and gently rubbed up and down, teasing. She nipped at one of his pecs and he arched his back. Kira grinned.

"Harder," Santi gasped above her. "Kira, please."

Oh. That was interesting. Very interesting indeed. Kira squeezed a little harder, making her touch a little more languid at the tip, and Santi squirmed. His breaths were getting shorter, he'd actually put one knee up to anchor himself to the bed. Kira, whose leg was looped over his, felt every movement, and found that she liked it, too. She varied her speed, listening to when he cursed or tried to hold back a groan, smiling when he arched his hips.

"Shit," he gasped, and his hips jerked. "My god."

"I think you mean Kira," she giggled, loving the effect she had on him. She took the condom from the side and handed it to Santi (his hands were drier, if clenched a little harder). He slipped it on.

"You're really going to take everything, aren't you?" he asked, as Kira pushed herself up off of the bed and kissed him, placing a hand on his hip so he knew she wanted him on top.

"Only if you're willing." She kissed him again, tracing the ridges of his jaw, the hollow of his collarbone, the little pebble of his nipple. Santi groaned and arched his hips against her again, and the way he gripped the sheets before he told Kira he was barely hanging on to his control.

"Santi," she said in a low, whispery voice, her fingers fluttering over his chest, flicking her tongue against his dark brown nipple, making him hiss. He lowered his hips, and she positioned her hand between them so he could feel it when she slipped her fingers inside herself. Kira moaned into his ear as she touched her clit, slightly swollen and begging for attention. "I want everything."

"Why?" he asked.

"Because I'm not scared," she told him. "Because I'm happy. Because you're you."

"Come here," he said, gripping her waist and pulling Kira's hand away. He sucked at her fingers, tasting her. Then he slid a hand under Kira's back and hauled her up a little higher, enough that her back was resting against the pillows. He grabbed an extra one and slid it behind her head.

"This is supposed to be about you," she told him.

"I'm happy when you're happy," he assured her. Then, he grasped his covered cock and swiftly entered Kira, thrusting up, and now it was her turn to anchor her feet to the bed.

Now it was totally his game. Kira grasped the hair on the nape of his neck, her free hand digging half-moons on his arm as Santi thrust upward. He gave her no room to set the pace, no patience for the water's encouragement to slow down. And it felt. So. Perfect.

Kira had never been the kind to sleep around. Sex carried its stigmas with it, no matter how she tried to shake it off. There was always that tiny bit of fear in the back of her mind that her partner could hurt her, that people could talk.

But when she was with Santi, she could ignore that. She could fully surrender herself to the absolute pleasure of him filling her up so well, could make the noise she wanted, express her desires.

"Slower," she could say, or, "Oh, not there," and she would be heard.

With him, she could be brave.

Kira grasped Santi's shoulder while he pressed a tender kiss on her cheek, and all she could hear was the sound of their gasps, the protestations from the bed, his occasional calling of her name.

And when he came, it was with a shout, his neck tense and his jaw tight, like she'd stolen his every breath.

"We should shower," he told her, after they both came down from the rush, after he cleaned himself up and she did, too. She lay against him now, her head on his shoulder. How strange that she felt completely comfortable sitting like this. Like they just…fit. And there was nothing else but the two of them in that bed; the entire world seemed to quiet down for once.

What had her oracle card called it? That line from *Practical Magic*. "A love that even time will lie down and be still for."

"It's sunny," Kira noted, looking out the window. Rain fell in thin, silent sheets, even with the sun only just starting to set. "A tikbalang is getting married."

"Oh no."

"I wonder what kind of food they serve at tikbalang weddings?"

Santi groaned, leaning his head back. "This is the 'centaurs wearing pants' question all over again."

"I just realized, they can have cake!" Kira gasped excitedly. "If they can drag race down C-5, they can eat cake."

"Okay, they can have cake." Santi shook his head. "Carrot cake. I admit defeat."

"I think you just accepted the fact that I'm always right," she told him.

"I've always known that," he chuckled. "But really, we should shower."

"You're ruining the magic." She tutted her lips at him, shaking her head. "Seven minutes."

"Three."

"Five," she said, smiling.

"Okay," Santi said softly, and she caught the tension under his voice, caught the moment he seemed to be deciding how to say whatever it was that was on his mind. She waited, content to let the water quiet his thoughts enough, temper his feelings to say what he needed to say. "I really do want to stay, you know."

"I know," Kira said softly. She turned so she could wrap her arms around him. She wished the fix was that easy. "I know."

Chapter Thirteen

January 18
Hotel Villa

A note on white chocolate: some might argue that
the lack of cacao in white chocolate disqualifies it
from the name. Those people are wrong. White
chocolate is made with cacao butter and is
wonderful if you just give it a shot.

"Alert the media, your favorite brother has arrived,"
Miro Edades V. Santillan announced as he walked into
Hotel Villa for the first time.

Santi, who had been on his way somewhere else,
stopped. He was stunned. In keeping with the great
Santillan family tradition, Miro had never walked into
Hotel Villa before. For him to walk in more than a week
after the rest of his family, Santi couldn't interpret it
as anything other than a bad omen.

He never really begrudged Miro and his choices.
Mostly because Miro was his younger brother, and
Santi's defenses tended to lower around him. Santi had
been told that his brother needed his care, his patience,
his understanding. But when push came to shove, Miro

always had the option of saying, "no." And because Santi had no sense of boundaries when it came to his brother, he would never make him change his mind.

Santi hadn't seen Miro since New Year, he realized, when he'd left his brother to deal with his grandfather after he had accused Santi of "going native." He should have called, explained why it was a horrible thing to say. But there had been no reason to see each other, no reason to talk, so they hadn't. But it was made clear. Everything Miro ever asked for was given, while Santi needed to "deserve" it.

A tiny pang of missing his brother hit Santi, even as Miro stood in his lobby. But Santi wasn't naive enough to think that it was why Miro had showed up.

"Did you miss me, Kuya?"

What a loaded question, Santi thought, hugging his little brother anyway, because yes, he missed him. He missed the two of them facing the family together, looking at each other from across the table like, "can you believe that just happened?" They hadn't done that in a long time. Because Santi left, because Miro was always itching to be somewhere else. There was that undertone of anger in his voice again, and Santi didn't know what his brother wanted from him. If Santi's exile had truly mattered to Miro, his brother would have fought for it, the way he fought for that penthouse in Makati. Couldn't he at least try to be civil with Santi, instead of blaming Santi for things that he couldn't control?

"It's good to see you," Santi told him, as Miro wriggled out of the hug.

"Whoa," he huffed at his brother. "You do hugs

now? That's weird. People might actually think you like me."

"We wouldn't want that," Santi sighed, awkwardly pulling at the hem of his shirt and running a hand through his hair, slightly embarrassed. "What can I do for you, Miro?"

"Well." Miro was looking around the space like their mother had, although he was a lot better at hiding his feelings. "I was actually on the way to Laiya for a shoot, and the office thought I should get this to you."

He handed Santi a folded piece of paper. The Carlton Group letterhead was obvious, even without him having to unfold it. But the fact that Miro was sent on a special detour to make sure Santi saw it meant it wasn't going to be good. A letter of intent?

Santi frowned down at the notice, and felt his heart sink to his stomach when he opened it and saw the contents.

This letter is to signify the interest of the Carlton Hotel and Resort Group, Inc., to purchase land and properties under the ownership of the Luz Holdings, Inc., in particular Lot. No. 2XX8-42 in Lima, Batangas...

The letter was marked received by Luz Holdings. Which meant that Kira's family knew. That she could know, that his grandfather wanted the Laneways, and he hadn't told her. His stomach roiled with acid, and he swallowed down the panic that was threatening to rise. How did Kira's family react when they found out? Did they tell her? Did she already know?

All the fantasies he'd built up in his head were

slowly starting to crumble, and the things he held close
to in Lipa faded at the edges. Santi breathed through
his panic, doing his best not to show Miro how terrified he was. His grandfather no longer had the ability
to wait for him. Petty as it was, Vito's message was
clear. *I can take everything that ever mattered to you.
I have control.*

There was a second page attached, a memo that really was just made to infuriate Santi.

*We are excited to announce an exclusive part-
nership between Carlton Hotels and Resorts with
Altair Chocolates. Starting January 30, Altair
Chocolates will be named the exclusive choco-
latier of all Carlton Hotels and Resorts, including
Hotel Villa and Carlton Beach Club Mandaue.*

Santi felt his jaw clench with restrained fury. His
hands went cold, and it felt like his body had gone on
lockdown, keeping everything inside. His immediate
thought was that this was his fault. How stupid must
he be, to underestimate his grandfather's desire for
control? He shouldn't have introduced her to them.
He should have gotten her away as soon as he saw
her. It wouldn't have taken much for his grandfather
to ask about Kira, and now she was going to lose everything she had ever built, because of him. The Laneways, Gemini, things that she loved and was proud of,
risked getting lost. It floored him that this was what
it came down to. That his grandfather would be willing to hurt her.

"You need glasses," Miro told him, pulling Santi out
of his thoughts. Santi realized his brother was watch-

ing him very closely. Likely any reaction Santi had right now was going to make its way back to Manila. He might as well take full advantage.

"Maybe I do," Santi said darkly, before he ripped up the memo, crumpled it in his hands and tossed it in a nearby bin. Miro's eyes went wide, like he'd just seen something very interesting indeed.

"He's not going to be happy," Miro warned him. A kindness, maybe. "That's basically a threat."

"He's never going to be happy. And he threatened me, too."

Which was the problem, wasn't it? Even if Santi did leave this all behind to go to Manila, his grandfather would still exert his control, would still twist them all together. He wanted Santi to give up everything…for what? He looked up at Miro, who was still looking at him like he didn't know Santi at all.

"Did you know this was what he sent you here for?" he asked through gritted teeth, wondering again what was going on in his little brother's mind.

"Does it really matter, Kuya?" Miro shrugged, betraying no real emotion. Or maybe he really didn't care about Vito's and Santi's power plays, when he wasn't really involved. "You don't shoot the messenger. And you're not going to shoot Lolo. So really, you're just angry at yourself, because you put yourself in this situation, and now your girlfriend is going to lose a *lot* of business."

She was. Cold dread prickled at Santi's skin, his hands suddenly stiff and clammy like he was in the dead of a Japan winter again. He needed to fix this. Kira was not going to lose her business because Santi hadn't been brave enough to tell her what his grandfather wanted, or smart enough to keep her out of his sight.

"I should talk to Lolo."

"And say what?" Miro scoffed. "'Lolo, please don't take my girlfriend's business away?' You know what he wants from you, right?"

He was right. At this point Vito would only be appeased by getting what he wanted, and he wanted Santi back in Manila. Suddenly, after pushing him away for as long as he had. Santi frowned and considered the facts.

"How much trouble is Carlton in?" he asked Miro suddenly. And rare was the moment that Miro actually showed surprise. And if Miro knew that the Carlton was in trouble, then it had to be big. "Miro."

"Enough," Miro assured him. Because of course. How could Vito suddenly have a change of heart, and decide he wanted Santi close? He needed something from him. His time, his expertise, everything he was built up to become. "Everything you did for Villa? He needs to do that in *all* his hotels."

No wonder he'd gotten so upset when Santi brought up his profit margins.

"You think you can fix this without going back, Kuya? You can't," Miro said, shaking his head. "You're not as perfect as you think you are. Just let Lolo have whatever he wants. We never wanted for anything when we were in his good graces naman."

"I disagree," Santi said. Because he'd seen love that didn't want for anything. Because he knew what it was supposed to feel like. It shouldn't feel like someone had a hold on you, a chain to your wrist they could pull back anytime you asked for something.

"Then you must be a bigger idiot than I thought," Miro concluded, shaking his head.

"I guess I am."

"And you really must hate us."

"I don't," Santi said sharply, glaring at his brother. Didn't he know that was the hardest part about all of this? "I never hated any of them. Or you. You just make it very, very difficult for me to love you."

There wasn't much that Santi and his brother could tell each other after that. Miro left, but not before he had taken one last glance at the building. Miro had been five years old when the Santillans left Lipa, and Villa hadn't made the same impression on him as it had Santi, maybe. But there was…something in that last little look. Regret? Anticipation? Santi didn't know.

As it was, he knew that he was just putting off an inevitable confrontation with his grandfather, and at the moment, he wasn't brave enough for the fight. Not yet.

He was about to turn and walk back to his office when his phone started to ring. And Santi didn't know why, but he just had a feeling that something was wrong. There was nothing to indicate it, even a random phone call from Kira wasn't unusual. But there was something. A tension in the air, or maybe he was still angry over what his grandfather was trying to pull.

"Kira?" he asked.

"I just need someone to listen," Kira said, and the tension in her voice was so palpable he could almost taste it. "Talk this through out loud."

"Okay," he said, moving toward the parking lot, checking his pocket for his keys. "I'm listening."

"A BatElec transformer exploded, and they can't restore power until tomorrow," Kira began, speaking very quickly as Santi put her on speakerphone. Safety first. "And I need to harvest, temper and pack 150 bars of dulce de leche white chocolates for Eugene and Jenny's wedding by 8PM tonight. And that would be doable if I didn't have to move everything, and I don't even know if I have enough time, where I'm supposed to move, because of course I don't have a contingency plan—"

She continued to talk, finding more problems than solutions. Meanwhile Santi was darting and driving through Lipa like he'd been doing it his whole life, slipping into side streets and narrow areas until he made it to the Laneways five minutes faster than if he stayed on the main roads.

A miracle.

"I think I can call them and cancel the order," she said. "The couple won't be too disappointed, I don't think. Oh god, I hope I can still be a bridesmaid, I already had the dress, and you're already my plus-one!"

"Do you have a pen and paper?" Santi asked, pulling into a parking space at the Laneways, and sprinting toward Gemini.

"What?" Kira asked. "Santi, are you running?"

"I can help," he told her, quickly checking the time on his smartwatch. He could see Gemini Chocolates and its explosion of plants. And just seeing the Laneways and its facade already helped calm him, helped him think. "It's 4PM now. We need to break down all the steps you need to take, and find out…"

He made it to the door of Gemini, swinging it open with his arm. The rest of the shop, currently operating on candles and phone flashlights, looked at him in shock. What a sight Santi must make, in his jeans and boat shoes and smartwatch, sweating and panting because having abs didn't make you the best runner, squinting because he really did need glasses, and where was Kira?

"...if we really do have enough time," he said, striding to the back to swing open the door to the chocolate kitchen, where Kira was standing in the middle of the room with candles lit everywhere, her phone in her ear as she stood poised on her kitchen island with a pen and paper.

Santi's heart, which had been beating erratically since Miro left, slowed. The fear and the nerves he'd felt, the worry he carried when he saw the memo from Carlton, it all moved to the back of his mind. To him, there was nothing more important than helping Kira, right here, right now. This, at least, he was sure he could do.

"Kira," he said gently before he hung up.

She looked up. To his surprise, she put down the pen and marched across the room, her brown eyes blazing in the low light. Then she wrapped her arms around him and squeezed him tightly, burying her head in his chest like she needed to be sure that he was here.

"You came," she said. "I didn't ask you to come."

"I wanted to be here. I want to help," he assured her, because he could. If nothing else, he could move things.

"But what about Sunday Bakery?"

"Closed for the afternoon, because we had to install a new oven," Santi explained. "We can use the kitchen at my house. Bribe our friends, if we have to."

Because he had friends here. *She* had friends here. There were people that cared about Kira, cared enough to show up when she needed help.

"You're going to use OpMan to help me, aren't you," she said. Santi smiled and brushed his thumb against her cheek.

"Well, I do have an MBA." He shrugged. "I am excellent at Operations Management. Now tell me every step you need to take from harvesting to packing, and we'll make a process chart and move forward from there."

Then Santi got to work, resolute. He was going to help Kira with her chocolates, save her shop and the Laneways no matter what the cost. It all seemed hazy and impossible, but he knew how to break things down into steps, find bottlenecks and solve them. He was going to fix this. He was going to fix everything.

Chapter Fourteen

January 27
Cantina Kitchen
The Laneways
At the same time

Today's horoscope: Dig deep. There's something
under the surface. Mercury is the planet of
communication, logic and rationality, and you must
use your connection to the stars to help overcome
the hurdle. It's only in retrograde if you let it be.

Three hours later, Gabriel and Kira were pouring the
last of the tempered white chocolate into the molds.
Tempering white chocolate, with its lack of cocoa sol-
ids, was an eleven over ten on the scale of difficulty,
but the tempering machine cut those problems in half.
Thank god for Ate Tiana Villa's aircon kitchen, and
her even more blessed generator.

"How are we doing?" she asked, sweeping into the
space, peeking at Kira and Gabriel's work.

"Getting there," Kira said, allowing herself a little
sigh. "Did I already thank you for letting us take over

your space? I already forgot. I think I'm slightly delirious."

"You have," Ate Tiana laughed. "And I told you guys I don't mind, Thursdays are slow. I especially like that you have my cousin reorganizing my pantry."

The entire party looked over toward the kitchen pantry, where sure enough, Santi was lifting boxes and putting them back. He seemed a tad on edge, something Kira had noticed since he'd walked into Gemini that afternoon, when she'd asked for his help. Out in the dining area, Sari Tomas and Kira's staff had taken over one of the long tables and created a whole chocolate-wrapping assembly line. It was really quite impressive. Even Sam, Sari's sister, had showed up to help.

"You know I never thought I'd get the chance to actually hang out with him." Tiana chuckled before she turned to Kira. "This is actually nice. If you didn't have a blackout and a big order to deal with, of course."

"He seems happy to help." Kira grinned.

"That's the way he's always been." Tiana shrugged. "I can tell he kind of needs to blow off some steam, though, so I proudly showed him the mess that was my pantry. But I think he's just about done. I'll check on him."

"Have fun!" Kira chirped, watching Ate Tiana saunter toward her cousin. Santi spotted her right away and said something, which Tiana responded by patting his arm and saying something that made him smile warmly. But the smile was off of his face the moment Ate Tiana turned away.

Definitely on edge, Kira thought, biting on her bottom lip. Between that and filling this custom order, she was…exhausted. But a lot less than she would be if she attempted to do this without help. Teaching Gabriel to use the tempering machine while she did it manually was a lot easier than wrangling all the chocolate herself, and she had to admit, Sari made a tighter, crisper fold on the foil than any of them could ever achieve.

"I have to say," Gabriel said, tapping the mold on the marble countertop to get rid of the air bubbles in the chocolate. "Very sexy of our boy Santi to do this."

"It *was* sexy, wasn't it?" Kira asked, smiling as she leveled off the chocolate already in her mold with an offset spatula. In the process of them figuring out what to do, he'd asked her to talk through her operations. He didn't question why she needed the chocolate to set for a few minutes before she started to temper it, didn't ask why she could only make a kilo in 40 minutes when it should be more.

He just helped. Listened, and gave her a clearer picture of how much time they had.

"He just...he knew what I needed, and I..."

Kira couldn't seem to find the words, but god, she felt the emotions. She carried it with her everywhere now, that squeeze in the heart whenever she thought about Anton Santillan. She made a sound, somewhere between a sigh and a laugh, which somehow encompassed how happy she was that Santi was in her life again, how nice it felt to be understood the way he understood her.

"Wow," Gabriel commented, after he'd placed his mold in the ref, and pulled the molds he'd used before that to pop out. "You love him, no."

"I..." Kira was slightly stunned. There was very little about the man that was unlovable, despite his protestations. He never asked questions when someone needed him, and the advice he gave was always practical. He was almost selfless, just as he had been when they were kids, and he would run in front of another kid in Ice Ice Water so Kira could escape. But he could be funny too, with a dry humor and a self-awareness that she found endearing.

But most of all, he looked at her like she mattered, when she spoke. He heard the things she said, from her thoughts about her BTS bias ("He's worldwide handsome! Who am I to deny his power?") to how alone she felt sometimes, doing what she did. Anton Santillan had become such an important part of her life that he was essential. But giving the emotion a name gave it power, and there was nothing left for her to do but surrender to it. "Yes. Yes, I love him. But there's something going on with him. He seems…"

"Angry?" Gabriel asked, and Kira was surprised that he noticed it, too. "Yeah. He's never going to talk about it."

"He will," Kira insisted. "He just needs a little time to process, maybe."

"Kira, he's a guy. And as another guy, I can tell you that admitting something is wrong, or that we're upset about something, is like the *worst*. We were raised to think we had to be tough, we had to be the one people rely on. It's the manly thing to do not to talk about your feelings. Kasi nga, lalaki. Laki. It's literally in our name to always be the bigger person."

"Ugh." Kira scoffed. "I don't accept that. It's not healthy! And he can't expect me to just accept that yeah, he's suffering, and I can't do anything? He can't carry it around by himself, whatever it is. He's literally organizing his cousin's pantry just to avoid it."

"I know." Gabriel sighed, and she appreciated that he seemed to understand her side as well. "But I realized these things because I grew up with six sisters who never let me get away with keeping anything to myself. Who does Santi have?"

Me, she wanted to say. *He has me.*

"I can make dinner," Santi announced, speak of the devil, walking up to Kira and Gab as they put the last of the chocolate molds in the ref to keep cool. Then Santi started to do that thing where he rolled up the sleeves on his button-down shirt, and very suddenly, Kira forgot what she was doing. Gab seemed to notice her distraction and nudged her with his elbow like, "girl, focus?"

Right, right. Feelings.

"I think I can whip us up some sisig quesadillas. Ate Tiana said she would teach me how."

"Santi," Kira announced from where she was standing, watching her boyfriend figure out dinner. She had no doubt he could, but there was a frazzled restlessness to him that was out of place. He didn't have to run to her that afternoon, didn't have to volunteer to make all the trips, didn't have to do all of this. "Is everything alright?"

"I'm fine," he said tersely, his voice suddenly sharp and caustic, like he was trying to cut something open. "Not everything has to be a crisis."

"Are you sure, dude, you seem a little…on edge," Gabriel noted, which made Santi look up at them both sharply. Kira was taken aback by the slight panic she caught in his eyes, but it faded quickly, and he looked away again.

"I'm fine," he insisted. "Just let me do this."

Gabriel turned to Kira then, as if to tell her that he would follow her lead on this. Kira made a shooing gesture, letting him know that she had this covered. Her friend promptly nodded and gave Kira's back a gentle, friendly pat before he walked toward the open dining area where Sari and Ate Tiana were talking.

"Who is the best girlfriend in the world, with the best chocolate folding technique and the most organized system ever?" he asked the room at large, which made Sari exclaim objections because of course praising her efficiency was the quickest way to her heart, and caused Sam to groan, "god, oo na! Ako na, ako na ang single!"

But neither Kira nor Santi seemed to hear that, not when he was busily starting his dinner prep and Kira was watching him carefully. She set her ten-minute timer for the chocolates to finish cooling before she unmolded and got them wrapped. Then she leaned against the ref door and watched him.

"Please don't look at me like that," he said without turning. "I just want to help."

"I know," Kira said, touching a hand to his broad back, which was tensed, muscles corded tightly. Then she hugged him from behind, burying her cheek on his back, wrapping her arms around his waist. She wondered what happened, why he was so intensely focused on helping her. "You know you've helped more than you needed to. Very knight in shining armor, even if the princess does do half of the saving herself. Thank you."

"I just wrote a list, Kira," he said, rubbing his hand over her arm as if he was reassuring her, continuing his work. "This was all you. And our friends."

Friends who had said "yes" so quickly that Kira was surprised by their enthusiasm. Even Ate Tiana, who had no reason to give them free rein over her kitchen or her generator tonight, had said yes in a heartbeat. Her friends were amazing. So was Santi.

"The list was half the battle, and I know you know that." She chuckled, and Santi said nothing in response, still rubbing her arm and burying himself in his task. Argh. "And you know you can tell me, right? Whatever it is. I can face it with you."

"Not yet." He shook his head, and the insistence of that, his vehemence to keep her out of it, made her heart ache. "I can still…not yet."

Still? she wondered. *How long am I supposed to wait?*

"Okay," she agreed. "But are you okay?"

"No," Santi admitted, placing his hands on the counter and dropping his head forward. "Everything is not okay."

"Okay." Her heart twisted in her chest, creating a dull ache for him. He looked so pained, and there was nothing she could do to help him, but wait. And wait. And wait.

"Happy New Year, by the way," Santi said, turning so he was actually facing her, and god, the pain in his face was so obvious, she couldn't believe she hadn't seen it before. He brushed a hand against her cheek, like he was trying to commit the moment to memory. He smiled. "I don't think I ever said it, when I came up to you."

"You didn't. But this is fun. I got tartufo and pesto for Christmas, sisig quesadillas for New Year," Kira noted. "I'm sensing a pattern."

"Don't forget bruschetta for Rizal Day," he said, catching her lips with his and making her melt into him, like untempered chocolate on your fingers. He did that so well. "Spanish bread for Three Kings."

"And really good dick year-round," Kira joked, and Santi absolutely blushed. Virgos.

"God almighty, please deliver me from all these horny people," Sam groaned behind them, making a show of squeezing past them to get to the water dispenser. "I just wanted water! You do not have to have sex in the kitchen right now, there is a knife!"

"We're having sex in the kitchen? I wish you told me," Kira said to Santi, who chuckled and resumed prepping.

"Water," Sam grumbled at nothing in particular. "I *just* wanted water."

"Thirsty ka, girl?" Kira asked, wiggling her brows at her friend, who gave her a massive eye roll.

"Okay *fine,* I am a little thirsty, but there is no need to rub it on my single ass!"

And it was while Kira continued to egg Sam on that she noticed the light fading a little from Santi's eyes. And while they lay together in bed that evening, too exhausted to do anything more than wrap their arms around each other and sleep, Kira didn't comment on Santi pulling her even closer.

Hours later, sometime between midnight and sunrise, Kira sat bolt upright on Santi's bed. It was *cold.* They had left the window open again, and the cold had seeped into the room, into Kira's skin. The wind whistled and made the trees look like they were content to party all night long, a branch in particular kept slapping against the window, telling her to wake the fuck up.

"Bitch, it is not even seven am," she groaned, blinking at her phone as it very aggressively informed her of the time. The sun had barely risen. "Santi...?"

She turned to Santi's side of the bed. It was those blessed few hours in the day where they were both usually asleep, but she was surprised to find his side of the bed empty. Frowning, Kira grabbed the blanket and wrapped it around her shoulders, wincing as her bare feet met the cold floor.

She slipped on her tsinelas and padded out to the living room, where she found Santi sitting on the floor, his back against his couch and his legs tucked under the new coffee table they'd picked up in Taguig. A now cold cup of barako was sitting on a coaster on the coffee table, seemingly untouched.

He was still just in his boxers, absently looking up at the Oscar Salita painting he'd brought to Lipa from his place in Ortigas. The painting was an abstract, soft, colorful shapes that took the shape of a woman with a basket of mangoes, and a man playing with a small child, another child in the background. The painting was vibrant and colorful, almost like the characters were constantly moving. But they seemed to carry a sadness about them, something in the painting's cool blues that made it less than perfect.

Santi looked more exhausted than Kira remembered, bruises under his eyes, looking at the painting while he absentmindedly stroked...a cat. The same cat that Kira had seen on his couch, apparently not an illusion. Because there it was, a fluffy white, brown and orange cat with green eyes, glaring at her like she wasn't worthy. And there he was, stroking it like the cat had owned him all his life.

"Santi?" Kira asked, and he jerked back to the room, blinking at Kira, narrowing his eyes a little, as if making sure it really was her.

"Kira, go back to sleep." His voice was strained and just…tired. Did he sound this tired earlier? "I'm…almost done with this."

"Done with what?" she asked, taking a tentative step forward. The cat glared at her, as if daring Kira to take it away from her current human scratching post. "Um, is that your cat?"

"I don't know who owns her." He shrugged as it (sorry, *she*) continued to blatantly nuzzle up against him. He may not know who owned her, but the cat seemed to definitely know whom she owned, if that made sense. "She just shows up at my door sometimes, asking for food and affection."

"Sounds familiar," Kira chuckled, sitting next to him on the floor, throwing the other end of her blanket over his shoulder. At least now Santi had a nice rug and a nice couch to lean against; she remembered the living room being particularly bare less than a month ago. "What's going on?"

He turned to her then, as if seeing her for the first time that evening, morning, early dawn, whatever.

"I can't fix it. I'm out of options, and I'm running out of time, and I don't want to run out of time," he admitted, pressing the heel of his hand over his right eyelid. She took his hand, and squeezed it lightly. She wanted to encourage him, to say, "yes, and…?" He looked so lost and defeated. She hated seeing him like this.

But he seemed to change tracks, and shook his head.

"Would you like to go to the beach?"

"We don't have to, Santi." She shook her head. The beach was a distraction, a shiny thing to dangle in front of Kira's eyes so she didn't notice that something was going on. She knew that, and she wasn't going to fall for it.

"Please. I just need to see something. And I think you need to see it, too."

The tension in his voice was all she needed to hear. That despair that he'd sunk into the word "please" undid her.

"Okay." She nodded. Then she looked at the cat again. "*You're* not coming."

Kira had a few things she left over at his house, clothes and underwear, and he had hotel toothbrushes, so they packed all of that. She got dressed, he got dressed, and they got in his flashy red Mercedes to drive two hours to Nasugbu.

"We're going where?" she echoed when he told her.

"Nasugbu," he said, keeping his eyes on the road. "We have a house in Playa Loro."

Of all the beaches in close range to Lipa, Nasugbu was not the most likely. They could have gone to Laiya two hours away, or Lobo. It was almost a three-hour drive to get to Nasugbu, the westernmost point of Batangas, and they could have driven to Manila in that time.

But no. Santi insisted that it needed to be Nasugbu. There was something they needed to see in Nasugbu.

So two, almost three hours later, they arrived at the gates of Playa Loro, the über-exclusive beach club for Manila's elite, a village full of beach houses and vacation homes, all facing the South China Sea. Kira didn't ask questions, not even when the guards waved them in without protest, when he drove through the streets like he had planned to come here all along.

They pulled up at a house at the very end of a road, a lovely, Spanish villa-esque three story, with a little circular driveway, marigold yellow walls and bougainvillea spilling over the walls in waves of magenta. There was even a tiled fountain in the driveway, beckoning people in.

A woman emerged from inside the house. She was small, at least a full head shorter than Kira. She wore a bright red apron and a tiny frown, but she immediately beamed when she saw Santi, even more (if that was possible) when she saw Kira.

"Twenty years," she scolded, waving a wooden spoon at them. "Twenty years you haven't come here, and all the advance notice I get is a *text* at 6 a.m.!"

"Sorry na, Tita Ria," Santi said, giving his aunt a kiss on the cheek. That was when Kira saw the resemblance. Santi and his aunt shared the same eyes, the same little frown when they were unhappy about something. "You know I've been—"

"Busy? You're swerte I was here. I was about to follow your Tito Johnny to Manila. Let me see your face properly, the hospital lights were too glaring," she said, pressing her hands, wooden spoon and all, to her much taller nephew's face, studying the lines and planes on it. And almost like there was a scar on it, she tutted her lips and shook her head. "Tell me. What happened?"

Kira saw Santi flinch, and suddenly, Kira knew why they had come here. Had known somehow that even this, a trip to the beach, was related to his grandfather. Because it was always going to be, wasn't it? His moving to Lipa, their meeting at the store, his decisions. They all tied back to this family, the family that couldn't seem to figure out how to love each other. Kira was tired of it, and she was barely involved.

"This is Kira Luz, my girlfriend," Santi said, pulling Kira from her thoughts, wrapping an arm around her shoulder, and she wanted to hug him and tell him that it was going to be okay.

"Ah!" Tita Ria exclaimed, beckoning Kira over. "The other place you needed to be, no? Let me take a look at you, hija. So pretty! And wow, your boobs are amazing."

"Um..." Kira said, feeling the urge to cover her chest as Santi blushed.

"Tita!"

"What! They are! I'm sure you knew that." Tita Ria laughed, waving a hand as she turned toward the house. "I'm Ria Marbella. I'm sure Anton has told you nothing about me."

"He's mentioned you," Kira said, glancing at Santi, who had the decency to look a little embarrassed. "He also knows I like surprises?"

"You're sweet, but he's dense," Tita Ria laughed. "I'm his runaway Tita, the one who stole the family beach house. Anton called and said he wanted you to experience the beach." Kira was about to comment that Santi hadn't exactly been forthcoming about the whole thing, when Tita Ria turned to her nephew. "Get your stuff. I'm putting you both in the big bedroom on the third floor, you know which one, Anton. I hope you're hungry, I have enough Vigan longganisa for a family of six."

"Six?"

"This is what happens when I don't get advance no-tice!" Tita Ria exclaimed, shaking her head. "Now go. We'll eat on the patio. Just like old times."

A weird look crossed Santi's face when his aunt said that, and they were left to their own devices. Through the open doorway, Kira could hear the soothing sounds of the waves, could smell that salt in the air. Her skin prickled, and it just knew. The water was a lot closer than she thought.

"She's your tita?" Kira asked him, watching as Tita Ria went back inside the house, speaking to the staff. "Like your tita-tita, or a parent's friend tita?"

"She's my real tita." Anton chuckled, but the mirth didn't quite reach his eyes. "We've been texting. She married Johnny Marbelle three years ago. It was in the news yata."

Kira vaguely recalled seeing something about the head of the Marbella Luxury group marrying one of the Carlton Hotels daughters, but there were so many rich families in the Philippines she hardly kept track.

"Anyway, she's my tita. Come here," Anton said, taking her hand. "This is what I wanted to show you."

They walked through the house, past the sunlit sunken living room that actually had a fireplace (in a tropical country?), past the open-plan dining area decked in more antiques and houseplants than Kira could count, Sanso prints in wooden frames, and *whoa*, was that an Edades painting? That was definitely a Mag-saysay-Ho. No wonder Santi had such excellent taste. This beach house was practically brimming with it.

But Santi walked them past all of that, to a set of huge sliding glass doors, which he pried open.

They stepped out on the patio made of red clay tiles, shaded with calachuchi trees, yellow bell flowers, gumamela and more plants than she could name. All of that greenery was just to frame the fact that the ocean was not more than ten feet away. She could feel the salt in her skin, taste it on her tongue. It was breathtaking. Philippine beaches always were, and gave Kira a sense of being safe. Home.

And the look on Santi's face let her know that he felt much the same way.

"Wow," she said as they left their shoes on the patio and walked out together, closer to the ocean, where the waves lapped at their feet as if in greeting. The sun was out, but it wasn't too bright. The December sea breeze whipped at them both. "Your tita's house is incredible."

"This used to be the family's beach house," Santi explained. "We came here almost every weekend, all of us, when I was younger. Lolo used to bring out a plastic chair right here. The closer to the water, the better," Santi explained, smiling fondly, taking her hand as they walked along the shore. "Of course his chair always sank when he sat on it. He said he wanted to watch me and Miro, but he kept getting knocked over. It was hilarious. I think he did it on purpose, too."

Then he pointed to the tall rock formation on their right, one that instantly made the beach private.

"Lolo and I used to explore that area beyond the rock, you can walk around it to get to a little cave at low tide," Santi told her. The fondness in his voice was almost painful to hear. It was hard to picture that the old man mocking his grandchild in the Villa lobby was the same man whom Santi was describing.

"And the family would always eat on the patio,"

Santi explained. "It was always too nice outside to eat inside. Mom would play something on the stereo, and Miro and Tita Ria would sing while my parents danced. We always had marshmallows and hot dogs on sticks for the bonfire. And Tita Ria assigned us the best room. It used to be mine when we stayed here. It has the best view of the ocean."

"Your tita said it's been twenty years," Kira noted as they walked toward a lone mangrove tree on the beach, where there was a little swing attached to a branch. Kira sat on the swing while Santi idly pushed the rope. "What did she mean?"

"Tita Ria and Lolo got into a fight about…something I don't remember, twenty years ago. I know she asked for the beach house, and they never spoke again. We were forbidden from coming up here, or speaking to her. I don't think she's spoken to my father since then, either."

"You must have missed her," Kira asked, trying to be gentle while still pushing.

"I did." Santi nodded. "But she was there when I opened Villa. It counted for something, when she showed up."

Kira scooted to the edge of the swing, and patted the empty space beside her, and Santi sat. It was a bit of a tight fit, but they made it work, both of them using their feet to gently rock the swing forward and back, forward and back.

"She made it out, somehow," Santi noted. "She seems happy."

"Why are we here, Santi?" Kira asked, looking out at the ocean like the answers could be divined from there.

"I came here because... I don't know. Maybe I needed to go back, find proof that my family was actually normal once. That we used to love each other. That deep down they loved me."

It was painful to hear, and it wasn't Kira's relationship with her family. And she knew she needed to be patient, needed to wait to coax the truth out of him.

But god, she was tired of waiting. Tired of hearing Santi beat himself up for being told he wasn't enough, when the man was So Utterly Perfect and Objectively Not An Awful Person. Anuba! He was wonderful! Took such good care of her, and the people around him. And he was so terrified of hurting people that he seemed cold, but Santi loved more deeply than Kira had ever thought possible.

How could his family not know that about him?

"You know that every time I experience something good," he said slowly, "at the back of my mind, a voice whispers. Tells me I don't deserve it, because I'm a bad grandson. Because I abandoned my family."

Kira's heart twisted in her chest. She thought about every happy moment she experienced with Santi—the wedding, sitting with him in Sunday Bakery, in the gardens of La Spezia, their New Year's, and all the moments in between. Did he mean to say that all those things were stained dark because his family wasn't there?

"You didn't abandon your family!" Kira said angrily, because god, why wasn't *he* angry? Why wasn't he railing against them and fighting for himself? "Santi, your family is *horrible*! Family doesn't treat you this way. They don't force your hand, or squeeze you out. They don't abandon you, or make you dissect everything they said just so you can convince yourself that they loved you. They shouldn't make good things feel like bad things. And you didn't do anything to deserve it!"

"To them, I did," Santi insisted. "Lolo released a memo making Altair Chocolates the exclusive distributor of all Carlton hotels, including Villa."

Kira's stomach dropped, and she had to grab the rope of the swing so she didn't fall. A wave of dizziness hit her as she realized the implications of Santi's sentence. Vito really was as horrible as every story Santi told. As horrible as he'd seemed on that one interaction she'd had with him. How could anyone who claimed to care, claimed to love their grandkid, treat them like this?

"Fuck," she managed to say. Because what else was she going to say? What else was there *to* say? She had waited, and waited for him to tell her everything. He could have told her on New Year's, and they could have maybe done something about it. But he hadn't, and it hurt. It hurt badly that he hid *this* from her. "You should have told me."

"I wanted to find a solution to the problem first." Santi admitted, dropping his shoulders. "Miro hinted that there's a problem in Carlton, which is why Lolo is acting like this. And if I want to keep helping you, if I want to keep our partnership alive, I have to go back to Manila just like Lolo wants."

"No," Kira said immediately, turning a little to face him. "No! Santi, don't go! They make you so miserable. You're so miserable now, and you're not even there!"

"I made a commitment to you, Kira," he reasoned, and he sounded defeated, like there was no other decision to be made. Kira refused to let that be the default.

"We're supposed to be business partners. And this is my fault. So if leaving will fix it, then…"

"No," Kira repeated, scrambling out of the swing so she could face him fully. Santi kept his eyes on his toes, his ankles buried in the sand as he lazily moved the swing. "This is not how you are business partners with someone. Partners do things together, they make decisions together. There has to be another way, I absolutely *refuse* to let that horrible man use you. You belong in Lipa, and with me, and everyone in the Laneways…"

"Did you know that he wants to buy the Laneways?" he asked her, and no, she did not. Kira wished she could just fall backward and lie in the sand. This was a *lot*. Almost too much, and she still couldn't believe that he had been carrying this around by himself. She understood how the Laneways was attractive, and profitable, but her family was never going to sell it. She was willing to bet it was going to be brought up at the family board meeting.

"I didn't," she admitted.

"I couldn't do it, because I know how much it means to you. And if I don't go, then he'll do everything to destroy everything I love in Lipa," he told her, and the pain in his voice fully made tears fill her eyes. She was sad, yes, but more than that, she was angry. Angry at the ways one man had managed to manipulate Santi, Santi who didn't want much in the world but to be loved. She was starting to sob, she realized, and she hated that her breath was unsteady, that her voice was unsteady, too. "I love you, Kira. I will not be the reason why you lose Gemini. And this will fix that."

"So…yun na yun?" she asked. "You're going to leave, and make yourself the hero, and you're just…

unhappy? And I'm supposed to just smile, let you go as you yeet yourself off of a cliff without a parachute?"

She shook her head. This couldn't be right. Between Gemini losing the Villa order and Vito almost buying the Laneways, and this? She couldn't wrap her head around any of it. How had Santi carried this around by himself?

It had to be solvable, surely it had. There were things they could still do, not that she could think about them at the moment. But Santi was already walking out the door, and she needed to remind him that he already knew what the better choice was. That he'd told her, that New Year's Day, what was truly, honestly in his heart.

I want everything with you, Kira. As long as you'll have me. I want to stay here in Lipa, I want to be happy here. There's nothing else.

"I love you too, you know," Kira told him. "As much as you're willing to go back to Manila for me, I'm willing to keep you, even if it means losing Gemini."

Truth. Because Kira knew if she had to, she could start over again, would do it all over again, if it meant having Santi stay. She was sure of it. As sure as she was that the best tsokolate was made with 70% dark chocolate, that the 50% chocolate bars were her favorite, and that her regulars would all come back even if she restarted the business from her bedroom.

She knelt in the sand, placing her hands on his knees, looking up at his pained face. He looked so hurt, and it killed her that it took so long for him to tell her all of this. If he'd told her sooner, then they would have figured it out sooner.

Hmmm. That wasn't very air sign of her.

"But what about…"

"Gemini? We haven't started figuring out a new plan for that, and you're already throwing in the towel." She managed to smile still. "You told me to face things head-on, and this is just a problem we have to face head-on. And I'll need someone to do the math, make those amazing process flowcharts that literally saved my butt last night."

He sighed. Kira wondered if she was getting through to him, even a little bit.

"I understand why you wanted me to see this, Santi," she said, finally. "But I think the people who used to vacation in this house aren't here anymore. And going back isn't going to make you happy."

Then she put her hands on his cheek, coaxing him closer to kiss him. He still had a decision to make, and she had a whole new business plan to try and figure out. But whatever happened, he had to know that not being together was not an option.

They were partners, after all.

Santi lowered his head, opened his knees so Kira could slip into his arms, so he could kiss her properly. She could taste salty tears, and she wasn't sure whose they were—hers, because she was so angry that her anger manifested in crying, or his. He pulled away and sighed, his arms still wrapped around her as he pressed his forehead against hers.

"You're absolutely right," he told her.

"As always?"

"As always," Santi agreed. He kissed her again, a little quicker this time. And she could have imagined it, but she thought she heard him say, "Thank you."

"Do you want to be alone for a little bit?" Kira asked. "Or do you want me to stay?"

"I think I need to be alone for a bit," he said, kissing the top of her knuckles. His eyes looked a little dull, like he was far, far away. "I'll see you in the house."

Kira nodded and rose, letting Santi help her dust the sand from her knees. She gave him a small smile like she was encouraging him before she headed back into the house, running into Tita Ria. They both squeaked in surprise, and Kira hastily wiped her tears with the back of her hand. Oh god, she was getting the sniffles.

"Oh dear," Tita Ria said, frowning. "What happened?"

"Nothing po," Kira said quickly, because how embarrassing that she had barely spoken to Tita Ria but was already crying in front of her. "Sand in my eye."

"That's a lot of sand, hija." Tita Ria smiled, placing an arm around Kira and leading her to the kitchen, where she was served a bowl of crushed ice, skimmed milk, shaved Japanese sweet corn, a smattering of frosted cornflakes and a scoop of vanilla ice cream on top. Damn, she did love a good mais con hielo. A tray of tissues was also discreetly passed her way. "Eat. Talk."

"I just don't understand *why* this family is so awful!" Kira exclaimed, shoveling the much-needed food into her mouth. Nothing like a good mais con hielo to cool the fevers of frustration. The ice cream and cornflakes just added that extra sosyal touch she was beginning to learn the Santillans enjoyed. "Um. Present company excepted."

"Naturally." Tita Ria smiled. "But I've asked myself that question for the last…fifty-six years, hija. I'm sure

Anton has, too. But after watching Infinity War, I realize that villains never know they're villains in their
own stories. They legitimately think that their way is
the right one, or they don't care? I don't know. I tried
to justify their actions before, but hic sunt dracones."

"Whose aunt?"

Tita Ria shook her head, still smiling. "Here be
dragons."

"So that's it?" Kira asked, slightly exasperated.
"They're just…bad?"

"Yes." Tita Ria nodded firmly. "And it's a hard
lesson to learn, especially for Anton because he was
raised to be the utusan. Harder still to accept when it's
your family, when you know the very, very teeny-tiny
amount of good they are capable of."

Kira felt her body deflate, because she really did
feel awful dumping on Santi the way she did. He really didn't deserve that, not after he'd helped her so
much. But as she looked at Tita Ria, she wondered if
she and Anton came here not to vindicate the Santill-
lans, but to ask for Tita Ria's help. Tita Ria, who had
already learned all the hard lessons, who still managed to be whole.

Maybe Santi brought her here because he needed
hope.

"I know he'll tell me eventually, but what happened?" Tita Ria asked. "It had to be bad, for him to
come here."

"I don't know. Vito happened," she guessed. "He
wants Santi to come home, but he doesn't know how
to say it, so he's burning everything Santi built to the
ground so he can have it. I know when we were kids,

they left Lipa because Vito demanded it from them. And I don't want to say it, but…"

"But?"

"He's terrible. And it's a toxic family relationship, and I can't stand seeing someone so wonderful and strong look so…lost. He's lost. He's ready to throw in the towel, but…he still loves them. Which is heart-breaking. And that's why they make him so miserable, because at the back of his mind he knows that this isn't how you love someone. And he doesn't deserve to be miserable, because Tita, he's so wonderful! Did you know that he *cooks*? He does this thing where he fries kesong puti so perfectly, and I—"

"What?"

"He just loves so deeply," she said, and her voice actually shuddered, as tears welled in her eyes. "So deeply. And they don't see it!"

Then she *really* started to talk. She told Tita Ria about Santi arguing with Vito about the employee loans, which led to Santi losing his job, about them meeting in Lipa, and his choice to go back. She told her about the two of them choosing to work together on Gemini, how Vito had taken it away after he met Kira at the lobby of Villa. She told her how unfair the family was, how hurt Santi was, how Kira was so *frustrated* about all of it.

"Tita," Kira said slowly. "I just don't understand why staying is even an option for him."

Tita Ria scoffed. "It sounds easy, no? Like, the answers are obvious. But when you're drowning, you think it's okay. Ganyan talaga, kasi family. It's hard to accept that the people who were supposed to love you can't do it the way you need it. Especially when there's someone who shows you how much better it is to be loved well. Just love him well, Kira. It means more to him than you realize."

Kira looked down at her bowl of corn. The ice was already melting. She turned her head and had a clear view of the beach from here, and Santi glaring resolutely at the sand like he could count every single grain there. She inhaled deeply, using the ocean breath she'd learned in yoga class to anchor her. Then she slowly released it.

"I know we just met," Tita Ria pointed out. "But you've done more to care for Anton than any of the family has in years. You'll figure it out together."

Kira looked out of the window, where they could both see Anton walking back and forth on the shore. There was nothing more she could do but to go upstairs and wait for him.

He had been right about the room, though. The room assigned to them was nice. The bed was soft and comfortable, the vanity mirror so Instagram-worthy she would have taken pics of herself if she wasn't so down, the rug so soft she could have slept on it if the bed wasn't already soft. There was a baul at the end of the bed that had a mother of pearl inlay, stuffed with more pillows and sheets, and photos on the walls. Most of them were of the halcyon beach days Santi mentioned, him and Miro always in beach shorts and big grins, Tita Ria with her sibling, and an old picture of the Santillan family with Santi's grandmother.

What happened to the family? she wondered. Money? Greed? It was difficult to tell. The pain was too old, too deep and too difficult to untangle without tugging hard.

Suddenly the room felt a little suffocating. Kira much preferred the balcony that faced the beach. There was a rattan lounger on the balcony on top of a banig from Samar, a woven blanket from Ilocos in a deep, midnight blue draped over the back for cooler nights. Kira felt like she could breathe with the ocean out here. So she did, staring out at the ocean, feeling her mind wander, her guilt settle, her heart ache.

As the sun set in the horizon, and her anger simmered, she knew she was being ridiculous. She needed to talk to Santi, sort this out, and…

"Kira." Santi's voice filled the room as he walked in. "I have food."

She looked up just in time to see him place a tray on the little round table beside the lounge.

As peace offerings go, Kira had to admit, it was *very* tempting. Santi offered her a buttered sourdough sandwich of some kind, stuffed with kesong puti and Vigan longganisa, a bowl of sliced fresh melon, buko juice and a bowl of cassava chips.

"Thank you," she said in a small voice as Santi sat in front of her. Kira took the sandwich and took a bite, and after a whole day of packaged snacks, it was extra delicious. "How was the beach?"

"Illuminating," Santi said, accompanied by a deep, weary sigh that made her heart wrench. "We should talk. I have half an idea to save Gemini. I have to make a few calls, Chloe doesn't really get up until past noon, but she'll listen, at least, and—"

"Santi," Kira said gently, taking his hands. "We can figure it out when we get back to Lipa. But I think we should talk about what *you* want first." She took in a deep breath, bracing herself for his answer. Whatever it was going to be.

"What do you want?"

His face softened then, a small smile finally slowly spreading on his lips as he looked at her. He squeezed her hands, and it was like he was himself again, with that smile she was now all too familiar with.

"This," he told her. "I want this, with you. I want to stay in Lipa and make a life there. I want Vigan longganisa and kesong puti by the beach, all the chocolate tartufo and the coffee with our friends. I'm happy to be here."

"Okay." Kira nodded, and nope, nope, she was not going to start crying again. "What about Vito? I think he's not going to give up on you so easily."

"He won't," Santi agreed. He looked back at the room for a second. "But he has nothing over me. I have to figure out how I'm going to do this, how I'm going to mentally reconcile the fact that my family doesn't know how to love me. But I won't be alone."

"You won't." She nodded, although her words were slightly muffled by the sandwich. Who was Tita Ria's longganisa supplier? Her mom would *love* this. "I just... I hate seeing you like this. And I hate that I can't do more."

"This is plenty," he assured her. "This is more than anyone has ever done for me."

"Did you talk to your Tita?" Kira asked.

"Yes." He nodded. "She's still hurting, after all these years. She's got a completely different life, but bringing up our family still hurts for her. I can't help but be terrified of being like her, alone in a big house by myself."

"Until twenty years later your nephew and his girl-

friend walk in," she said, trying to lighten the mood.
He chuckled. Success! "But she's not alone, Santi. She
has her husband, her work. It's not a bad thing, to make
the healthier choice."

He nodded. Maybe he wasn't quite there yet. But it
was going to be okay. She believed it would be.

"You helped me so much with Gemini, and I want
to help you with this, too," she said, when she finished
the sandwich. "Let me help you."

"I don't want you to get hurt," Santi told her. "This
isn't easy, or light. You think you're hurting now, but it
can get much, much worse, still. My family isn't going
to make it easy to be with me. I don't even know why."

"Because you're a prize," she chuckled, and he gave
her a look that said he appreciated the compliment,
but it really wasn't the time. "You are, though. You're
wonderful."

And it really shouldn't have been pleasant, Santi
suddenly kissing her, because she had longganisa
breath and butter on her fingers, but he did anyway,
his hands on her face like he needed her to breathe.

"So are you," he said, and Kira sighed deeply, letting her relief rush in.

"Longganisa breath," she warned him, crinkling
her nose.

"Really?" Santi asked, blowing in her direction, and
ugh, he had it, too. "Didn't notice."

He pushed her down slightly, so she was leaning on
the arm of the chair, and Kira opened her eyes to the
sight of Santi's face, still a little lost, worried, with a
blanket of stars behind him. Kira pressed her hand to
his cheek, making him look down.

"I love you, Anton," Kira said. "I love every part of you."

He kissed her again, and Kira poured her feelings into it. She wanted him to feel like it was safe to confide in her, that she could be a safe place for him as he had been for her.

He kissed the juncture between her jaw and neck, trailing his lips lower and lower to the valley of her breasts, licking and sucking at the crest of her curves. He licked her cleavage and tugged her sports bra up, like he needed more of her.

"May I," he said, and it was more a plea than a question. "Kira, may I—"

"Please," she said, taking the band of the sports bra that her boobs had buried and pulling it up and over her head.

Her bra had barely made it to the floor and Santi was already on her, squeezing one breast, flicking the nipple while his mouth did the same to the other. Kira gasped and shifted her hips to sit up higher, and Santi followed hungrily, nipping at the curve. Kira braced her feet on the lounger as she reached for the hem of Santi's shirt (he was wearing a Kurama shirt from Uniqlo, because of course he was) and helped him take it off.

"Hay, ka-gwapo," she sighed, because he really was. The moonlight softened the harder planes of his face and his body, and he just seemed to glow.

"You, too," he told her, and he smiled, truly and fully. And it was good to know he was here with her. That they had this, at least.

"Come here," she said, tugging the hem of his shorts so he could brace his arms beside her head. He kissed her forehead, and it was so tender and sweet that tears actually pricked her eyes this time. She wanted Santi to know how loved he was, how loved he made her feel.

Her shorts came off, then her underwear, then his shorts. He had a condom, because they bought some on the way, and slipped it on. Santi rubbed his cock against her thigh once, twice, and his fingers mimicked the motion on her clit, and Kira hoped to god Tita Ria wasn't home because there was no way she could keep her cries of pleasure to herself.

"Santi," she gasped. "I need you."

"I'm here," he said, taking a hold of himself and positioning himself so he could slip inside her, and it felt wonderful. Nobody had ever filled her the way he did, could make her feel so connected to another human. Kira wrapped her legs around his waist as they thrust into each other. They both liked it like this—a little rough, a little urgent, vigorous. Kira bit down on his shoulder and he groaned, thrusting a little harder. She squeezed her thighs and he cursed and swore.

"Tang-ina," he moaned, which was probably the most Batangueño he'd ever sounded. "Kira, Kira, tang—"

"Mmm." She smothered the rest of the curse with a kiss, grabbing his butt and using that as leverage to shift them both. Santi scooted higher on the lounge, and her legs went higher. At this point Kira was sure the stars she was seeing weren't the ones in the sky.

She could feel it, that all-too-familiar buildup inside of her, could feel that Santi was close, too. So Kira slowed slightly and put her hand on his cheek, getting his attention again. He looked down at her, dazed. She smiled, and waited.

He smiled back.

"I'm here," he promised, catching her lips in a kiss. "I'm here."

They moved together slowly, a bridge in the song, a moment together before they resumed their earlier speed. There was no need to drag this out more, no need to reassure each other. Now they could just feel, and be.

And when Santi's orgasm came, he started shouting and groaning, Kira dug her nails into his skin as her own release followed. Santi collapsed on top of her on the lounge, scooting down a little so his head was on her chest. Kira ran her fingers idly through his hair, looking up at the starry sky, waiting for their breaths to even out as the waves crashed against the shore beyond.

"Oh, I've been meaning to tell you," Santi said, as Kira's eyes lazily fluttered. The sea breeze did wonders for her sleep. "I looked up my birth chart. I'm a Virgo Sun, Cancer Moon and a Scorpio rising. I don't know what any of that means, but, there you go."

"Wha—oh my god," she said, laughing when she realized what he was saying. "That makes so much sense."

Santi's hands gripped her waist and he pressed a kiss to her stomach. And they both knew that things were only going to be much more difficult before they became better. But as long as they were together, they were going to figure it out.

Chapter Fifteen

January 29
Café Cecilia
The Laneways

Today's Horoscope: There is much to be gained by leaving your heart on your sleeve, and you know that better than anyone else, Gemini! Making yourself a bit vulnerable may inspire that vulnerability in your partner as well. Treat each other with care, all will be well.

Kira Luz was a firm believer in certain things that she knew had absolutely no basis in reality. When her palms itched from a soil allergy (it happened sometimes), she was sure she was about to come into some money. When people packed away the food while she was still eating, it meant she was never going to get married. Of course you had to go somewhere else after going to a funeral, the dead could follow you home.

And it wasn't necessarily because she believed them to be a hundred percent true, but those little beliefs, those practices were a part of her life now, and had led to good moments. When her palms would itch and she

actually found money. When she laughed off those su-
perstitions and got a boyfriend like Anton Santillan.
When those little last-minute convenience store trips
before going home led to conversations about life, and
death, and reminiscing just a little bit longer about the
person who passed. She was only human, and these
little things helped her make sense of a world that really didn't.

So she wasn't sure what to make of it when she kept
getting burned all day.

It started in her window garden, when she found
that one of her rosal leaves had a burn mark, which
seemed to have come from nowhere. She put the plant
in a slightly shadier spot and moved on. Then she made
it to breakfast, where her father was very obviously
waiting for her to bring something up, and burnt her
tongue on her arroz caldo.

"The meeting is in two days," he unhelpfully reminded her as she drank a cupful of water. "Are you
ready?"

She was not. Santi's half-an-idea was moving, but
it was slow going. It involved Chloe Aglia and some
kind of deal with Altair, but Kira had a strange feeling
that it wasn't going to turn out the way she wanted. So
she'd stayed where she was and tried to find an alter-
nate way. Her own way.

"The more plans we have, the better." Santi, ever
the Virgo, agreed. "We just have to pursue all the avenues until we run out of them."

So far, Kira had been meeting dead ends left and
right. She was already considering renting a smaller
space, considering renting just a small kitchen as a
commissary. Gabriel never used the kitchen in the

house he rented from them, maybe that could be her chocolate-making space?

But the burns just kept on happening. When she got to the Laneways and started to microwave a bowl of dark chocolate in fifteen-second bursts to make ganache, she'd burned the chocolate beyond use. When she pulled a tray of chocolate crinkles out of the oven, she'd forgotten that the pan was hot and burned the tip of her pointer and middle fingers.

"What is happening?" Kira muttered as she ran her hand under cool water. She didn't know if there was an old belief surrounding burns, but she took it as a bad sign. A very bad sign.

"Knock, knock," a deep voice said by the open door of the kitchen, and she turned to find Mang Roldan standing there, looking nothing like his fifty years of age, carrying half a sack of something in hand. He really did look like Keanu Reeves, especially with the beard. "Hmm. That didn't sound like me."

"Mang Roldan!" Kira said brightly, smiling at him as she patted her poor fingers dry on a towel. She must remember to add aloe vera on it later. "Not that I'm not happy to see you here, but did I expect to see you here?"

"Not really, but I realized I needed to pay you back for that cup of tsokolate and brownie," he told her, and Kira was about to protest when he held up a hand.

"Kira," he said gently (but then again, did Mang Roldan have a mode that wasn't gentle?). "That cup of tsokolate changed my life for the better. I feel I need to give you something back. So here."

He indicated the sack on the ground. Kira didn't need to open it to know what it was. She could recognize that heat that the bag seemed to radiate, recognized the sour scent in the air. Mang Roldan had brought her a sack of fermented cacao beans, at least five kilos of it, judging from the way it looked.

"Oooh, where are these from?" Kira asked, kneeling in front of the sack and untying the knot to reveal the treasure inside. Her eyes lit up at the sight of the beans, still in their little shells. Yes, the scent was almost pungent, but she was used to that pungency. There was so much potential in this little sack. They could be fruity, or raisiny, they could taste perfect with a little more milk, or truly stand out when they were dark. *What would you taste like?* she wondered. *I think you're going to be delicious.*

"Tomas Farm." He shrugged like it was no big deal. Which duh, of course. He was the farm manager there, after all. "This is the first batch we've managed to ferment, and I wanted you to be the first to try it."

"Wow, that's—wait." Kira gasped when she realized what Mang Roldan was offering her. Nearly fell completely on the floor, really.

When she started Gemini Chocolates, she knew that she couldn't make it from Davao beans forever. It would defeat the entire purpose of setting up the business in Lipa if she did. Especially when at some point in history, Batangas had been the only coffee and cacao supplier in the country (at one point Lipa had been the only place in the whole *world* you could find coffee, but that was a different story). The history of her family was in the land, in the trees that grew, and she knew that she was going to have to figure out how to get her Batangas beans soon.

She'd been waiting. She'd known Sam Tomas found

the cacao in the Tomas land in Sta. Cruz, but she didn't realize that they had cleaned up the area already. That they had even started fermenting the cacao.

Her hands were shaking. There was so much that these beans still had to go through to turn into chocolate—they needed to be sorted, cracked, winnowed, roasted, melanged, all of it—but there was no doubt in Kira's mind.

They were going to be amazing.

"Mang Roldan," she said, and she didn't realize she was about to start crying until she said his name. "This is…this is amazing."

"Ala eh. Like I said, I owed you," he said, smiling sheepishly. "I… I also tried to make tsokolate with it, just so you had an idea of the taste."

He handed her a thermos, and Kira immediately stood up, taking the thermos in her hand. She looked up at Mang Roldan with an excited smile.

"Should we try it?"

Moments later, after Kira helped Mang Roldan pour the cacao beans into an airtight plastic box, she offered him a mug of tsokolate again. His, this time. They sat across each other in the shop area, in that bistro table and those old chairs that Kira loved, a mug of the tsokolate in each of their hands. Judging from the scent, Mang Roldan had slightly burnt the cacao, but she didn't blame him. That was traditionally how the big manufacturers made their tableya, and the roast was going to be her contribution to the thing.

"I think we should toast?" she told him. "To love."

"To love," he agreed, with a nod. "And the people who remind us to be brave."

She took a sip. Kira let the chocolate melt slowly on

her tongue, spread warmly in her mouth. She closed her eyes.

Whoa.

Maybe it was because they were sitting in the bistro chairs in the shop and looking out the window. Maybe it was because she was sitting in a place that was so familiar to her, but Kira thought that the chocolate tasted like home. Something familiar, only just sweet enough but still comforting and delicious. There was a tapang to the chocolate, but only in the best ways.

But was it marketable? Did it have to be? Kira liked it, but would other people? Was that taste of home something only she knew, or would others recognize it, too?

The shop bell rang, and Kira looked up just in time to see Ate Nessie rush in looking completely frazzled, Mikaela close behind her with an equally worried expression. Mang Roldan immediately stood up from his seat and offered it to Nessie, and Kira was glad to see that Ate Nessie didn't shy away from the gesture, instead smiling at him. Mang Roldan grabbed the extra batibot chair one of Kira's staff handed him and offered it to Mikaela, before he stood behind Ate Nessie's chair.

"If you're going to tell me that Labander and Papermint decided not to take the space next door, I already know," Kira said with a little smile, because the tsokolate had put her in a good mood. "Sayang though, the labanderia/print shop idea sounded intriguing."

"No," Ate Nessie said, taking Roldan's mug and looking at him for permission. When he nodded, she took a deep gulp of the thing. "Wow. Mmm. Sarap."

"Ate Nessie," Mikaela said with a tiny voice. "We came here to…"

"Right! Hija!" Ate Nessie said, suddenly taking Kira's hand. "Does he have a plan? Tell me he has a plan!"

"Huh?" Kira asked in confusion. "Who has a plan?"

"Si Pogi!" she exclaimed, gasping when she realized Kira had no idea what she was talking about. "You don't know. Hesusmaryosep. San Sebastian." She made the sign of the cross and turned to Mikaela, who looked equally worried. "She doesn't know."

"Ah," Kira said, her shoulders dropping. "Santi."

"I said si pogi, right?"

"My mom works at Villa," Mikaela explained. "She told us about you, and Santi's family at the Villa lobby."

"Yes, well, it wasn't my finest moment." Kira winced. "No regrets, though."

"Good." Ate Nessie nodded, before she told Mikaela to continue.

"We also know about the memo," Mikaela said like she was bracing for impact. "The one where he was giving all the chocolate sales to Altair Chocolates."

"What? I should go to Villa," Mang Roldan suddenly said from behind Ate Nessie. "Speak to Boss Santi."

"I'll call Alfred!" Mikaela exclaimed. "We'll tell everyone to stop going to the breakfast buffet!"

"I'll join you," Ate Nessie agreed. "I'm also going to tell his Lally, he's going to be in *so much* trouble—"

"No, no, wait." Kira held her hands up to get them to stop.

Kira Luz believed in the universe. She believed in the alignment of the stars, in the positions of the moon having power over how the seemingly random moments of her life came together. But all of that was meaningless unless she actually chose to do something about it. There was only so much the universe could do. Right now, she had no doubt that Ate Nessie, Mang Roldan and Mikaela all came back for a reason. And Kira wasn't going to let the moment go to waste. She felt a surge of love for all of them, how they came back when they needed her.

"I know about the memo," she told them, prompting more confusion, but she assured them with a shake of her head that it was fine. "Santi has some things to figure out with his family, clearly. But I could use some help on this."

She remembered Santi standing in her kitchen laying out a plan with a pen and paper. Kira grabbed the same and outlined her own plan. She was going to throw half her presentation out the window, but bahala na. Especially when this could turn out much better than any deal she had with Carlton.

During their family dinner forever ago (it was last month, god time *flew* by), Kira's family had outlined Gemini's two options—increase her sales, or lower her costs. While Santi continued to work on increasing sales, Mang Roldan's gift was the perfect way to lower her costs.

She wrote down a list of all the things she needed to find out, of all the tasks that needed to be done. By the time she finished, Ate Nessie was looking at her like she was a completely different person, Mikaela was already processing the information, and Mang Roldan was waiting for instruction.

"Mang Roldan," Kira said. "I need to talk to Sam Tomas. Is she at the farm?"

"Yes."

"Good. Can I hitch a ride with you? Ate Nessie, I'm sure my parents have gotten wind of this, can you—"

"Assure them that you're an adult and you can handle this yourself?" she asked wryly. "Maybe. I'll have to make bonete."

"Use my kitchen if you need," Kira said with a nod. Things did tend to go smoother when there was bread around. Kira stood up and picked up her list, ticking off two items before consulting it again. If she didn't like lists before, she was definitely understanding their appeal now. "Mikaela, I need to run numbers on this, for sure."

"I'm free. I'm free all day," Mikaela said immediately, nodding. Kira thanked her, and was about to head to the kitchen to grab her stuff when Ate Nessie gasped.

"What about pogi boy?" she asked. "Si Santi?"

Kira inhaled sharply, using that breath to steel her. Because she really wished she could go to him, and ask him what the hell happened, listen to what he had to say. But there was no time for that. Santi would come to her if he needed help. Right now, she needed to help herself.

"He'll be okay," she said. "He knows what he has to do."

Meanwhile.
Carlton Hotels and Resorts Head Office.
Pasig City.

The Carlton Hotels and Resorts Head Office was established sometime around Santi's twelfth birthday. He'd seen it grow from a single-unit office, to a whole floor, then two floors. He knew where each department was, knew employees that had known him since he was in diapers. Knew what colors the walls used to be, how old a particular piece of furniture was, could remember when the hardwood floors were installed.

And yet he didn't feel that same sense of nostalgia that he expected as he walked into the Office of the Chairman. It was just another place to him, another thing he didn't feel connection to. How strange.

"Home at last," Vito announced as Santi walked into the room stuffed to the brim with every single award the Carlton had won, all the accolades it had earned with and without Santi's help. Vito's office had a stunning view of a mountain range a province away, Santi was never sure which. There was, as always, a cup of unfinished coffee on the desk, stacks of seemingly random scratch papers where Vito wrote most of his notes and calculations, and a framed photo of Miro and Santi on his desk. Not for the first time, he wondered where the man with the plastic chair at the beach in Nasugbu was. Maybe he was long gone, or maybe he was still here. Maybe Vito did love him, and this was the only way he knew how.

But Santi wasn't going to spend the rest of his life convincing himself that it was the truth, wasn't going to spend his life trying to justify his grandfather's actions. He had way too much self-respect for that.

"You've finally come to your senses," Vito said as Santi stood in front of his grandfather, trying to keep his expression neutral. He'd rehearsed his speech several times over when he was drafting it, when he was finalizing it. He practiced on Kira, practiced on the Cat (he didn't have the heart to name her quite yet), to himself on the drive over. He was a Virgo, after all, and Virgos made plans and rehearsed those plans.

But right now, he knew he was going to have to wing it a little.

"I won't stay long," he announced, ignoring the way his grandfather's face dropped. "How did you know that Kira owned Gemini Chocolates?"

If Vito knew what Santi was about to do, he didn't let it show. "Your staff was very tight-lipped about it." Vito huffed. "But as it turns out, your brother is very good at looking other people up. At least he's useful for something."

"I see." Santi sighed. He should have known Miro had dropped him somehow. He wondered vaguely what he got in exchange for the information. A car? Another condo? Would it be enough, for Miro to finally forgive whatever he thought Santi had done to him? "I wanted to give you my answer in person. You asked me to consider moving to Manila, before you forced my hand. And I've considered it."

"And?"

"I say no."

"No?"

"No to coming back to the Carlton, no to Manila, and everything you were thinking of offering to me. You already made me leave once, and I really don't want to come back."

"I wasn't giving you the option to say no," Vito said, his fist clenched on the desk. His nurse nearby peeked at them, ready to jump in if he needed it. Good.

"And isn't that exactly the problem?" Santi asked. "You taught me to always have an exit strategy, and here's mine."

"You are a part of my legacy, Anton. There is no exit from that," Vito said, and the words sent a shudder down Santi's spine. But he said nothing, and continued to say nothing, as he watched his grandfather.

He concluded that the old man from the beach didn't exist anymore. Vito was too old, too attached to his money, too used to using it to control others to still be the same man. But then again, Santi wasn't that kid from the beach anymore, either. He was older, and much smarter. He was willing to do anything for the people he loved, because he was the best person for the job.

Vito was born mid-October, and it occurred to Santi that if he'd told Kira that, she would have known exactly what brand of evil Vito was. She would have told him that Vito was born on a Libra-Scorpio cusp, making him prone to drama, indecision and heavy criticism. People born under the cusp were notorious for testing their love, cynical and judgmental. A horrible match for an earth sign, she would say.

Because Kira knew everything.

And when she didn't, Santi did. It made them a great team, really.

So, here were the facts, in no particular order;

1. He was probably never going to see or speak to his grandfather again, after today, even if he wanted to. It made him sad, but he was ready to accept that. It was that or keep throwing himself into the Tokyo subway train loop that was the Santillan family, and he really couldn't put himself through that anymore.

2. Santi was exhausted by all of this. He really wished he was eating a cookie right about now. Or chocolate. Maybe both.

3. But he was going to do it anyway. Because he was wonderful. And smart. He was downright brilliant. And damn it, he was going to stay in Lipa.

4. And, that the next thing he said was probably going to give Vito a lot to think about.

(He also knew that his own silence was killing Vito. The man never did enjoy silence.)

Santi wished he was a saint, or a bigger person. Then he would be able to swallow his pain, his pride, and just be the perfect grandson. He was neither of those things. Oddly enough, he was proud of himself for that. He was wonderful, the way he was.

"What do you want from me, Lolo?" Santi asked instead. "You don't need to control me. I already love you. And your money isn't why."

It was hard to describe the look on Vito's face, but Santi had studied his grandfather's faces, his expressions long enough to read them as quickly as he could make them. Surprise gave way to hurt, only to be replaced with a sneer.

"You must really be naive to think that love has anything to do with this," Vito said in response. "You still need me, Anton."

That was the problem, wasn't it? Vito had horribly miscalculated. And need couldn't be the basis of love, especially now that Santi was old enough to know himself better. Oh, it could be a foundation—he and Kira built their relationship around a childhood promise just like that—but love needed choosing, action, listening, devotion. It was a verb that was reciprocated, grew and moved.

Money had its limits. So did control. And Vito had used them both to replace love, and made his family believe that an iron grip was the only way to make sure somebody stayed, and loved you.

Anton had learned the hard way that it wasn't true.

"You know, I'm actually very happy in Lipa," he told Vito, looking out at the view and imagining his home there. He pictured Gabriel behind the counter at Sunday Bakery, Kira wreaking havoc in Gemini, Sari watching from her windowsill in Café Cecilia. "After everything you did, it's something you never quite managed to take away from me. The only thing I need right now is to live as happy a life as I can, and I'm sorry that it seems to kill you inside when I do."

He looked down at his grandfather. "But one day, and I hope that day doesn't come soon, you're going to leave this earth, and you can't take your legacy with you. Then my parents will follow, and by that time, everything will fall to me and Miro. The hotels, the resorts, the money, whatever is left. And I fully intend on giving away everything I can. The legacy you're so proud of will no longer exist, and nobody will remember the Carlton. I'm okay with that. But I don't think you have that much time to figure out a game plan."

Santi knew he was going to do the math on this eventually—he would probably have to sell his condo in Ortigas, he wouldn't need it anymore. He would have to figure out a way for Gemini to make whatever Vito had taken away, and he was meeting Chloe Agila after this. Vito would likely come for Villa out of spite, but Santi already had a plan for that.

Those were easy costs. Calculable costs.

But he had to admit, seeing the fury in his grandfather's face? Was absolutely priceless.

Chapter Sixteen

> Today's Horoscope: Some things are just meant
> to be.

There were always places to escape to, if one knew where to look.

When Kira and Santi were kids, that place was the secret corner of the Azotea Ballroom. Of the many, many special events that they celebrated there, it was nice to have a corner of the ballroom that you could make your hideout, a place where the adults couldn't find you, a place that wasn't as boring as whatever was going on inside.

The ballroom was designed as a large floorspace with terra-cotta-colored tiles in an elegant ogee pattern. The outside was separated from the inside by large sliding doors made of sturdy wood, with blue glass on top of the windowsill. With the ballroom's high ceiling and the ability to let in as much air as needed, it wasn't hard to imagine why it was always booked solid.

This hidden corner in the ballroom wasn't really secret, because there was a batibot chair, a small round table strategically placed with a vase of flowers that were always different, but you needed to move the ballroom's sliding door just right to get to it, and of course Santi knew exactly how to get to it.

This was where they'd made their first promises. After Kira thwacked him in the head and gave him his scar, because he told her he was moving to Manila, and he was all bandaged up, he pulled her hand and they escaped to this little corner of the ballroom.

"Sit," she remembered Santi saying, stubborn even as a kid.

"*You* sit," she'd insisted, because even as a kid she'd been stubborn, full stop. "I have something to say."

Even from where she was sitting, Kira could hear the chatter of the Luz clan inside. Business had been properly conducted, the family plans were set in place for the year. All that was left was the best part—lunch.

But Kira didn't really feel like eating right now, even if the bagnet kare-kare had looked tempting. Right now she needed time to herself, to process what had happened in that ballroom.

The sudden, but soft downpour of rain made it feel like there was a strange magic in the air, and made Kira want to stare out at the garden all the more. The ballroom was bordered by tropical plants, mostly birds of paradise, and capiz lanterns that lit up the space. There was a bamboo fence behind the plants, but it was the side of the property that faced a still-empty lot. Kira listened to the falling rain, listened to the music, and closed her eyes.

She'd done it. It had taken two sleepless nights, a lot of her and Sam Tomas talking and asking each other questions in circles, ordering a *lot* of takeout until they finally remembered that Sari was much better at this stuff, and asked for her help. But they'd done it.

If Kira worked alongside Tomas Coffee Co. and paid the farmers' family members seeking part-time employment to ferment and sort the beans for her, she would create a whole supply chain that actually reduced her costs, enough to meet her deadlines on the return on investment.

Enough to save Gemini, and for Kira to keep her place in the community that she loved being a part of. Giving her the chance to play with the Batangas cacao, finding out her flavors was just the fun part.

She had to admit, seeing her family's slightly stunned faces at her presentation was delightful. Just about as delightful as Tito Nicos bringing up the Carlton's letter of interest to buy the Laneways, and every Luz in attendance laughing like it was some cosmic joke. Her cousin Kuya Uno looked aghast, until his own father explained it to him.

"We would never sell the Laneways, Uno," Tito Nicos explained. "It's a safe space for anyone in our family who needs it. And someone will always need it."

Kira laughed, and hot air blew out of her. The cool air of December and January had dissipated, and summer was creeping its long arm into the tropics. Thank you, global warming, but summers in Lipa always came in hot and angry, even when it was raining. Heat just settled under the skin like you were walking through a hot swamp. The night air was cooler, but it was still early evening, and the rocks on the ground seemed to be radiating heat, more so when the rain fell on them.

With summers came better things. New things.

"You have to promise that you'll come back. When I'm old, like, thirty, and when I need you most. Like a knight in shining armor. With a horse and everything!"

The funny thing about princesses waiting for knights to save them was that eventually they would figure out a way to save themselves. The knight was simply the getaway vehicle. Or maybe the knight was the one that believed in them, so the princess believed in themselves.

Something like that.

Kira rested her elbow on the table next to her, and her chin on her palm. Who would have thought that making business presentations about supply chains to her family would be so exhausting? The vote to keep Gemini running had been unanimous, helped along by samples of the new chocolate.

Inside, she heard cheering and roars of happiness (because it wouldn't be a family event if someone didn't roar of happiness). Just as Kira was about to check it out, the door suddenly slid open, revealing Kuya Kiko glaring at her.

"Gah!" Kira exclaimed, practically falling off of the metal chair. "Kuya, what the hell!"

"What do you mean, what the hell, I wasn't exactly being subtle when I said, 'Kira, are you here, how the fuck does this door work?'" Kiko said, taking the second batibot chair and looking out at the view. He smelled a little like kare-kare and Kira's stomach grumbled. Maybe the dramatic muni-muni was best done *after* lunch. "You missed the proposal. Apparently Kuya Uno wanted to move back to Lipa to be with his girlfriend. When the board officially voted for him to take over the Laneways, he proposed."

"That's...sweet?" Kira asked, unsure how romantic a board meeting proposal was. But maybe it was a thing for his cousin, to move back. It certainly had been for Santi.

"It was a little dramatic for me. Pero I guess the couple is happy?" Kiko shrugged. "Makes you think."

Kira gasped and turned to her brother. "Kuya, if you want to go to the States to get married, I will support you one billion percent, I will officiate the wedding if I have to, I will bully anyone who says it's not legal."

"I appreciate the sentiment, Kiki, but Jake and I decided we wouldn't think about marriage until it's available here, and I don't think it's going to happen in our lifetime," Kiko explained, a wistful little smile on his face. "I think it's more than enough for now for us to stay together the way we are, to decide on these things together."

"Were you guys always so wise that way?" Kira asked, sighing as she leaned against her chair. "Sana all."

"Definitely not." Kiko laughed with all the wisdom of a man in a two-year relationship. "Half our issues were because we kept waiting for the other to say something. It gets easier, but it's always like pulling water from a stone."

She hadn't even realized that she was scowling until Kiko gave her leg a playful kick. "Hey, watch the skirts, bro!"

"Kasi naman, who wears long skirts to a board meeting!"

"I do! And so does the Duchess of Sussex, leave me alone. Lola Luz said I looked very professional, okay."

"Kiki. You know it hurts my heart to see you brooding. It's like hearing a sad puppy whimper," Kiko laughed. "Is this about Santi?"

"Maybe." Bless Kuya Kiko, who probably didn't know what was going on, but had noticed Santi's absence in the meeting.

"Whatever it is, just remember it's a conversation. You have to find the happy that you both can live with."

"You don't let the other sacrifice themselves to freeze in the sea." Kira nodded, because she'd pulled the *Titanic* card from her movie oracle cards that morning. She'd thought it was a bad sign, but to be fair, it was one of the top earners in the world at some point. Kira explained as much to Kiko.

"You still use that oracle deck?"

"Kuya, it's me. Of course I still use it. Unlike some Tauruses who sold my last Christmas gift to them."

"It was the thought that counted!" he exclaimed, brandishing the fountain pen he'd bought to replace the one she got him. Something about the nib being "too thick."

"But did I tell you that deck used to be mine?"

At Kira's wide-eyed stare, he chuckled. "Shocked, bes?"

"You gave me a *secondhand* gift?" She gasped in mock horror.

"Excuse me, not secondhand, sentimental," Kiko corrected her. "I was so desperate for guidance when Jake and I first started dating that I got that set off of the Internet. I don't know if I really *believed* in it or not, I mean, one of the cards just says, 'phone home.' But it was comforting. It made me feel a little less…"

"Less alone," Kira agreed, nodding. Because it really did. Oh, she knew there was some ridiculousness to all of this, her trust in the stars, in plans and divine beings, that pulling a random card from a pile meant anything, but it was comforting.

And it never steered her wrong so far.

"Exactly," Kiko agreed. Then he shifted uncomfortably in his seat, and Kira was pretty sure it wasn't because batibot chairs were the least comfortable things to sit on. "Listen, Kira. I think we were a bit too hard on you last time, when we talked about Gemini…"

"Medyo lang?" Kira asked, raising a brow because she was going to need him to grovel a little more.

"Okay, we were a *lot* hard on you about the Gemini thing," Kiko admitted sheepishly. "And I'm not making excuses for what we said, but you actually did it. You found your own way to save it."

She didn't know about saving. There were a lot of things that could still go horribly wrong. But as long as she stuck to her goals, and faced her issues head-on, she knew she would be okay. *No fear,* as the Swan Princess movie taught her.

"I actually stepped out here because I got a call from Chloe Agila," Kira explained to her brother, feeling a little smug, and rightly so. "Apparently, Altair Chocolates has been made the exclusive distributor of the Carlton Hotels."

"What?" Kiko said. "Even—"

"Even Villa." Kira nodded. "It's why I had to redo my entire presentation. It's why Santi isn't here."

"Shit." Kiko winced.

"Shit talaga," Kira agreed, frowning. It was why she still hadn't left that corner of the room, despite the fact that the call had happened about an hour ago. "But apparently, the order is too big for Altair to do by itself. So Chloe wants to start a, what did she call it, a collective? She wants chocolate makers all over the country to pool together our resources to make chocolates that we will sell to the collective, and the collective will sell to Carlton, or any other client that's interested in Filipino chocolate. So instead of one maker getting all the contracts, we share them all."

"Wow," Kiko said, and Kira nodded again.

Chloe had come to Kira with the proposal to make something she didn't think was possible—a new community, full of chocolate makers from this country, sharing the same problems, selling their chocolates together. There were things to work out, of course. So many details, still. But it was *something*. And it felt right.

Chloe said over the phone that Kira was the first person she'd called about the proposal. And Kira knew that there was only one person who could have led Chloe to her.

I just need someone to believe in me. For once in my life.

And he had. He always had.

"I couldn't have done it without the people around me, you know," Kira pointed out. "People who don't complain when I need something, people who listen when I need it. People who make me strong. Like you guys."

Kira smiled at her brother, and that vote of confidence from him meant a lot more to her than she would ever be able to express. But it felt like they were on equal footing somehow.

"What do we do about Santi, then? Do you need me to kick his ass? I know he's tall and can cut me in half with that jaw of his, but I can totally take him."

"Oh god. Huwag na." Kira laughed. "You just had lunch, and he's got terrible eyesight."

"Sure ka? I'm super sober no," Kiko insisted, before he burped, and both Luz siblings wrinkled their noses. "Or not."

Eventually she found her way back into the ballroom, and back to her own plate of bagnet kare-kare, which really was its own level of deliciousness. By the time she joined the family in the festivities, she threw herself into the role of being the consummate pamangkin—talking about how she made her tsokolate so good (it's all in the fresh milk, tita!), if the SM really had Uniqlo (yes, Tito) and what time the next Mass at Redemptorist was (there's one at 5 p.m., po).

"Is it true that the owner of this hotel is your boyfriend, hija?" Tita Maricel, married to Tito Nicos and always up to date with the chika, asked. "That suplado one, the one that looks like an oppa?"

"Um," Kira said, unsure how to answer a question that was suddenly way too complicated. *Yes, he's still my boyfriend. He still owns the hotel...probably.* Ugh, too many minefields. She decided to smile instead.

"Ay look at that smile," she cooed. "I'm looking forward to attending another wedding in this ballroom. Did you hear about the governor's son's wedding here?"

It was the perfect opportunity to escape to the buffet table, which was looking a lot less laden with food than it had been when Kira first left the ballroom. She was contemplating the kuchinta when someone stood next to her and started to put brownies on his plate. A *lot* of brownies on his plate. Kira tried to stifle a little giggle, only for Uno Luz to stop mid-take and look at her oddly.

"This is for me and my fiancée," he explained. Kuya Uno had been stiff and standoffish throughout the board meeting, like he wasn't quite sure how he'd ended up in a ballroom of a boutique hotel in Batangas. But hey, if he was comfortable enough to ask someone to marry him here, maybe he would do well.

"No, Kuya, I'm just glad you're enjoying them." Kira smiled. "They're made with Gemini chocolate."

"Are they?" he asked, then had the decency to look slightly embarrassed. "I should know that."

"Well, you're still learning." Kira shrugged. "And I'm happy to help if you need it."

"Thank you," he said with a little smile. "You know, I was worried that you were going to be dramatic about this whole, 'me looking into your business' thing."

"Oh, I get it. It's something everyone has to go through; it's normal, it's not devastating. I've heard all the reasons why I shouldn't have worried." She shrugged. Easy to say now, but… "And maybe you thought I would be dramatic because the last time we actually talked, I was twelve, and you told me Kurama would never love me," she said with a quirked brow, because Scorpios held grudges like nobody's business.

"Well…yes," Kuya Uno admitted, and Kira really appreciated that it was impossible for her cousin to hide his embarrassment. It made his Wharton-educated ass seem a lot more approachable. Even if he was still a bit of an ass. Was there such a thing as a half-ass? "But you know it's not personal, right? It's just business."

Kira sighed. She picked up the second kutsinta. She freaking deserved it, if she was going to have this conversation. "Kuya Uno. If you still think that, then I think you have quite a lot to learn about the Laneways."

She really did wish him all the best. She also had no doubt that Ate Nessie was going to have him wrapped around her middle finger very soon. "It's not personal to you, but it is to me. It's personal to the shop owners, to the family, and to everyone there. You saw how quickly they shot down the Carlton Group's letter of intent."

"Right." He frowned. "I did think that was the wrong move, to not even consider…"

"It's land. It's not going away anytime soon." Kira shook her head. He still didn't get it. "It's a safe space, Kuya. And honestly, it could be yours too, if you need it."

That made him pause. He looked at Kira like she was a completely different person, like he hadn't really seen her until now. Which wasn't fine, but it was more his loss than hers.

"I…" he finally said. "I suppose."

Kira couldn't help herself. She laughed, leaving her cousin completely bewildered as she went to join the rest of the family making plans for Christmas.

It was later in the evening when Santi finally showed up. At this point, the Luz family was now in full family reunion mode, and it wasn't a family reunion without "Dancing in September" playing in the distance. Technically they were well over their number of hours rented on the venue, but the staff of Villa didn't seem in any rush to kick them out. Even if they were already discreetly bringing out the coffee and the dinner menu.

Kira had the kind of family that stuck around for events, just to make sure nobody else needed an extra hand, offering rides home to anyone who needed it. So after she smiled at a few titas and titos, assured them that no, she was definitely *not* next to get married, she escaped again. Out of the ballroom and to the walk-way that connected it to the hotel, a long winding path in brick that had a trellis with pothos plants to protect the person walking from rain.

She was standing at the entrance of the ballroom, leaning against the wall and brooding like a princess in a tower, when her knight in shining armor *finally* showed up.

It was funny, watching Santi walk to her now.

He'd done it before, of course. The man liked a good, dramatic walkup. But New Year had been about Santi taking a stand, showing her nothing but only his best side as he came to her. Back then, she had seen his determination, his arresting but quiet strength. New Year's Eve he was striding toward her with Darcy's sheer confidence and hope, *as I had scarcely ever allowed myself to hope before.*

It was hard to believe that the man that had frustrated her, challenged her—so stubborn that only Vigan longganisa sandwiches had gotten through to him— was the same man walking up to her today. Santi was walking to her with a smile. Hesitant, but he was there. He also looked exhausted, like he was in desperate need of a hug, and then a nap. He still made her heart sing. He still believed in her. He still had a savior com-

plex that she knew was going to cause them a *lot* of
trouble in the future.

But he was here. Just as he said he was, that New
Year's Eve. She didn't know where he'd been, what
happened with his grandfather. She didn't know what
the future would look like for the both of them. But she
had a sneaking suspicion that it was going to be okay.

"Hey," she told him, smiling, although she knew it
wasn't her brightest, or her best. "You're late."

"Hi," he said, stopping just in front of her, tucking
his hands into his pockets. He'd pushed up his sleeves.
And not only was it slightly distracting, it also told her
that he hadn't missed the board meeting just because.
Things had been done. "I'm sorry. I've been talking
to lawyers for the last two days. Name a form of communication, we've probably done it."

"Morse code? Messenger hawk? Coded messages,
skywriting?"

"Okay, maybe not," Santi sighed. "How was the
meeting?"

"Are you moving back to Manila?"

There was a moment where Kira thought that he
would tell her that he was. That he had decided to take
the hard way out and leave. But the moment came as
quickly as it passed. She knew better now.

A familiar song filled the air. "Moon River," playing on a violin. One of her cousins was probably asked
to perform for the adults, as standard family reunion
practice.

She'd just recognized the song when Santi took
those last few steps to her, wrapped his arms around
her, and kissed her like there was no tomorrow. The
kiss was gentle and soft, but it seared through her.

And while the kiss was good, the hug was even better. Kira was able to bury her face in his chest and smile, was allowed to hold as close to him as he would allow. Santi didn't tell her to stop, and held her just as tightly.

Air filled Kira's lungs as she inhaled, breathing in the smell of Santi, so tangible and real. Every bone in her body seemed to melt into him, and it was the sweet, sweet feeling of relief. Relief that she had her answers, that she could finally stop waiting, that she'd managed to do this. That *they* had managed to do this.

And strangely enough, it was like she'd lived this moment before, a thousand other times in another thousand lifetimes. All of them with this sweet happiness, with this person. They had both come out of their journeys by themselves, but couldn't have done it without the other. It was like the end of the movie, when the two leads would reunite, and the camera would pull in close, to capture them in a kiss.

Then there would be a big dance number. Kira had always loved those.

"I told him to take everything," Santi said. "And he will. But he's not going to get what really matters. *This* is what really matters. And I'm staying."

She heard him release a shaky sigh. And she felt his body shake, and her shoulder get wet, just a little. They were both too old for his shit.

"I saved the business," Kira announced. "The family agreed to give me more time, and I set up a whole supply chain to provide beans."

"A whole supply chain?"

"You would be so proud. I made a process flowchart and everything."

He pulled away from her as she wiped at her nose

with her sleeve, and his eyes were red-rimmed. Kira looked into the face she knew so well. The one she would get to know more of. She smiled, and this time it filled her whole heart, the one that he held. She kissed him again. And this time, it didn't feel like a goodbye.

It felt like a promise.

Chapter Seventeen

February 18
Sunday Bakery
The Laneways

Tempering: heating and cooling chocolate to stabilize it, to give it a smooth and glossy finish.
Exact temperatures are required, and can be extremely frustrating. But when you manage to make it happen, it's the best feeling ever. Totally worth it.

"I don't understand," Sari said, frowning at Kira from her seat in Sunday Bakery's dining area. "So do they live happily ever after?"

"Not yet," Kira explained, shaking her head. "Sari, this is a K-drama. All loose ends have to be tied nicely before you get to the wedding scene. Maybe someone gets amnesia at the second-to-the-last episode. After a car crash! Gasp!"

"Oh god." Sari, practical Capricorn as always, rolled her eyes. "That sounds exhausting."

"That's *drama*, girl!"

"Bro! Stop. Hoarding. The chocolate," Gabriel hissed at Santi before he pulled the plastic tub containing squares of white chocolate Kira had made an hour before.

It wasn't Santi's finest hour, coming and asking Kira to explain to him what she had told the board. She let him ask his questions, let him talk while making chocolate, until he ran out of things to say, and she handed him a square of the dayap white chocolate.

"I appreciate your help, Santi, I do," she'd assured him. "But I'll come to you if I need help. Now can you tell me if this flavor combination is good, or amazing?"

The chocolate was white, and had a slightly caramelly sweetness to it, made with dayap rinds and a dayap flavoring that one of the titas from Haraya had offered to her as a sample. The experiment resulted in a slightly fruity chocolate, with a gorgeously subtle floral aftertaste, and just the tiniest kirot of sour from the key lime.

There was more than enough left for today's brainstorming session at Sunday Bakery. Santi and Gabriel were currently fighting over the last few squares from a one-kilo batch they whittled down quickly. Gabriel was vehement on his insistence that it was unfair that Santi felt the need to take away the one thing that was making him happy, and—

"Excuse me, the *one* thing?" Gabriel's girlfriend asked, and let nobody ever face Sari Tomas's wrath in a brow-raising contest because they were sure to lose. Sari opened her palm toward Gabriel to give her the tub. "Hand it over, dimples."

"But, Sari!"

"I can always make more, guys," Kira assured them, totally amused at her friends fighting over her chocolate. Santi knew that amusement in her tone, she was genuinely happy about their reaction, but god, she'd made something pretty magical.

Santi would have been the first to refute the existence of magic, but maybe the thing about magic was that it was something you made. When you managed to make things align perfectly, when things went the way they should, you called it magic.

And right now, despite all the mess he'd managed to make, the mess they were now going to try to clean up, and the mess that his family made, it seemed magic still had a way of coming through. Looking at Kira, at her happiness, he was happy to be a part of it.

"I still think I can make it better," she was saying. "I get that initial snap when you bring it out, but it doesn't last! Tempering is *such* a bitch."

"It's *your* bitch, though," Gabriel assured her, licking bits of melted dark chocolate on his fingers. Santi concurred with a nod, still savoring the little square he'd managed to purloin before they handed the tub to Sari. God, this stuff was addicting. Not that he ever stood any chance against Kira's chocolate.

"Also, shh, the chocolate will hear you," Sari chided Kira, covering the top of the tub with her hand. "Is this the chocolate you're selling to Chloe Agila?"

Santi inhaled sharply, lest the feelings that bubbled up in his chest accidentally burst out of him, and wouldn't that be embarrassing? But he was just so damn proud of Kira, for never being afraid of what her business threw at her, for doing things her way. He wanted to do everything he could to help her, to make sure that she was happy in this thing that clearly made her so happy.

Love just didn't seem to encompass how he felt for

her. Neither did the word "girlfriend." (Wife, maybe, but that was another thing entirely.)

"Not this," Kira chortled, shaking her head, and Santi gave in to the urge to reach for her hand in front of her friends, because he could, because he wanted to. He squeezed it, and saw the little blush that appeared on Kira's cheeks, which made him smile. "There's still a lot of things to hammer out with the collective, but I think I want to keep this chocolate just us for now. I can do that now."

Lightness had surrounded Kira ever since the board meeting. Santi wasn't ashamed to admit that he was jealous of the happiness she'd managed to achieve, the realization that she'd done enough, that she could keep on doing what she enjoyed, with all its heartaches and impossible-to-temper-ness.

"By the way, I've been thinking about what you can do with your retained earnings," Santi said. "Now that you're seeing a profit, you can set a percentage aside, grow that, and then reinvest it in something your family might find worthwhile. Like set up a scholarship fund, or a small business loan."

Kira's face lit up at the thought. "Santi, that's amazing! I have to pitch it, but—"

"Hoy hoy hoy, lovers and do-gooders, Wonder Boy and Choco Girl," Gabriel said, successfully grabbing a square from the tub in Sari's hands, grinning at his girlfriend's mock indignation. *Wonder Boy?*

"Choco Girl?" Kira snorted. "Boo."

"Okay, okay." Gabriel admitted defeat. "We can save the world later. I thought we were supposed to be figuring out how to rescue Wonder Boy's hotel from the clutches of his evil family?"

Santi tilted his head slightly as he considered that. One would think that he would be offended that his friend was calling his family evil, but oddly enough, he felt…okay with it. His family was what they were.

Was he still terrified he would end up like them? Of course. But he really was trying not to be. He was going to have to make peace with the facts that had presented themselves, which were the following:

1. His family loved him. They really did, or else they wouldn't claim to need him as much as they did.

2. But that didn't mean that it was enough. They just loved other things more. And that was okay. That was their problem, not his.

3. Santi had found the kind of love he needed somewhere else. Here.

4. And he was going to make damn sure every day that he would make his family here feel loved. That they would never doubt how important they were to him.

He felt the squeeze of Kira's hand, and he gave her a soft smile back. There was no doubt about it. He belonged here with her, with the place that welcomed him back, the place that made him feel valued in a way that he could give.

Now if only they could figure out how things were going to be settled. After Santi left Vito's office, his grandfather sent a letter saying that Santi was no longer allowed on the Villa premises. And no matter what Chloe said, Santi was *not* happy about Gemini losing the contract to Villa because of his grandfather's pettiness. Emotionally manipulating Santi was one thing; deliberately harming someone else's business was another.

And, because he was petty, and extra bitter, he did *not* want Villa to end up with the Santillans. Not to mention his Lally would kill him if it did.

"What's your end goal, Santi?" Sari asked, still cradling the slowly diminishing tub of chocolate as Gabriel served fresh-from-the-upstairs oven pan de sal, along with this incredible (if he did say so himself, and he did) dip thing Santi made of smoked tinapa with cream cheese and ebiko. There was also a carafe of dalandan juice, and water, and really, did you need anything else? "What are we trying to achieve here?"

Santi looked at the spread of food, at his friends passing around the warm, impossibly pillowy-soft bread. He contemplated the steam that rose from the bread as he split his own roll, and added a generous helping of the spread to the sandwich. Nobody protested, or told him he took too much. Nobody asked him to make their sandwich for them. Santi held the finished sandwich in his hand. It was very easy to tell them what he wanted, now.

He handed the finished roll to Kira, who accepted it gratefully. The little moan of delight she made when she took a bite made Santi smile.

"Happily ever after?" he asked. "Is that too much to ask?"

"Aw—" Kira began, but was cut off by Gabriel.

"Aww! Stop," Gabriel cooed, pinching Santi's cheek playfully. "God, you are adorable when you're being sweet."

"Isn't he?" Kira giggled. Santi was not used to being praised like this, and pretended to be way too absorbed in making his own pan de sal while Sari laughed and rolled her eyes. The shop door opened then, signaled by a bell that Gabriel attached, and in walked Ate Tiana Villa, her eyes way too focused on the pastry case to notice her cousin and friends occupying the bakery tables.

"Please tell me they still have those Birthday Cake cookies left, I have a *need*," she announced, walking to the case, her eyes scanning the contents.

"I've got them!" Gabriel sprung up from his chair like a mushroom, making Ate Tiana jump in surprise and turn to the little brain trust that had gathered around the pan de sal and spread. Her brow rose at the sight.

"This is a bakery and a sweets shop. What are you doing with Ton-Ton's tinapa spread?" she asked, taking the seat Gabriel graciously offered, as Santi passed the bread and spread to his cousin, who made herself a sandwich as well. One does not simply ignore tinapa spread.

"We needed brain food," Santi explained. Then Kira jumped in and told his cousin about everything that happened with Lolo Vito, and why they were stuck at the moment. Santi was actually tired of rehashing and reliving the story over and over, out loud and in his head, and was grateful that Kira jumped in when she did.

But when she finished, they were met with a confused stare from Ate Tiana, who looked at Santi like she was surprised he hadn't come up with the answer yet.

"Hoy," Ate Tiana said, making herself another sandwich. This spread really was addicting. "Have you really not talked to Lally?"

Kira's and Sari's heads shot to Santi, and he very

much felt like a mouse caught in a corner, or the first time he saw the Cat walking into his kitchen (she wasn't his cat, therefore Santi couldn't call her anything else, despite her living with him for the last week) and she'd been completely surprised that he lived in it.

"What does Lally have to do with this?" he asked.

"Dude." Ate Tiana rolled her eyes. "Kaya pala, she's been bugging me to talk to you. She got an offer for Hotel Villa from the Marbella Hotel and Resorts. Apparently your Tita Ria called her, and she's married to—"

"Johnny Marbella." Santi's brow rose. The Marbellas were Carlton's biggest competition, just because they had partnered with the Langbourne Hotels from England and had the backing to run smaller, boutique hotels. That they were interested in Villa made sense, as it fit in perfectly with the brand, but… "Is Lally interested in selling?" Santi asked.

"Yes!" Tiana exclaimed. "She just has to terminate her lease with you to do it."

"Lease?" Sari echoed. "Santi, you didn't *buy* Villa?"

"No, I rented it from my grandmother," Santi explained. From the way Kira and Sari exchanged shocked looks, it seemed the gossip circles had gotten something wrong. Santi would have laughed, but he was too stuck on his grandmother wanting to sell her hotel. "It was the smarter choice."

"It was his exit strategy, because of *course* he has an exit strategy," Tiana said by way of explanation, which was true.

When Santi took over the hotel, he'd promised his Lally two things—that he would restore the hotel to its former glory, and that he would never take it away from the Villas. Everyone had just assumed that Santi bought it, but it hadn't felt right, completely taking it from them. His company held the usage rights to the land and the hotel, as well as the Hotel Villa name. It was Santi's company that held the franchise agreement with Carlton.

"Yes," he agreed. "But I didn't want to terminate the lease because Gemini was at stake. Lally could still say no."

"Oh. Oh!" Kira exclaimed, because of course she understood. This was her job, after all. "If you convince your Lola to pre-terminate the lease, all she has to do is return your deposit—"

"Made with Lolo's money," he pointed out.

"And Vito won't have any say in the hotel anymore. Then she can sell to the Marbellas if she wants!"

"Which she already said she wanted to do, which you would have known if you actually went to *see* her, Ton-ton." Tiana rolled her eyes at him. "God, you are *so* wrapped up in your own problems sometimes."

"I didn't want to bother her," Santi argued. "She's 85! She must have other concerns."

"She's only 85, and her main concern has been you, especially when everyone heard your Lolo was coming back and taking over the place," Tiana explained.

Santi sighed and immediately recalled his grandmother's stern face, how she thinned her lips when she was annoyed. He hated that the next time he saw her, it was to ask her to give up the lease with his company. Another reason why he hadn't wanted to take this exit strategy.

"She's rich, thanks to you, twice over. The improvements you made to Villa increased its value ng bong-gang-bongga, and that fund thing you put her deposit in, earned way more than she ever thought she needed."

From the counter, Gabriel chuckled as he waited for the cookies to finish warming up. "Damn, Santi," he said. "Do your hands itch, like *all* the time? Money just walks up to you, no?"

"I placed her deposit in a bond fund that matures this year." Santi shrugged. "I thought it would be better for Lally if her money worked for her. It's easier if you do your research."

"Wow," Sari said, shaking her head before she turned to Kira. "What's it like to live with a peak Atenista, bro?"

"Pare naman. First of all, Gab and I are Ateneans and *we* don't talk like that." Kira chuckled, ignoring Santi's frown while he muttered, "You do, a little."

"Second of all, he doesn't just talk like an Atenean, he talks like a guy in School of Management that wears boat shoes, a polo shirt and khaki shorts to school every day."

"A mood," Gabriel concurred from behind the counter. Sari the UP grad was almost rolling on the floor laughing.

"Third of all," Kira added further. "He's generous and lovely, and he's really good in bed. He's stubborn, and a pain in the ass sometimes, but he's *my* pain in the ass, and I love him."

Santi knew his friends were making fun of him, but it still made his heart melt to be a part of all of this. He wanted to hug Kira, but he knew that they were never going to hear the end of it, especially from Ate Tiana, so he resolved to squeeze her hand instead, unable to hide his little grin.

"Wait, so it's resolved?" Sari asked, slightly confused. "The Villas pre-terminate the lease and the hotel is just…free?"

"I'll pay Lolo Vito the deposit," Santi amended. "I've made a few investments myself, and I have enough. Lally shouldn't have to lose money for my mistake. As I said, I was more worried about Gemini, but—"

"Yeah, I saved myself before the knight could, this time," Kira noted, her nose wrinkling even as she grinned. "But I think I'm more than happy that he's going to stick around."

It felt good to hear. And maybe, that lightness Kira had been carrying around her rubbed off on him, too.

Two weeks later, Santi paced the empty restaurant, trying his hardest not to watch Ate Tiana as his cousin frowned down at the memo in her hand. It had taken Santi most of last night (and a lot of this morning) to draft the memo explaining the situation to his employees, how Santi had the Marbellas ensure that nothing would change for the employees or their suppliers, except management would change.

The first thing he did after that brainstorming session, fueled by white chocolate and good food, was to drive to Mahogany, deep in the heart of the bayan, to see Lola Leona Villa. Lally had been happy to see him, which Santi didn't expect, or think he deserved. But she accepted his mano anyway, before pressing a hand to his cheek.

"Hay ikaw. Ka-tigas ng ulo," she'd tutted. "Thank god."

He didn't realize that he needed that validation until

she gave it. And after that merienda where she chastised him for being stubborn, for not seeing her, for not bringing Kira (because of course she knew he was with Kira), for letting someone like Vito Santillan walk all over him, Santi had settled into a routine of going to see Lally once a week to get her to boss him around and make lunch. Most of the time they were with the Villa family lawyer, discussing the sale of the hotel, once with Tita Ria, and more than a few times with Kira or the cousins.

After the Villas issued their notice that they wanted to pre-terminate the lease, and news got around that the Marbellas were interested in the hotel, Santi paid his grandfather the pre-termination deposit on the rent.

Santi had not heard from his family since. He didn't hear from Miro, his Aunt Joyce, not even his parents. Not that it was a huge loss, but it was a loss anyway. He would be lying if he said it didn't hurt. He didn't regret the choices he made, not one bit. But it felt like he'd left a very, very old piece of himself with them, and they refused to believe that Santi wasn't that same dutiful golden boy anymore.

There were better things to look forward to, even if he knew that the piece of his heart he'd left in Manila would always feel like a hole in his chest. The Santillan family was content to ignore what had happened, but when Santi met with the Tito Johnny, he'd said that Vito had nothing but awful things to say about his grandson.

"I get it." Tito Johnny shrugged. "Family, am I right?"

"Exactly," Santi had chuckled. "Now should we talk

about how you're going to maintain all of Villa's current contracts with its suppliers and employees?"

The new routine suited him, Santi liked to think. And with Villa no longer a factor, and La Spezia being set up somewhere else (there was an available spot in the Laneways, last he heard), it was more than enough to make him feel like he'd made the right call. Looking at his office no longer conjured up memories of walking into Vito's office and imagining himself there; walking through Villa and speaking to the staff didn't remind him of his family anymore.

He felt free, freer than he had ever been allowed before.

"I knew you would figure it out," Tiana said, lowering the memo and shaking her head. "You've always been smart."

Santi was raised to think that being smart was a given. Of course he was smart, how else was he going to help the family if he wasn't? Over time that smartness had gotten him in a lot of trouble. But as long as he used it to help other people like this, to keep transitions like this one smooth, he was happy to have it.

"It doesn't sound too personal?" Santi frowned.

"You ran this place for three years. Of course it's personal, Ton-ton," Ate Tiana said, tapping his shoulder. "This isn't *You've Got Mail*."

"I haven't seen that K-drama."

"Ha? It's a movie." Ate Tiana laughed. "Anyway, I'm off. My girlfriend was complaining that she needed help with this super-special last dinner at the restaurant that *somebody* insisted on."

"I could cook, I told you," Santi mumbled. Ate Tiana's girlfriend Lydia was Santi's head chef, and he knew well enough to get out of their way when they had something up their sleeve.

"Boss Santi, I know you love cooking for Kira, but you just can't make a chocolate tartufo like I can," Lydia explained, walking into the office as she wrapped an arm around his cousin's waist. Tiana gave him a little wink and a twirl before the happy couple skipped out of Santi's soon-to-be former office. Santi chuckled and looked down at the memo on his desk, and exhaled. It still felt right. He was going to miss Villa, of course, but this was for the best.

"Miro?" He heard Tiana's voice outside.

"I need to see my Kuya, please—"

"I'm in here," Santi announced, reading the memo one more time.

"Kuya!" a voice exclaimed, and the desperation in it made him look up immediately to see Miro, his hair mussed (which told Santi he'd been twisting it with his finger, a nervous habit of his). He walked into Santi's office and collapsed in the guest chair.

"You didn't say hi to Ate Tiana and her girlfriend," Santi chided him.

"Who?" Miro asked, his brow furrowing in confusion. Santi shook his head and resumed his work. He was going to have to send the memo out to his department heads today.

"Never mind," Santi said. "I'm not sure why you're here."

"I need you to know," Miro said, leaning forward in his seat, his eyes completely clear even if his voice seemed a little nervous. "Kuya, I didn't know Lolo was planning on ruining your relationship. I thought he was curious about your life! I trusted him, and I didn't know they were going to hurt you. I got the penthouse in exchange, but…"

Santi inhaled sharply. He had a feeling Miro wasn't as innocent as he seemed, but he wasn't declaring that he was returning the penthouse, either. And yes, he was aware that it was dramatic, but he *was* a Scorpio something. He should be allowed to be dramatic sometimes.

"You can't be mad at me," Miro continued, unaware of Santi's feelings. "If you're mad at me, then I'm just like them. And Kuya, I don't want to be like them. Please, Kuya. I don't want to be like them."

It gutted him, to see the worry on Miro's face, the pain there. But Santi had gotten hurt too, and it wasn't going to be easy for him to trust his brother again (maybe ever, but who knows).

"I needed you, too," he said softly, trying to take the sting out of the words—but the way his brother winced, he knew he'd failed. He had needed Miro; he needed him when he was fired, when he was opening the hotel, then the restaurant. Needed Miro to say something after that lunch with Lolo, or when he'd showed up at Villa with those letters. "I'll always be your brother, Mi. But I can't be in the same room as our family right now. I hope you understand, I'm still recovering from the hurt they caused, that you caused. Maybe one day, when I can make sense of it all. But right now, I'm not there yet."

"I didn't think you *could* get hurt," Miro said, his face completely crumpled and miserable now. Santi realized that this was his brother's true face—someone that wanted desperately to be loved, just as much as Santi, so much that he turned a blind eye when someone was trying to use him. Santi didn't know if it made Miro naive or willfully ignorant, but it was up to Miro to face that.

"It's a wonder, the things the Lipa air can do to a heart," Santi said, standing up from his desk to walk Miro gently out of the office. "But thank you for talking to me, Miro. I'll…call. You can call too, but I might not pick up."

"I don't know how to ask for help," Miro said, his gaze a little far away. "I never realized that I was traumatized by our own upbringing until Vito told me what I did to you. Kuya, he was *proud* of himself, what kind of sicko—"

Miro stopped. He must have noticed that Santi's jaw was suddenly stiff, that he hadn't moved a muscle since he brought it up.

"You don't want to talk about it," his little brother concluded.

"I don't," Santi agreed. "But I'm not the only person out there that can help you."

"Santi!" Kira's excited voice said at the end of the hallway leading to his office. She appeared like a vision, walking down his hallway in a soft pink dress, the kind that swished every time her hips swayed, the kind that molded perfectly over her gorgeous décolletage. Santi shifted his weight one foot to the other. "I'm a genius!"

"I'm not going to deny that," he said, leaning against his doorframe like Miro wasn't there. "But why?"

"I finished my meeting with Chloe Agila, and she gave me a tip on the white chocolate, which led me to think about chocolate silk and how to use it to temper things. Long story short, I did it. I bought another tempering machine so I don't die inside every time I make chocolate, even small-batch ones. Can we eat, then celebrate, i.e., have sex?"

"Kira," Santi said, trying his hardest not to laugh. "You remember Miro, my baby brother? He came to visit."

Kira stopped mid-walk, her face white as a sheet as Miro chuckled beside Santi and gave Kira a polite, Instagram-friendly wave. Santi saw the moment his brother put on that influencer mask, but the mask didn't fit quite so tightly over his face anymore.

"Hi," Miro said, grinning. "I have heard nothing but terrible things about you from the wrong sources, so I'm going to assume you're wonderful."

"Well, I am pretty great," Kira said, showing off an uncharacteristic shyness by tucking her hair behind her ear.

Miro smiled, and the hole his family left in Santi's chest significantly filled.

"This feels wrong," Kira said, sitting across him an hour later, after Santi had seen Miro off. She was frowning slightly even as she speared her fork into her fig and honey salad with greens from Blossoms Farms and a bit of the burrata made with Luz Creamery. "It feels like your grandfather won, somehow, because Lally ended up selling the hotel."

"The hotel was always Lally's, Kira," Santi reminded her gently, tossing his burrata in with the rest of the salad to add a bit of flavor to the usually flavorless cheese. "It was never mine, and I'm okay with that. I was worried about Miro, I wanted to talk him through his problems with me, but he seems to have found his own way. He said he's looking for help, and I'm trying not to be optimistic, but…"

"You want to be optimistic." Kira nodded, smiling. "It's okay."

"And La Spezia is going to be smaller, but it will still be the best."

"Well, if it's still the best." Kira pretended to roll her eyes, smiling as he felt something warm against his ankle.

"Are you really playing footsie with me at my own restaurant," Santi asked, trying to oh so casually sip his wine, when Kira lifted her foot higher and he nearly jolted in surprise.

"Apparently I am." She giggled. "And this is your last meal here. I want it to be memorable."

Santi smiled at her over the candlelight. Strangely enough, this last time he was going to eat here with her was the first time they did together. There was just never enough time before, not enough opportunity. But the soft lighting from the candles made Kira look like she was glowing, her eyes sparkling as she sat across him, trying to act like running her foot up against his leg was totally casual and easy.

"Your chocolate tartufo." Bruno put down the single plate that contained Lydia's now signature dish. Inspired by a dish of the same name sold in Rome, the innocent-looking ball of chocolate and whipped cream topping didn't seem like much. But when Kira ran her spoon through the whipped cream, chocolate chunks and ganache gave way to the ice cream, then the strawberry jam and the brownie inside. It was Kira on a plate, she liked to say, and she ate the dessert with gusto.

We'll have this again, Santi thought, slowly and deliberately licking his spoon. *As long as I'm with her.*

Epilogue

"Come on, come on, there's nobody here," Kira whispered, tugging Santi's arm insistently out to the fire escape that connected Sunday Bakery's kitchen and Café Cecilia's coffee lab, the perfect spot to look out into the city. The all-too-familiar December breeze felt a little more special, more like a caress tonight than anything. "I didn't think people would do fireworks this year!"

"I didn't think we would be breaking into Sari's coffee lab today, but it's been nothing but surprises with you," Santi said, only mildly sarcastic.

They made it to the fire escape, just in time for one of the nearby neighbors to start shooting fireworks up in the sky, one bigger than the other.

"Clearly we were wrong to underestimate Lipa," Santi agreed, looking up as the sky lit up gold, blue, green and red. Whoever had managed to secure the fireworks (which had been impossible for them to find), they had to be really close by; Kira could almost reach up and touch the lights. Not that she was going to, and it was obviously a fire hazard, but it made the night all the more magical. Like the universe was giving her heartfelt approval.

Kira felt Santi's arms wrap around her from behind, and she leaned her head against his chest, feeling safe enough to take a deep breath.

"Hey," she teased. "Social distancing kaya."

"We're a single household now," he teased back. "Unless I married someone else in the church this morning?"

"Yes, that was my evil twin," Kira giggled, enjoying the feeling of her new husband's body wrapped around hers. "It's been our plan all along to seduce you, marry you, have a happily ever after with you."

"Scary," he said dryly.

"Terrifying," she chuckled. "But exciting. And lovely. And happy, and hopeful."

"All the good things," he agreed.

They'd been in this position several times now, but this time felt different. The first of many things they would do together as a married couple.

They almost didn't push through with the wedding. It felt ridiculous to spend any amount of money, to risk everyone else, just because Ate Nessie couldn't stop commenting about how Kira was "living in sin" with Santi and the Cat.

But they found a way, inviting only Kira's family to the ceremony and a guest list of less than twenty for the dinner Santi made for everyone at La Spezia's al fresco dining space on the Laneways. Everyone got a mask, locally made soap and sanitizer, and an option to join the festivities via video.

It was more than enough for them.

"Miro texted," Santi said. "He said he had to go, but make sure I said congratulations, or best wishes. Maybe it was good luck."

"I'm glad he could come." Kira grinned, still watching the fireworks.

Santi hadn't been sure that his brother was coming, and despite his insistence that he would have been fine either way, Kira thanked the freaking stars above when Miro Santillan showed up in a mask that matched his tie, and the best-smelling hand sanitizer Kira had ever had the pleasure of being sprayed into her hands. He sat at the very back of Bolbok church and volunteered to man the video chat.

Before that, the brothers Santillan talked mostly on the phone, and in-person conversation was both difficult and a little awkward (especially that one time they tried video chatting), but they had each other's backs.

"Someone had to tell your mom to mute herself."

"I had no idea how she got the Zoom link to the wedding," Santi said apologetically. "But I thought it was funny."

"She called you a traitor."

"Lally told her to go fuck herself. I'd say things are even." Santi shrugged, and Kira turned to look at Santi. There were still days when he would get nostalgic and sad about his family. In fact, it made for a lot of their struggles—that she felt they lingered around them like a ghost, that he couldn't totally move on. But he was a lot better about talking to her about it now. "Lolo was online, too. I don't know who set it up, and his camera was off, but he was there."

Kira was about to say something to the effect of asking if it was a good thing, when her phone vibrated.

In her dress. Santi's grip loosened as he raised a brow at her.

"Did your boobs just—"

"What? It was my pocket, get your head out of the gutter, husband," she said, pulling her phone from the pocket of her creamy dress. She'd taken inspiration from Princess Beatrice's wedding dress when she commissioned her own from at least three local seamstresses and paid premium for it. It was a thing of cream and gorgeous silver shimmery beads, and she felt like a full-on princess, which was the point. The pockets had been on her insistence, much to the chagrin of the mananahi. "The home baking association at Haraya ordered three kilos of 60% dark chocolate triangles this morning, I just wanted to make sure the tricycle didn't miss them or something."

She realized Santi was giving her a look, and she slipped her phone back into her pocket. "Not that I don't trust that your website works! I'm just…making sure. You've rubbed off some of that Virgo-ness on me."

"Hey, Trike Express works, and you know it." Santi shrugged, because of course the man who realized he could use local tricycle drivers to make deliveries in Lipa for a profit share had earned that. "And I wouldn't be mad if you admitted that you've become a bit of a workaholic."

"Only a *little*," she conceded. But hello, it was a pandemic, and she was allowed to celebrate that her business was still afloat. A lot of the stores on the Laneways had relied on the rent holiday they offered, even after all of the Luzes' plans for the year had been scrapped.

It was a struggle, but they had no other choice but to take things day by day. Surprisingly, Gemini found a whole new market in selling chocolate to local home bakers, both casual and enterprising. Stress baking did wonders for your mental health, and only god would get in the way of a Bantangueño when they decided to open a home baking business.

"So," Kira said, confirmation received and all. "We just made a whole new set of promises to each other. How do you feel about it?"

And with the lights of the fireworks, and her phone officially telling her it was midnight, Kira's new husband pulled her in close, and brushed the side of his nose against hers. Then he kissed her.

And in that kiss, Kira found herself asking the universe, praying to God and to any star that would listen, for hope. Hope that they would stay together, that they would get through this, that things will be okay.

She had to keep believing in that.

"Like the universe said, 'yes,'" Santi said, grinning. "Finally."

* * * * *

Acknowledgements

It takes a village to write a book, and I am extremely grateful for the people in my village! First, to Gabbie, my chocolate-maker sister, who always provided writing fuel when I needed it, and invented white chocolate so good that it will make the hardest-hearted Capricorns weep. It's me. I'm the hardest-hearted Capricorn.

To KB, the Best Beta Reader and Bangtan chingoo, who cheered me on while I was in the peak of my rewriting phase, and keeping me on track. Your help was invaluable, as always. To Layla, Light of My Life (naks!), fellow enabler and one of my favorite people of all time, saying "yes," To another panicked beta reading message, and providing the insights that I feel just made this story so much better. You always remind me to love myself, and my characters are all the better for it. To John, for their critical but encouraging eyes. I complained a lot (to myself mostly) about their questions about emotional beats, but I think it was all for the better. They saw the story I was trying to tell, even when I wasn't too sure myself.

You know that feeling of being seen? They all made me feel seen, or at least my story, and what I wanted to say. So you have my eternal thanks.

Thank you to my other sisters—Celine, Michelle, Roselle and Frances—for getting me an oracle reading for my 30th birthday, and for encouraging me to look at the universe through the stars. And to Kelsey for being the guide!

Mom and Dad already got all the thanks in *Sweet on You,* but extra thanks for never asking to read my books. And the boys—Ram, Rom, Gijo and Rowell— you are useless for book writing, but I love you just the same.

All gratitude will always go to the #romanceclass community, for everything they do, and being one of the lights in this very dark time.

And to LDW, just for being himself. Hay, ang gwapo mo, ha.

About the Author

Carla de Guzman writes contemporary romance, and believes in a happily ever after. Her books *Sweet on You* (published by Carina Press), *If The Dress Fits* and *The Queen's Game* are explorations of her favorite tropes, places and food.

For her, there is always something new to share with the world through her art and her writing in order to give her readers maximum amounts of kilig. She believes that every person needs a safe space, and she hopes her books provide that, too.

She is a part of #romanceclass, an online community of writers, readers and creators of Filipino romance in English, and will always say yes to a café invite.

Website: www.carladeguzman.com
Twitter/Instagram: @carlakdeguzman

For barista and café owner Sari Tomas, Christmas means parols, family and no-holds-barred karaoke contests. This year, though, a new neighbor is throwing a wrench in all her best-laid plans. The baker next door—"some fancy boy from Manila"— might have cute buns, but when he tries to poach her customers with cheap coffee and cheaper tactics, the competition is officially on.

And Baker Boy better be ready, because Sari never loses.

Keep reading for an excerpt from
Sweet on You *by Carla de Guzman!*

Chapter One

December 1

To Sari Tomas, finding the right café was like finding the perfect pair of jeans. She loved cafés that welcomed you inside like you walked into someone's inspiration board come to life, except the coffee was much better, the desserts were delicious, and the music was excellent. If you were extra lucky, there would be food, and that food would be good too.

After having spent her life in and out of cafés for studying, hanging out with friends, or just spending time with herself, Sari had always longed to open up a little place of her own. Somewhere she could always be useful and needed, somewhere that she could come to every day and work.

Their grandmother had run Tomas Coffee Co. for thirty-five years. She had done it all by herself, but when Sari, Sam and Selene took over, they decided on a different approach. They agreed to split the business according to the things they were good at, and the things they wanted.

Selene, the oldest, who loved the idea of running things and being in charge, ran the corporation from

Manila. She got the condo in Makati City, with room
for her sisters when they needed it, of course. Sam, the
youngest, who was only twenty-three then, had no idea
what she wanted to do, and was willing to do anything.
So she went down to Los Baños to learn agriculture
and farming, and took over the Tomas Farm, growing
their famous robusta beans.

And Sari, the middle child, who longed for a café
of her own, learned the fine art of roasting coffee,
creating signature blends for clients, got Café Cecilia. Named after their great, great grandmother who
started the company, the café had been a side project
that their grandmother put aside, until Sari picked up
the lease from the Laneways and transformed it into
her dream café.

The hundred-square-meter shop was everything
she had ever wanted. It had a light, airy ambience
thanks to the old warehouse windows that overlooked
the Laneways, a carefully crafted mix of eclectic and
comfortable furniture after scouting trips to Tagaytay and Ermita, patterned Machuca floor tiles, a two-
group espresso machine that gleamed in baby blue,
and plants. A *lot* of plants that thrived in the sunlight
that streamed in to the place, and made the café feel
a little more welcoming. Sari wanted Café Cecilia to
be the neighborhood place, much like the cafés she'd
enjoyed in Manila and abroad.

Every day, Sari would go to the café and spend time
on the floor, even when really, the place could run itself by now. But she enjoyed it, and couldn't bear to
stay away for very long.

And for the next three years, it was perfect. Sure, her
food selection wasn't the best, and her pastries were all

pre-packaged from a factory, but it didn't really matter to customers who were here for the coffee and the vibe.

Until one day in November, when suddenly it mattered, *very* much. Sari was very calmly tasting a new coffee blend in her lab on the second floor when she was knocked off her feet by the dull, heavy sound of a hammer. A sharp sound of a drill had followed, then the acrid smell of welding, both coming from the then-empty shop next door.

A bakery, Ate Nessie had told her conspiratorially. *Some fancy boy from Manila is opening a bakery right next to you.*

Suddenly, the food in Café Cecilia was very important, and for the last month, Sari had felt like a headless chicken, running around and sourcing suppliers, only to be met by reasons like "we can't deliver outside Manila," "no way you can get it fresh every day," or "can't you just make it yourself?"

Now it was the first of December, and based on surreptitious, totally not constant peeking over the manila paper-covered windows, and the feigned ignorance of the deliveries being made to the shop, Sunday Bakery was ready to open their doors to the world. And Sari was not ready.

It was competition, after all, and if Sari couldn't be the best, what was the point?

"You're obsessing," her younger sister Sampaguita singsonged, her arms full of Christmas lights and ribbon as she caught Sari glaring at the bakery's window. Sari was aware that everyone was getting tired of it, but she couldn't help it. Every time she stood on the street outside the café and stared down at their doors, so close together they were practically one door, she just…didn't like it. It made her stomach flip in a bad way, made a sour taste swirl around in her mouth. She couldn't have that. Not when she made a living out of her own taste buds.

"It's Christmas, Ate. Lighten up." She held up a length of twinkle lights and shook it at her older sister like it was all the Christmas magic she needed. Sari huffed and shook her head.

"It's been Christmas since September," she pointed out. "And I wasn't obsessing. I was…observing. Scouting the competition."

Sunday Bakery looked innocent enough from outside. The aesthetic was half lab, half London Underground, made of all white subway tile on the walls, patterned mosaic floors, neon letters and phone camera-friendly lighting. They had half the seating capacity of Café Cecilia, and not as many plants. Sari was also definitely not always thinking about the fact that inside Sunday Bakery was a den of jewelled, sugary delights waiting for the innocent customer to try, test, taste. She'd smelled the butter on the pain au chocolat, seen the perfect frosting swirls on cupcakes, heard the snap of cookies. And while coffee was a jolt to the system, a great dessert was pure sin on a plate.

Therefore, it was the enemy.

Sari had no plans of interacting with Sunday Bakery next door. She'd seen the Mummy movies enough times to know that you couldn't just take jewels all willy-nilly. But the pastries and their other sinful siblings continued to tempt her, tuning her senses to locate them before they came too close. She could smell a baked good from a mile away.

"In short, you have an irrational dislike of the

bakery next door, because you want to try his baked goods." Her younger sister shrugged, tugging at a tangled string of lights.

"Sam, don't make it sound dirty." Sari frowned, taking the mess of twinkle lights from her sister and carefully untangling it. "All this sugar and sweetness in the air is going to mess with my nose and my taste buds."

"I'm just saying. You've never liked change, or new things, and this bakery is a new thing."

"Can we please focus on what we're supposed to be doing?" Sari sighed in frustration. "The Christmas decor is not going to put itself up."

Technically, Café Cecilia was already behind on their Christmas decor. The other stores on the Laneways—Kira's chocolate shop, Meile's flower shop, Kris' cookies, had all put up their Christmas decor around the same time Sunday Bakery next door started construction. And even that was a little late, as the malls put theirs up in September. One could argue that Halloween wasn't really a huge holiday in this country. There was little fun in dressing up for Halloween when the malls had already decked the halls with boughs of Christmas sales.

But Sari was a stickler for tradition, and in the Tomas family, decor was put up exactly on the first of December. While for her parents, that had been a simple, "put up the decor," to their house help, Sari took a more hands on approach, and naturally recruited her little sister to provide assistance. There were twinkle lights to string across her storefront, deep red poinsettia plants in pots to place in the window boxes, and candy cane coffee to serve. The most serious of café owners would have scoffed at Sari serving something so pedestrian, but she didn't much care when it came to spreading the holiday cheer.

Now if only she could feel just as charitable for her neighbor.

"Parol coming through!"

For the grand finale of the decorating, Sari rounded up her staff, an electrician, and her sister Sam to make sure the parol was perfectly placed. The parol was a thing of beauty, a five-foot, star-shaped lantern made from capiz shells that cast a soft yellow glow when lit. It was their grandmother's, specially purchased in Pampanga as a gift from their grandfather. Making sure the parol hung in a place of prominence was one of the many traditions Sari took to heart. So they hung it by the window of Café Cecilia, year after year, guiding their guests into the café like a shimmering beacon.

Kylo, Sam's big black rescue who Sari believed was part horse, tilted his head to the side and barked, making Sari jump from her spot on the street where she'd been supervising.

"Really?" she asked the dog, who seemed to not care that he'd nearly killed his part-owner and flopped to the ground at her feet. Sari rolled her eyes and got back to the task at hand, supervising the perfect parol placement. "A little to the right. Forward. A little more. No, that's too much."

"How about this, ma'am?"

"That's perfect." Sari nodded, bending down and absently scratching behind Kylo's ears as she watched. "Sam?"

"Yup!" Her sister called from inside.

"Turn it on?"

The parol lit up and the rest of her staff started to

clap. Excited chatter filled the space, and people who were casually strolling the Laneways ended up stopping and watching too. Sari's staff were happily taking photos, posing with the giant parol to post on their social media. Some of them approached Sari joking about Christmas bonuses and how excited they were for the Christmas party happening in a couple of weeks.

"Relax, guys, it's just a parol," Sari laughed, but the sight of the bright star did make her heart feel fuzzy and grow three sizes. Memories of being a little girl looking up at this very same parol, clutching a little cup of tsokolate in her hands as her family sang Christmas carols by the tree filled her, and made her smile. They were old memories, ones that no longer rang true, but the joy she had was still there.

"We good?" Sam asked, poking her head out of Café Cecilia's door.

"Yup. We're good." Sari nodded. She was just about to herd the entire group inside, they had plenty of time to pose with the parol later, when "Noche Buena" started to play from unseen speakers. She turned her head in the direction of the music, and two staff members in specially embroidered aprons bearing the Sunday Bakery logos stood outside their shiny, new shop, holding a tray of soft little pillows of mamon that smelled absolutely heavenly and impossibly caramelly for sponge cake.

"Sunday Bakery's soft opening! Please try our browned butter mamon!"

"Oooh!" Sam actually exclaimed beside her sister, her eyes lighting up at the sight of free food. Even Kylo seemed to be sniffing his nose appreciatively in the direction of the baked goods. In her panic, Sari looped her arm around her sister's, then her free fingers through her dog's collar. She saw her staff starting to move in the direction of the bakery, and cleared her throat.

"Okay, everyone inside! Coffee isn't going to serve itself!" That got their attention. Ordinarily Sari wouldn't have minded her staff stepping out for a second when there was free food out, or when a huge parol was being put up, but not from next door. "Come on, Kylo."

The dog seemed to grumble, but followed Sari inside anyway, after a couple of tugs on his collar.

The rest of the staff were talking eagerly about Christmas plans, Secret Santa wishes, and possible dance numbers for the Christmas party. They had been like this since September rolled around, but Christmas was so close she could feel it in the air and taste it on her tongue.

With one last little scowl at the bakery and their mamon, she strode in to Café Cecilia. Now this, this was an area she knew to be absolutely *hers*. She knew which plants were growing where, which of their dining chairs had a slight wobble, which table got the best light in the afternoon. Sari knew every song on the playlist, every blend they used, remembered how she came up with each one in the coffee lab upstairs.

This café was home to her. Some days she felt it was the only home she would ever know.

Sari immediately went back to work, wiping down the countertops, checking the temperature of the pastry case, making sure that the gleam of the robin's egg blue coffee machine was pristine. As always, she had a peripheral view of Sam as she sat on her usual spot

behind the counter. Even Kylo knew where he was supposed to be—at his corner of the café where he didn't
get in anyone's way. Sari's regulars started to come in
for their mid-morning brews, and everything was as
it should be.

Except she could smell something in the air. A
sweet, heavy scent, one that slid lazily across the space
where it didn't belong. Sari wrinkled her nose. She had
the sudden image of fluffy pancakes being drenched
in golden syrup, imagined a little blob of butter melting with the syrup on the pancake's warm and fluffy
surface. Her father knew how to make his pancakes
extra fluffy and bouncy, and the memory of post-fight,
post-drama family mornings with pancakes had no
business being here.

"What is that?" Sari asked nobody in particular.

"It's probably from next door," Sam responded, not
looking up from her phone.

"Ugh. It's making the café smell like pancake
syrup."

"You're exaggerating."

"When have I ever exaggerated, Sampaguita?" Sari
had spotted her sister moving behind the counter to
raid the pastry case and handed her sister several nap-
kins for whatever pastry she was about to get. Spill-
age was inevitable.

"I have to admit, it's not like you," Sam agreed. "I'm
taking a cookie."

"It's that bakery next door," Sari closed the pastry
case after her. "They're overpowering the neighborhood with sugar and gluten and sweetness."

"Eugh. This is awful." Sam swallowed the bit of
cookie she already ate and wrapped the rest in the nap-

kin, gently nudging it forward into a space where Sari knew Sam could conveniently pretend it didn't exist.

Being the older, more mature sister, Sari decided to ignore the little dig at the pastry. Goodness knows she beat herself up about it more than her sister did. But she sniffed instead. Sari didn't open her café to peddle pastries, she was here to dispense legally allowable stimulants in proper dosages, sometimes with milk and sugar. She was *not* supposed to feel bad because her pastries were…average.

She was a coffee shop, and she was happy with being just that.

But as a responsible business owner, she really should have known better. This was the Philippines, after all, where market consumerism was driven by trends and the Hottest New Thing that someone copied from someone else. The food industry was a dog eat hot dog world, and when competition came in, the ones left behind were the ones who closed up shop first.

"Then stop stealing from me." Sari rolled her eyes. "Do you want coffee?"

"Always."

At least that, she could still do. Sari slipped a saucer underneath Sam's discarded cookie and handed it to one of her staff to take to the back. When she came back, Sam had just finished rummaging through her gigantic canvas bag for a tumbler, which she held up to her sister with a cute smile that only bunso kids could manage.

"Do I want to clean this before I put coffee in it?" Sari wrinkled her nose at the tumbler, which had definitely seen better days.

"A-*te*," Sam huffed, blowing stray strands of hair

away from her tanned face. Ah, the long suffering sigh of being the youngest. Sari was not familiar. "That's clean, duh."

"I was kidding. Barako?"

"Hot as the devil, sweet as sin, and acidic like my heart, please."

Sari smiled, because Sam always said that, and Sari liked that she always said that. Some things, at least, she knew she could trust. Sam, a clean countertop, a good pull of espresso, and that a little bit of brow gel and great lipgloss could fix anything.

But as much as there were things she could trust, there were things she definitely couldn't. Her parents, who in their own ways never really grew past their teenage years, the guy who tried to sell her ice cold water for three euros when she'd been wandering the hot streets of Rome on vacation, and the bakery next door. The bakery next door where she could hear the slow cadence of "Thank God It's Christmas" clashing over the sweeter melodies of "Bibingka," and she hated it.

"And anyway, who opens a business just before Christmas?"

"Oh, we're still talking about the bakery?" Sam almost sounded bored from where she was sitting, and the thing was, Sari was aware that she was being boring. But she couldn't help herself. She was just so… perturbed. Perturbed by a bakery next door.

"It's bad business practice. I'm sure there's a feng shui rule against it."

"We're not Chinese, and Christmas doesn't count in feng shui."

"And yet you insist that the foot of your bed shouldn't point to your bedroom door."

Sari turned to the percolating coffee maker—barako was traditionally made on a stove, but she wasn't a traditionalist, and prioritized using a blend that had Liberica beans, instead of whatever alternatives other coffee brands were touting these days. Their grandmother, who had always been a scion of propriety and had banned the use of red lipstick among her granddaughters until they were married, had been known to drink heaping cups of the country's strongest, punchiest coffee. A bit too strong for Sari, but Sam's favorite. Sari held up the coffeepot, ready to pour, when it happened.

The bell to the shop rang, a bright, tinkling sound that cut through the music while Sari carefully poured Sam's coffee and stirred in a spoonful of brown sugar. Sari heard her staff politely greet the customer as they came up to the counter, heard the opening of a box as they studied the menu. Sunday Bakery, the box announced in big, bold, black and gold letters. Ugh. Their packaging was nice. Pretty enough to be eye-catching, enough for anyone who happened to see it to guess that there was some luxurious, sinful treat inside.

The customer was telling her cashier about the baked good she'd just purchased next door, looking for suggestions as to what she could drink with it. And the world moved in slow motion as she tore the hot pink sticker with a flick of her thumb and opened the box. Sari inhaled. She smelled the usual culprits—butter, sugar, chocolate, all deep and rich and much stronger than any baked good she'd ever smelled. But then there was an unexpected scent that lingered in the air. Was that…*banana*?

Her head shot up from where she was standing behind the counter. The scent had been subtle, but it came to her nonetheless, like a disturbance in the Force. Unexpected. But then again, did anyone ever really expect bananas?

Barako would go perfectly with the customer's cookies. A punch of strong coffee would cut through the sweetness, maybe a bit of milk to soften up the contrast between the cookie and the coffee. The combination reminded her of road trip snacks, ones they'd always had on hand when the drive from Manila to Lipa used to take four hours instead of two. Their mother had been on a health kick, so it was all banana chips for their girls, until their father gave up and got them Jollibee. Their mother had gotten angry and yelled, and their father yelled back, all the way to Lipa. It was the kind of yelling that made Sari press her hands to her ears and shut her eyes, wishing she could click her heels and just fly away somewhere else. Anywhere but where her parents were.

She shook her head, because she refused to feel anything about a baked good that wasn't even hers to begin with.

The customer smiled and ordered an iced Americano, which wasn't a bad choice either. Without prompting from her store manager, Sari got to work, using their finer, more floral Selene blend to match the scents in the air as the customer took her seat, smiling at Sam. Sari's hands were moving in sync with an invisible beat as she pulled the espresso, poured it into a mug with ice before adding the water to make the

Americano. She knew this fruity blend would work well with the customer's pastry the same way she knew how to pull espresso from her beans.

She was about to put the coffees on the serving table when she heard the customer eat…whatever it was. *Crunch.*

Really, this was getting ridiculous. Sunday Bakery next door had been officially open for one day.

"Iced Americano for Leala," she called a little too loudly, placing the ceramic mug with her logo on the serving counter. She wanted to fight baked goods with coffee, even if it was all in her head. "Barako for Sampaguita Corazon Tomas!"

The customer was a little dazed as she looked up, and Sari could see the crumbs she brushed off her skirt. Tiny, innocent little things that were now in her territory. *Must remember to sweep the floor*, even if it wasn't her job, even if she didn't have to.

"What is that?" Sari asked the customer when she came to retrieve her coffee, and it sounded more like an interrogation than it did friendly conversation. Sam, who was reaching for her own coffee, flattened her lips into a thin line to stop herself from laughing. "In the box?"

"Banana chip and cacao cookies," the customer said hesitantly, clearly confused. "They're from the bakery next door."

"Of course they are," Sari grumbled, and turned her head to the wall she shared with Sunday Bakery, glaring at it like it was going to crumble if she glared hard enough. She certainly endeavored to try.

To her customer, (or to anyone else, really), it may have looked like she was seething, and she was, just a tiny bit. Give her a backwards baseball cap and a flannel shirt, and she was Luke the diner guy from *Gilmore Girls*. She was already dispensing the coffee anyway.

"Uh, can I have my coffee to-go instead?" her customer asked, edging slowly away from the counter and looking desperate for someone else, anyone else to attend to her needs. Sari opened her mouth to acquiesce to the request when Sam crossed the counter, took the customer's cup of iced Americano and deftly transferred the contents into one of the robin's egg blue paper cups, popping a biodegradable lid on and handing the customer her coffee.

"Here you go, have a great day, and merry Christmas!" Sam chirped, giving the customer a polite but unnecessary bow. She smiled back, taking the cookie and its scent away with her.

Sari felt her shoulders drop, and she hated that they did. She briefly wondered if her great, great grandmother, Cecilia Tomas, had ever felt like this. She was the one who started the Tomas Coffee Co. right here in Lipa, seeing herself, her farm and her staff through wars and natural disasters to make sure it was passed on to her granddaughters. Cecilia had had her husband at her side to help her learn how to properly cultivate and care for the coffee, the side Sam had taken to like a fish to water. Sari's grandmother Rosario had their grandfather to help her learn how to truly expand the business, selling to big chains and groceries in Manila and Batangas, the part of the business that Selene now looked after.

The specialty coffee blends and the café? They were all new, all Sari's. Sure, they used to have the café across from the Cathedral, but that was mostly just because Lola Rosario's friend had owned the building and needed a renter when they fell on tough times. The first version of Café Cecilia had been an afterthought, until Sari told her sisters definitively that it was the part of the business she wanted.

Selene still said that it was one of the few times she'd ever seen Sari so decisive.

She was supposed to be better than this. She'd owned this place for three years, with coffee that her family has been serving for generations, but with decor and blends that were all her own. Sari wasn't going to fail just because a bakery opened next door.

"Do you…do you want to talk about it, Ate?" Sam asked, always the most sensitive among the three Tomas sisters.

Sari wanted nothing more than to curl into a little ball and tell her baby sister that she was a little worried about it, but quickly decided against it.

"No," she said primly before she grabbed a tray and started to load it with mugs and a little jug of locally produced fresh milk, a rarity in the Philippines. It was one of the reasons why Sari had loved the idea of opening her café here, where she had access to fresh, local ingredients without having to think about the logistical nightmare it would have been if she were in Manila. "I'm all right."

"You're always all right," Sam muttered under her breath, and Sari pretended not to hear.

"I have to go upstairs and prep for barista class."

"Need help with that?"

"No."

"Cool." Sam shrugged as she and Kylo followed Sari up the stairs to the coffee lab/her office on the second floor. Juggling a tray of coffee mugs and milk, Sari nearly fell back when Kylo wriggled between them and reared up on his hind legs to scratch at the door.

"Oh my God, Sam, your beast—"

Sam pulled Kylo's collar back and opened the door for Sari. The big black dog squeezed between the sisters and bounded into the room with zero regard for the expensive things inside and flopped on the daybed by the window, a throw pillow between his paws to drool on. Sari watched the dog resume his nap with a wistful sigh before she walked over to her work station and placed her precarious tray of things on the counter.

"Your dog is too big," she told her sister.

"You love him." Sam closed the door behind her.

"Don't you have a farm to tend to?"

"The coffee beans literally grow on trees, Ate. There's not much to do at the moment." She shrugged, and Sari frowned, immediately going into big sister mode. Sure, Sam was in the café most days, but the way she said it made Sari wonder if her sister was trying to say something else. The thing with being an older sister was that over the years, Sari had learned to read her siblings as easily as she could a list of instructions, even when they tried to be inscrutable.

"Are you excited about the Christmas party?" Sam asked, getting up from the table to walk around Sari's space, picking up the mister and misting the plants. "I mean, I know you and Ate Selene dominate the karaoke contest every year, but you really have to give me and Kira a chance, she's super determined to win."

"I make no promises." Sari grinned, because her Christmases had fallen into a familiar and comforting pattern, and winning the Annual Christmas Party Karaoke Contest was just par for the course.

She briefly wondered how the Sunday Bakery's attendance at the party would change up the dynamic. Not much, if she had anything to say about it. She was determined not to let her new neighbor mess up her Christmas joy, no matter how good their browned butter mamon had smelled.

Don't miss Sweet on You *by Carla de Guzman,
available now wherever ebooks are sold.*

www.CarinaPress.com

Also Available from Carla de Guzman

If the Dress Fits *(2021 Edition)*

Martha and Max have been best friends for as long as they can both remember. From weekend calls to pasalubongs, they're practically attached at the hip. So it didn't feel like too much of a stretch for Martha when she called Max her "boyfriend" on the day she needed someone the most. Titas need no other reason to pounce, even more so when your cousin is marrying the man you used to be in love with.

Luckily for her, Max has had tons of practice being her perfect fake boyfriend, since he's in love with her and all.

To purchase and read more by Carla de Guzman, visit www.carladeguzman.com and wherever ebooks are sold.